LILL
ology
novel
medi
royal
mona
found
and a
in Ge

JOHN BROWNJOHN is one of Britain's foremost translators from French and German. His work has won numerous awards on both sides of the Atlantic, including the US PEN Prize, the Helen and Kurt Wolff Prize, and the Schlegel-Tieck Prize on three occasions. He lives in England.

Lilli Thal

MIMUS

Translated by

John Brownjohn

ALLEN&UNWIN

This edition first published in 2005
First published in Germany by Gerstenberg Verlag, 2003

Allen & Unwin
83 Alexander St
Crows Nest NSW 2065
Australia
Phone: (61 2) 8425 0100
Fax: (61 2) 9906 2218
Email: info@allenandunwin.com
Web: www.allenandunwin.com

National Library of Australia
Cataloguing-in-Publication entry:

  Thal, Lilli.
  [Mimus. English]
  Mimus.

  ISBN 1 74114 702 6.

  I. Brownjohn, John. II. Title.

  833.92

Cover and text design by Sandra Nobes
Set in 10.5 pt Galliard by Midland Typesetters, Maryborough
Printed by McPherson's Printing Group, Maryborough

10 9 8 7 6 5 4 3 2 1

– CONTENTS –

- CONTENTS -

– MONTFIELD –

'*... BUT THE SORCERESS avenged herself on the prince by imprisoning him in a stone tower without a roof. Deprived of shelter, he was scorched by the sun and soaked by the rain and snow. And the sorceress commanded a raven to fly over the tower once a day and let fall a thimbleful of water and a morsel of food as black and bitter as wormwood...*'

Tanko fell silent. The other boys sitting beside him on the tree trunk stared at him expectantly. Florin could feel the prince's parching thirst, the taste of wormwood on his tongue.

'What then?' Senna insisted. 'What happened to the prince after that?'

Lost in thought, Tanko bent and picked up a round piece of moss from the forest floor. Stroking it as if it were a furry little animal, he went on:

'*The prince groaned aloud in his distress, but all that answered him was the silence of the sky and the howling of the wind. And the sorceress, having considered how to increase his sufferings, commanded an eagle to—*'

The boys gave a jump, startled by a loud snapping of twigs in the undergrowth.

'What an impressive sight,' said a familiar voice. The four youngsters sprang to their feet at the sound of it. 'There they sit like a row of ringdoves, the future masters of Moltovia, shuddering at some old wives' tale. Why trouble to go to the exercise yard? Let old Count Ursio teach his straw dummies to fence!'

The bushes parted and a grey-haired man stepped into the clearing. Short and wiry, he was nimble and vigorous in his movements and had a face like tanned leather. Although Count Ursio was very old—or so he seemed to his pupils—he still wore the leather tunic and iron shin armour of a swordsman. He proceeded to examine the four youngsters like an officer inspecting his troops. Having looked daggers at each of them in turn, he came to a halt in front of Tanko.

'Why not finish your story?' he demanded, rocking belligerently on his heels.

Tanko stared at the tips of his toes in sheepish silence.

Count Ursio drew a deep breath. 'Teller of fairy tales!' He spat out the words like the coarsest of insults. 'You're nothing but a dreamer!' he barked like a furious mastiff. 'Go take your tales and sit with the washerwomen! It's no wonder any farmer's lad can unhorse you! You aim to be one of the king's knights? A fairground huckster—that's all you're fit for! I'll give you a handbell, then you can join the clowns and fire-eaters and entertain the rabble in the streets!'

Radbod, who was standing beside Tanko, tittered despite himself. He would have done better not to, because Count Ursio promptly rounded on him.

'And what of you, my boy?' He pressed Radbod's head back with two fingers under his chin to force the youth to look him in the eye. 'What will your noble father say if I send you home to your fine castle? What if I advise him to tie you to your nursemaid's apron strings for another few years before he sends you back to the royal school of knighthood?'

Although nearly thirteen, Radbod was—much to his sorrow—short for his age and slender. He swallowed this insult with his lips pressed tightly together.

'But here's the biggest buffoon of all!' The old count left Radbod and drew himself up in front of Senna, who was almost a head taller. 'You think you're the best of this wretched bunch? You hope to succeed Sturmius as the prince's bodyguard?' The louder his voice became, the more Senna seemed to shrink. 'Tell me something: What would you have done if a horde of vile Vinlanders had burst in on Tanko's fairy tale? Uttered a spell and turned them into toads?'

Senna tried to speak. 'But Count Ursio, there aren't any Vinlanders so close to Montfield Castle, you know that full well.'

'Look over there!' barked the old fencing master. With out-stretched arm, he indicated a tall youth leaning on his sword at the edge of the clearing. 'Is Sturmius sitting down with you fools? No, he's keeping watch as befits the prince's bodyguard. He's a dependable fellow!'

Sturmius gripped the hilt of his sword, trying not to look too proud of himself.

The old count walked past them all again. 'A washerwoman . . .' he growled contemptuously, 'a babe in arms . . . a buffoon . . .' He clasped his hands together as if in prayer. 'Holy St. George, noblest of warriors, assist me! See to it that these youngsters grow up at last!'

Florin bit his lip to suppress a grin. 'You've forgotten me, Count Ursio,' he said politely.

The count gave a little bow. 'It does not behove me to rebuke you, Your Highness,' he said. 'You must always set your companions a good example—no one knows that better than you.'

He took an hourglass from the pocket of his tunic and set it down on a tree stump. 'You'll all be at the exercise yard before the glass empties,' he growled. 'Complete with armour, swords and shields—or you'll regret it. And don't take it into your heads to turn the clock back!' With a last menacing glare, he disappeared into the trees.

'Brrr!' Radbod shook himself like a wet dog after a rainstorm.

'Trust the old fox to steal up on us on foot!' said Senna. 'We'd have heard his horse half a mile away.'

'If he had his way, we'd never leave the castle,' Tanko said plaintively, 'and would go to bed armed to the teeth.'

'Count Ursio sleeps in full armour every night,' Florin added. 'What on earth will he do if peace really comes?'

'He'll invent some new threat,' Tanko predicted, 'and bully us even more. To Count Ursio, sword drill and swordplay are as necessary as breathing.'

'It looks as if we'll be fencing in the rain,' Radbod said, with an appraising glance at the sky. 'But who cares?' He mimicked Ursio's voice. 'What will you do in battle, you milksops? Ask the vile Vinlanders to hold off until the weather improves?'

Tanko cast a worried glance at the sand in the hourglass. 'We'd better go.'

'There's no hurry.' Cool as a cucumber, Senna produced an ivory pin from his pocket. Having carefully dipped it in some pitch oozing from the tree trunk, he bent over Count Ursio's hourglass. 'First I want to know if he survives.'

'If who survives?' Tanko stared at him.

'The prince in the tower, of course,' Senna replied as he neatly thrust the pin through the hourglass's leather case. The pitch clogged the trickle of sand, which stopped abruptly. 'Just imagine, a thimbleful of water and a morsel of wormwood a day! Our prince grumbles if ten of his favourite dishes fail to appear on the table at once.' He nudged Florin in the ribs. 'It's a miracle you remain so thin, Your Highness.'

'Food certainly sticks to *your* ribs,' Florin retorted. 'Three years at Montfield Castle have doubled your girth as well as your height!'

'Don't be envious!' Senna withdrew the pin with a jerk. 'Well, friends,' he said contentedly, 'now we've solved that problem, what would you say to making a little detour on the way to the exercise yard?'

'The hideaway!' Florin and Radbod exclaimed together.

The hideaway was an abandoned hermit's hut that stood not far from Montfield Castle, concealed by a thicket of fir saplings and bramble bushes. The boys had stumbled across it by chance while hunting deer—a meeting place during the winter days to come.

'But we can't!' Tanko eyed the useless hourglass apprehensively.

'No one touched it,' said Senna. 'It simply stopped. Count Ursio should fill his hourglass with finer sand.'

'He'll flay us alive!'

Senna sighed impatiently. 'How can anyone who thinks up such exciting stories be such a coward himself?'

It was true, Florin reflected. Tanko's storytelling seemed to use up all his courage, wit and spirit of adventure.

'To the hideaway,' Senna said firmly. 'And you, my prince,' he added, bowing with a flourish, 'will take the lead. You know you must always be foremost in setting your companions a good example.'

Halfway there, the heavens opened and the rain came down in sheets. The boys raced off followed by Sturmius, Florin's bodyguard, who was hampered by the sword at his belt. They reached the hideaway laughing and soaked to the skin. With a little bow, Senna and Radbod opened the rickety wooden door for Florin as a matter of course, only to slam it in his bodyguard's face a moment later.

'An excellent idea of yours, Sturmius, to stand guard outside!' Radbod shouted through the door. 'You're a dependable fellow!'

'Poor Sturmius,' Senna said pensively. 'Fancy having to stand guard in the rain . . . Being the prince's bodyguard is a dull job. I shall have to think twice about it.'

'You do that,' said Florin, well aware that Senna was itching to assume the post. He looked round the hut. Two weeks ago he had talked one of the royal foresters into secretly making the place more comfortable for them. It was now clean and snug, with fresh rushes on the floor and sacks of straw to sit on. Dry logs were stacked beside the brick-lined hearth.

'Wait.' Radbod produced a tinderbox from his pocket. 'We'll soon have a fire.'

Before long, flames were leaping up the chimney. The boys pulled the sacks nearer to the fire and spread their sodden cloaks to dry.

'My father has a mind to replace Count Ursio,' Florin confided. 'When he returns from Frankenland, Duke Bonizo may become our instructor in the arts of war.'

'Truly?' The youngsters' eyes lit up. Duke Bonizo's renown as a warrior was legendary.

'Then they'll have to enlarge the school at last,' said Radbod. 'Our dormitory is already bursting at the seams.'

The royal school of knighthood numbered twenty pupils. King Philip had founded it so that his only son, the future king of Moltovia, should not grow up in isolation. The teachers were learned monks and experienced soldiers whom he had summoned to the royal court from all over the country, and every noble family in Moltovia yearned to have at least one son educated in the prince's company.

'Duke Bonizo must be commanding your father's bodyguard now,' Senna said enviously. 'If only we had some news from them. A fast-riding horseman could have been here long ago.'

'Except that he would have had to set off as soon as they got to Frankenland,' Radbod objected. 'Why would King Philip send a courier if there's nothing to report?'

'Well said,' Tanko remarked, warming his hands at the fire. 'You'll see, a courier will arrive in the next few days. And, just to prevent you from bursting with curiosity, I'll tell you what news he'll bring.'

Florin smiled at his friend. 'Are you a soothsayer now, as well as a storyteller?'

'Who knows?' Tanko replied with an air of mystery. 'At all events, the beginning of my story is the plain truth. So listen.' He settled himself more comfortably on his sack. *'Once upon a time there were two kingdoms, Vinland and Moltovia . . .'*

'Forget about Vinland,' Senna growled. 'Vinland can go to the devil for all I care, but Moltovia will exist for ever!'

'Don't interrupt!' Tanko scowled at him. *'The two kingdoms were at war, a war so old that its beginnings were shrouded in mystery . . .'*

'As old as I am,' Senna said drily. 'Fourteen.'

'Yes, and every babe in arms knows why it started,' Radbod chimed in. 'Theodo of Vinland had fastened his greedy gaze on our silver mines, that's why.'

Tanko folded his arms. 'I've had enough!' he said firmly.

'No, go on,' Florin pleaded. Listening to the facts of their own story told like a legend was mesmerising. 'For my sake.'

'Very well,' Tanko said graciously, 'but only for your sake.'

'It was an endless, merciless war—merciless for the most part because neither kingdom could defeat the other. There were spells of deceptive calm during which the warriors licked their wounds and the harassed inhabitants breathed again. Thereafter the warring armies clashed with redoubled ferocity, plundering towns and villages, burning homes and churches, and ravaging the fields. As in Moltovia, so in Vinland.'

'That's true,' Florin said quietly. Even though the war had never come within a hundred miles of Montfield Castle, thanks to an ingenious ring of fortifications, he had heard enough about its horrors from his father's generals.

'Things continued in this manner, year after year,' Tanko went on, *'until one spring, when King Theodo of Vinland—'*

'This spring,' Radbod amended.

'. . . one spring,' Tanko repeated, glaring at him, *'when King Theodo quite unexpectedly sued for peace. Moltovia's royal court greeted this approach with deep suspicion . . .'*

That was putting it mildly. The first envoys from Vinland to reach Montfield Castle were thrown into a dungeon before they had a chance to pass on a single word of Theodo's proposal, and were only released at King Philip's express command.

'. . . *but Theodo continued to send Philip envoys day after day, and they never tired of conveying the same message: the King of Vinland wishes to make peace with Moltovia.*'

Until the day came when we simply had to believe it, thought Florin.

'*Early that summer, negotiators from the two kingdoms met at the Relling, the river that marks the frontier between them. The Vinlanders pitched camp on the west bank, the Moltovians on the east, and the loudest-voiced among them bellowed their conditions across the water . . .*'

'That would have been a job for me!' Senna said exuberantly.

'*By the time they were hoarse, it had been agreed that the warring kings should meet in person. Not in Vinland or Moltovia, but on neutral territory: in Frankenland, at the court of King Ludvik . . .*'

'Where they dine on snails and frogs' legs,' Radbod put in with a shudder. 'Let's hope our people take a good look at the fare that's set before them!'

'*The sun was beating down when King Philip, escorted by a magnificent retinue, set off for Frankenland . . .*'

That had been six weeks ago. Since then, Montfield Castle had seemed deserted. Over three hundred men, including the whole of the Privy Council, had accompanied King Philip on horseback.

'*And two weeks later they reached the capital of Frankenland safe and sound.*'

'Now you're playing the soothsayer,' Senna objected.

'But that's what the couriers will say,' said Tanko. 'They'll report that the King of Vinland was awaiting King Philip with impatience.' The corners of his mouth twitched. 'They'll report that he's a fat, bald, toothless, evil-smelling fellow with flat feet.'

The other boys giggled. 'Come, come, Tanko,' said Florin, 'you've no idea what Theodo looks like.'

Tanko closed his eyes. '*To hymns of praise and the ringing of church bells,*' he went on solemnly, '*the two kings exchanged the kiss of peace and pledged eternal friendship. The elaborate festivities held to celebrate their pact continued for a whole year. But the finest festivity of all was the marriage of Moltovia's crown prince to the princess of Vinland.*'

Radbod and Senna burst out laughing. 'It's lucky you aren't a genuine soothsayer,' Senna exclaimed.

After glancing at Florin's face, Tanko said hesitantly: 'At all events ... *peace had been restored, and they all lived happily ever after.*'

'God grant it may be so,' Florin said earnestly.

'Sounds almost too good to be true,' Senna said gruffly. 'And now, Tanko, tell us what the eagle did to the prince in the tower.'

AT the evening meal the boys listened in silence to a lecture from Chancellor Artold crammed with words like duty and example, responsibility and respect. Count Ursio sat beside him with his arms folded and a look of extreme satisfaction on his face.

He would probably have looked less smug had he heard the chancellor's whispered words as he bade the boys goodnight.

'How in the world does one get an hourglass to stop?'

'Pitch,' Florin whispered back.

'Senna, I suppose?' Chancellor Artold gave an admiring nod. 'The crafty young devil! It still amuses me to remember the tripwire he installed outside the dormitory of our learned monks, not to mention the inflated fish bladder he hid beneath a cushion on Monsignor Federino's chair.' He chuckled at the memory. 'The reverend gentleman almost sank through the floor in shame, it made such an appallingly vulgar noise . . .'

'By your leave,' Florin said with modest pride, 'the inflated fish bladder was mine.'

'Ingenuity is a gift from God and, as such, beyond praise,' the chancellor said, straight-faced. 'In the immediate future, however, you and your companions had better apply your ingenuity to Euclidean geometry and Latin grammar. Otherwise, everyone will think I'm an old fool who allows young scamps to lead me by the nose!'

———

THE next morning Florin was woken by a prolonged ratatat on the door of his bedchamber.

'Your pardon, Highness,' he heard the chamberlain call, 'but it's time. Petitioners are already standing in line outside the castle gates.'

'What did you say?' Florin struggled into a sitting position.

The door opened and Count Marrod entered the room. Although it was still early, he was already wearing his official black robe complete with the insignia of his office, a gold chain and a bunch of keys. 'Surely you hadn't forgotten what day it is?' he asked with a smile, drawing back the curtains round the bed. 'Chancellor Artold will not be best pleased, I fear.'

Audience day! Florin shut his eyes for a moment, then leapt out of bed.

'Where's Ramon?' he asked. 'Why didn't he wake me?'

The reason soon became clear: a sleepy grunt issued from his valet's bed in the corner.

The chamberlain cleared his throat. 'I shall await Your Highness in the throne room,' he said, and shut the door quietly behind him.

'Ramon, get up!' Florin stripped off his valet's bedclothes. 'You heard: they're all waiting.'

'I'm making haste, my prince.' Ramon raised his tousled head from the pillows. 'But first,' he gave a hearty yawn, 'I must somehow pry open my eyes.'

Soon afterward, with a half-eaten slice of plum loaf in his hand, Florin was sprinting toward the throne room followed by Sturmius, who had been waiting outside the door of his bedchamber, already booted and spurred. Count Marrod had still to open the castle gates, fortunately, so at least he didn't have to thread his way through a crowd of petitioners. Even so, it was disagreeable enough to hurry to the throne past all the bowing and scraping clerks, civil servants, sentries and pages.

'Punctuality is the adornment of kings, my prince,' Chancellor Artold said with a frown. 'May we begin?'

While Sturmius took up his position behind the throne with sword drawn, Florin hurriedly stuffed the last morsel into his mouth and sat down.

Six months ago, on Florin's twelfth birthday, King Philip had invested his only son with the title of regent—the traditional way of accustoming a crown prince to his responsibilities. Florin was proud of this honour and his father's trust.

However, he could happily have dispensed with many of his new duties. *Giving audiences*—he remembered how magical the words had sounded to him at first. Receiving people from all over the country, listening to their troubles and cares, making sensible and fair decisions . . . He now found his Latin lessons more exciting than these weekly audiences. The petitioners' concerns were always the same: requests for exemption from taxes, complaints about high import duties, requests for privileges, complaints about predatory provincial governors, requests for royal safe-conducts, complaints about exorbitant rents and rates of interest . . . Ninety-nine out of a hundred such decisions Florin thankfully left to Chancellor Artold—after all, who cared about interest rates and import duties? When evening came and the castle gates were shut at last, his head was full to bursting with polite phrases and standard responses, and his lips stiff from smiling patiently.

'Why do we have to see all these people?' he had asked his father. 'They always come out with the same old things, either requests or complaints. Audiences are dull and tedious.'

'If you find them too much for you,' his father had replied, 'what of our Heavenly Father? Imagine how many requests and complaints are ringing in his ears every moment of the day and night. What if there came a time when he'd had enough of us mortals and our petty concerns?' King Philip took Florin's hands in his. 'Being a future king by God's grace, don't you think you owe the Almighty a few hours of patience now and then?'

His father was right, and Florin never complained again. Instead, he devised a little game—'the hat oracle'—to entertain himself during those endless days. He was playing it now.

'A tattered grey velvet cap,' he muttered to himself as the first petitioner came before him. 'The man's a villager. I'll wager he starts with 'Your Royal Highness' and is involved in some dispute with a neighbour.'

'Your Royal Highness,' said the small, dark-skinned man in front of him, 'I thank you most humbly for your indulgence in lending an ear to my trifling request. Your magnanimity is a boon to the entire country, your benevolence—'

'Your request, my good man,' Chancellor Artold admonished him.

'Er, yes, of course.' Abruptly losing the thread of his well-rehearsed speech, the man cleared his throat. 'My evil neighbour, may God punish him for it, has been deceitful and treacherous enough to move the boundary stones between our properties . . .'

Florin secretly awarded himself full marks.

The next person to approach the throne was a young woman.

A snow-white lace bonnet, thought Florin, as she curtsied to him. She's newly married, and her husband has sent her because he can't pay his taxes this year. She'll begin with 'Gra—'

'Gracious Prince,' the woman began in a low voice. 'My beloved sister and I wish to devote our lives to God at the convent of St. Clara, but we lack the gold shilling which every nun must pay into the convent treasury on admission. If you, most bountiful prince . . .'

Although Florin had only predicted her first words this time, the oracle proved right surprisingly often: a priest's black hat inevitably meant some question about church dues, a baker's white cap about the price of bread. The more audiences Florin held, the more accurate his predictions became. Besides, guessing made the time pass more quickly.

A commotion had broken out in the antechamber. Chancellor Artold, sitting stiffly behind his desk, looked up indignantly. 'What is it?' he demanded.

'I'll go and see.' Count Marrod went out, only to reappear in the doorway a moment later. 'Good news, my prince!' he called. 'Couriers from your royal father have just arrived.'

'At last!' Florin turned to Chancellor Artold. 'May they come in at once?'

'But of course.' The chancellor laid his pen aside. 'The audience is adjourned.'

He signed to the chamberlain, who went out again and promptly returned with the couriers.

The five men hadn't even paused to brush the dirt of the road off their cloaks and boots. Florin noticed their smell as they approached the throne: the stench of dust and lathered horses and the exertions of a long, hard ride. He glanced at their headgear out of habit: all five wore woven leather caps with long cords attached, presumably to secure them when travelling at a gallop.

Caps of this kind are new to me, he thought, full of anticipation. I've no idea what these men are about to say.

One of the couriers was carrying a sealed parchment scroll. Florin glanced briefly at the green wax seal of a leaping wolf. It was the royal emblem of Moltovia, which also adorned the signet ring on his own finger.

The man bowed. 'Your Royal Highness.' Then, with another bow in the direction of the desk: 'Chancellor Artold.'

'Count Tillo,' Artold replied coldly. 'The court of Moltovia has seen you but seldom in recent years. What brings you here?'

Florin eyed the man with curiosity. He had never seen Count Tillo before, but he knew that his family castle was near the borders of Vinland.

'We come as envoys from King Philip, and—'

'Why should His Majesty send you, rather than one of his usual couriers?' Artold broke in curtly, and Florin was puzzled by his icy tone.

'For a very simple reason, worthy chancellor,' replied Count Tillo. 'The king's men are fully engaged in preparing for a new era.' Solemnly, he spread his arms wide. 'The war between Moltovia and Vinland is at an end!'

'God be praised!' said Florin and Count Marrod simultaneously and with heartfelt relief. The clerks and pages also murmured prayers of thanksgiving. Still seated behind his desk, Chancellor Artold alone looked totally unmoved.

'King Ludvik of Frankenland proved a successful mediator,' Count Tillo went on. 'The two kings have signed a treaty and sealed it with the kiss of peace. We have come straight from Bellingar, Vinland's royal castle, to bring you King Philip's news.'

'My father is in Vinland?' Florin asked in surprise.

'And has been these ten days past. King Theodo expressed a wish to mark the signing of the treaty with a grand festivity at his court.'

A festivity—just as Tanko predicted, Florin thought happily.

'Your father accepted the invitation with pleasure,' said Count Tillo. As he drew nearer to the throne, Florin noticed a diagonal scar on his right cheek. When the man smiled, as he did now, it wriggled like a worm. 'On the morrow of their kiss of peace, the two kings set off for Vinland with their retinues. But it's best you should read this yourself.' Count Tillo moved to hand the scroll to Florin.

'By your leave,' Chancellor Artold broke in. 'I wish to examine the document first.' He held out his hand with an imperious air.

An uneasy silence filled the room while Artold was reading.

'This communication undoubtedly comes from His Majesty,' he said in a slightly more agreeable tone. 'Signature, seal, secret cipher— there's no doubt of it.'

He came out from behind his desk and handed the parchment to Florin. 'Read the letter yourself, my prince. It will please you.'

Florin positively devoured the letter with his eyes. While reading it, he felt joy well up inside him like a sparkling fountain.

'My father wishes me to attend the festivities,' he said with shining eyes. 'But . . . that's wonderful news!'

It was all he could do not to whoop with delight. The war was over, his father was King Theodo's guest, and he himself would soon be riding off to Vinland ...

Out of the corner of his eye he saw Chancellor Artold almost imperceptibly shake his head.

'Surely I can go?' he said quickly. 'It's my father's request and my own express wish.'

Instead of answering, the chancellor turned to Count Tillo. 'I presume you wish to accompany His Highness to Vinland?'

'Those were King Philip's instructions,' said the count, and his companions nodded in confirmation.

'Don't misunderstand me, Count Tillo,' said Artold, returning to his desk, 'but your escort is insufficient for the prince's protection.'

For an instant Florin saw Tillo's eyes flash with anger, but a moment later he inclined his head. 'Then what do you suggest, chancellor?'

Artold picked up his pen. 'I shall assign you twenty soldiers from the garrison of Montfield Castle.'

'Twenty is too many,' Count Tillo said dismissively. 'An escort of that size would attract attention. The more inconspicuous we are, the better.'

The chancellor nodded. 'Very well. In that case, five of our best men.'

Count Tillo seemed about to raise another objection, then he bowed. 'My thanks for your assistance, Chancellor Artold.'

'When do we set off?' Florin asked excitedly.

'Preferably at once,' said Count Tillo. 'However,' he added, looking down at himself, 'it will probably take us until tomorrow to make ourselves look less like highwaymen and more like the members of a royal escort.'

'We could leave at once, for all I care,' Florin said delightedly. 'How long will it take us to ride to Vinland?'

Count Tillo eyed him appraisingly. 'Twelve days, at a guess.'

'How many days did you take to get here?'

'Ten.'

'Then you'll also do it in ten with me,' Florin said firmly. After all, riding and climbing were the two royal disciplines at which none of the other boys could match him, not even Senna.

'Of course, my prince.' Tillo's scar writhed again, and Florin tried not to stare at it.

Chancellor Artold gave the men a curt nod. 'The chamberlain will show you to your quarters. Be our guests at dinner tonight.'

The entrance to the throne room was still thronged with jostling petitioners.

Florin fidgeted as if the seat of the throne had transformed itself into a red-hot grate. He longed to tell his friends the news before they heard it from the clerks or pages . . .

Chancellor Artold cleared his throat. 'You'll be setting off for Vinland tomorrow morning, Prince Florin. Do you consider that a sufficient reason for cutting the audience short?'

Florin gazed longingly through the window and down into the castle courtyard, where his fellow pupils at the school of knighthood were just saddling their horses. 'No, Chancellor Artold.'

The chancellor bent over him. 'It would be arrogant to disappoint so many people,' he whispered, inverting the big hourglass on his desk. 'Two hours more, my boy. Then I'll end the audience.'

Florin sighed quietly, then sat back on the throne and watched the chamberlain lead the next petitioners in.

A leather helmet with silver buckles. He's a soldier—a captain, at a guess—and his opening words will be . . .

———————

AS usual, the chamberlain consoled any disappointed petitioners by handing out 'audience sweetmeats': small sugar loaves stamped with Moltovia's heraldic beast, the wolf. Some people whispered that many petitioners stood in line just for the sake of the treats.

Chancellor Artold, who had ended the audience and was making notes, looked up as the chamberlain passed the desk. 'Marrod, my friend,' he said casually, 'I should like a word with you as soon as I've finished this.'

Florin was halfway to his bedchamber when he halted, struck by a thought. He knew that the chancellor always made decisions on his own. If Artold had asked the chamberlain to confer with him, he must have something important on his mind.

Abruptly, Florin turned back—and bumped into his bodyguard, who was as usual following at his heels.

'Sturmius, I left my father's letter behind. No, stay here,' he added quickly, when the youth made to come with him. 'It, er . . . would set my mind at rest if you guarded my bedchamber for once. We'll meet there.'

'As you wish, my prince.' Sturmius strode on with a self-important air while Florin hurried back on tiptoe. Just beside the throne room was a cramped, stuffy little chamber lined with cabinets in which Chancellor Artold's clerks filed away his documents. To prevent them from freezing in winter, a grating had been inserted in the foot of the wall to admit some warmth from the throne room's massive fireplace. It wasn't the first time Florin had eavesdropped at this grating, lying flat on his stomach.

'Count Tillo, of all men,' Chancellor Artold was saying, and the displeasure in his voice was unmistakable. 'Why should King Philip have appointed him his courier and the prince's escort? Any other man would have been preferable.'

'You heard what he said,' the chamberlain replied. 'He alone could be spared. Artold, you know as well as I that the kiss of peace won't be the end of it. Soldiers must be withdrawn, occupied territories returned, prisoners of war exchanged—such matters will require negotiation. King Philip needs all his closest advisers at his side.'

'Be that as it may,' Artold growled, 'it's only with the greatest reluctance that I shall entrust the prince to his care.'

'You're too suspicious, my friend,' Marrod said indulgently. 'The letter was in the king's hand, you made certain of that for yourself. After all, there are sound reasons why Prince Florin should attend the peace celebrations.' The chamberlain lowered his voice. 'He's young, but who knows? Perhaps he'll be betrothed on this occasion.'

Florin's sense of guilt at eavesdropping disappeared in a flash. He pressed his ear to the grating so hard it hurt.

'Then a marriage to Vinland's princess has been agreed?' said Artold.

'Count Tillo told me so earlier,' the chamberlain replied. 'It would be the best way to ensure a lasting peace. Provided, of course, that the two young people take to each other.'

On the other side of the grating, Florin shook his head in amazement. Did Tanko genuinely possess second sight?

'All these years of war and hatred,' murmured Chancellor Artold. 'Marrod, old friend, are they truly to end at last?'

'If it be God's will,' the chamberlain said solemnly, 'and if all concerned keep the faith, yes.'

'You're right,' Artold said abruptly. 'I'm imagining things again, old fool that I am. Of course the prince must attend the festivities. It's just that . . . You're aware of Count Tillo's reputation?'

'You mean that he has remained on excellent terms with Vinland's royal court throughout these years of war? Yes, so I've heard, but no one has ever accused him of committing treason against King Philip.'

'He's a fox, for all that,' said the chancellor. 'I don't trust him.'

Florin heard Artold push his chair back with a jerk. 'Why Tillo, of all men?' he repeated. 'Why did the king have to choose *him* as an escort? If anything happens to the prince on the way . . . It doesn't bear thinking of!'

'Come, come, Artold,' the chamberlain said soothingly. 'Bid Captain Albero accompany the prince. He would let himself be cut to ribbons for the boy's sake.'

'Send Captain Albero to me at once,' said the chancellor. 'He'll find me next door in the document chamber.'

Count Marrod laughed. 'Documents and deeds—your proven means of banishing worries. In such cases, I prefer a slice of venison pie and a jug of red Malvasian.'

Florin had heard enough. He stole out of the document chamber on tiptoe.

By the time he joined his friends at dinner that night, they had long been informed of the peace treaty and his forthcoming journey to Vinland. He was, however, able to tell them one unexpected piece of news.

'Betrothed?' Senna, Tanko and Radbod exclaimed simultaneously, with genuine dismay.

'Ssh!' Florin glanced quickly at the other end of the table, where a frozen-faced Artold was seated beside Count Tillo. The old chancellor's documents had clearly failed to restore his spirits. 'I'm not supposed to know.'

'Tanko,' Senna said faintly, 'you're a soothsayer, after all. Florin betrothed to King Theodo's daughter—ugh!' He shuddered. 'My condolences, Your Highness. I'm glad *I'm* not a crown prince!'

'You've never met her,' Florin protested.

'Nor have you,' Senna retorted, unmoved. 'What's more, you can't even choose. Theodo has a whole brood of sons but only one daughter.'

'Let's hope she's pretty, at least,' Radbod said thoughtfully. 'That would make the fact that she's a Vinlander easier to endure.'

'Stop it,' said Florin. 'We're now at peace with Vinland, don't forget. King Theodo is an admirable man and his daughter a charming damsel. Besides, I can always say no.'

'Then arm yourself with a good excuse,' Tanko advised. 'If she turns out to be cross-eyed—'

'—with a wart on her nose—' Radbod amplified.

'—a crooked neck and flat feet—' added Senna.

'—you can still decide to become a hermit instead of a king,' Tanko concluded.

'Florin,' Radbod said with a smile, 'don't you understand? The truth is, we envy you so much we're almost bursting. You're going to ride to Vinland to join your father. You'll be welcomed as an honoured guest, attend grand banquets and festivities. Ah, if only we could come with you!'

'Instead of which we'll rot here in the castle,' sighed Senna, 'being tested by our Latin master and barked at by that old mastiff Ursio.'

'And we certainly won't set eyes on any delightful Vinlandian princess,' Tanko chimed in. 'Which reminds me, have I ever told you the sad but true story of the Prince of Karinth, who asked for the hand of a king's daughter in marriage? . . . *The luckless fellow never suspected that his chosen bride was under an evil spell. A delightful damsel by day, she turned at night into a huge black spider that promptly ensnared any man it could capture and sucked him dry. On their wedding night, when the prince joined her in the bridal chamber* . . . Oh, never mind,' he said hastily, noticing Florin's grim expression, 'it's only an old wives' tale.'

IT was late when Florin entered his bedchamber. Ramon, his big feet perilously near the hearth, had fallen asleep while waiting. Muriel's door was ajar, and her snores drifted through the crack. The old nurse-maid stoutly defended her privilege of sleeping in the cubbyhole next to Florin's bedchamber. He hesitated for a moment, then tiptoed over to her bed.

Seen by candlelight, Muriel's face looked as tiny as a shrivelled raisin, but she was inoffensive only in her sleep. By day she turned into a cantankerous old spitfire whom the other servants referred to simply as 'the She-Dragon.' Yet to Florin, Montfield was as unimaginable without Muriel as it would have been without the old lime tree in the castle courtyard.

His mother had died when he was two, and Moltovia had never acquired another queen in her place.

'This court is like a monastery,' Muriel used to say, wrinkling her nose. 'It lacks womenfolk. King Philip should have taken another wife long ago. Every royal court needs a queen and a bevy of cheerful ladies-in-waiting. And you, my boy, need a mother.'

'But Muriel, I've got you,' was Florin's standard response. First, because he knew that Muriel would be pleased, and secondly because it was true. Muriel had been his mother's nursemaid, and to him she was grandmother, mother and nursemaid all in one. She had looked after him for as long as he could remember.

Florin was jolted out of his reverie by a smothered curse from next door. He gave Muriel's cheek a quick stroke, then slipped back into his own bedchamber and surveyed the scene. Ramon, his face contorted with pain, was hopping up and down on one foot in front of the hearth.

'Did you roast your foot?' Florin asked sympathetically.

'Ouch, that hurts, by all the fires in hell!' Ramon exclaimed. 'I was just about to stoke the fire for you when—'

'Nonsense,' said Florin. 'You fell asleep.'

'I may have dozed off for a moment,' Ramon conceded. 'No wonder, when you stay up half the night like an owl. Into bed with you, my prince, or you can dispense with sleep and ride off at once.'

He hobbled over to Florin's four-poster, drew the curtains and threw back the eiderdown. Then he held out a basin of water.

'I shall miss you, Ramon—you, Muriel and Sturmius,' said Florin while washing his hands and face. 'I'd like to take you with me.'

'No, no,' Ramon growled, 'I'm your valet, so it's only right that I should remain in your bedchamber until you return.'

'Hm,' Florin said dubiously. 'If I know you, you'll spend more time in the maidservants' chambers than mine.'

Ramon shook his head gravely as he pulled Florin's silk nightshirt over his head. 'Notions of that kind, my prince, are truly unbecoming in someone of your tender years.'

But I'm old enough to be betrothed without being consulted, thought Florin—betrothed, what's more, to a princess I've never met. Still, let's wait and see. It may not turn out badly after all. My mother was a princess from a neighbouring kingdom, and my father loved her beyond measure . . .

'Er, Ramon,' Florin said cautiously, 'how will I know whether I like a girl or not?'

'By her smell,' Ramon replied without hesitation. 'If she smells of apple pie or freshly baked cinnamon cakes, she's the right one for you. If she reeks of herrings and sour milk, on the other hand, don't touch her, however pretty her face may be. And now stop daydreaming—it's late.'

He adjusted Florin's pillows and carefully pulled up the bed-clothes. 'Sleep well, my prince.'

– ACROSS THE FRONTIER –

IT OUGHT TO be possible, thought Florin, to keep such days like jewels in a casket. Whenever an audience became especially tedious, I would only have to lift the lid and feast my eyes on them.

They had now been riding across country for three days, and he was enjoying every moment to the fullest. Immediately after their departure he had felt a trifle lonely and wished that his friends were with him, Radbod in particular. With every mile they put between themselves and Montfield Castle, however, he was more and more overcome by the wanderlust that makes migratory birds take wing.

Count Tillo, who knew every hill and crossroad they passed, answered his questions with inexhaustible patience. He nearly always smiled as he did, but Florin managed to ride on his left and avoid the sight of the scar on his cheek.

Their route took them across meadows, through shadowy woods and along the banks of streams where midges danced and their horses' hoofs sank deep into the soft soil. They avoided the well-trodden, much-frequented trade routes.

'For your safety's sake, my prince,' Count Tillo explained when Florin asked the reason. 'Many disreputable characters travel the high roads: footpads, highwaymen and Vinlandian mercenaries, none of whom would shrink from robbery and murder. God forbid you should fall into their hands.'

Florin nodded politely, although there seemed little danger of this. After all, he was accompanied by ten experienced fighting men with sharp swords concealed beneath their inconspicuous cloaks. In the lead rode Chancellor Artold's escort, whose commander, Captain Albero, clapped his hand to his sword hilt if a bird so much as fluttered into the air. Count Tillo's men formed the rearguard.

They halted for the night at inns and monasteries, where they passed themselves off as ordinary wayfarers. This filled Florin with impish glee, because the innkeepers and other guests naturally mistook him for the soldiers' stable boy. He insisted on unsaddling his escorts' horses and pulling off their boots in turn—which embarrassed them immensely. For once, he could help himself to food at table and sleep on straw like his companions. No one guessed, however, that two of them kept watch over their 'stable boy' all night, seated on uncomfortable wooden stools to keep themselves awake and cradling their drawn swords on their laps.

Having made good progress despite their circuitous route, they reached the Argentian Range on the fourth day. Florin had never been so far west before. His few excursions had taken him south, to the court of his uncle, King Guido of Arelia. It was probable, he reflected, that he had seen less of Moltovia than any other boy at the royal school of knighthood. King Philip seldom permitted Florin to go travelling and visiting with him. He would have preferred to keep his only son shut up in a cabinet like some precious glass goblet. High time for a change!

A convenient high road led along the valley that crossed the Argentian Range, but Count Tillo spurned this. Instead, he conducted the party along a mule track halfway up the mountainside. Before long the terrain became so impassable they had to dismount and lead their horses by the bridle. Boulders, drooping branches and juniper bushes blocked the view ahead until, all at once, the slopes across the valley could be glimpsed through a gap in the trees. Florin gave a start. Instead of a mountainside green with trees and bushes, he saw bare, jutting crags and huge, black, yawning holes. It looked as if some giant had split open the mountainside with an axe.

'What's that?' he asked.

'Not an agreeable sight, is it?' Count Tillo replied. 'But if one knows what lies hidden in those clefts in the rock, one's heart rejoices.'

He made a sweeping gesture that encompassed the whole area. 'Your treasure chamber, my prince: the silver mines of Argentia.'

Towering, glittering mountains of silver—that was how Florin had always pictured the silver mines of Argentia, not these gaping wounds in the rock. Did the miners have to crawl into them like worms to get at the silver?

'For as far as your eye can see,' Count Tillo said beside him, 'the slopes are threaded with veins of silver. Not for nothing has this district been hotly contested since the war began.'

When they came down out of the mountains, Florin saw for the first time what war had done to his country and its people. Crops had been burnt to ashes, trees loomed up like blackened stumps, empty windows stared out of ruined houses like sightless eyes. Villages that must once have been prosperous were abandoned and laid waste. Not a living soul remained there. Deer were grazing on pastureland behind woven fences and wild boar wallowed in village ponds. Foxes and wild dogs roamed the deserted cottages.

Wild beasts had become villagers and house-dwellers, and the only objects bearing witness to humankind were graves: low mounds of soil carelessly shovelled together, devoid of headstones and adorned at most with rough wooden crosses.

What made the deepest impression on Florin was a hunting lodge. Although it looked bright and cheerful from a distance, he saw as they drew nearer that its windows, too, were gaping holes, that the lime tree in the courtyard had been felled and the well filled in. He did not see the most terrible sight until they rode on: impaled on the points of some tall iron railings were cats—dozens of contorted, terribly mutilated feline cadavers. Cats with their eyes put out, with scorched tails, paws cut off and bellies slit open. And, in the air, a cloying stench of decay and putrefaction.

Florin averted his head.

'Who would do such a thing?' he asked in disbelief.

'War,' said Count Tillo. 'It turns castles into ruins and men into beasts.'

Florin remained thoughtfully silent as he rode on. What a strange quirk of fate. He was bound for Vinland to celebrate the coming of peace, but the horrors of war were confronting him at every step. It was as if the Almighty wished to show him the true blessings of peace on earth.

'God be praised that peace will now prevail,' he said.

'Yes, indeed, my prince,' Count Tillo agreed. 'God be praised.'

On the afternoon of the seventh day their progress was unexpectedly delayed by the Relling, the river that marked the frontier between Moltovia and Vinland. All that remained of the bridge that had linked the two kingdoms were some charred beams protruding from the water, and no ferryman could be found.

It wasn't until they had ridden ten miles downstream that they encountered a young fisherman who, in return for a bright silver shilling, rowed them across the river in his ramshackle boat, one man and one horse at a time.

On the other side of the river the countryside gradually began to change. Moltovia's mountains, gorges and dense forests gave way to broad, open plains, marshland and fields with a view to the far horizon.

'What the Vinlanders conceive of as mountains we Moltovians call molehills,' Count Tillo remarked with a smile. 'You'll see, even the hill on which Bellingar Castle stands is in truth a low mound of earth created by the hand of man.'

Scattered among the fields and marshes were small, wretched-looking villages made up of half-timbered cottages with thatched roofs. Ducks and geese quacked and cackled in their pens and thin, shaggy dogs yapped at the passing horsemen. To Florin's relief, the houses were still occupied and the wells intact.

'The inhabitants are too poor to make looting worthwhile,' Count Tillo explained. 'No soldier in search of plunder troubles to dismount hereabouts. Vinland's prosperous regions, its grain stores and gold deposits, are far away in the south and west of the kingdom.'

ON the evening of the ninth day, the party had been riding since dawn across sparsely inhabited tracts of land. Although modest in size, the secluded hillside monastery where they planned to spend the night was the largest building in all that region.

'We'll be in no danger up here,' said Count Tillo as he dismounted and pulled the rope of the doorbell. 'The pious brethren have sworn a vow of silence: they're forbidden to utter a word outside their monastery walls. Let us give them a treat and disclose your true identity. They can tell their novices about it for decades to come!'

When the brother porter heard who was seeking admission, his eyes widened and his jaw dropped. He hurried off to inform the abbot of their exalted visitor—indeed, he forgot to open the gate in his excitement, so Florin and his companions remained standing outside like humble petitioners.

Twilight was creeping westward across the countryside, which

seemed from the monastery hill to stretch away into infinity: pastureland, streams fringed with trees, harvested grain fields in which shocks
of corn were arranged in rows like little hunchbacked dwarves. All was
as calm and peaceful as if the world had never been otherwise since the
dawn of creation. Was it only three days since they had left the ravages
of war behind?

Florin looked at the sun, a small orange disk hovering above the
skyline. 'The end of the world must be somewhere over there,' he
mused aloud. He thought of the stories Tanko had told about the edge
of the world: about the dog-headed creatures that dwelt in clefts above
the fiery abyss, or about the bird folk who surveyed the countryside
from their enormous eyries, seized the unwary in their talons and
carried them off. 'What is it like?' he asked.

'Alas, my prince,' said Count Tillo, and his scar writhed, 'I fear
that we shall not reach the end of the world despite your fine horse-
manship. We will, however, reach Bellingar Castle—tomorrow night,
what's more.'

Butterflies stirred gently in the pit of Florin's stomach. Bellingar,
the lion's den, King Theodo's castle . . . What would it be like to be a
guest there?

By the time the brother porter opened the outer gate, all the
monks had lined up like a flock of grey birds to welcome Florin. They
bowed low, then conducted him proudly into their monastery, an
unpretentious timber building that was their dormitory and refectory,
library and seminary, barn and henhouse combined. A small chapel
with a belfry had been built of rubble nearby.

As the guest of honour, Florin was accorded the monastery's only
bed: that of the abbot himself. Whatever was to blame—the bran bread
the brother kitchener had baked for supper or the musty odour
emanating from the bed curtains—he took a long time to get to sleep.
Restlessly tossing and turning beneath the thick eiderdown, he
watched by the light of a candle stub the backs of the two sentries

seated like statues at the foot of his bed. When he finally fell asleep, he lapsed at once into a sinister, confused dream.

HE was walking along a forest track, but not alone: his companion wore a nobleman's doublet and had the head of a fox—with a scar beneath the right eye.

Forest creatures lay dying on either side of the path: squirrels, hares, badgers, roe deer, stags. Mouths flecked with bloody foam, they fixed Florin with their dull-eyed gaze.

'What happened here?' he asked.

The fox-headed man pointed into the shadowy depths of the forest. 'Have you not noticed the wild beast, my prince? Look, there it goes through the trees.'

Quickly though Florin turned his head, the beast in the trees was quicker still. He caught a glimpse of two glowing eyes and a flash of gold. At the same time, his nose detected a pungent, feral smell. A jackal? A lion?

Fear turned his blood to ice. Seeing a light up ahead, he hurried toward it. The wild beast, hidden in the undergrowth, kept pace with him.

Florin broke into a run as if his life depended on it. With a cry of relief he reached the edge of the forest—and found himself on the brink of an abyss. He swayed, but just managed to recover his balance. Stretching away in front of him was a grey, cheerless, endless plain unbroken by tree or bush. Sable-winged birds were circling above it.

'Welcome to the end of the world,' the fox-headed man said from behind him. 'You're expected.'

'MY prince!'

Florin sat up with a start, roused by the sentry's low voice.

'Your pardon, Highness,' the man said with a bow. 'It seemed you were having a bad dream.'

'I was,' Florin murmured in relief. 'Many thanks.'

After early mass and a morning meal for which the brother kitchener dished up some apple pie as hard as rock, they set off again. About a mile beyond the monastery they came to a wide river which, Count Tillo assured Florin, flowed straight toward Vinland's royal capital and Bellingar Castle.

They rode fast, and Florin's fearful dream images were dispelled by the exercise and the cool morning air. It's just that everything is suddenly so near, he told himself. To me, Vinland's court used to seem as strange and sinister as the end of the world, and all at once I'm nearly there.

The riverbank was lined with willows and hazel bushes. Startled flocks of waterfowl rose into the air as they rode by, big birds with black plumage and white crests such as Florin had never seen in Moltovia. They occasionally passed fishermen's cottages or watermills, and Florin watched the fishermen skilfully keeping their craft head-on to the current as they cast their nets. Near one wooden pier some little boys were splashing in the shallows while women laundered sheets and spread them out to dry on the bank.

Florin's excitement grew with every mile. He had seen the scars of war on his journey; now he was riding into a peaceful future. Like these people beside the river, everyone in Vinland and Moltovia would be able to live unharmed and without fear. If *that* wasn't reason enough to celebrate!

Florin began to picture the festivities. What was the court of Vinland like? What did they eat and drink there? As long they didn't dine on snails and frogs' legs like the Frankenlanders! There would doubtless be music and dancing. Was the princess fond of dancing? He hoped he wouldn't offend against any unfamiliar customs and conventions. On the other hand, what could happen to him with his father at his side?

Count Tillo's voice broke in on his thoughts. 'Wouldn't you care to rest, my prince? It must be long past midday.'

Florin considered this. 'How much farther is it?'

'If it be God's will, we shall get there by sunset.'

'Then let us ride on,' said Florin, far too impatient to stop now.

'As you wish, my prince.'

THE nearer they drew to the royal capital, the busier the river became. It was like a mirror that reflected the life around it. Florin saw cargo vessels laden with timber and barrels, rafts crowded with horses and people—even a small oared galley with an unfamiliar orange flag flying from its mast.

By the time he sighted the city's walls and church towers, the tall willow trees had steeped the river in shadow.

Vinland's royal capital was a substantial place, Florin noted as he rode through the city gates at Count Tillo's side. The well-paved streets were flanked by streams and remarkably free from rubbish. The ground floors of the handsome stone buildings were occupied by shops, taverns and artisans' workshops. As they were riding across the spacious marketplace, which was enclosed on all four sides by shady covered walkways, ten or more churches began to ring their bells for evening service, creating a din that must have carried far beyond the city walls.

Passing along narrow lanes and through stone arcades, they came once more to the river. Captain Albero's horse had just set foot on the bridge that spanned it when a black-robed old woman dashed out of the bridgekeeper's house. Before the startled soldiers could stop her, she had leapt in front of Florin's horse.

'Woe unto thee, poor wretch!' the old crone cried shrilly, her grey hair loose on her shoulders. She hopped up and down, drumming on a billet of firewood with a marrow bone. 'Disaster threatens!'

Florin took no notice of her words, too busy trying to prevent his frightened horse from trampling her into the cobblestones.

The woman herself was heedless of the danger. 'Turn back, thou bird of ill omen, before it's too late!' she screeched, drumming on her piece of wood. 'The warning voices have spoken!'

'Easy, easy,' Florin told his horse, which was dancing on the spot with flattened ears and rolling eyes. 'For Christ's sake, old woman, what do you want of me?'

'Flee for your life!' she screamed. An instant later she was surrounded by armed men. They were not Count Tillo's men, Florin was surprised to see, but strangers who had suddenly appeared from nowhere.

'Away with the crazy old witch!' Count Tillo commanded brusquely, his face pale.

Two of the men seized the old woman and dragged her off.

'Let me go, you devil's spawn!' she wailed loudly. 'The voices, the voices—I must sing my song!' She turned to Florin with her arms above her head. 'Hearken to me, prince of misfortune! Do not cross this bridge!'

'Let us ride on,' Count Tillo commanded.

Once Florin was across the bridge, he turned and looked back. The crone had evidently eluded the men's grasp, because she was now standing motionless on the bridge like a coal-black raven, one arm raised in warning.

Florin shivered at the sight. 'She addressed me as prince,' he said in a puzzled voice. 'Did she know me?'

'The crazy old witch also called you a poor wretch and a bird of ill omen,' replied Count Tillo, still looking shocked. 'A demon must have scrambled her wits.'

Florin couldn't shake off the strange incident. 'What men were those?' he asked thoughtfully. 'They seemed to appear from nowhere.'

'Soldiers of the king,' Count Tillo said curtly. 'They're responsible for keeping order in the city. But now let us ride on quickly, my prince. You must be weary, and I want you safe behind Bellingar's walls before nightfall.'

BELLINGAR, Theodo's royal castle, stood a good three miles outside the city—near enough to be supplied with goods by the townsfolk but far enough for the noble courtiers to be able to ride and hunt in peace. When Florin reached the royal forest after a brisk gallop across fields and meadows, he quickly forgot the old woman's babblings. With its centuries-old beech, oak and chestnut trees with trunks bigger than three men could span, arms outstretched, King Theodo's forest was no less beautiful than that near Montfield Castle.

'It's September,' thought Florin with a thrill of pleasure. After the festivities King Theodo would invite them to go hunting—he was bound to. While the members of his escort surveyed their surroundings even more warily than before, Florin imagined himself riding through the forest at his father's side, accompanied by a pack of excited hounds. King Philip would be able to shed his starchy, regal manner. They would grill venison together over the fire and sleep beneath the stars . . .

The trees thinned and they rode out into the open. At last it loomed up straight ahead of them: Bellingar Castle, a massive fortress whose weight seemed to flatten the hill on which it stood. And it was red! Florin thought for a moment that his eyes had been deceived by the twilight, but as they drew nearer he saw that the castle's walls, ramparts and turrets were constructed of pale red granite.

Fluttering high above the battlements were banners depicting a lion with claws extended. Florin gulped at the sight. The lion was Vinland's heraldic beast, and as closely associated with King Theodo as the wolf was with his father.

'Any wolf that enters a lion's den must expect to be torn limb from limb . . .' Florin had suddenly recalled the old fable of the wolf and the lion. Then he shook his head at his nonsense. Wouldn't the heavenly kingdom envisioned by the prophet Isaiah be more appropriate, where the lion and the wolf dwelt together in peace?

When he rode through the outer gateway behind Count Tillo, Florin marvelled at how spacious the castle was. Montfield Castle was built on a precipitous rock and had space enough only for a moat and strip of grassland, whereas Bellingar's hill was big enough to accommodate pastureland, orchards, a big jousting yard, servants' quarters and more than sufficient stabling.

The castle itself was enclosed by a ring of walls and towers. A single gate protected by a heavy portcullis led to this innermost area. Florin saw dozens of heavily armed sentries with archers on the ramparts above them.

'Open the gate!' a captain called from the ramparts. The portcullis was raised with a rattle of chains, and grooms hurried over to attend to the horses. Florin had scarcely slid from the saddle when the portcullis fell back into its iron seating with a crash.

Torches were already blazing on the walls of the castle courtyard. A sentry emerged from the shadows beside the gate and marched up to Captain Albero.

'If you and your men would follow me,' he said politely, 'I'll show you to your quarters.'

The captain looked hesitantly at Count Tillo.

'You can take my men as well,' the count told him in friendly, reassuring tones. 'We're at our journey's end, Captain Albero, and you've truly earned a rest. Have a bath, eat your fill, and be sure to sample some Vinlandian wine. The prince will gladly dispense with your services until tomorrow morning.'

Captain Albero bowed to Florin. 'May we take our leave then, Your Highness?'

'Of course, captain, and thank you,' Florin said absently. His attention had been captured by the big, brightly illuminated, round-arched windows over the gateway. They were awaiting him up there—the thought made his heart beat faster.

'Come,' said Count Tillo.

The chamberlain was standing in the entrance hall. Florin almost giggled at the sight of him, his sullen grey face went so badly with his pale blue silk coat.

'Welcome to Bellingar Castle, Your Highness.' He bowed and handed Florin a goblet of cold spiced wine. 'Vinland's court is honoured by your presence.'

His tone was polite, almost grovelling, but Florin had hardly put the goblet to his lips when the man snatched it from his hand.

'With your permission, I shall conduct you to the banqueting hall at once,' he said.

Florin was puzzled. Shouldn't this discourteous servant have first shown him to his quarters, or at least brought him a basin of water in which to wash his hands?

The man in the silk coat seemed unaware of his surprise. 'The king awaits you with impatience,' he said urgently.

'Which one?' Florin asked with a smile.

The chamberlain looked at him inquiringly. 'What do you mean?'

'Well,' said Florin, astonished that the man had failed to understand his question, 'I suppose that two kings are awaiting me: Theodo, King of Vinland, and Philip, King of Moltovia, my father.'

For some reason the chamberlain seemed utterly disconcerted by this answer. In defiance of all etiquette, he stared at Florin with his mouth open, swaying slightly as if the ground were quaking beneath his feet. He did not recover his composure until Count Tillo said sharply: 'Would you now be good enough to conduct the prince upstairs?'

'Your Highness, Count Tillo,' the chamberlain said with another bow, 'if you would follow me!'

What a heart-warming welcome, thought Florin, as he followed the chamberlain up the stairs. Were all Vinlanders like this? Suddenly remembering the planned betrothal, he felt a nervous stitch in the pit of his stomach. But why worry about the Vinlanders? He would soon be reunited with his father and his father's closest noblemen, many of whom he greatly admired. He was tempted to dash past the chamberlain and into the banqueting hall, but that would be unbecoming in a prince.

The antechamber was brightly lit by torches in wall sconces and the big double doors were wide open. Another court official was awaiting them on the threshold. Attired in a blue silk coat like the chamberlain, he might have been the latter's younger brother but for the way he glared at him, which was anything but fraternal.

'Who's that?' Florin asked Count Tillo in a whisper.

'The royal master of ceremonies,' Count Tillo whispered back. 'He and the chamberlain are said to be the best of enemies.' The scar on his cheek writhed, but his smile was more of a grimace. How tense the count was looking all of sudden, thought Florin. Was he unnerved by the prospect of confronting two kings at the same time?

'Count Tillo, you have carried out your task to the letter,' Florin told him reassuringly. 'I shall tell my father how much I enjoyed our journey together.'

'Most gracious of you,' Count Tillo replied, but he didn't look Florin in the eye.

At that moment the master of ceremonies rapped on the floor with his gold staff of office.

'Our noble guest,' he called loudly into the banqueting hall, 'Florin, Crown Prince of Moltovia!' With a pompous gesture, he signalled to Florin to follow him.

'Aren't you coming?' Florin asked when he saw Count Tillo turn to leave.

'My mission ends at this door,' replied the count. 'Go in, my prince. Don't keep King Theodo waiting . . . or your father.'

When Florin was out of earshot he added softly, 'God help you, Prince of Moltovia.' Then he turned on his heel and hurried downstairs as if all the hounds in hell were after him.

– BETRAYED –

FLORIN WAS OVERCOME by a strange sense of familiarity as he followed the master of ceremonies across the banqueting hall. The triple round-arched windows, the two ornate fireplaces with their crackling logs, the great banqueting table between them, the elevated royal throne at its centre—the resemblance to Montfield's banqueting hall was as perfect as a mirror image. Even the location of the pinewood torches in their iron sconces was identical. Who knows, thought Florin, perhaps the architect of Montfield Castle and his team of masons had moved on to Vinland two centuries ago. The one striking difference was the ceiling: here, Montfield's familiar heavy beams had been replaced by an airy vault such as Florin had never seen except in a church. It was sprinkled with golden stars that glittered mysteriously in the torchlight.

'Does it please you to be here?' a voice asked softly.

Florin's gaze had been directed at the ceiling, which was why he noticed only now that he had reached the throne. It stood on a dais like his father's, so the man who had spoken was looking down at him. Youthful in appearance, he was slim and lithe, with smooth, olive-skinned features, curly jet-black hair, and sparkling white teeth.

They'll report that he's a fat, bald, toothless, evil-smelling fellow with flat feet . . .

Florin had to suppress a grin at the memory of Tanko's words. Seldom had his friend been so sorely mistaken.

Behind him, the master of ceremonies cleared his throat, and Florin suddenly realised that all present were waiting for him to reply.

'It pleases me greatly, Your Majesty,' he said. He pointed to the star-spangled ceiling. 'It seems your court has enlisted the vault of heaven itself.'

'Heaven is close to us indeed,' King Theodo said with a smile. 'Vinland enjoys God's special protection.'

Only a few weeks ago Florin would have laughed this idea to scorn. Now he nodded politely, at the same time looking around for familiar faces from Moltovia. But in vain—only Vinlanders were seated at the royal banqueting table. Florin did his best to meet their gaze in a frank, self-assured manner. They might be foreigners, but he was aware of their status: they were Vinland's most influential dignitaries— men without whose advice and consent the king made no decision of importance. The seating order at King Theodo's table corresponded exactly to that which was customary at Montfield Castle. The places of honour immediately beside the king were occupied by bishops in cere-monial red vestments. Somewhat further away sat the Privy Councillors with their heavy gold chains of office, the black-robed royal judges, and the country's foremost noblemen. Even the hounds beneath the table were lying in the same position as those at home.

'What a pleasure it is to be able to welcome Moltovia's crown prince.' Although King Theodo spoke in a low voice, Florin caught the words with ease: everyone in the room fell silent as soon as he opened his mouth.

'Come, sit down.' Theodo took hold of Florin's hands and drew him closer. 'No, here beside me. By your leave, Father Gelasius . . .'

With a courteous bow, the bishop at Theodo's side vacated his chair and a page showed him to another place.

King Theodo smiled at Florin. 'Are you weary after your journey?'

Florin firmly shook his head. 'I would happily have ridden many miles farther,' he said. It belatedly occurred to him that his host might think this rather discourteous. 'But I'm very glad to be a guest at the court of Vinland,' he added quickly, 'and I thank you for inviting me to the celebrations.'

'To the celebrations, yes,' Theodo repeated, lost in thought. 'We have every reason to celebrate and give thanks to God.' Abruptly, he clapped his hands. 'Let dinner be served!'

How strange, thought Florin as pages and maidservants deposited platters and dishes on the table. Since when was food served before the arrival of the guests of honour? It would be cold long before King Philip and his men came to table. Were Vinlanders so unmannerly? And where were the Moltovians supposed to sit, given that every chair was occupied save the place of honour immediately opposite Theodo?

The roast venison gave off a tempting aroma, and Florin, who had eaten nothing since his meagre slice of apple pie that morning, felt his mouth begin to water. But no one at table made any move to touch the food. The atmosphere in the room felt peculiar—an almost imperceptible vibration, like a current flowing beneath the surface of a calm stretch of water. Florin had detected the same tension in Count Tillo and the chamberlain. Only King Theodo seemed perfectly calm. 'It's good that you aren't weary,' he said. 'There are great things in store tonight.'

Florin's eyes roamed the banqueting hall once more. He simply had to ask, or he would explode with impatience.

'Where's my father, King Theodo? And where are the members of his retinue?'

'Be patient a little while longer,' Theodo replied. 'Your father will soon be with us. There was—' he hesitated for a moment, 'some trouble with his attire.'

Knowing his father, Florin found it hard to suppress a smile. Although King Philip was extremely frugal in almost every respect, he set great store by dressing correctly. Moltovia's court tailors dreaded his rebukes.

Surreptitiously, Florin examined Theodo out of the corner of his eye. Over his dark doublet the King of Vinland wore a black velvet coat whose sole adornment was a clasp in the shape of his heraldic lion. The bishops in their vestments of red and gold brocade resembled gaudy idols in comparison.

Florin looked down at himself and stifled a sigh: his father would greatly disapprove of his dusty travelling cloak and crumpled doublet, but he hadn't been given an opportunity to change. Furtively extracting his rings and golden amulet from the little leather pouch in which he'd kept them during the journey, he put them on. They would have to do for now.

He surveyed the room once more. Where was the queen? Where were the princes and princess, the wives of the courtiers and their children? Apart from a few youthful pages, he was the only boy in the room.

He shook his head in puzzlement. A banquet without the queen? But wait, how could anyone in the castle have known that he and his escort would arrive on this particular day? Of course, he thought, feeling relieved, that explained it: tonight was just a modest function held in honour of his father and himself. The grand banquet had been set for another day.

'The grand banquet,' King Theodo repeated as if Florin had uttered his thoughts aloud. 'The most glorious banquet this court has ever witnessed.'

'When will it take place?' asked Florin.

'Tonight,' the king replied with a smile. 'Here and now.'

Florin was dumbfounded. Was this supposed to be the grand cele-
bration? He didn't wish to be impolite, truly not, but Moltovians were
better at celebrating. They did so with music, dancing and games—
entertainments of which the Vinlanders had apparently never heard.

King Theodo seemed to read his thoughts from his expression.
'You lack entertainment?' he asked. 'Be patient a moment longer.'

He nodded to the master of ceremonies, who almost imperceptibly
returned his nod and left the room.

Theodo gaily clapped his hands. 'The night's diversions are about
to commence!' he cried. 'Watch closely, young Prince of Moltovia, so
that you miss nothing!'

Florin stared at the doorway in suspense. What would appear
there? Conjurers? Acrobats? Exotic beasts? But his joyful anticipation
quickly gave way to bewilderment when, instead of jugglers or
dancers, soldiers came marching in armed to the teeth with swords
and pikes.

'What does this mean?' Florin looked at Theodo inquiringly.

'Just wait,' said the king. 'We shall soon have some sport.'

Still more soldiers entered. With mounting uneasiness, Florin heard
a hoarse-voiced captain bellow an order and saw the soldiers divide
into two ranks, forming an avenue that led from the entrance to the
banqueting table.

Harsh words of command and a rattle of chains could be heard
issuing from the doorway.

'Now,' said King Theodo. 'Now watch!'

Hemmed in by guards, a man had appeared on the threshold.
Florin had to crane his neck to see him. The man's head was bowed,
his clothing hung in tatters, his skin was a mass of welts and dark
bruises. The heavy iron shackles about his wrists and ankles made it
hard for him to walk, but the soldiers prodded him with their pikes
like bear-baiters. Just in front of the table he stumbled and almost fell.

The guards hauled him to his feet, and for a moment the candlelight illuminated his face.

'Duke Bonizo!' Florin shouted the words despite himself. Wide-eyed, he saw the duke forced to his knees in front of the table with a spearpoint pricking the back of his neck.

'I see that our program of diversions has already captured your attention,' said King Theodo. 'But this is only the start.'

Florin seemed to hear the king's voice from a long way off. As if under some dire magic spell, he could only stare at the doorway through which more prisoners were being herded. They resembled the band of captured pirates he'd seen displayed in the marketplace at home a few weeks ago. They were ragged, filthy and in chains, yet he recognised each one: Duke Bonizo, the bravest of Moltovia's warrior noblemen; Count Etigo, King Philip's faithful friend and Florin's godfather; counts Gilbert, Bertin and Bernold, supreme commanders of the army; Count Abram, administrator of the royal castles; white-haired Duke Quentin, vice-president of the Privy Council; Judge Hilduin, chief justice of the royal court of arbitration . . . All had accompanied King Philip on his peace mission to Frankenland. Moltovia's highest-ranking noblemen were being paraded here like footpads and murderers.

At length there were twenty prisoners kneeling before the banqueting table, held in check by the spears and pikes of their guards. But King Theodo paid them no heed; he was looking intently at the doorway.

In that moment Florin knew what would happen. He wanted to cry out, but no sound escaped his lips. He wanted to jump up, but remained frozen to the spot. As if in a trance, he heard the master of ceremonies announce: 'The King of Moltovia! Make way for the mighty King of Moltovia!'

When his father was hustled in, half naked and in chains like the rest, Florin began to tremble. The trembling started in his legs, crept slowly up into his chest and arms, and finally took possession of every part of him. He could not stop it. Helpless and shaking all over, he could only stare at King Theodo when the latter said: 'This was a sight worth waiting for, don't you agree? Your father's ceremonial robes are truly sumptuous.'

Prodded by the soldiers' pikes, King Philip tottered toward the banqueting table. The assembled company clapped and jeered loudly at the sight of him.

'Welcome to Vinland, proud monarch!'

'Where's your army, King of Moltovia? Did you lose it on the way?'

'I'll wager you never imagined it would be like this, Wolf of Moltovia!'

When the guards dragged King Philip in front of the throne, Florin saw that he was bleeding from a number of small stab wounds. Then Theodo raised his hand. Silence fell, broken only by a loud crack as a log split open in the fireplace.

'Welcome, Philip.' King Theodo inclined his head as if in deference to his guest. 'We've been waiting for you. Now partake of our banquet.' With a smile, he indicated the place of honour across the table from him.

King Philip's only response was to spit on the floor at his feet. Theodo's eyes narrowed, but his lips continued to smile as before.

'It seems you fail to appreciate my hospitality,' he said softly. 'What is your son to think of such discourteous behaviour?'

King Philip saw Florin then, and his face froze in horror. He made a desperate attempt to break free, but the vigilant guards tugged at his chains so mercilessly that he abandoned the struggle with an agonised groan.

'My surprise has been a success,' Theodo said, his tone suggesting that he had presented Philip with a particularly valuable gift. 'Or doesn't it please you to have your son at your side on this auspicious occasion?'

'Pray to God, Theodo,' King Philip retorted. 'Pray to God that your own sons never learn the truth about their father. Burdened with such a disgrace, how could they ever again raise their heads before God and the world?'

Florin listened to his father, listened to King Theodo, and understood not a word of what passed between them. One afternoon years ago, before he'd learnt to swim, he had given Muriel the slip and fallen into a pool in the forest. He remembered his utter bewilderment as its green waters closed over his head. That was just how he felt now; drowning in dark eddies of insanity. Surely a strong hand would reach down and haul him from the depths? 'My sons,' said Theodo, in the same soft voice in which he had bidden Florin welcome shortly before, 'will some day rule the united kingdoms of Vinland and Moltovia. They will be rich and powerful and justly proud of their father, who has rid the world of you vermin. So have no fear for *my* offspring. You would be better advised—' he put out his hand and gently stroked Florin's cheek, 'to fear for your own.'

To Florin, Theodo's touch seemed to burn his cheek like a branding iron.

'What are you, Theodo of Vinland,' King Philip demanded hoarsely, 'a man or a fiend? Only the devil can have inspired you to lure the boy to your court.'

'But father,' Florin said haltingly, in a desperate attempt to make sense of the situation, 'you yourself invited me to the festivities.' Swiftly, he felt for the letter in his wallet, unrolled the parchment and held it up like a talisman against the incomprehensible. 'Surely this is your seal?'

King Philip nodded. 'My seal,' he said. Then, grimly: 'My signature, too.' He turned to King Theodo with his eyes blazing. 'Murder and treachery are not enough for you, it seems. You were vile enough to forge this letter!'

Even as his father was speaking, Florin involuntarily ran his fingers over the parchment. His mouth went dry: they had encountered an almost imperceptible bulge where a skilful forger had affixed his father's seal and signature to the letter with silken threads as thin as cobwebs, so as to avoid the telltale smell of glue. Why in the world had neither he nor Chancellor Artold noticed anything?

'I'm a truly forbearing man, Philip,' Theodo said calmly. 'Despite your impertinence, I invite you once more to sit at my table.'

Again he pointed to the empty chair, and again King Philip spat contemptuously.

'Think it over well.' Theodo waved his hand at the dishes and platters in front of him. 'This will be your last nourishing meal. In the dungeons you'll have to accustom yourself to different fare.'

'Most beloved king,' a loud, mocking voice said suddenly, 'it's said there's some delicious game to be hunted in your dungeons.' Florin, who had been listening with bated breath, gave a start. 'King Philip will be able to hold some magnificent banquets down there: spiders' legs and centipedes in rats' blood sauce—even the royal kitchen-master will turn green with envy!'

Universal merriment greeted these words. 'Where are you hiding, Mimus?' called a man at the lower end of the table. 'Come, you donkey, show yourself!'

'Have you missed me already, noble sirs?' the voice demanded. 'Have you, all you gluttons and drunkards who cram their bellies at my king's table?'

A figure detached itself from the gloom behind a pillar and slowly emerged into the glow from the fire. The flames cast tall, flickering shadows, and Florin was at first unsure if it was human, the stooped creature that stood there sniffing the air in all directions. It had the face of a man, but its head was surmounted by long ass's ears and its body sheathed from head to foot in an iridescent skin striped green and yellow, like that of a frog. Every movement it made was accompanied by the tinkling of bells, a sound so shrill it hurt the ears.

'Mimus,' King Theodo said reproachfully, 'you're neglecting your duties. I dislike being kept waiting for my entertainment.'

It dawned on Florin that the tinkling frog must be Theodo's court jester. Many kings and princes kept jesters for their amusement, but he had never seen one before. His father had a deep-rooted aversion to clowning and masquerades. Hospitably though monks and scholars were received at the court of Moltovia, jugglers, clowns and itinerant entertainers were turned away at the castle gates.

'My sweet king,' the jester said, performing an exaggerated bow, 'why summon me when you've already assembled such a splendid band of buffoons?'

He bounded into the midst of the kneeling prisoners, pinched the cheek of one, tweaked another's ears, and grinned derisively at the impotent rage on their faces.

'What's this I see, you noblemen of Moltovia?' he cried in mock astonishment. 'Your attire is utterly unsuited to this festive occasion. I can't believe it!' He went right up to King Philip. 'The mighty King of Moltovia has actually forgotten to don his crown! How fortunate that I can come to his aid. Hold him tight!' he bade the guards.

Florin drove his fingernails deep into his palms as the jester extracted a fistful of steaming offal from his pocket and deliberately dumped it on his father's head. Blood and filth ran down King Philip's cheeks. A simultaneous yell went up from all present. The Vinlanders bellowed with derision and delight, the Moltovians with rage and detestation. A moment later, heedless of his chains and the pikes levelled at him, Duke Bonizo flew at the jester's throat.

'Let him be, my friend,' Florin heard his father say calmly. 'He's only a jester!'

Four guards hurled themselves at Duke Bonizo, whose hands had fastened on the jester's throat like a vice.

'Ow, help me, damn you!' screeched Mimus, his bells tinkling ever more loudly and shrilly. 'He's throttling me!'

King Theodo was watching the scene with undisguised glee, Florin saw. The jester continued to bawl until the guards at last succeeded in hauling Duke Bonizo off and bludgeoned him to the floor.

'My poor Mimus!' said Theodo, laughing heartily at the jester, who was clutching his throat and fighting for breath. 'It wouldn't surprise me if one of your knavish tricks cost you your life one of these days. But I promise you,' he went on with a cursory glance at Duke Bonizo's writhing, groaning figure, 'that anyone who lays hands on you will pay a heavy price!'

Florin's heart missed a beat as Theodo turned to his father. King Philip had shaken off his ignominious crown and was standing motionless between his guards. The two kings exchanged a long, silent stare, their mutual hatred almost tangible in the air between them. Then, in response to a swift gesture from Theodo, the guards forced Philip to his knees.

'That's better,' Theodo said contentedly. 'Worms belong on the ground.'

'You and your jester are two of a kind,' King Philip retorted, his voice shaking with fury. 'This display of yours is pure buffoonery!'

'Buffoonery, you call it?' Theodo pointed triumphantly to Philip's chains, to the kneeling prisoners and the pikes pricking their necks. 'I call it victory—a victory won by me, the victor, over you, the vanquished. Or had you forgotten that we two are at war?'

'You know as well as I that the peace treaty was signed and is now in force,' said King Philip.

'Peace treaty? To what do you refer?' Theodo surveyed the room with feigned incomprehension. 'You yourself, Philip, in your boundless arrogance, frustrated my attempts to make peace. King Ludvik of Frankenland and all these men here—' he indicated his henchmen, 'are my witnesses.'

'Liar!' shouted one of the prisoners. Almost casually, a guard drew back his fist and dealt the man a blow that sent him sprawling.

'God in his heaven knows that you lie, Theodo of Vinland,' said King Philip. 'And here on earth my papers will bear witness to the truth.'

'Ah, yes, your papers.' Theodo heaved a rueful sigh. 'Let us hear what you have to say on that subject, Chancellor Benedict.'

Theodo's chancellor rose from his chair. He was young, barely half as old as Chancellor Artold, and his pointed nose and dark, beady eyes lent him the appearance of an overgrown rat.

'Law and custom prescribe that the papers of a captured foe be honourably preserved,' he declared in solemn tones. 'For that reason, Philip of Moltovia, I ordered your document chest to be guarded like the apple of my eye. But there's no remedy for stupidity, alas, and one of the night watchmen left his tallow candle burning on the chest. Here, Your Majesty,' the chancellor continued, shaking with suppressed laughter as he produced a tiny funeral urn from his pocket, 'are your papers!'

'And there's no peace treaty among my own papers,' King Theodo said casually. 'You see, Philip? We're still at war, and it breaks no divine commandment or earthly law to treat a defeated enemy as one pleases.'

Still on his knees, King Philip drew himself erect. When he spoke, he seemed taller than Theodo on his throne.

'Shame on you, King of Vinland! We kneel before you as prisoners, but our captivity is a thousand times more honourable than your victory. You feigned a wish for peace, treacherously signed the treaty, exchanged the kiss of peace with me for appearance's sake—and all the time you were intent on our destruction!'

'Your memory has played a trick on you,' declared Theodo. 'There never was a treaty or a kiss of peace. You yourself proclaimed that the war should continue.' He raised his hands. 'And Vinland, with God's help, has won it.'

'Lies, all lies,' King Philip said scornfully. 'What traitor's reward did you promise King Ludvik of Frankenland in return for bearing false witness against me?'

'Come to your senses, Philip,' Theodo said with mock concern. 'You've lost your wits.'

But King Philip continued. 'In order to seal our supposed friendship, you invited us to your court—where we arrived, all unsuspecting, two days ago.'

Only two days ago—it flashed through Florin's mind. So Count Tillo had delivered him at the crucial moment. The trap had been laid with care.

'As honour and custom prescribed, we surrendered our weapons,' King Philip went on, 'but the swords and pikes of your soldiers were already awaiting us.' Florin saw the sorrow in his eyes as he went on. 'You slaughtered my unarmed men like cattle, and each of them was worth a hundred Vinlanders. The blood of my gallant subjects be on your head, Theodo of Vinland!'

Theodo gave a mocking bow. 'Well howled, Wolf of Moltovia!' he said. 'We've listened to you for long enough. Now be silent and hear the Lion of Vinland roar!'

He shouted the last words at the assembled company, and the Vinlanders broke into exultant cries.

'Long live King Theodo! Long live the Lion of Vinland!'

Theodo raised his hand and the hubbub ceased at once.

'Philip of Moltovia,' he said coldly, 'you have lost the war, but you lack the courage to admit it. Instead, you bemoan the loss of your slaughtered wolf pack like an old woman.'

He indicated the prisoners with a contemptuous gesture.

'There are enough mangy curs left to provide you with a fitting escort on your final journey. But fear not, Philip.' Theodo spoke very quietly, but his dark eyes blazed with anger. 'You will not die at once. I shall grant you leave to become acquainted with every little stone, every speck of mortar in your dungeon. You'll fight for your bread with rats and measure the time by the drips that fall from the ceiling. Every sin you have ever committed in your life you'll rue a thousand times over!'

Florin was shocked to see his father, who had defied Theodo so proudly, bow his head in silence. What did King Theodo mean?

'Only then, Wolf of Moltovia,' Theodo went on in the same calm tone, 'will you set off on your final journey.' He glanced at Florin. 'Followed by this brat of yours.'

'Spare the boy,' King Philip said hoarsely. 'He's innocent.'

Theodo laughingly shook his head. 'He's flesh of your flesh. I intend to exterminate every last one of you. From this day forth, it will be as if your pestilential family had never existed!'

'You're an affront to God, King of Vinland!'

'On the contrary,' Theodo retorted calmly. 'God is with me. I've never been closer to paradise than I am tonight.'

'The paradise of rogues and hypocrites,' said King Philip. 'The garden of Eden of murderers and traitors.'

'Watch your tongue,' Theodo said softly, 'or I'll have you silenced.'

'People of every land,' King Philip went on loudly, 'will speak of your disgraceful deed. Theodo the traitor, Theodo the murderer, Theodo the jackal—the world will devise a fitting name for you.'

'That's enough,' said Theodo. 'Shut his mouth!'

The guards gagged Philip with a piece of rag—a sight that promptly restored Theodo's spirits. 'Pardon the discourtesy,' he said, 'but at my court, jests are the sole prerogative of Mimus, my fool. As to nicknames, Theodo the Avenger would be far more to my taste. But now you can think it over, long and thoroughly.'

He paused for a moment with his head bowed as if waiting for an answer. Then he said: 'You're right, Philip, we've exchanged pleasantries long enough.' He clapped his hands. 'The scissors!'

A young maidservant came up bearing a pair of scissors on a velvet cushion.

'Dearest king, permit me to do it!' begged the jester, who had evidently recovered from Duke Bonizo's assault. 'Barbering kings is my favourite pastime!'

He pranced in front of King Philip, chanting:

> *'Snip away until he's shorn,*
> *bald as babies when they're born.*
> *Ere King Philip meets his fate,*
> *cut the hair from off his pate!'*

The jester made to take the scissors, but Theodo caught him by the arm.

'No, Mimus,' he said. 'We mustn't begrudge Philip of Moltovia the pleasure of a last caress from a maiden's gentle hands.'

He nodded to the girl, who proceeded to wield the scissors.

As if turned to stone, Florin watched tuft after tuft of his father's thick hair fall to the floor. When the job was done Philip of Moltovia was kneeling, shorn-headed, in front of Theodo. Florin tried to smile at his father, but he sensed how tremulous and wretched his smile must seem: his father was defeated.

The hush that reigned in the banqueting hall was broken by a laugh like the bleating of a goat.

'Look at King Baldilocks!' scoffed the jester. He took a fool's sceptre from his belt, raised it above Philip's head, and bowed derisively. 'Greetings, o *hair*less, *land*less, *power*less monarch!' he cried, cracking him three times on the skull with the wooden bauble.

Florin burned with unbridled hatred. He longed to wring this monster's neck like Duke Bonizo, until he choked on his own malevolence!

The jester was still capering round his father when Theodo gestured to him to stop.

'Take the prisoners out,' he commanded.

One by one, the kneeling men were yanked to their feet and lined up between the soldiers as if in readiness for some grotesque minuet.

One of the officers pointed to Florin. 'Is he also to be put in chains, Your Majesty?'

'Later,' said Theodo. 'The wolf cub may keep me company for a trifle longer.'

Chains clanking, the prisoners were driven out in turn, King Philip last of all. Florin saw him pause in the doorway and turn his head. At the same moment, the guards roughly urged him onward.

Without really seeing, Florin stared at the spot where his father had been standing a moment before. He felt as if something had been ripped from deep within him, leaving a gaping wound that oozed with pain and fury. It was only when the sound of laughter came to his ears that he raised his head and gazed with smarting eyes at all the unfamiliar faces round the table. He was alone now—alone and at the mercy of these beasts.

'Let the banquet commence!' cried King Theodo. 'Eat and drink till your bellies burst—and think meanwhile of the luckless wolves for whom lean times have come early this year!'

'Nevertheless, my king,' said the jester, who was prowling in front of the table like a restless cat, 'there's one dish with which your captives must be plied in abundance.'

'And what would that be?' asked Theodo.

'Thin air, then they can tighten their belts!'

'That they shall have in plenty,' said the king, nodding contentedly as a page filled his goblet. 'They shall be regaled with the bread of adversity and the water of affliction, as Isaiah so aptly says. Or was it Jeremiah, Mimus?'

'Why ask me, my sacred king?' the jester retorted. 'Is it I whose godfather is a bishop, or you?'

'Merciful heaven, remind me not of Bishop Quirinius!' Theodo rolled his eyes. 'That man of God will be tormenting me again tomorrow morning. His catechisms are more painful than the red-hot pincers of Master Antonius.'

Quick as a flash, the jester bent his ass's ears into a bishop's mitre and hooked the bauble over his arm like a crosier. Then, with a devout expression, he made the sign of the cross over Theodo. 'Look into your heart, my son,' he said in a deep, sonorous voice, 'and seek the sins that lurk there!'

'Not bad, Mimus,' the king exclaimed with a laugh. 'That was Bishop Quirinius to the life!'

'But how are you to find those sins,' the jester went on unctuously, 'when your heart is so black that they're invisible?' He bowed his head in thought. 'I have it,' he continued in his own voice. 'I shall present Bishop Quirinius with a keg of the chalk the maidservants use to polish table silver. Perhaps he can use it to scour your heart clean.'

King Theodo joined in the general merriment.

'May I offer a suggestion?' the jester went on gravely. 'Feed Bishop Quirinius to your pikes. Then you can sin to your heart's content, the pikes will be amply fed, and the good bishop will achieve martyrdom and go straight to heaven.' He turned to the bishops present. 'Yes, that's the way of it, venerable Sir Beer-Belly, Sir Wine-Bibber and Sir Foul-Breath.'

In view of Theodo's laughter, the three ecclesiastics contorted their faces into a sour smile.

'But you, my sacred king,' Mimus intoned with devoutly upcast eyes, 'will always, for the rest of your life, say a paternoster before every bowl of pike soup.'

More laughter on all sides.

'Your tongue is nimble tonight, Mimus,' said Theodo.

'Yes, but it grows weary.' The jester pulled a woeful face. 'See how limp it is!' In proof of this, he stuck out his immensely long tongue. 'It badly needs refreshment,' he added, staring fixedly at a bowl of apples.

'You old glutton!' King Theodo laughed and tossed him an apple, which he greedily devoured.

He eats like an animal, thought Florin.

'What are you staring at?' The jester slunk up to him, still chewing the remains of his apple. 'It's better to fill one's belly than belie one's hunger.'

'Go on, Ass's Ears!' called someone. 'Give the wolf cub from Moltovia a drubbing!'

Amid roars of laughter, the jester took a napkin from the table. Having dabbed his lips and pretended to wipe his backside, he abruptly slapped Florin across the face with it. 'Well, Goggle-Eyes, do you accept my challenge?'

Florin hesitated for a moment. Then he retorted fiercely: 'Better to light a fire than fight a liar! Better to worst a jester than jest with the worst!' He relished the look of surprise on Mimus's face. If this creature fancied he could make him look a tongue-tied fool, he was mistaken—he knew the game too well. The boys at Montfield Castle called it 'word-fencing'. They had played it like maniacs all summer, much to the annoyance of the brethren, their pious tutors, who condemned it as a sinful perversion.

'Better to be quick to cut than cut to the quick!' he cried angrily. 'Better to rap another's knuckles than knuckle under!'

The jester raised his eyebrows admiringly. 'Better to chain a captive than be a captive in chains.'

'Better to ruin a plan than plan someone's ruin,' Florin countered swiftly.

'Better to sit enthroned over a loser than lose your throne.'

'Better to betray a traitor than treat a betrayer.'

'Better to sing over your wine than whine as you sing.'

'Better to slay a fool than fool with a slayer.'

'Help! Come to my aid, sweet king!' Mimus plucked at his ass's ears in mock despair and made as if to crawl beneath the table. 'This youngster has a sharp tongue. Master Antonius will have to prune it for him.'

'And whet your own at the same time, old fool,' Theodo said

sarcastically. 'It seems to me you've met your master.' He eyed Florin thoughtfully. 'If not your master, certainly your pupil. I'll make you a gift of the little rascal. Well, how do you like the idea?'

Florin saw Mimus glance up at him with a look of sudden alarm. Or had he been mistaken? The jester recovered his composure in a trice.

'Many thanks, my king,' he replied obsequiously, 'but you'd do better to give him to her.' He pointed to a white she-hound stretched out in front of the fire. 'One can never have too many dogs—' he shook his long ears with a tinkle of bells, 'but one donkey at court is enough.'

'Two donkeys can go hee-haw in turn,' Theodo insisted. 'No, Mimus, I mean what I say. You'll take this miserable scion of the house of Moltovia and train him to become a court jester. At least he'll earn his keep.' The king's eyes flashed derisively. 'I hereby appoint you a master of the jester's art.'

'A master!' Mimus screeched in delight. 'Did you hear that, all of you? I'm a master, a master of the jester's noble art!' He jumped up, seized the nearest page and hurled him to the floor. 'Down on your knees before me, you miserable worm!' The boy resisted fiercely, and the jester hit him on the head with the wooden bauble. 'I'll teach you to show a noble master due respect!'

The page tried to seize him by the collar, but Mimus dodged behind the throne and thumbed his nose at the page from there.

'Don't let your newfound distinction go to your head, Master Mimus!' the king said with a smile, curtly waving the page back to his place. 'Although, if you do so, there will at least be *something* in your empty skull!' He turned to Florin. 'As for you, jester's apprentice, work hard and don't disgrace your father. I shall expect you to enter-tain us at the grand banquet to be held on the day I have him beheaded.'

'I can think of a fine song for the occasion,' cried Mimus. He jumped on to a chair and proceeded to sing at the top of his voice:

'Poor King Philip lost his throne,
rued his fate with many a moan.
In a dungeon dark he lay,
till there dawned that fateful day
when, his prayers having said,
poor King Philip lost his head.'

'What a pity,' he said to Florin, 'that your father will be unable to hear my ditty. But never mind, frogs and toads thrive in the castle sewers. They'll croak his headless majesty many a fine melody!'

Florin glared at Mimus, choking with fury, and the green and yellow stripes swam before his eyes. Whatever happened, he would never have anything to do with such an evil creature. When the jester reached for him, he thrust his outstretched hand aside with all his might and ran.

His attempt to escape ended ignominiously. Before he could reach the doorway, the guards drove him into a corner like a hunted hare, seized him and dragged him back to the throne by his hair.

'Before I forget,' said King Theodo. 'Nobody in this room will reveal the parentage of my little jester—not unless he wishes to pay for that disclosure with his head. But now, Mimus, take your apprentice away before I change my mind and have him hanged on the spot.'

– THE JESTER'S
SECOND SKIN –

'YOU NEED NO tuition,' Mimus purred as he led Florin out of the banqueting hall. 'Only a perfect fool attempts to escape with three dozen guards in the room. You can thank your lucky stars the king didn't make you run the gauntlet!'

Ahead of Florin the jester, whose ass's ears swayed to and fro in time to his footsteps, and behind him a guard armed with a pike—such was the escort that accompanied Florin down the same stairs he had run up so expectantly. How long ago had that been?

Down below in the castle's big entrance hall, soldiers were crowding around the portal. With a wild flicker of hope, Florin looked for Captain Albero and his men, but all the troopers' leather caps and iron helmets bore the lion emblem of Vinland.

That's right, Florin thought bitterly, you've done your duty: the prisoners are safely under lock and key. Now you can enjoy your leisure!

Fresh, cold night air came wafting through the doorway, which was wide open. Florin took an involuntary step in its direction, only to receive a painful prick between the shoulder blades from his escort's pike.

'No, you don't!' the man said gruffly. 'Follow the jester.'

They crossed the entrance hall and climbed another flight of stairs, then made their way along an endless passage. The sound of voices and laughter grew steadily fainter until all that Florin could hear were the jester's tinkling bells. It was as if he and his companions had left the world behind them and were being engulfed by a shadowy realm devoid of life and light. Without the guard's torch, it would have been pitch-dark. There were no sconces in this part of the castle.

The jester came to a halt at last. 'Where am I?' thought Florin. His bewilderment intensified when his nose detected the pungent smell of animals. There had to be stables nearby, yet they hadn't left the castle.

Mimus opened the door to a gloomy chamber. 'In you go,' he said, taking Florin by the arm.

The guard barred their path. 'Not so fast!'

He held his blazing torch so close that Florin retreated a step. Unmoved, the man shone the light on him from head to foot.

'You won't be needing *those* gewgaws any more.' With a jerk, he wrested the gold chain and amulet of St. George from Florin's neck and examined them with a satisfied grin. Then he roughly pulled the rings off his fingers. 'Gold and gold go well together,' he said spitefully. 'But if need be—' he drew his dagger and cut the clasp off Florin's cloak, 'I'll make do with silver!'

He rolled the cloak into a convenient bundle, then ran his eyes over Florin once more and proceeded to loosen the laces of his doublet.

'Nice warm wool,' he said approvingly. 'And that,' he went on, feeling Florin's shirt collar, 'is fine linen.'

He unbuttoned the shirt without more ado.

'Please don't,' Florin entreated.

'No need to concern yourself,' said the soldier, who was now fiddling with Florin's belt buckle.

'At least leave me my breeches!'

'Believe me, my friend, you'll soon be getting far finer attire,' the man sneered as he pulled Florin's breeches down. 'Think yourself lucky: the brave Moltovians who escorted you here have no further need of clothes at all!'

Not until Florin was standing stark naked did the soldier step aside with the bundle of clothes beneath his arm. He gave the jester a nod. 'Now he's yours.'

'Some shear sheep, others hogs—that's what I call fair shares,' grumbled the jester. 'You get gold and a woollen coat, I get a naked whippersnapper.' He nudged Florin in the ribs, sending him stumbling into the pitch-black chamber. 'We must make sure you don't give me the slip,' he muttered. Before Florin realised what the jester was doing, he felt something cold and heavy close round his ankle. A chain clanked. Then a padlock snapped shut.

'It's only for your own good,' Mimus said curtly. 'Now go to sleep. Hey, brave soldier!' Florin heard him run quickly after the guard. 'Wait for me! Leave me the torch at least—and a tiny little gold ring!'

The door slammed shut. Florin groped around for somewhere to lie down in the darkness, but the chain attached to his ankle drew taut after only two steps. All that his fingers encountered was a sprinkling of straw on the floor. Spreading his arms as wide as he could, he scraped it together into a heap, sank down on it and pressed his fists to his eyes. His ears still rang with jeers, mocking laughter, tinkling bells. A chaotic jumble of images danced behind his closed eyelids: Duke Bonizo sprawled on the floor; his father kneeling before Theodo; the maidservant wielding the scissors; Mimus capering round his father like the devil incarnate; Mimus with the bunch of steaming intestines in his hand; Mimus . . .

Suddenly, without warning, Florin's stomach heaved. Retching, he tottered over to the wall and vomited bitter bile—interminably, again and again—until he crept back to his heap of straw shivering with cold and exhaustion. He fell asleep almost instantly.

———————

WHEN Florin awoke the next morning, he forgot for one brief, blissful moment where he was.

Still half asleep, he surveyed his surroundings by the grey light of dawn. He was bewildered to note the stamped mud floor, the straw, the walls of rough-hewn stone—until his memory suddenly returned like a punch on the jaw. He was a prisoner, a prisoner in Bellingar Castle, and condemned, moreover, to become King Theodo's jester . . . He sprang to his feet, heedless of his leg-iron, and fell headlong. Groaning, he rubbed his forehead.

'Why make such a diabolical din at this hour?' From a heap of straw beside him there emerged the shaven head of a man Florin had never seen before. Or had he? Something about the pale, puffy face seemed familiar. He stared at the stranger until, after quite some time, he realised that the man must be Mimus the jester, but without his ass's ears and shimmering jester's motley. His grey sackcloth smock made him look as unremarkable as a common or garden manservant.

'What are you doing here?' Florin asked with a puzzled frown.

'I most humbly beg your pardon if my presence here intrudes on your royal privacy,' said Mimus, giving his shaven head a thorough scratch, 'but I've dwelt and slept in these sumptuous quarters for the past fifteen years.' He yawned and sank back into the straw.

'Oh, no, you're not going back to sleep!' Florin insisted, suddenly wide awake. 'Remove this chain at once!'

'There's time enough for that,' the jester grumbled. 'Sleep comes first.'

'Release me this minute!' To underline his peremptory command, Florin stood up straight as a ramrod—and promptly took another tumble over the accursed chain. 'Let . . . me . . . go!' he hissed between gritted teeth, rubbing his ankle.

'Listen to me, you little . . . er, prince.' Mimus lay back with his eyes shut and didn't budge. 'I may be a jester, but the notion of making *you* a jester didn't originate in *my* head. You can thank the king for that.' He opened one eye with a perceptible effort and squinted at Florin. 'I don't want you. All I want is some peace and quiet, so kindly hold your royal tongue!' He shut his eye, turned over on his side and heaved a sigh. 'Too late, here comes Rollo.'

Florin, too, could now hear footsteps and muffled oaths in the passage outside. A moment later the door opened with a crash and a short, prodigiously fat man entered. Panting and grunting, he carried in two bowls and two buckets of water. His threadbare knee breeches were kept up by a calfskin halter encircling his huge belly, and above them he wore a woollen jacket that seemed to consist entirely of pouches and pockets.

'Get up, Mimus, you old sluggard!' The man's voice was as deep and gruff as a bear's. 'I already heard: you've got yourself a little Mimus. The dwarf will crack your dirty jokes for you, is that it?' He emitted a rumbling laugh and deposited the two earthenware porringers on the floor with a crash. 'And I, devil take it, will have to cope with two of you from now on!'

'Permit me to introduce you,' said the jester, still comfortably stretched out on the straw. Even on his back, he contrived to sketch a mocking bow. 'Rollo the bestiarius—the master of the wild beasts.'

Bestiarius . . . Florin was mystified. There was a bestiarius at Mont-field Castle, too, but he was responsible for looking after the hawks and hounds. What had this person to do with him?

'He brings us our food,' the jester went on, 'so be polite to him.'

'He's right, dwarf,' said Rollo, breathing heavily, 'be polite to me. Mimus and the monkeys are nuisance enough. May the Holy Virgin protect me from another pest!' He quickly kissed a medallion on a chain round his neck before turning his attention to Florin. 'Well, I'll be damned,' he exclaimed as Florin hurriedly covered his nakedness with straw, 'a shrinking violet. Where did the king get him?'

'The little pigeon flew to him of its own accord,' said Mimus, propping his chin on his hands. 'It fluttered in, all unsuspecting, and stuck fast to the royal lime-twig.'

'Enough of your jester's nonsense,' growled Rollo. 'Well, it's all the same to me how he came here.' He bent over Florin. 'Let's have a look at you, little Mimus.'

His rough coat brushed Florin's face, his breath reeked of beer and onions. Florin shrank back as far as he could, but his chain was too short. Quite unmoved by his desperate attempts to fend him off, the bearlike bestiarius kneaded Florin all over like a lump of dough. Having pulled up his eyelids and inspected his eyes, he expertly prised his jaws open.

Florin went rigid with mortification. Just the way our bestiarius examines a newborn puppy, he thought. He had an urge to spit in Rollo's moon face, but a residue of common sense deterred him.

'He seems healthy enough,' the bestiarius remarked to Mimus. 'Make sure he washes himself well before you put his motley on.' He let go of Florin and rummaged in his innumerable pockets. 'Where did I put it, by all the fires of hell?' he grumbled. At last he found what he was looking for—a linen bag, which he hurled at the jester's head. 'My wife and the seamstresses toiled at it all night long, confounded waste of time that it was! Adieu, you jesters!'

The door shut behind him with a loud crash, and Florin heard him lumbering up some stairs.

Mimus sat up, still yawning, and pulled the porringers toward him. 'Well, Your Highness, breakfast is served.' He pushed one of the bowls in the direction of Florin's feet. 'Bon appétit.'

The bowl contained lukewarm millet gruel. It tasted of nothing at all, but Florin hungrily gulped it down. His stomach was beginning to feel better, but his head was still in a whirl. Had the shimmering figure of last night, the jester who had spouted all those malicious remarks, anything in common with this thin, pallid man who was silently spooning up gruel beside him? Florin kept glancing at him out of the corner of his eye. Although hard to believe, it was true: the bruises Duke Bonizo had left on the jester's throat were proof enough.

'Why did you do it?' Florin blurted out despite himself.

The jester didn't reply until he had carefully scraped his porringer clean. 'What are you talking about?' he said.

'Don't play the innocent!' Florin said angrily. 'You mocked my father—you struck him and crowned him with a handful of stinking offal. Why?'

'To amuse King Theodo,' Mimus replied. 'That's my purpose in life. And, from today, yours too.'

'You don't say!' Florin laughed derisively. 'And what if I don't care to play the fool for that godless, treacherous king?'

'In that case,' said the jester, laying his empty bowl aside, 'I can think of an admirable inscription for your gravestone:

> *Here lies a prince from Montfield's court.*
> *His wits were as dull as his life was short.'*

'Think again!' Florin snarled. 'You'd do better to devise a funeral oration for yourself and that king of yours. If you keep us imprisoned here much longer, you'll bite the dust before you've completed it!'

'By all the Furies,' screeched the jester, 'what a terrifying prospect! No more, I beg you, or I'll soil my breeches with fright! Nevertheless,' he went on calmly, 'until that time comes, we play by King Theodo's rules. Anyone who doesn't play the game is brushed aside like fly dirt—like this!' He flicked an imaginary speck of dust off Florin's nose. 'Speaking of dirt,' he said, pushing one of the buckets toward Florin, 'I think a little cleansing of your princely person wouldn't be amiss.'

Florin cautiously dipped a finger in the bucket. 'This water's as cold as ice,' he said plaintively. 'I'll catch my death!'

Mimus regarded him with amusement for a moment. 'With your permission, my prince,' he said, then picked up the bucket and tipped it over him. 'Beg pardon, Your Highness, did I splash you a trifle?' he inquired innocently, thrusting a scrubbing brush into Florin's hand. 'I fear you'll have to fend for yourself. It's my servants' day off. The lazy rascals have idled for fifteen years. I ought to complain to the king.'

So saying, the jester washed himself from head to foot. He cleaned out his ears with an iron ear-pick, then set to work on his teeth with powdered chalk and a length of waxed thread. 'You must clean your teeth regularly and chew fennel and aniseed,' he mumbled, before spitting the powder across the room. 'Foul breath will earn you a beating.'

Satisfied that he was clean enough at last, he proceeded to don his striped jester's costume, which fitted him like a second skin. Now, by daylight, Florin could see the countless little bells that tinkled so loudly when he moved. Clearly visible on the right leg of the costume, as though branded on Mimus's upper thigh, were the arms of King Theodo of Vinland. His feet were shod in thin cloth slippers with upturned toes.

'Handsome footwear, those.' Florin pointed mockingly at the jester's feet. 'What do you do if it rains?'

Mimus didn't reply. He pulled on a close-fitting cap with long ass's ears and big bells sewn to it. Last of all, he girded on a belt to which he attached a leather pouch, an inflated pig's bladder, and his fool's sceptre.

Florin watched the process of transformation, spellbound. What now confronted him was a monster—half man, half beast. The shimmering, froglike body was surmounted by an ass's head with a human face resembling a mask.

'Tell me when your eyes pop out,' Mimus said gruffly, 'and I'll help you to look for them.' He picked up the linen bag Rollo had brought and thrust it into Florin's hand. 'Come, open it,' he urged, folding his arms with relish. 'Now it's my turn to gawk.'

For an instant, when Florin took out the costume, his skin went completely numb. Then it began to itch as if a thousand ants were crawling hither and thither across his body. He stared in dismay at what he was holding in his hands: a jester's cap with ass's ears, a striped garment adorned with bells and Theodo's coat of arms. It was Mimus's costume, only smaller.

'This is a badge of shame,' he said brusquely. 'I refuse to put it on!'

'It's a magnificent costume,' said Mimus, bowing derisively, 'and comes from the king in person—with his best regards, what's more.' All at once his tone became serious in the extreme. 'You'd do well to wear it.'

'Never! I shall never do so!'

'My prince, the choice is yours,' said Mimus. 'Coloured stripes or streaks of blood? Ass's ears or no ears at all? The jingle of bells or cries of pain?'

Florin glared at the jester. Did he seriously mean those threats?

'Don't let it come to that,' Mimus went on, as if he'd read Florin's thoughts. 'Our merry monarch stands no nonsense in such matters.'

Gritting his teeth, Florin slipped into the tight-fighting garment with the help of Mimus, who removed his leg-iron, only to replace it immediately afterward. The shrill tinkling of the bells rang in his ears. He picked up the fool's cap and tried to pull it over his head, but in vain. Looking at Mimus once more, he pictured his own face beneath the ass's ears with a mixture of horror and fascination. Abruptly, his stomach somersaulted again. What would become of him if he put the cap on now? Would he still be a son of God, or would he have joined the race of demons, like the bird- and dog-headed creatures that dwelt on the edge of the world?

'Wait,' the jester said suddenly, 'first you need shearing.'

'Don't you dare!' Florin clutched his long hair in horror. Then he bowed his head dejectedly. '*Barbering kings is my favourite pastime,*' he said, mimicking the jester's voice. '*Snip away until he's shorn!*'

'So you paid close attention last night,' said Mimus, taking a razor from his pocket. 'Anyone with a head as full of nonsense as yours needs nothing on top. Keep still, or I'll cut off your royal ears as well.'

When the job was done he inspected his handiwork with satisfaction. 'Smooth as an egg,' he said. 'The lice can now go skating on your pate.'

Florin couldn't resist running his hand over his shorn skull. Could that really be *his* head?

'Nice and airy, eh?' said Mimus. He pulled the jester's cap over Florin's head and eyed him appraisingly.

'You make a handsome donkey foal,' he said. 'Hee-haw, hee-haw! Let's see how quick the little creature is to learn.' His eyes glittered in challenge. 'I'm sure you're acquainted with the rules of jousting, noble prince, but what of the rules of jesting?'

Florin emitted a contemptuous snort.

'Let's start with the simplest matters,' Mimus continued imperturbably. 'Rule number one: you may remove your jester's motley and cap only when retiring for the night. Rule number two: these honourable regalia—' he produced a bauble and an inflated pig's bladder from his pocket, 'must go everywhere with you.'

Florin looked with distaste at the transparent pig's bladder, which contained a handful of dried peas. 'What's *that* for?'

'Well,' Mimus said in a businesslike voice, 'you can use it as a rattle or knock precious goblets off the table with it. If the opportunity presents itself, you can hit someone over the head with it—' the jester was getting into his stride, Florin could tell, 'or burst it close to a courtier's ear, or prick it on a bishop's mitre. But the best place for it of all—' he was now looking positively transfigured, 'is beneath the buttocks of the noblest lady present!' He eyed Florin expectantly. 'Well, what do you think of this splendid appurtenance?'

'It's revolting!'

'If you say so.' The jester shrugged. 'Perhaps you'll like your other companion better.' He tossed the pig's bladder into a corner and picked up the bauble, which took the form of a fool's head on the end of a baton. 'I'm now your best friend,' he croaked, as if the head itself were speaking. 'You must talk to me every day or I'll tell the king!'

'Stop it!' Florin had gone pale. 'Your foolish twaddle turns my stomach!'

The bauble seemed to hop up and down with rage in Mimus's hands. 'Did I hear aright?' croaked the wooden head. 'This fine gentleman thinks he's a cut above me, but I'm his spitting image. Look at me, Prince Mimus: I'm you and you're me!'

The carved face beneath the jester's cap seemed to grin sardonically. With a violent sweep of his hand, Florin knocked it aside.

'Ugh, how discourteous,' said Mimus, reverting to his normal voice. 'Ah, well, you'll soon get used to each other. Better a wooden friend than none.'

He rummaged in his pocket again and took out a parchment with writing on it. 'Have you acquired the art of reading, noble sir? Have you, Prince Mimus?'

'Don't call me Mimus,' Florin said angrily. 'That's your name, not mine!'

'Wrong,' the jester said amiably. 'All jesters are called Mimus. My predecessor's name was Mimus. So is mine. And so, from today, is yours. Well, little Mimus, can you read?'

Florin preserved a stubborn silence.

'Of course you can read,' Mimus said firmly. 'The erudite monks of Montfield must surely have taught the king's son that much, even if they can't tell apples from pears in other respects.'

'What business is it of yours, you monster?' snapped Florin, and the bells on his costume tinkled shrilly. 'May you choke on your own bile!'

'Heigh-ho, I can see I shall have some sport with you!' said the jester. Without warning, he sprang at Florin and hurled him to the floor. 'By tonight,' he said curtly, tossing the parchment at his feet, 'you'll know every word of this by heart!'

Florin heard the door shut, then silence fell. If only it weren't for this confounded leg-iron! The fetter round his ankle was a trifle loose, and for a while he strove to pull it off. Wild with rage, he eventually gave up, squatted down on the straw and reached for the parchment.

It was a list of riddles. A hundred and fifty riddles—Florin counted them—written in a small, spidery hand. Fancy having to learn such rubbish! he thought, staring at the parchment. All at once he was assailed by an overwhelming sense of unreality. When would he at last awaken from this ridiculous dream? His father, King Philip of Moltovia, had vanished into Theodo's dungeons. Likewise his loyal men, if they hadn't all been slain on the spot. And he himself? A chained-up figure in jester's motley charged with learning a hundred and fifty riddles by heart!

'How droll,' he said aloud, simultaneously laughing and crying until the tears ran down his cheeks. 'How exceedingly droll!'

WHEN Mimus returned early that evening Florin was lying on the straw, staring at the ceiling. He had tossed the parchment heedlessly aside.

The jester picked it up and sat down. 'Now show me what you've learnt,' he said. 'The moment of truth has come.'

'The moment of truth?' Florin sat up. 'Wait, I'll ask you a riddle on the subject.' He'd been itching for this moment all day long. Now he drew a deep breath. 'Pay attention. He's ugly as an ape, cowardly as a hare and stupid as a donkey. Who is he?'

'Who on earth can it be?' The jester pretended to think hard. 'With the best will in the world, I can't imagine!'

'It's Mimus the jester,' Florin blurted out. 'It's you! And here's another riddle. He's even uglier than an ape, even more cowardly than a hare and even more stupid than a donkey. Who is he?' He paused for a moment, then: 'It's Theodo, the jackal in king's attire!'

The jester rolled his eyes. 'What wit! What subtlety!' He eyed Florin with an air of boredom. 'Has noble sir vented his anger sufficiently? Might he now be gracious enough to ask me a few of the riddles he's learnt?' He gave a hearty yawn. 'I don't have all the time in the world for princely tomfoolery.'

He waited, but Florin's silence persisted. 'So you haven't learnt a thing,' Mimus said after a while. 'The scullions will be delighted. Tomorrow you'll be down on your knees, scrubbing the kitchen floor in their place.'

Florin sat up with an involuntary start. He still said nothing, but his eyes blazed.

'It's quite simple,' Mimus explained. 'For every day of mine you fritter away to no purpose, you'll make yourself useful elsewhere. You can wield the fragrant latrine ladle or turn the well-wheel in step with the oxen.' He grinned at Florin's look of fury. 'We'll find some suitable tasks for you—I'll select them with the greatest care.'

'I shall be yesterday,' Florin said suddenly, 'and I was there tomorrow. Who am I?'

'Today,' Mimus answered without hesitation. 'Well,' he said impatiently, 'go on, don't dawdle!'

Florin deliberated. 'What is no sooner spoken than broken?'

'A word of honour.'

'*Your* word of honour, perhaps,' said Florin. 'Consult the parchment: "Silence" is the correct answer . . .' He deliberated again. 'It's lighter than a feather, yet no one can hold it for long. What is it?'

'A fart.'

Florin almost grinned despite himself. 'Wrong again,' he said. 'A breath.'

'Aha, so the greenhorn knows better than the master,' Mimus

jeered. 'Wait, now I'll ask *you* one: He goes on all fours in the morning, walks on two legs at noon and three legs in the evening. Who is he?'

Florin had memorised all one hundred and fifty riddles and their answers, so he didn't have to think for long. 'A man,' he said, 'but that's a stupid riddle.'

'Stupid?' said Mimus. 'You didn't understand it, that's why you think so!' His tiredness seemed to leave him in a flash. 'Watch this!' He got down on the floor and crawled along on all fours, babbling like an infant. The next moment he jumped up, seized an imaginary spear and marched briskly up and down. Then, all at once, he became immensely old. Bent double and leaning on an invisible stick, he hobbled over to Florin.

'Now do you understand?' he asked in an old man's quavering voice. He looked truly comical as an old dodderer with ass's ears, but Florin didn't bat an eyelid.

Mimus straightened up again. 'Don't clap too hard,' he said drily, 'you'll get blisters on your hands. Next riddle: It hears without ears, talks without a mouth, and answers you in every language. What is it?'

'An echo.'

'Holes in a row?'

'A chain,' said Florin, glaring at his leg-iron.

'Wrong,' said Mimus. 'Theodo's empty-headed courtiers standing in line.'

Florin couldn't help grinning at last.

'Well, well,' Mimus said with feigned astonishment, 'I thought His Highness's face had rusted over . . . However,' he went on with a satis-fied nod, 'your head seems free from rust. That will help you.'

'Help me to do what?' Florin's smile vanished. 'Rattle a pig's bladder? Converse with a bauble?'

Mimus laughed. 'There's a trifle more to being a royal jester than that,' he said, and Florin detected the note of pride in his voice. 'Take these riddles. You'll see, they can work wonders. You've been toiling away all night, the courtiers are yawning, a shoe hits you on the head, and the king is thinking of having you flogged. At that moment you ask: "What is lighter than air and growls like a bear?"—and they all rack their brains. Ask them another riddle, and another, and they'll forget they were about to give you a good hiding.'

'Well,' Florin couldn't help asking, 'what *is* lighter than air and growls like a bear?'

'That you'll learn in due course,' said Mimus. 'That and a thousand other things.'

I won't do anything of the kind, Florin told himself. He'd had time to think during that long, lonely day. He would hold his peace and pretend to cooperate—*that's* what he would do. Mimus surely wouldn't keep him chained up forever. Then he'd be off in a trice, out of this terrible place and away from the jester's eternal blathering! There were horses in the castle, likewise spears and swords with which to fight off pursuers . . .

Mimus had gone over to the window. 'It's time,' he said after an appraising glance at the position of the sun. 'I must return to the king. If you grow bored, have a chat with your new friend.' He attached the bauble to Florin's belt. 'He's not exactly talkative, but he'll always give you a hearing.' He gave the carved head on his own fool's sceptre an affectionate pat, then made for the door. 'Goodnight.'

'Stop,' Florin said quickly. 'Wait. One last riddle: It belongs to me, but it's empty and it rumbles. What is it?'

Mimus paused on the threshold. 'The belly that will sing you to sleep. We eat tomorrow morning, not before.'

'But I'm starving!'

'*An empty belly keeps your wits nimble,*' said King Theodo's soft voice from the doorway. Florin spun round—and saw the grin on Mimus's face. 'And our king ought to know,' the jester went on in his own voice. 'His own belly is always full.'

'But—'

'No buts!'

Crash. The door had slammed shut.

To take his mind off the gnawing sensation in his innards, Florin read through the riddles once more. Some of them he'd known already. The old court physician at Montfield Castle had used them to distract boys from the bitter potions he administered to cure their fevers.

Nightfall came all too soon. Florin lay down on the straw and strained his ears in the darkness. It was very quiet; all he could hear from time to time was a faint sound of snuffling and whimpering. So he hadn't imagined the animal smell last night. But since when were livestock kept *inside* a castle, especially as he'd noticed the big stables outside the castle walls when riding in. On the other hand, what else was this wretched chamber—in which the jester, according to him, had dwelt for fifteen years—but a stable?

'Everything here is foolish,' Florin muttered, shaking his head. 'Everything but the fool himself.'

Once again, images began to whirl in his head: he saw Mimus prancing around his father, saw his father kneeling impotently before Theodo, saw the courtiers' grinning faces . . .

What was his father doing at this moment? Florin dared not picture the dungeons too vividly. If only he could see and speak with him, however briefly, he wouldn't feel so miserable. Never before had he been truly alone. He'd been surrounded day and night by people concerned for his welfare and quick to fulfil his every wish. Ramon, Muriel, his overzealous bodyguard Sturmius, even stern Chancellor Artold and grumpy Count Ursio—he was fond of them all, and they returned his affection. Not to mention his friends Senna, Radbod and Tanko—friends with whom he had only to exchange a look to know that they shared his thoughts. O Holy St. John, patron saint of all good friends! He missed them so much, his belly ached with sorrow . . . Or was it hunger?

They were all still at home, suspecting nothing, taking it for granted that he was safe and happy at his father's side, a much-loved guest at the royal court of Vinland!

He laughed bitterly at the thought.

Nobody at the court of Vinland loved him. Nobody in this place cared whether he was full or hungry, healthy or sick, alive or dead. If fire broke out now he would perish horribly at the end of his chain. 'A shame about the new costume,' the bestiarius would grumble—and carelessly bury his charred remains in some corner or other.

What had the jester told him this morning?

'Anyone who doesn't play the game is brushed aside like fly dirt . . .'

Florin had a vivid mental picture of King Theodo's hate-contorted face. There was no doubt about it: that man wouldn't hesitate to kill him on the smallest pretext. What went on in his head? It was monstrous of him to have lured a fellow monarch into a trap by means of a false and blasphemous oath and confined him in a dungeon like a criminal. Other lands waged wars and their kings were sometimes captured—treated in an honourable manner befitting their rank and released as soon as possible—but King Theodo, in his incomprehensible hatred, cared nothing for the law, either human or divine.

'And for that, you royal perjurer,' Florin muttered, 'you'll roast in hell—in the hottest flames reserved for traitors!'

But until then . . . Florin's chain rattled as he turned over on his side.

Playing the game, acting the fool night after night—what would it be like? How would it be to confront those courtiers, that pack of baying hounds, and sing or dance or ask riddles—or whatever else a poor jester had to do—whenever one of them snapped his fingers?

'I won't do it,' he said resolutely. He would escape at the first opportunity, then word of Theodo's cowardly betrayal would spread like wildfire. Moltovia's generals would have mobilised their forces even before he, Florin, had fought his way home. Many of King

Philip's loyal retainers were still free: influential noblemen like Senna's father, the doughty Baron Henried, or Count Essrin, Radbod's father. With their help, Chancellor Artold would be able to muster a powerful army. Florin's uncle, King Guido of Arelia, would join them with his own troops, and then . . .

'And then,' Florin muttered, 'God help you, Theodo, you breaker of oaths!'

Still picturing with grim satisfaction how King Theodo would kneel, whimpering for mercy, amid the shattered ruins of his castle, he fell asleep.

– THE DONKEY HUNT –

IT WAS FIVE days before the jester removed Florin's leg-iron. He
thrust a sheet of closely-written parchment into his hand every
morning, then made himself scarce until nightfall. Even though Florin
felt sick with hatred at the very sound of the jester's bells outside the
door, he put on a brave face for the 'examinations' to which Mimus
submitted him. Instead of crumpling the parchment into a ball and
stuffing it into the jester's mouth, as he dearly longed to do, he reeled
off the jokes and riddles he'd memorised. He was dominated by one
thought alone: escape!

At last, on the sixth day, the long-awaited moment came. To
Florin's surprise, the jester unlocked his leg-iron after their morning
gruel.

'Today you're going to learn to fly,' said Mimus, spreading his
arms in a grandiose gesture, 'to soar aloft on the wings of poetry. A
chain would weigh you down.'

Gingerly, Florin felt the fiery red weal the iron shackle had left on his ankle. But that didn't matter. The chain was gone and the door was never locked—he'd noticed that. His heart began to beat faster. Would it really be that simple? Softly, though! He mustn't show anything! The jester was still squatting on the straw in front of him, never taking his eyes off him for a moment.

'I want to hear a rhyme for every word I say,' Mimus commanded. 'Sheep?'

'Sleep.'

'Deer?'

'Beer.'

'Cattle?'

'Rattle,' said Florin, grinding his teeth. What nonsense! Even the moon-faced bestiarius would manage to think of rhymes like these. It was all he could do to stop glancing at the door.

'Rabbit?'

'Habit.' What rhymed with 'escape'?

'Hound?'

'Sound.'

'Hornet.'

'Er . . . What?'

'Up to now,' said the jester, 'I fancy you've found my rhymes too easy. Hornet?'

Florin thought. 'Bonnet,' he suggested half-heartedly.

'Come, come,' jeered Mimus. 'Surely you can do better than that?'

'There isn't a rhyme that fits.' Florin was literally quivering with frustration.

'You can't think of one, that's all. Pay attention . . .' Mimus raised his forefinger. 'Hornet . . . Torn it! There, doesn't that melt on the tongue like butter?'

'Show-off,' Florin muttered under his breath.

But the jester had sharp ears. 'Very well, what rhymes with "show-off"?'

'As you wish,' Florin said impudently. 'Big-mouth, braggart, boaster, bloated idiot. They all rhyme with Mimus.'

'By Sancta Simplicitas, the patron saint of all blockheads!' Mimus cast his eyes up at the ceiling. 'I fear we shall have to give the poetic furnace a good stoke beneath your backside! Here . . .' He handed Florin a sheet of parchment and a stick of charcoal. 'From A for apple to Z for zebra. Give me one rhyme for each letter of the alphabet, if I may make so bold.' While speaking, he attached the bauble and pig's bladder to his belt. Florin bent over the parchment, scarcely daring to breathe. If the jester left their stable now, would he remember the leg-iron?

'Enter the service of the Muse of Poetry,' Mimus declared as he ceremoniously walked to the door, 'and you'll be able to soar like an eagle! Adieu, my prince!' He performed a perfect, courtier-like bow, then he was gone.

For a moment or two, Florin stared in stupefaction at the leg-iron lying untouched beside the wall. Then he pulled himself together with an effort.

It's time, he thought. What are you waiting for? Run for it!

He hurriedly tore the pouch, bauble and pig's bladder from his belt and the fool's cap from his head. His heart was in his mouth. Theodo would make short work of him if he were caught trying to escape, but he mustn't let fear stop him.

He darted to the door and listened. What if the jester was lurking outside, ready to drag him back amid peals of mocking laughter? Warily, he opened the door a crack and peered out. The passage was quiet and deserted.

'Then God be with me!'

He ran off as if the furies were at his heels. Those bells! Why hadn't he changed this accursed costume for the smock he slept in? But never mind, he was free! Joy surged through him. No more airless stable, no chain, no Mimus plaguing him with stupid jester's tricks . . .

Praise be to the Muse of Poetry, he thought exuberantly. A few rhymes and he was indeed soaring like an eagle. He suppressed a nervous giggle. Poor Mimus! When Theodo discovered that he had escaped, the jester would have to devise a devilishly good excuse . . .

How long the passage was. Closed doors to the right and left of him, then an open doorway from which issued the heavenly scent of fresh-baked bread. Peeking inside, Florin glimpsed a floury kitchen table and some baskets filled with dough. A woman's voice called after him, but he ran on, his heart beating time to his footsteps.

Every bend in the passage might conceal guards . . . Careful, careful! But he couldn't bring himself to be careful, he could only run, on and on, after all those days of inactivity. Would the passage never end? A flight of steps . . .

'God be with me!' Florin breathed a sigh of relief when he sighted the entrance hall. By some miracle, it was deserted. He threw his weight against the heavy door. The creaking of the hinges echoed from the vaulted ceiling, but no one came running. He squeezed through the crack, grazing his shoulder in his haste, but he paid it no heed. He was outside!

God had heard his prayer.

The daylight was dazzling. For one uneasy moment he could see nothing at all after the permanent gloom of the jester's stable. He blinked repeatedly until the sunlit courtyard swam into view. Footsteps and voices could be heard on the battlements, but never fear, the sentries' attention was directed outward. Don't hesitate, go on! Summoning up all his courage, Florin ran straight across the courtyard and nestled against the cold stone wall immediately below the battlements. The sound of footsteps was even louder now. His heart was beating like a roll on a drum, but he had to press on. Still hugging the wall, he darted to the inner gate.

The portcullis was raised. He couldn't see the sentries, but he could hear their voices.

'A four, a two and a six. That makes twelve.'

'What's got into your eyes: pigeon dirt? A four, a two and a five make eleven. Hand us the cup.'

With his back to the wall, Florin sidled through the gateway. He could now see the sentries. Four of them were standing round a barrel, throwing dice, and his confounded bells were tinkling fit to rouse the dead.

'God be with me!' None of the men looked up as he tiptoed past.

God was with him: he had struck the sentries blind and deaf. Florin set off at a pace that burnt his throat with every breath. Past the servants' quarters, past the stables. What if he stole a horse, but what if the stable boys overpowered him? He hesitated for a moment, uncertain what to do. Glancing over his shoulder, he felt dizzy with terror: at least a dozen archers were patrolling the inner battlements. Florin saw them, saw their iron-tipped arrows flash in the sunlight, but they didn't see him! God was on his side. He must press on without a horse, just press on . . .

Now for the outer wall, the outer gate. 'Please God, let it be open!' Florin prayed breathlessly. 'Let it be open!'

The outer wall came into view. The gate was wide open.

God was still on his side.

Not a sentry in sight. He was in luck. Hope surged in his breast like a bird taking wing. If only his father and his father's men were with him . . . Florin could see the road that would take him down the castle hill. He could see fields, and beyond them the forest that would shield him from view.

He didn't see the horsemen in the paddock beyond the stables until it was too late.

King Theodo, accompanied by his equerries and one or two retainers, was inspecting some foals at pasture. Although very close, they would fail to see him like the sentries and archers. No one could see him. God had rendered him invisible and was guiding him through a host of enemies . . .

'There he is!'

Florin's bird of hope plummeted like a stone. He heard one of the men derisively imitate the sound of a hunting horn. 'After the donkey!' cried another. 'My king, may I catch him for you?'

'Quarry as rare as this?' Theodo said with a laugh. 'Don't you dare! I shall run him down myself!'

The king's horse reared as he dug his spurs into its flanks. Florin took one look at Theodo's face and ran. He knew he was done for, yet he continued to sprint for the outer gate, whose opening seemed to mock him: 'Look, this way lies freedom, but not for you—not for you.'

The king's hoofbeats grew louder and louder.

'Hey, hey, hey!' Theodo's henchmen shouted and clapped their hands like beaters driving game.

The king drew level with Florin. He would seize him at any moment.

'Hey, hey . . .' Florin ran on. The gateway was very near . . . The forest . . .

Theodo overtook him, a leather lasso in his hand. His grey stallion pranced on the spot.

'Stand still like a good little donkey!'

The king's tone was playful, but the noose that cruelly tightened round Florin's neck was no plaything. He clutched his throat with both hands in a vain attempt to loosen the constricting thong, but Theodo pulled him steadily nearer. At last he grabbed him and flung him across his saddle.

'Run away by all means, little donkey,' he whispered as they rode back through the gateway and into the castle courtyard. 'Run away as often as you please.' His gentle voice was unendurably close to Florin's ear. 'But always be mindful of your father when you do so. Your escapades will cost him dearly!'

Once outside the portal, he pitched Florin off. 'Take him back to the jesters' stable,' he ordered some men who stood ready to hand. 'And tell Master Antonius—' he uttered the name deliberately and with relish, 'to expect me down below.'

MIMUS was already waiting for him. 'View halloo, my prince!' he cried, as if Florin had just broken cover like a hunted fox. 'How long did the king take to run you down?'

Florin didn't reply, nor did he resist when the jester pulled the fool's cap over his head and chained him up again. The king's final words were still ringing in his ears: '*Tell Master Antonius to expect me down below!*' What horrors underlay them?

'You've been neither gutted nor stuffed,' Mimus said suddenly in a different tone of voice. 'The king hasn't harmed a hair of your head, if my eyes don't deceive me, so what ails you?'

Florin's overpowering anxiety got the better of him. 'My father . . .' he said, and broke off. 'Who is Master Antonius?'

The jester gave him an unfathomable look. 'You'll make his acquaintance soon enough,' he said. 'Antonius is a charming, entertaining fellow, and a master of his trade. He's King Theodo's dungeon-master and torturer-in-chief.'

Mimus unlocked Florin's leg-iron before he left the stable at nightfall. 'I suppose,' he remarked casually, 'we can now dispense with that.'

It wasn't until Florin was staring into the darkness on his own that he grasped the full significance of those words. He was well and truly shackled, with or without a leg-iron. Theodo had him in the palm of his hand. They were mere castles in the air, all the fine plans that had kept up his spirits during those dismal days chained to the wall. Life in a dungeon or a jester's motley—, those were his sole alternatives.

FLORIN was in one of Theodo's dungeons, a rough-hewn cavity in the rock with stout iron bars over the entrance. He watched in horror as a big chunk of rock broke off the roof and crashed to the ground. Two more big chunks came crashing down. The whole hillside was collapsing on top of him—it would crush him like a grape in a winepress. Desperately, he rattled the bars and cried for help. Nobody answered.

More lumps of rock came thundering down behind him. Florin hurled himself at the bars with all his might. They were rough—they were tree trunks, and their bark tore his hands. Now he was toiling through a trackless thicket. He heard his father's voice quite close at hand: 'Have a care, Florin. We dwell in a dark forest filled with turmoil and terror.'

He could make out his father riding not far ahead, a vague, shadowy figure amid the trees. Argos, his stallion, shimmered white against the gloom.

Florin strove to catch him up. He ran as fast as he could, panting and stumbling. 'Wait for me, father,' he called. 'Let me ride with you. I'm so weary.'

But the dark figure neither paused nor turned.

'Please wait,' Florin called again. Mustering all his energy, he sprinted after the horseman. Branches lashed him in the face, thorns lacerated his legs. Slowly, he caught up.

'Come no nearer!' His father's voice sounded almost imploring.

'Take me with you, father, I'll never find my way out of here alone!' Florin overtook the horseman and planted himself in his path. King Philip brought the stallion to a halt with a tug on the reins.

'On your own head be it,' he said. 'See what Theodo has made of me.' And he threw back the hood of his cloak.

Florin recoiled. Seated astride the horse in front of him was a dwarf no bigger than a child of five, a grotesquely misshapen creature with a massive hunchback. But it was Florin's father, for all that. The face and voice were his.

'What has he done to you?' Florin cried in dismay.

The dwarf gave a rueful smile. 'You tried to escape, had you forgotten?' He pulled his hood down and gripped the reins. 'I cannot help you, Florin. You are bigger than I—fend for yourself.'

The white stallion set off again. The horseman raised his hand in a familiar gesture of farewell, then vanished into the gloom without a single backward glance.

FLORIN sat up with a start. In the final moment of his dream he'd thought he felt a comforting hand stroke his forehead, but there was no one there, only the jester, who fixed him with an ill-humoured stare.

'Would you be kind enough to sob a little less loudly in your dreams?' asked Mimus.

Florin turned his back on the jester without replying. He didn't want to think; his only wish was to go back to sleep as soon as possible—without dreaming this time. 'Almighty God,' he prayed despairingly, 'even though you have deserted me, please protect my father!'

– AGONY OF MIND –

'IF YOU LIKE,' Mimus said the next morning, 'I'll show you round your new home.'

Home! Florin spat contemptuously, but when the jester turned in the doorway and beckoned, he followed him. The prospect of leaving this cheerless stable was too alluring.

Mimus began by conducting him back to the entrance hall. 'Let's start at the end,' he said, indicating the double doors with a grand gesture. 'The end of the world!'

The notion that double doors could constitute the end of the world was almost comical. 'What do you mean?' Florin inquired suspiciously.

'I mean we aren't permitted to leave the castle,' said Mimus. 'That's the third jester's rule, and it must be strictly obeyed!'

'Don't say you've never been outside these past fifteen years?'

'Only in my dreams,' the jester replied pensively. Seeing Florin's startled expression, he went on: 'It could be worse. No snow on my head in winter, no sunstroke in summer, and the king cherishes me like a father.'

'I don't believe you,' Florin said firmly. 'Nobody stopped me yesterday.' Abruptly, he opened one of the doors and stepped over the threshold—only to bump into a pair of crossed pikes. The sentries motioned him back inside without a word.

'You won't get out,' Mimus said, shrugging his shoulders. 'The portal is guarded day and night.'

'But yesterday . . .'

'Yesterday was an exception. They wanted to have some sport with you. Come now.' The jester set off up the stairs. 'There's plenty more to see.'

Florin followed him, irritated by the incessant tinkle of the bells on his costume. How could the jester endure it day after day?

Mimus conducted him to an ornately carved wooden door on the second floor. The two sentries who flanked it were leaning on their pikes with an air of boredom. 'Beyond this door lie the royal family's apartments,' the jester explained. 'We enter them only at the king's bidding.'

'And if you jesters don't remove yourselves in double-quick time,' one of the sentries growled, 'we'll throw you down the stairs—with or without the king's bidding!'

As if scared to death, Mimus leapt backward. 'A miracle!' he cried. 'The furniture spoke!'

He eyed the two men with his head on one side, and clicked his tongue in disapproval. 'What exceptionally shabby, worm-eaten pieces! It's a disgrace. The chamberlain should really take better care of the royal household.'

Before the sentries knew what was happening, he had leapt between them and grabbed them by the nose.

'You see,' he said, twisting their noses so hard that the men yelped with pain, 'even the handles won't turn properly! But now—' he gave each nose another hearty pinch, 'they're all nicely oiled again. Run for it, little Mimus!'

So saying, he released the sentries. The two men raised their pikes, seething with fury, but Mimus dodged them, nimble as a lizard, and raced down the stairs after Florin. He paused on the next landing.

'What's the matter with you blockheads?' he called impudently. 'Won't your wooden legs work?'

'Just wait till we catch you!' a furious voice called down. 'We'll skewer you like a brace of squealing piglets!'

Florin cast an anxious glance up the stairs.

'Never fear,' Mimus said with a grin, 'those prize specimens can't leave their posts. They're like chained-up watchdogs. You can torment them to your heart's content—as long as you don't venture too close to their pikes.'

Several windows were set into the sides of the stairwell, presumably to render the king's descent from his apartments to the banqueting hall as light and pleasant as possible. Florin turned to Mimus inquiringly.

'Go on.' The jester made a gesture of invitation. 'It isn't forbidden to look out.'

From here they had a panoramic view of the entire castle precincts: the ramparts, towers and walls, the iron-bound gates. Seeing the soldiers in the watchtowers and the archers on the battlements, Florin could imagine how they had sneered at his ludicrous attempt to escape. Mimus was right: he needed no schooling in jesterdom. He had fallen into King Theodo's trap like a perfect fool.

His gaze travelled across the crenellations of the inner wall and came to rest on the servants' quarters. From up here they looked pleasant enough, with freshly whitewashed walls, green wooden shutters and shingled roofs. All the doors were open and brisk activity reigned. Farmhands in knee breeches were toting bales of hay to the stables and stacking sacks of oats. A stable boy was leading two horses to pasture.

Seated beneath a pear tree laden with fruit that glowed yellow in the sunlight, an old woman was darning woollen socks as she chatted to a young nursemaid with three little children on leading strings and a tightly swaddled infant in her arms.

Florin thought of the servants' quarters at Montfield, of the long wooden tables round which they gathered after work to sup together and play cards. As a little boy he had sometimes joined them with Muriel. He could still recall the taste of the sweet malt beer he was offered, which he'd never sampled since. There was something comforting about the memory, and he wondered why the jesters, too, didn't lodge down there in the servants' quarters.

'We jesters dwell in the Monkey Tower,' Mimus said beside him, as if he'd divined Florin's thoughts. 'You can't see it from here, it's on the north side.'

Why Monkey Tower? Having asked himself that question, Florin realised a moment later that he didn't want to know the answer at all.

Mimus pointed to the servants and farmhands with an air of disdain. 'Those folk down there toil in the sweat of their brow.' He made a sweeping gesture. 'Whereas I, on the other hand, am the king's favourite. Though not,' he added, 'the only one. Come, it's time I introduced you to our neighbours.'

On their way back to the Monkey Tower they passed the big castle kitchen. The morning hurly-burly was in progress beyond the half-open door: pots were clattering, soup was bubbling, fat was sizzling. Florin longingly sniffed the scent of roast chicken that assailed his nostrils.

The jester tugged at his arm. 'Don't trouble to beg, they'll give you nothing. The king's word is law in this castle.'

Next to the kitchen was a long row of wooden doors secured with heavy bolts and padlocks.

A shiver ran down Florin's spine at the sight of them. 'Are those the dungeons?' he asked apprehensively.

'Here, directly beside the kitchen?' Mimus laughed. 'Even our king isn't as cruel as that. The dungeons are far below ground, where they belong. These—' he indicated the barred doors, 'are storerooms. The chamberlain wears the keys on a golden chain round his neck. He has to account to the king for every last hen's egg.'

Mimus led Florin back into the Monkey Tower, but outside the door to the jesters' stable he turned right and set off up a narrow spiral staircase.

On the first floor he put a finger to his lips. 'Ssh! First I'll see if the distinguished gentleman is in the mood to receive us.'

A door was ajar. Mimus peered cautiously round it. The next moment he wrenched it wide open. An overpowering stench of wild beast smote Florin from the dark chamber within.

'Permit me to introduce you,' Mimus cried ceremoniously. 'Zito, my arch-rival for His Majesty's favour!'

At the sound of his voice, a gigantic bear rose to its feet. Florin, who had never seen such a huge beast at close quarters, started back in alarm. Then he saw that Zito was secured to the wall by a massive iron collar and chain.

'It's just as well,' said Mimus, who had followed the direction of his gaze. 'Master Bruin can turn quite vicious. The king likes to have him led in when his privy councillors become too long-winded. Zito's appearance always helps the noble lords to reach a swift decision.'

Florin looked round. From the low ceiling to the straw on the floor, the bear's quarters were identical with their own stable.

At least we have no iron collars, he thought, eyeing the bear with a touch of compassion.

'Rollo is the only person who can approach Zito,' Mimus went on. 'They not only look like father and son, they love each other in the same way.'

'Mimus, you evil blabbermouth!' The bestiarius had climbed the stairs behind them unobserved, carrying a bucket of turnips in each hand. 'Any more of your impudence and I'll feed you to Zito for breakfast before you've even opened your eyes.'

'That would be a mistake, Rollo.' Quick as a flash, Mimus snatched two turnips and tossed one to Florin. 'I'd give him diarrhoea. Think of the mess!'

Rollo merely grunted. He walked past them and emptied out the turnips at Zito's feet. To Florin's amazement, the bestiarius didn't turn a hair when the huge animal planted its paws on his shoulders.

'Good boy,' he murmured, ruffling the bear's matted fur. 'You give me far less trouble than these accursed jesters, may Beelzebub take them!'

'Are you aware, Rollo,' jeered Mimus, 'that every oath costs you another hundred years in purgatory? Alas, when I reckon up your score! Be sure to get a nice warm place beside the devil's furnace!'

Rollo's moon face broke into a supercilious smile. 'You don't frighten me, Donkey-Ears,' he declared. 'Purgatory will end sooner or later, and then I shall enter the kingdom of heaven. You, on the other hand,' he continued, thumping Mimus on the chest, 'will end up in Abraham's sausage boiler, like all brute beasts, and be transformed into some new kind of creature.'

He produced a honeycomb from the depths of one of his many pockets and held it in front of the bear's muzzle. 'Here, my lad, enjoy your meal.'

Mimus tapped Florin on the shoulder. 'Let us leave father and son to commune in familial bliss. Brother is waiting.'

'Brother,' who lived on the floor above, turned out to be a full-grown wolf, and he was unsecured.

'Never fear,' said Rollo, who had followed them. 'He's as harmless as a lapdog. One of the king's huntsmen reared him from a cub.'

'But he's free.' Florin stared in surprise at the big grey wolf, which was digging in the straw with its muzzle and eyeing them warily. 'Why doesn't he run off?'

'Because he's the biggest coward imaginable,' Rollo said scornfully. 'Watch!' He stamped his foot, and the wolf promptly slunk into a corner. 'Our fearsome wolf would never dare get past Zito, still less you jesters.'

Mimus grinned at Florin. 'Then he should cherish a truly fraternal affection for you, being a wolfcub in donkey's clothing.'

'Don't listen to his nonsense, my boy,' growled Rollo, 'or warts will sprout from your earlobes.'

Florin followed Mimus and the bestiarius to the stable on the top floor. When Rollo opened the door, Florin realised at once how the tower had acquired its name. Four monkeys lived up there, all of the same breed. Pretty creatures with pale brown fur and black faces, they wore pinafores like little children—pinafores, Florin was disconcerted to note, made of the same striped cloth as his jester's costume. The monkeys greeted Mimus and Rollo with enthusiasm but were wary of approaching Florin.

'We'll soon accustom them to you,' said Mimus, plucking two of the creatures from his head. 'The king likes to see his monkeys and his jesters perform together.'

Bear and wolf, monkeys and jesters . . . Florin's head began to spin. 'Keep away!' he snapped, as Rollo laughingly tried to perch the smallest monkey on his shoulder.

The bestiarius turned to Mimus with a puzzled frown. 'What ails the dwarf?'

'He's weary—,' said the jester, 'weary of descending step after step, ever downwards.'

'Eh?' Rollo looked mystified. 'The Monkey Tower hasn't as many stairs as all that. I trudge up and down them a dozen times a day.'

FLORIN paused outside the door to their stable. 'I don't understand,' he said. 'The king summons you to him every day—he thinks the world of you, so why does he compel you to live like this?' He made a gesture that encompassed their wretched quarters. 'Like a beast among beasts?'

As if he were the master of ceremonies in person, Mimus rapped the floor with his bauble. 'By your leave,' he said, pointing gravely to himself. 'Mimus the jester, favourite of the king and highly esteemed member of the royal menagerie, along with Zito the bear, Brother the wolf, and the monkeys. His Majesty is so fond of his pets that he suffers us to dwell merrily together in his vicinity: in the Monkey Tower.'

He laughed at Florin's grim expression. 'There are many advantages to being a royal pet,' he declared. 'We don't have to work; we're entitled to a new costume three times a year, like the monkeys; we're given our daily bowl of gruel; and—most important of all—if we please the king, he feeds us little tidbits with his own hand.' He chuckled again. 'I'm sure you'll learn to appreciate the latter privilege in due course.'

'If you put up with such treatment,' said Florin, 'you're truly no better than a beast.' The jester's words disgusted him. He had never before encountered a person so lacking in pride.

Mimus seemed unconcerned by his scorn. 'Pay attention, my princely pupil,' he said, giving Florin an encouraging prod with his bauble. 'In order to enter the exalted circle of royal favourites, you must now embark upon your lessons.'

'I did so long ago,' Florin retorted impudently. 'What else have I been doing hitherto?'

Mimus gave him an amiable smile. 'Limbering-up exercises. Let's start, then. What skills do you possess, little Mimus?'

'What business is it of yours?'

'So it's true what they've been saying at court,' said Mimus. His eyes glinted. 'The Crown Prince of Moltovia is a shining example to all the young knights in the land.'

'That goes without saying,' Florin retorted. 'As a future king, I have to—'

'Because,' the jester broke in, 'he's the stupidest, laziest, greediest of all.'

'You . . .' Florin was speechless with indignation. 'You vile, insolent—'

'Convince me of the opposite,' Mimus said imperturbably. 'What can you do?'

'Things of which a fool like you can only dream!' Florin snarled. 'I can ride, swim, fence, hunt, fish, wield sword and lance . . .' He broke off for a moment, recalling his various disciplines. 'I've studied law, philosophy, geometry, grammar, oratory, Latin and Greek—'

'Pardon me, o walking fount of erudition,' Mimus interrupted mildly, 'I was speaking of skills, not of useless lordly pastimes. Let us try again. Can you—' he proceeded to count on his fingers, 'play the bagpipes? Perform a graceful pirouette while dancing? Turn cartwheels and somersaults? Croak like a frog? Crow like a cockerel? Play the tambourine?'

Florin just stared at him.

'I see,' sighed the jester. 'Your training will require a goodly amount of work. Sing me a song.'

'Over your grave!'

'Go on, sing!'

Florin had a sudden idea. The jester wanted a song? Very well, he should have one. He had picked up a satirical ditty from the soldiers at Montfield Castle, so he proceeded to sing it as loudly and discordantly as possible:

'King Theodo is a man of mettle
whom no one e'er defeats in battle.
When reckless enemies venture close
the king his victory fanfare blows:
his churning innards fill the air
with thunderous farts beyond compare.

His soldiers cheer, his foes fall back,
his servants quickly wipe his crack.
For Vinland's king, with might and main,
has soiled his breeches yet again.'

'What an enchanting melody! What poetic delicacy!' jeered Mimus. 'Moltovia's elected court poet is a swineherd, no doubt. But watch this!' With a single bound, he went into a handstand and promenaded round the room on his palms. 'I shall teach you to do that. And . . .' Balancing on one hand only, he fished a leather ball out of his pocket, tossed it into the air and deftly caught it with his feet. 'And that, too!'

'Show-off,' Florin muttered.

The jester landed on his feet with the agility of a cat. 'Can you do a headstand?'

'No, I can't.'

'A handstand?'

'No, I can't.'

'A cartwheel?'

'No, I can't,' Florin repeated mulishly.

'No, I can't! No, I can't!' the jester mimicked. 'But you could open your mouth wide enough the night we first met, Prince No-I-Can't! "*Better to light a fire than fight a liar!*"' he warbled in Florin's voice. 'What put that flash of inspiration into your head?'

'I was furious,' said Florin, as if that explained it.

'I see,' the jester muttered thoughtfully. The next moment he drew back his arm and dealt Florin a hard blow on the chest with his bauble.

'Ouch!' Florin exclaimed. 'Why did you do that?'

'To infuriate you,' Mimus explained, all innocence. He raised the bauble again. 'Let me know when you're furious enough to do a headstand.'

'Stop that at once,' Florin snapped, 'or I'll—'

'Or you'll what?' the jester demanded sharply. 'Methinks his royal highness still hasn't grasped that I'm his teacher—his *master*! When I click my fingers, you'll jump. When I tap my foot, you'll dance. And if you don't . . .'

'Go on,' Florin said scathingly. 'What then?'

The jester spread his arms. 'Then run away again,' he said. 'You couldn't do the king a greater favour.'

Florin lapsed into embittered silence.

'Your jester's course of instruction will take the following form,' said Mimus, sounding just like one of the learned monks at Montfield's royal school of knighthood. 'In the mornings I shall teach you how to flex and contort your limbs. In the afternoons, when I'm busy elsewhere, you'll study quietly, and at night you'll recite all you've learnt by heart. And if you're an obedient, willing little donkey who works hard and gives his master perfect satisfaction, you'll find life with me paradise on earth!'

IN reality, the rules that governed Florin's new existence were cruel and relentless. He more than once felt he would explode at any moment. If only he could at least have gone outside now and then! It was late September, the time of the great autumn hunts, and not a day went by but a party of boisterous huntsmen assembled in the courtyard after morning Mass. When Florin heard the clatter of hoofs, the shouts and laughter, the blare of hunting horns, he clamped his hands over his ears. His yearning for the forest, for sunlight and fresh air, was like an all-consuming fever. If only he could once have ridden with them, galloping across fields, meadows and streams until the morning air stung his eyes and his heart beat a wild, rapturous tattoo . . .

Instead, he was buried alive in the Monkey Tower. While learning riddles and rhymes by heart he paced restlessly from one corner of the stable to the other. A newly caged beast must feel like this, he told himself—cooped up and fretful.

His one small taste of freedom came at noon. As soon as the bell of the castle chapel struck twelve, Mimus stretched out on the straw.

'The hour of St. Desidia,' he explained, 'the patron saint of sluggards. The noble lady's invitation may not be spurned.' So saying, he
turned over on his side and instantly fell asleep.

During this free period the jester allowed his pupil the run of the
castle. Florin roamed every floor, but they were solitary, joyless excursions. No one ever addressed a word to him, whether page or scullion,
soldier or chambermaid, errand boy or washerwoman. They all stared
at him as if he were some exotic beast.

Which is just what you are, he told himself grimly. Get used to it,
little Mimus.

But how could he get used to contemptuous glances? To the shrill,
incessant tinkling of bells? To his one bowl of gruel a day and the
hunger that stole over him by midday and plagued him so sorely at
night that he couldn't get to sleep?

But even more of a torment than hunger and jester's bells was
Florin's concern for his father. He had no idea what Theodo and his
torturer-in-chief might have done to him, and he was so racked with
fear and uncertainty that he broached the subject with Mimus.

'How do I know that my father isn't already dead?' he asked in
despair.

'He isn't,' Mimus replied firmly.

'You can't be sure of that.'

'Yes, I can,' was the jester's calm retort. 'Headsman, priest and
jester are present at every execution.'

During the long, cold nights when Mimus was entertaining King
Theodo, Florin lay awake on the straw and pined for home. He missed
simply everything and everyone: Muriel and Ramon, his warm bed, his
beloved falcon, his friends, their afternoons in the forest, their meals
together, their pleasant evenings round the fire.

When he pictured life at Montfield Castle going on without him,
sorrow gnawed at his belly like a malignant worm. His father's throne

would now be occupied by some fat, ill-tempered governor appointed by Theodo. His equally fat and ill-tempered son would be sleeping in his, Florin's, bed. He would bully Ramon and Sturmius and simultaneously try to ingratiate himself with his, Florin's, friends.

He recalled Theodo's triumphant words to his father: *'It will be as if your pestilential family had never existed!'*

What if that really happened? What if those at home simply forgot him in the course of time, as if he were dead and buried? Then he would be truly alone—abandoned by God and man alike. At the thought of this, Florin burrowed into the straw and fretted until he finally went to sleep.

———

WHEN one of Bellingar's inhabitants *did* speak to him on his next tour of the castle, Florin could happily have dispensed with it. He was just climbing the stairs when three pages descended them side by side, leaving no room for him to pass.

'Out of the way, fool!' one of them snapped.

The trio had already passed Florin when the page in the centre swung round abruptly. Leaving his companions, he planted himself in Florin's path. Florin now recognised him as the pale-faced, arrogant youth whom Mimus had struck with his bauble on that first disastrous night.

The page stared at Florin with a look of surprise and disbelief in his blue eyes. 'So they really did it,' he said softly.

'Come on, Raoul,' one of his companions called impatiently. 'Why concern yourself with the jester?'

'Because I know something you don't,' Raoul replied in a self-important voice. His initial surprise was giving way to undisguised and malicious glee. He put his hands on his hips and looked Florin up and down.

'What elegant attire,' he sneered. 'You now look as much of a fool as your master.'

While speaking, he began to kick Florin on the shin, gently at first, then harder and harder. Intrigued by this sight, the other two converged like hounds scenting blood. Each of them was a head taller than Florin.

'Three against one,' he said angrily. 'What valiant heroes you are!'

Raoul gave Florin a shove that sent him staggering into the other pages' arms. 'You're wetting yourself with fear, little Mimus,' he said with relish. That he knew exactly who his victim was seemed only to spur him on the more.

'You're as much of a coward as your master. You jesters are a lily-livered bunch—you feel strong only when clinging to the hem of the king's robe. Hold him tight,' he commanded his friends. 'I'll teach him a lesson he won't forget in a hurry.'

When Florin hugged his body protectively and felt the bauble in his belt, it occurred to him that he wasn't defenceless. Count Ursio had trained him to fight at close quarters almost daily since his eighth birthday. The solid wooden sceptre would be his sword.

The three young courtiers had no notion of swordplay. When Florin drew the bauble from his belt, Raoul's evil grin became broader still.

'Do you know what happens to a dog that bares its teeth at its master?' he asked. 'The master thrashes it until it licks his feet, whimpering for mercy. And that's just what I'm going to—aaargh!'

Florin had taken careful aim and thrust the bauble between his ribs, where it would hurt most. While Raoul was hopping up and down like an injured frog and gasping for breath, Florin swiftly eluded his two companions' grasp. A moment later he was raining blows on all three pages from above. Heads, shoulder blades, ribs, elbows; with remarkable accuracy, the bauble struck the aiming points marked in red on Count Ursio's straw dummies. The old fencing master would have been proud of him.

When Florin finally let them be, they stood there panting, fists clenched and faces crimson with rage, but they didn't dare lay hands on him again.

'Well, how about it?' Florin brandished his fool's sceptre menacingly. 'Shall we begin again from the beginning?'

Raoul glared at him furiously and muttered something unintelligible. Then the three pages turned on their heels and hurried down the stairs. With a sigh of relief, Florin replaced the bauble in his belt.

'What manner of demon are you?' Another youngster was peering out from behind a pillar. Florin promptly gripped his bauble again.

'By all the archangels,' the boy said hastily, emerging from his hiding place, 'I mean you no harm.' About Florin's height, he had coppery hair that encased his head like a helmet and a broad, good-natured face sprinkled with countless freckles. He was wearing the dirtiest smock Florin had ever seen.

'You led them a nice little dance,' he said, looking impressed. 'I doubt if any courtiers have ever received such a drubbing before. Did the king buy you from a troupe of entertainers? Who else would have taught you those tricks?'

'Hm . . . yes,' Florin replied vaguely.

The boy scrutinised Florin's face. 'You haven't been long at court. At all events, I've never seen you before. You're a court jester like Mimus, aren't you?'

'Hm . . .' Florin shrugged his shoulders.

'Well . . .' said the red-haired youngster, and Florin could tell from his pitying expression that he took him for a simpleton unable even to string three words together. 'I must be going.'

Standing there, Florin saw the boy give him several backward glances as he walked off.

ALTHOUGH the Almighty had evidently forgotten him, Florin prayed as he had never prayed before. At night, when his rumbling belly refused to let him sleep, he sought God's assistance. He prayed to St. Florin, his patron saint, and to St. Barbara, who had been imprisoned in a tower like himself and couldn't fail to understand his needs.

He prayed for his father and his friends at home, and he never forgot to include King Theodo in his prayers. Fervently, he wished him blindness, gout and consumption all at once. And, if God were unprepared to strike down the godless, perjured king quite so unmercifully, Florin prayed that he would at least be afflicted with a scabby head and a face full of warts.

On Sunday mornings all the church bells in the city rang. Their clangour penetrated even the Monkey Tower's stout walls. Florin had noticed that Mimus never seemed to pray. The jester merely threw him mocking sidelong glances when he said his morning and evening prayers, and now he was not even preparing to attend Sunday Mass.

'Does no one say Mass in this place?' Florin inquired.

'Of course,' Mimus replied.

'Is the chapel outside the castle walls?'

'No.'

'Then why don't we go to Mass like all good Christian folk?'

'Go, by all means.'

By the time Florin finally found the entrance to the chapel, every last pew was occupied. As at Montfield, Sunday Mass in Bellingar Castle was attended in force by the inhabitants and their servants. From the saddler's family in the nave to the royal family in the gallery, they all gathered together before the same altar. Florin remained standing at the back beside the entrance. The chaplain and two adolescent servers were lighting the many candles by the altar, a procedure that took some time. Florin's gaze was drawn to the big stained-glass windows behind the altar, which outshone all the candle flames put together.

They were unearthly in their beauty. To Florin it seemed as if heaven itself were shining through the windows into the chapel's gloomy interior. He had never realised before how many shades of blue there were: the luminous, triumphant blue of Heaven, from which Christ was returning to earth on the Last Day; the soft, majestic blue of the cloak in which Mary was swaddling the Child; the multi-coloured, dynamic blues of the water on which Jesus was walking, as if on dry land, toward his disciples. Even the jaws of Hell were a bottomless dark blue chasm into which unfortunate sinners were tumbling without hope of redemption.

Florin remembered how proud everyone at Montfield Castle had been two years ago when the chapel's opaque horn window panes had been replaced with new leaded glass. Compared to these heavenly windows, the ones at home were plain to the point of poverty.

How much money had Theodo paid for this splendour? Whose blood had he shed in order to acquire it?

Almost simultaneously he felt ashamed of his envious thoughts: extolling the beauty of Heaven was always pleasing in the sight of God.

He clasped his hands together, intending to offer up a silent prayer. The little movement made his bells jingle—only briefly, but the chaplain at the altar craned his neck. Catching sight of Florin, he walked swiftly down the aisle toward him.

'What are you doing here, you wretched creature?'

Florin was utterly taken aback. All heads had turned in their direction. The children in the last pew gazed at him wide-eyed.

'I should like to attend Mass, Father.'

The man in the grey cassock stared at him as if he'd just discovered a rat in the communion bread cupboard. 'Divine service violated by the presence of monkeys and jesters? What next! God does not suffer his temple to be defiled.'

Florin was standing beneath the gallery reserved for the royal family, so he couldn't see if the king was present. However, he gathered from the way the chaplain kept glancing upward that Theodo was following events below.

'God will not turn away anyone whose soul is in need,' he said stoutly.

The chaplain's eyes darted upward once more. 'A jester has no soul,' he hissed. 'In a jester, the place where the immortal soul dwells in us human beings is occupied by a mass of putrid air. And now begone with you!'

Florin looked past the priest's gaunt grey figure at the heavenly stained-glass windows. He squared his shoulders resolutely. What the chaplain said meant nothing. He knew he wasn't a soulless jester; he was a child of God like all present, and God had welcomed him to his sacred abode. He wouldn't budge an inch from the spot . . .

Then he heard the king's voice overhead.

'Bestiarius, take the fool back where he belongs: the Monkey Tower!'

Florin slowly retreated. It was unendurable, the thought of Rollo dragging him out like a mangy cur in front of all these people.

'I'm going,' he muttered.

He returned to the stable with his head bowed. Mimus studied his face attentively. 'Well,' he asked, 'did you pray for our souls?'

'What souls?' Florin said bitterly. 'I've just been denied one.' He straightened up with a jerk. 'You knew they wouldn't admit me, didn't you?'

'Yes,' Mimus replied quietly. 'Many things must be experienced in person. It's the only way to understand.'

'To understand what?' snapped Florin.

'The jester's peculiar nature,' Mimus told him. 'He's nothing. Neither this nor that, neither fish nor flesh, neither man nor beast, neither God's nor the devil's. That's why the priests hate us most of all. And we them.'

'Oh, spare me your blasphemous nonsense,' Florin said unhappily. What now? How could God forgive his sins if no one would hear his confession? If he were not permitted to attend Mass, how was he to

know the difference between good and evil? It was like being abandoned in a desert without water.

'Do you at least have a prayer book?' he asked.

'What for?' the jester retorted. 'Does Zito pray? Do the monkeys?'

'You speak of animals,' Florin said indignantly. 'You and I are
human beings who owe the Almighty praise and thanks.'

'Amen,' said Mimus, casting his eyes up to heaven. 'You still
propose to pray, even though God has just turned you out of his
house?'

'Not God,' Florin said firmly. 'Only the king and his arrogant
chaplain.'

– PUPIL AND MASTER –

'I'VE SOME NEWS for you,' Mimus said casually over their morning gruel. 'Your life of idleness is at an end. This evening you're to display your amazing talents to all and sundry!'

Florin dropped his spoon into the bowl with a clatter. '*What* did you say?'

'It's true, I fear,' sighed the jester. 'The king wishes to satisfy himself of your progress. No doubt you'll ruin the fine program of entertainment I've devised for tonight's festivity.'

'Festivity? What festivity?'

'The annual bootlicking contest to which the king treats his toadies,' Mimus explained. 'A grand spectacle. The entire royal household will be present, including the queen, the crown prince and the princess.'

Florin would have felt no different had the jester hit him on the head with a club. He had put up with everything until now—homesickness, hunger, humiliation—but to be paraded before the court as a jester was the most terrible prospect of all. And he had no choice, if he wanted to prevent his father from coming to harm.

'Stop daydreaming,' Mimus said impatiently. 'To work! I've no wish to be a laughing-stock on your account!'

'As if you needed me to be anything else!' Florin muttered.

Compared to what followed, the learning of rhymes and riddles seemed a serious, dignified occupation. The jester strapped a tambourine to Florin's waist and made him beat time to his ditties. He compelled him to put a live frog in his mouth, turn somersaults when he clicked his fingers, fire peas from a peashooter, rattle his pig's bladder, dance a jig with his bauble, and ask riddles while standing on his head. And he nagged him incessantly.

'Call those somersaults? You're rolling around like a nag with the colic!'

'You're supposed to sing, not bleat like a sick goat!'

'Your tongue is as slow and slippery as a slug. Remember this: the tongue is your sword. You must always keep it whetted and oiled!'

The later it got, the less satisfied Mimus became with Florin's efforts. Finally, the boy lost his temper.

'Leave me be!' he snarled. 'You're training me like a monkey!'

'You think so?' Mimus retorted. 'I'd long ago have whipped a monkey as disobedient as you.' For the hundredth time, he thrust Florin's bauble into his hand. 'Go on, one last little dance. Kick up your heels!'

'If you enjoy hopping around like a chicken with gout, do so yourself!' Angrily, Florin hurled the fool's sceptre into the straw. 'If you think I'm going to perform your monkey tricks in front of the court, you're mistaken.'

'Really?' Quick as lightning, Mimus grabbed Florin by the ears on his fool's cap and drew him close. 'Listen to me, noble princeling,' he purred. 'Your fate is a matter of total indifference to me. If your illustrious head rolls off the executioner's block tomorrow, I shall kick it over the battlements in person.'

'And break your toes, I hope,' Florin put in fiercely.

'Unfortunately,' the jester went on, 'we're both in the same boat tonight. If you're a bad pupil, I'm a bad master. If you drown, I shall drown with you!'

'Ah, so that's the way the wind blows,' sneered Florin. 'The gallant gentleman is wetting himself with fear. I'm to act the monkey and save his miserable neck!'

'And, as it happens, your own,' Mimus retorted sharply. 'So dance!'

While Florin, grinding his teeth, was capering around in the most idiotic fashion, Mimus went to the window and looked out.

'Time to go,' he said. 'Remember this: when the sun shines through the crack between the battlements and the castle wall, the king awaits us.'

'Very interesting.' Florin was panting with exertion. 'Then he must await us at nightfall in summer and in the afternoon in winter.'

'What a clever little fellow you are.' Mimus gave him an affectionate smile. 'Boredom sets in far earlier in winter, didn't you know that?'

With practised movements he attached the bauble and pig's bladder to Florin's belt and tweaked his fool's cap straight. 'You're in luck, by the way,' he said complacently as he pushed Florin toward the door. 'Tonight you'll witness a choice example of the jester's art. I shall be presenting one of the court officials with a, er . . . very special mark of distinction.'

'Like the crown you set on my father's head?' Florin asked bitterly.

The jester remained impassive. 'Something of the kind, yes.'

'Do you enjoy doing Theodo's dirty work?'

'That depends. Tonight, at all events, my victim will not be innocent. Chief Justice Bernardo is a scoundrel. It won't hurt him to receive my nice little award.'

FLORIN entered the great banqueting hall at Mimus's side. The master of ceremonies turned his back on them with an air of disdain, but their bells more than compensated for his failure to announce them: nearly every head turned in their direction. At that moment Florin would have given anything to be able to exchange his fool's cap for a cloak of invisibility. He involuntarily recoiled, but Mimus grabbed him roughly by the arm.

'No mistakes now,' he warned, towing him along.

Despite his distress, it struck Florin that everything had changed since that first night. There were no soldiers in evidence, no raucous shouts or clanking weapons. Instead, music and perfumes filled the gilded, brightly illuminated hall. As if in an attempt to turn night into day, huge chandeliers had been lowered from the ceiling, and their hundreds of candles bathed the guests in a radiant glow. The gold and silver tableware vied in brilliance with the jewels of the ladies-in-waiting. The air smelt simultaneously sweet and pungent. The flag-stones were strewn with herbs, and rose petals floated in big silver bowls. Up in the minstrel gallery, flautists and lutenists were playing.

The banquet was already in full swing. Maidservants with wreaths of flowers in their hair were carrying in platters laden with roast pigeon, quail and partridge, the sight of which made Florin's stomach turn somersaults. He marvelled at the red and white wine that gushed in seemingly inexhaustible streams from a golden fountain at which guests could help themselves to their hearts' content.

And he'd thought that banquets at the royal court of Vinland would be poor affairs!

Wherever he looked he saw jubilant, expectant faces. Just as at Montfield, this night was the high point in a courtier's life: a welcome opportunity to emphasise one's own importance, bask in the king's favour, and—last but not least—outshine each other in splendour of jewellery and elegance of attire.

And, also as at Montfield, the children cared nothing for this display of magnificence. The younger ones played with the dogs beneath the table and fed them tidbits; the older ones played chess or cards. Sitting over there were three boys with their heads together. They looked almost like—

'Come on!' Mimus's voice brought Florin down to earth with a bump. The jester made for a pillar near the fireplace and pushed Florin into its lee. 'We'll wait here,' he whispered, and instantly seemed to turn to stone. Nothing moved but his eyes, which roamed the room unceasingly.

Florin stood beside him with his back against the pillar. Almost despite himself, his gaze strayed to the king's throne.

There he sat, Theodo the godless, perjured king. Florin's prayers notwithstanding, he was free from warts and clearly in the best of spirits. Seated beside him on another throne was a tall, pale-faced woman with a gold band in her brown hair.

So that is what it's like when there's a queen at court, Florin thought as he looked at her. Queen Elina held herself straight as a ramrod, but her face wore an exhausted, terribly earnest expression, as if even a smile would have been too much for her.

Florin's gaze moved on. The boy beside King Theodo had to be the crown prince, the girl beside him the princess. Both were about his own age. Sitting there at table side by side, they looked like an inverse copy of the royal couple: the prince lean and lanky, with his mother's pale skin and shadows beneath the eyes; the princess olive-skinned and of medium height, with Theodo's dark eyes and curly hair.

'*Let's hope she's pretty, at least!*' Florin felt a sudden pang as he remembered that conversation with his friends at supper in another world. Theodo's daughter was pretty enough, but who cared now?

As if she had sensed his gaze, the princess suddenly raised her head. Florin saw her give a start at the sight of him. She eyed him in surprise, then nudged her brother in the ribs and whispered something in his ear.

Florin tried desperately to banish every thought from his head. He mustn't reflect on what he looked like to them: a ridiculous, froglike creature bedecked with bells and surmounted by ass's ears. Sooner or later he would go mad with shame. Involuntarily, he pressed closer to the pillar, and his bells tinkled softly.

'Keep still!' hissed Mimus.

'What are we waiting for?' Florin whispered apprehensively. Whatever lay in store for him, he wanted to get it over.

Mimus didn't move. 'You must watch your audience closely,' he muttered between his teeth. 'Too soon, and they quickly grow bored. Too late, and they're drunk or asleep. Choose the ideal moment, and you've as good as won the day.'

The ideal moment came when a foppish lackey in red silk livery, with a curly wig and powdered cheeks, was bending over one of the silver bowls to replace a rose that had fallen out.

'Theodo's valet,' Mimus said happily. Taking a run at the man, he dealt him a kick on the rump that pitched him head first into the bowl. He was back in his place a fraction of a second later. 'His name is Marsus,' he went on, as if nothing had happened.

A voice rang out from the king's throne. 'Mimus, come here!'

Before Florin knew it, the jester had given him a push that sent him staggering sideways. 'Do as you're told, little Mimus! The king called you.'

'It was *you* I called, you old fool!' Theodo said sternly. 'Come here!'

'No.' The jester calmly remained in the lee of the pillar. 'Methinks there's a storm brewing. I shall wait until it has passed.'

At a signal from the king, two pages seized the grumbling jester and dragged him before the throne like a sack of oats.

'What's this?' King Theodo demanded reproachfully, pointing to his valet, who was spouting water and mopping his face with a silken cloth.

'A gargoyle?' Mimus suggested. Everyone laughed except Marsus, who angrily brandished his fist at the jester. 'No, wait,' cried Mimus, 'I want to try again.' He slunk up to the valet and loudly sniffed him. 'Marsus has just renewed an old acquaintance,' he announced. 'He has never once encountered water since his baptism—hoppla!' Nimble as a lizard, he dodged the valet's fist and rapped his silk-stockinged shins with his bauble.

'Admit defeat, Marsus,' Theodo said with a laugh. 'He's more than a match for you. But tell me, Mimus,' he went on, looking at Florin as if he had only just spotted him, 'what's this you've brought us?'

'The jester has given birth,' called one of the guests.

'He showed no sign of being with child,' quipped another.

'Permit me to explain.' Mimus preened himself on being the centre of attention. 'We jesters are like mushrooms in the woods. This little offspring of mine—' he took Florin's hand and dragged him in front of the throne, 'sprouted from the ground overnight. He needs to be kept a trifle moist, that's all.' So saying, he took a pitcher of wine from the table and made to empty it over Florin's head.

'Stop!' said the king. 'I wish to inspect your offspring in all his glory.'

Florin had been listening to their banter with only half an ear—he was too busy bracing himself for the inevitable, but it was no use. Now that he was standing before Theodo, he could scarcely breathe for the hatred and humiliation that constricted his throat.

'Turn round, little Mimus,' the king commanded. 'Now take the bauble in your hand. Yes, that's it . . .'

Theodo gazed at Florin for what seemed an eternity. So did the queen, the prince and princess and everyone else in the banqueting hall. Even the children interrupted their games to stare at him.

'The fool's sceptre suits you admirably,' Theodo remarked. 'All you need is a crown between your ears, and one could justly call you Prince Donkey-Ears.'

Florin saw the knowing grins on many faces, saw the pages nudge each other. His gaze fastened on the gold knife lying beside the king's plate.

Go on, you perjured king, he thought. Go on, poke fun at me. If your knife is sharp enough, you'll soon be called King No-Ears!

Theodo, who had followed the direction of his gaze, gave a delighted laugh. 'What impious thoughts are going through my pious little donkey's head,' he said derisively. 'A shame the chaplain declined to say Mass for the beloved beasts of the field.'

Mimus feigned surprise. 'Yet Father Anselm is usually so fond of animals,' he said. 'I've heard he has a special liking for goats.'

Florin failed to understand why everyone guffawed at this remark, but he hoped the arrogant chaplain was present and had heard himself mocked.

'The time has come, Mimus,' said King Theodo, never taking his eyes off Florin. 'Show us what your pupil can do.'

'Pupil?' screeched Mimus. 'Pupil be damned! He's a good-for-nothing, a numbskull, a blockhead—a disgrace to any teacher! He can't do a thing, not a thing. Would you care for a sample?' He cuffed Florin and commanded: 'Fly!'

'You see?' he said at once. 'The booby hasn't budged an inch from the ground. My other pupil does me credit. When I tell him to fly, he flies!' From his pocket he produced a lively though very dishevelled sparrow and tossed it into the air. The bird promptly fluttered up to the vaulted, star-spangled ceiling.

Florin couldn't have said when and where Mimus had caught the sparrow, but he had no time to ponder the question. The very next moment he felt something struggling in his hand: a frog.

'Into your mouth with it,' Mimus hissed.

Although Florin retched a little, he obeyed in response to a keen

glance from the jester, who felt in his pocket once more. This time he
brought out a mouse. 'Watch *this* obedient pupil of mine,' he called
loudly. 'When I tell *her* to sing—' he pinched the creature's tail until it
uttered a plaintive squeak, 'she sings.' He tossed the mouse into the
lap of a horrified lady-in-waiting and turned to Florin.

'When I bid *him* sing, what comes out?' He dug his elbow into
Florin's ribs, causing him to open his mouth. Everyone roared with
laughter when the frog escaped with one mighty leap.

'This youngster hasn't the brains of a sparrow or a mouse,' Mimus
grumbled. 'Tell me yourself, my sweet king, what am I to do with such
a pupil?'

'Well,' said Theodo, 'perhaps he can do other things. Have you
tried swordplay?'

Mimus was quite unprepared for this question. He blinked in
surprise, then cried quickly: 'Your Majesty wishes to see a swordfight?
Very well!' Grasping Florin's thumb, he held it up and stationed his
own thumb alongside. 'Brave Sir Mimus challenges fearsome Sir
Mimus the Younger to a duel!'

Florin couldn't help admiring his ingenuity. The jester swooped on
every new idea like a falcon.

'Let's see,' Mimus said, thinking aloud. 'Our knights need
helmets—' he quickly snapped two candle-snuffers off their handles
and placed them on his and Florin's thumbs, 'and swords.' With an
impudent grin, he snatched up the king's and queen's silver toothpicks.

'The swordsmen are armed!' he cried in a thunderous voice. 'Let
the duel commence!'

He clicked his tongue in imitation of hoofbeats and charged
Florin's thumb with his own, brandishing his toothpick wildly.

'Take that! And that!' he bellowed as his toothpick inflicted painful
pricks on Florin's skin. 'Defend yourself, you villain!'

'By all means,' Florin hissed. Gripping his own toothpick, he went over to the offensive in his turn. Cut and thrust, parry and disengage, then renew the attack—his thumb fought a thoroughgoing duel. However, he had to take several counterthrusts. Although the jester knew nothing about fencing, he was as nimble as an adder and ruthlessly exploited every lapse of concentration.

Out of the corner of his eye, Florin saw children crowding round them and many adults rising from their places at table to watch the proceedings. It was too comical, the way the 'knights' rode back and forth, hurling savage oaths at each other and exchanging blows until the toothpicks rang. It was good sport, pure and simple.

'What do you say now?!' Florin cried triumphantly. With one well-aimed thrust, he had skewered Mimus's thumb like a sausage.

'Have mercy, mighty Sir Mimus the Younger!' the jester wailed in a quavering voice. 'I'm dying!' Smitten with terrible convulsions, his thumb writhed in its death-throes.

'Pull that toothpick out!' he whispered in Florin's ear. 'I feel like a spitted suckling pig the butcher forgot to slaughter.'

'Serves you right!' Florin whispered back. He left the jester to writhe awhile longer before he extracted the toothpick with a jerk.

'The winner of this heroic encounter,' Mimus bellowed, raising Florin's thumb on high, 'Sir Mimus the Younger!'

Florin's thumb bowed in acknowledgment of the children's applause.

'You see, Mimus?' said Theodo. 'Even your good-for-nothing pupil is good at something.'

To Florin, the king's words were like a deluge of icy water. Fiercely, he pulled the snuffer off his thumb. How could he have been so thoughtless? He had allowed himself to be lulled by the jester's antics. Worse still, he had enjoyed it! What would his father have thought of him, playing the buffoon in front of their enemies?

He saw the princess lean over and whisper something to her father. Theodo nodded, then beckoned a maidservant bearing a dish of pastries.

'My daughter thinks you've earned a reward, little jester.' He tossed Florin a pastry.

Its scent was overpowering, and Florin's decision to reject any recompense from Theodo promptly evaporated. For all that, he had enough self-control to eat it slowly, one modest mouthful at a time. He refused to expose his weakness by wolfing it like a famished beast in front of everyone.

Mimus squinted longingly at the pastry. 'What of my reward?'

Theodo shook his head. 'You'll have to work harder. The night is still young.'

'How unjust!' pouted Mimus. 'This little good-for-nothing crams his belly and I have to watch. Just wait, you rascal!' He brandished his bauble threateningly. 'You'll pay for this!'

He dragged Florin behind the pillar by his ass's ears. 'You could have done worse,' he whispered, 'far worse.' For one brief moment his face relaxed. 'Take a rest,' he said with a smile, winding a rag round his injured thumb. 'Chief Justice Bernardo is about to attend a trial he won't forget for as long as he lives.'

Screwing up his eyes, he stared fixedly at a corpulent, exceptionally well-dressed man at the lower end of the king's table. Even as he did so, the face beneath his fool's cap transformed itself into a mask: watchful and malevolent, with glittering gaze and mouth turned down at the corners in scorn. He looked just as he had that first night, when Florin learnt to hate him.

A falcon, Florin thought again. A bird of prey trained to kill quarry for the king.

When Chancellor Benedict rose and proceeded to read out the names of court officials, Mimus gripped Florin's arm. 'The bootlicking contest is beginning,' he whispered. 'Now pay attention.'

Each of the men summoned went up to the throne and received a gift from the king. When Chief Justice Bernardo's turn came and he stepped forward, he did so with a self-satisfied smile on his lips.

Mimus thrust a peashooter into Florin's hand. 'When he's standing in front of the throne, bombard him with peas,' he whispered. 'But mind you don't hit the king!'

While the judge was being presented with a gold cup, Florin put the peashooter to his lips and aimed at his head. He succeeded at the first attempt: Bernardo spun round. Seeing that the two jesters' attention was focused on him, he gave a start.

'Why so fearful?' Mimus slunk up to the judge like a tomcat whose mouth is watering at the sight of a plump rat. Elegant gentlemen and court dignitaries had been clustering round the throne like moths round a candle. They now scattered in all directions as if the judge had been suddenly afflicted with leprosy.

'That's a fine gift you've received.' Mimus tapped the gold cup in Bernardo's hand. 'I, too, have a reward for you. Let us play a game together!'

The judge turned to Theodo indignantly. 'Most gracious king,' he quavered. 'I have no desire to be plagued by this simpleton. I refuse to—'

'You shall play,' the king said quietly.

Bernardo turned pale.

'Hurrah,' cried Mimus, 'this will be an amusing game!' He turned like lightning and gave one of the nearby pages a resounding slap. 'Don't stand there goggling!' he commanded. 'Bring me a chair!'

Florin saw the page flush with anger and clench his fists as he drew up a chair. Remembering his clash with Raoul, he scanned the room for him. The next moment he felt a vigorous dig in the ribs.

'Accompany me on the tambourine,' Mimus hissed. Then he patted the seat of the chair invitingly. 'Climb up there, Your Worship.'

'Most gracious king!' Chief Justice Bernardo turned to the throne once more in search of help, but Theodo, who had raised his goblet and was smilingly toasting the assembled company, paid no heed to his look of entreaty. The judge laid his gold cup aside with a gesture that invited sympathy, then mounted the chair.

'Now bend over,' Mimus commanded him. 'Spread your arms and raise one leg behind you.' He beckoned to Florin with a false air of anxiety. 'Hold his foot tight. If he falls, he'll leave a grease spot on the flagstones.'

The judge, in his sumptuous fur-trimmed doublet, wobbled helplessly on one leg. He had to flail his arms to keep his balance. Titters could be heard.

'Ah, yes, crooked paths often end in quicksand.' Mimus circled the chair appraisingly. 'Now for our game. The rules are simple: I ask questions, you answer them.' He tweaked Bernardo's earlobe. 'Understand?'

The judge grunted with exertion. 'Get on with it! Ask your questions, you confounded fool!' Beads of sweat were rolling down his plump cheeks and into his ermine collar.

'Then tell me, Your Worship,' the jester asked loudly. 'The fines you imposed last year—how much did you pay into the royal exchequer?'

'According to the record—' Bernardo began, but Mimus interrupted him.

'Oh, did I forget to mention it?' he asked, sweet as sugar. 'You must crow your answers like a cockerel. What's more,' he added, patting Bernardo's arm, 'you must flap your wings at the same time.'

'Your Majesty!' The judge teetered so perilously on his chair that Florin had to hang on with all his might. 'Bethink you of my position, my services to the crown . . .'

'You'll do as the jester says,' Theodo commanded.

'Well,' Mimus resumed, 'what were you about to tell us?'

A long silence ensued. Then Bernardo whispered: 'Cock-a-doodle-doo.'

'What was that?' Mimus cupped one of his ass's ears. 'I couldn't hear. You must speak more loudly.'

'Cock-a-doodle-doo! Cock-a-doodle-doo!' crowed the judge, flapping his arms. Everyone roared with laughter.

'Silence in court!' cried Mimus. 'I shall translate: according to the record, the noble chief justice imposed fines on the king's behalf totalling three thousand gold pieces.'

While he was speaking, two footmen carried in a massive chest with the heraldic lion of Vinland stamped in gold on its lid. A murmur ran round the banqueting hall when they tipped out its contents before the king in a big, glittering heap.

'And here,' Mimus said with a broad smile, 'is the money in question.'

He took a gold piece and held it up against the candlelight. 'How bright it is,' he said in mock surprise. 'I thought these coins would be encrusted with blood and tears—Chief Justice Ruthless!'

'I always act in the king's service,' Bernardo gasped. 'The law must be strictly enforced, and—'

Casually, Mimus smote him on the head with his bauble. 'Haven't you forgotten something?' he demanded.

'Cock-a-doodle-doo!' crowed Bernardo. 'Cock-a-doodle-doo!' His doublet was now so dark with sweat, he might have fallen into a horse trough.

'That's right,' Mimus said approvingly. 'But look, what's this?'

The two footmen entered bearing another chest, this one adorned with a scarlet griffin.

'My personal treasury!' Bernardo bellowed. 'How dare you . . . Cock-a-doodle-doo!' he crowed hastily, as Mimus raised his bauble.

The footmen emptied the contents of the chest at Theodo's feet, a heap of gold as big as the first.

'Tell me, judge,' said Mimus, bringing his face within inches of Bernardo's, 'where did this gold come from?'

'Cock-a-doodle-doo! Cock-a-doodle-doo!'

'I see.' Mimus nodded as if he'd understood. 'Likewise fines payable to the king. Tell me something else, judge: why is this money in your chest, not the king's?'

'Cock-a-doodle-doo!'

'Because you cheated His Majesty, that's why!' the jester exclaimed gleefully. 'You failed to record half of those fines and pocketed them yourself!'

'Cock-a-doodle-doo!' There was a note of despair in Bernardo's voice. 'Cock-a-doodle-doo!'

The Chief Justice was a frightening sight. The blood had drained from his cheeks, his teeth were bared, his lips blue.

Mimus stepped back a pace. 'I wonder,' he said, 'what His Majesty will say to that.'

'Cock-a . . .' Bernardo's voice failed. He drew two or three whistling breaths, then toppled over sideways, wrenching his leg from Florin's grasp. He hit the ground like a stone and lay motionless, face down.

Two young men jumped up from the table and gently turned him over on his back.

'Has Judge Bernardo two sons only?' cried Mimus. 'What a shame—four horses are required for quartering a convicted criminal, one to each limb.'

The elder of the two slowly straightened up. 'That will not be neces-sary,' he said in a dull voice. 'My father has not survived his disgrace.'

'He has merely spared himself a walk to the scaffold,' King Theodo said coldly. 'You both know the penalty for embezzling royal dues.'

The younger son made the sign of the cross over his father, then turned to Mimus, who was standing beside him with his arms folded. 'What a miserable wretch you are,' he said in a voice of loathing. 'I pity you from the bottom of my heart.'

The jester returned his gaze impassively, his face an impenetrable mask.

A tense silence reigned while footmen carried the judge's corpse from the banqueting hall.

'Lord-a-mercy,' Mimus said suddenly, 'I forgot something important!'

One by one, the self-important, gorgeously attired courtiers bowed their heads and averted their gaze as he walked along the tables with slow, deliberate tread. 'I should have warned Bernardo not to crow like a cockerel on Judgment Day.' He shrugged his shoulders with mock regret. 'Now he'll end up in the devil's chicken broth!'

The tension vented itself in a roar of mirth. The musicians struck up again, the guests laughed and chatted, and the banquet resumed its course—more loudly and boisterously than before.

'My compliments on your malevolence,' King Theodo told Mimus contentedly. 'You deserve a reward, you old fool.'

And he tossed the jester a pastry.

Florin watched Mimus cram it into his mouth. Your reward for a man's life, he thought.

————————

THE banquet went on far into the night. The musicians had stopped playing long ago, but the king and a handful of his henchmen continued to sit over their goblets of wine. Mimus leant against his pillar and sang love songs in a low voice while Florin, who could scarcely stand for weariness, beat time on the tambourine.

Theodo rose at last and gave a hearty yawn.

Florin had just exchanged his jester's motley for his nightshirt when he heard voices outside the stable door. He cautiously stuck his head out—and hurriedly withdrew it when two sentries glared at him.

'Why are they there?' he asked Mimus in surprise.

'For our protection.' The jester removed his fool's cap and gave his bald pate a good scratch. 'Judge Bernardo had sons. He had friends and retainers. They might take it into their heads to roast us in our straw.'

'Yes, but . . .' Florin stared at him in dismay. 'What about tomorrow? What about a week from now?'

'A pinch of danger seasons the soup of life,' the jester replied dryly before scraping the straw into a heap, as he did every night, and subsiding onto it with a pleasurable sigh.

'How do you do it?' Florin asked when they were sitting over their gruel the next morning. 'When you're in front of an audience I don't recognise you.' He studied the little grey man at his side with a thoughtful expression. 'You seem to become taller. Your face changes. You speak differently. It's as if . . .' He broke off.

'Yes?' Mimus thrust a spoonful of gruel into his mouth.

Florin shuffled his feet. 'Does some demon assume mastery over you?' he asked eventually.

The jester didn't take his question amiss. 'Several demons are at work inside me,' he said. 'Their names are practice, practice and more practice.' He smiled. 'Who knows? Work hard, and you too may gain some success in the noble art of jesterdom.'

'The noble art of jesterdom?' Florin pulled a face. 'People laugh at you, that's all. Don't you mind it that they treat you like a fool? You're no idiot.'

'No, I'm not,' Mimus replied gravely. 'I'm the court jester. When you're that, laughter becomes praise and derision acclaim. Mark this well, little Mimus.' He gave a wry smile. 'As long as people laugh at you and mock you, they're satisfied. If not, better pad your backside.'

'How long have you been Theodo's court jester?' Florin asked. 'He can't be much older than you.'

'Theodo had just turned sixteen when the old king died. He received me as a gift to mark his accession. I was five years younger.'

'Almost as old as I am now,' Florin said pensively. 'How did you come to this?'

Mimus had carefully scraped his porringer clean. Now he laid the spoon aside. 'We boys used to play on the village green every day. One morning, some of the king's horsemen rode into the village.' He stared into the empty bowl as if it contained an image of that long forgotten day. Having watched us playing for a while, they asked the way to an inn. Guess who couldn't keep his big mouth shut? "Here in the village there's naught but a lice-ridden peasant tavern," I told them. "But if you ride down the road for two miles, then turn left and follow the farm track for another three miles, you'll come to a fine inn perfectly befitting gentlemen such as you."'

'Well?' said Florin.

'I'd sent them to a watering-place for oxen,' said Mimus. 'How proud I was of my prank! Little did I know that the horsemen had been combing the country for weeks in search of just such a blabber-mouth. That evening they knocked at our door, thrust a few gold coins into my mother's hand and bore me off.'

He fished a last grain of oats out of the bowl with his forefinger. 'I arrived here on the day of Theodo's coronation—I, a peasant boy who had never set foot outside his native village. I was carried away by all the splendour, the music, the sumptuous fare, the elegant attire . . .'

For one fleeting moment Florin had a vision of the boy who had run up the stairs with shining eyes—just like himself on his first night here at court.

'On that very first day I thought: Now I shall live in the lap of luxury.' Mimus emitted a rueful laugh. 'That idea persisted until I found myself lying here in chains, weeping with hunger and homesickness. Then the delusion was over.'

'Have you never tried to run away?' asked Florin.

'A dozen times, I suppose,' Mimus replied. 'Once I even succeeded in reaching home.' He deposited his empty bowl on the floor. 'My mother kissed and cuddled me. Then, lured by the prospect of another gold coin, she locked me up in the hen coop until the king's lackeys arrived.'

'And then?'

'Well,' Mimus said with a shrug, 'Theodo devised some effective ways of curing my itch to run away.'

'And you never saw your mother again?'

'Oh, yes.' The jester picked up a blade of straw and twirled it between his finger and thumb. 'She visited me now and then—and begged a few coins from the bestiarius each time.' He fell silent for a moment, lost in thought. 'She died ten years ago.'

'Just like my mother,' said Florin. 'I can scarcely remember her.'

'Did your father never marry again?'

Florin shook his head. 'No woman ever took his fancy after her death.'

The thought of his father was too distressing. He quickly changed the subject. 'Who trained you?'

'Mimus—the jester before me. He had already put in thirty years' service at court when I arrived. I learnt everything from him.' The jester smiled at the recollection. 'He had a hard time with me—I couldn't even read or write.'

'What became of the old Mimus?' Florin asked.

'One day, when he discovered that I was better than him at everything, he lay down on the straw and never got up again.' Mimus grinned at Florin. 'Lucky for me you present no threat from that point of view. Even as a doddering old man, I'll still be more than a match for you!'

'That won't apply,' said Florin. 'The king will have me killed long before that.'

'Who knows?' Mimus countered. 'If you play the game nicely he may forget who's under those ass's ears. Then you'll simply be little Mimus forevermore.'

'What a prospect,' Florin muttered dejectedly. Another thought struck him. 'You weren't always called Mimus. What did your mother call you—I mean, what is your real name?'

The jester seemed to ponder for a moment. 'I fear I've forgotten,' he said offhandedly. 'It's too long ago.'

Florin was horrified. How could a person forget his own name? For an instant he pictured himself oblivious of any name but Mimus after countless years of service as a jester. If he could no longer recall who he was, who *would* he be?

However hard the jester worked him, this question haunted him for the rest of the day. That night it accompanied him into his dreams.

———————

FLORIN was standing at the mouth of a cave so huge that its end was lost in darkness. Lined up against its rocky walls were long rows of cowled, shadowy figures. Knowing that one of these men was his father, Florin wanted to go to him. He had taken a step forward when a small, ice-grey dwarf leapt in front of him.

'Are you looking for your father?' asked the dwarf, busily brandishing a list. 'What's your name?'

Florin didn't reply. He pushed past the little creature and set off along the ranks.

'Father?' he cried, unable to distinguish any of the faces beneath the cowls. He didn't dare touch any of the shadowy figures, so how was he to find his father? He walked on. 'Father?' he called again, hoping for some word or gesture that would enable him to recognise King Philip, but the men neither spoke nor moved. Exhausted after passing thousands of them, he returned to the mouth of the cave and said: 'Can't you point my father out?'

'What's your name?' the dwarf asked again, tapping his list. 'If you don't know who you are, how do you propose to recognise your father? Tell me your name, then you'll have saved him.'

Florin racked his brains. He knew he'd forgotten his name beyond recall, and the knowledge rent his heart.

'Who are you?' The dwarf's voice rang in his ears. 'Your name? Your name? Your . . .'

———————

STILL half dreaming, Florin once more felt a hand stroking his brow. He lay quite still, enjoying its comforting caress until he became aware that he was asleep no longer. Cautiously, he opened his left eye a trifle—and the stroking stopped abruptly.

The jester was bending over him with a scowl. 'You make as much din as a flock of young ravens,' he grumbled. 'If you persist in dreaming as loudly, I shall turn melancholy from lack of sleep. Kindly dream you're a fish!'

– THE ROYAL CHILDREN –

AT NOON THE next day, while Florin was practising headstands against the wall, a peculiar creature appeared in the doorway. It looked like a fat, glossy caterpillar with wings, and Florin wondered anxiously whether all those hours upside down had addled his brain. It wasn't until he had blinked several times that he recognised the wings for what they were: the tails of a red silk coat worn by Marsus, Theodo's valet.

'The king is lunching with his family today,' he announced solemnly, 'and wishes to be entertained at table by his little jester.'

Crash! Florin lost his balance and collapsed on the floor in a heap—yet again! He glanced helplessly at Mimus, who gave him a reassuring nod. 'You're familiar with the rules of the game by now. Just take your cue from me.'

But when Mimus made for the door, Marsus tapped him on the shoulder.

'Not you,' he said firmly. 'Only him.'

'Only me?' Florin's throat went dry in an instant. 'I won't go on my own.'

The valet's powdered face contorted itself into a grin of pure pleasure. 'There'll be trouble, then,' he said to Mimus. 'Trouble for this young whippersnapper, but more especially for you, you dung beetle. I shall enjoy conducting the pair of you downstairs to Master Antonius.'

'I won't go!' Florin repeated, struggling violently as Mimus attached the bauble and pig's bladder to his belt. 'Not on my own! I can't . . .'

'A Sir Won't-Go goes to the dogs!' the jester snapped. 'A Sir Can't-Go gets fed to the ravens. Make haste, or the king will be angry!' And he thrust Florin outside.

Florin followed the valet through the carved wooden door and into the royal apartments with his head buzzing like a beehive. They crossed a small antechamber comfortably furnished with all manner of chests and upholstered benches, then made their way down a long passage to a door which Marsus opened to reveal a small dining room.

Afternoon sunlight was streaming in through the windows, making the dark, polished oak floor gleam and casting a warm glow over the walls, which were painted red and gold. A handsome dining table was already set with white linen and silver plates and goblets, but the room was still deserted.

'Go and stand beside the plate cupboard,' the valet told Florin, pointing to it, 'and hold yourself in readiness. But don't dare touch anything with your grubby jester's paws!' So saying, he went out and shut the door behind him.

Florin was too agitated to stand still. His bells jingled maddeningly, and he longed—not for the first time—to rip the confounded costume from his body. He felt like a trapped beast. How in the world could he escape?

'Are you rehearsing for your performance?' inquired a mocking voice. 'A lively little jester's jig, perhaps?'

The princess had tiptoed into the room. Florin stared past her at the half-open door, convinced that the rest of the royal family would appear at any moment.

She interpreted his glance correctly. 'You still have time. My mother's maidservant is braiding her hair, and my father is going through the household accounts with his chamberlain. Strain your ears, and you'll hear him shouting from here.'

'Oh, er, yes,' Florin said feebly. At the same time, he felt his heart start beating again.

The princess eyed him up and down, and he sensed that his cheeks were burning. 'A prince in jester's attire,' she said scornfully. 'That comes of choosing the wrong father.'

Florin's rage was such that he forgot his fear. 'How fortunate you chose the right one,' he retorted. 'Brave King Oath-Breaker, whose word is worth less than a monkey's fart!' To his great satisfaction, he saw her dark eyes flash angrily.

'You're courageous,' she said. 'That remark could cost you dear. One word from me to my father, and you'd regret it for days on end.'

'Run and tell him, then!' snarled Florin, who had ceased to care.

The princess gave him an appraising look. 'I may do just that,' she said casually. 'First, though, tell me something. What is it like to become a donkey overnight? Hardly a bed of roses, I imagine?'

Florin was still seething with rage. 'At your court, princess, there are more donkeys than in any donkey train, and—'

'Ssh!' She had raised her head and was listening. 'Your prayers are answered,' she said spitefully. 'Here comes my father!'

Florin experienced a renewed flicker of fear as the valet, bowing low, held the door open for the king and queen and their five sons, followed by a small retinue of ladies-in-waiting, footmen and nurse-maids. Leaning motionless against the wall, he saw the princess greet her parents with a curtsy and kiss their hands.

'Were you waiting for us, Alix?' Theodo asked his daughter with a smile. 'I trust the time did not hang too heavy?'

'Not at all, father,' Alix replied innocently before taking her place at the table beside her mother.

Father Anselm said grace. Then footmen carried in the food and filled the silver goblets with fragrant mulled wine. The atmosphere was cheerful and animated, and everyone seemed to be enjoying their communal meal. Even the queen, who had looked so pale and exhausted the night before, conversed in lively fashion with an elderly, horse-faced lady-in-waiting. The king took his youngest son on his lap, fed him little morsels with his own hand, and listened gravely to his important child-ish confidences. Theodo looked peaceable and relaxed at table—a sight that troubled Florin far more than the icy disdain to which the king had previously subjected him. What right had this person—this monster!—to sit with his family in the guise of an affectionate father? What right had he to expect him, Florin, whom he had robbed of everything, to watch this happy scene—indeed, to contribute to everyone's enjoyment?

Despite himself, Florin began to fidget uneasily. The jingle of bells attracted Theodo's attention.

'Watch closely,' he told his little son. 'See what the jester does.' And, to Florin, snapping his fingers: 'Commence!'

Florin's head was whirling like a top. What was he to do now? Sing, dance, recite a rhyme? Each alternative struck him as equally intolerable. He pictured himself darting forward, jerking the tablecloth away, and tipping everyone's fully laden plates into their laps. Would they find that amusing? At least *he* would have something to laugh at, albeit not for long. *What in God's name could he do?*

'Tell us a story!'

It was the second of the king's young sons who had blurted this out. A sturdy lad some ten years old, he already wore doublet and hose unlike his younger brothers. Florin glanced quickly at the king, who nodded his assent.

A story . . . Florin's head was still spinning. He had never told a story before, but then, remembering Tanko, he drew a deep breath and took a step nearer the table.

'*Long, long ago,*' he began, only too aware how reedy his voice sounded, '*there lived in a village some good, upright folk. They sowed, ploughed and harvested their fields, and their storerooms and barns were always amply filled. Their children and cattle were well fed, their life followed an orderly course.*

'*But one day—and not even the old goatherd, who knew everything, could say whence it came—the village was visited by a fearsome dragon as big as a war chariot. It spat fire and devoured everything within reach of its jaws.*' Florin surreptitiously scanned the dishes on the table. '*Steamed trout, pike soup, roast pigeon and partridge, roast beef, pancakes, apple pie, nut bread, butter, grapes, pears, plums, figs, marzipan—everything without exception.*'

'Why, the dragon ate the same as us!' the little prince cried, and everyone laughed.

'Yes, some remarkable coincidences have been known to occur,' Florin told him gravely. '*Unlike you, however, the dragon had an irresistible urge to devour the villagers. It would only too gladly have swallowed them whole, but they all, from the youngest babe in arms to the ancient crone who gathered herbs, had taken refuge in the little village chapel and nailed the door shut behind them. Bellowing with rage, the dragon assailed the door with its fiery breath. The iron nails glowed red under its onslaught . . .*'

Florin paused, drew a breath, and pretended to think.

'Go on!' urged the king's little son.

'*But, rage as it might, the dragon failed to burn the door down. St. George the Dragon-Slayer, to whom the chapel was dedicated, saw to that . . .*'

A long-time favourite of the boys at the royal school of knighthood had been the story of Fitz the stable boy, the only villager brave enough to take up arms against the dragon. They made Tanko tell it again and again, and it had improved with every telling. Now that Florin himself was recounting it, he heard Tanko's voice in his head, pictured his expression, his smile, and sensed that his own nervousness was subsiding. He finished the story in a calm, firm voice:

'*So the dragon finally bit the dust. When Fitz returned to the village he was acclaimed, as befits a hero, and given the name Fitz Dragonblood. But despite his heroic name, Fitz Dragonblood gave every dragon a wide berth for the rest of his days—and who could blame him?*'

'More! Don't stop!' clamoured the young princes.

'That will do for today. Little Mimus will have plenty of occasions to tell you stories,' Theodo assured them. He held out the bowl of plums. 'I'm content with you,' he told Florin. 'You may help yourself.'

The luscious, dark blue plums were redolent of cinnamon and honey. Florin gulped avidly, then suppressed his greed and calmly took a single plum.

The king had been watching him with a sardonic smile. 'Still proud, Prince Donkey-Ears?' he asked. 'We shall see how long *that* lasts. The beasts in my menagerie have no pride.' He reached into the bowl himself and filled Florin's leather pouch to the brim. 'Now trot back to your wise old master!'

'I DON'T believe it!' Mimus exclaimed when Florin returned to the stable. 'Your head is still on your shoulders! How did you accomplish such a miracle?'

'Here.' Florin emptied his pouch on the straw. 'Help yourself.'

'Oho!' Mimus eyed him sarcastically. 'Were you as successful as *that?*'

'I had to tell the princes a story,' said Florin. 'Not a very hard task.'

'If you find it easy, you're one up on me.' The jester mumbled the words indistinctly, having stuffed three plums into his mouth at once. 'Theodo's sons regularly burst into tears at *my* stories.'

'I can well imagine,' said Florin.

Mimus had scarcely spat out the stones when he crammed his mouth once more. The little heap of plums was melting like snow in the sun, and Florin regretted his generous invitation.

'The queen and the crown prince didn't spare me a glance,' he remarked.

Mimus shrugged. 'What do you expect?' he said. 'The queen doesn't converse with the dogs under the table, either.'

Florin sucked a plum thoughtfully. 'The princess spoke to me, though.'

'Watch your step with her,' Mimus growled. 'She's every inch her father's daughter—looks as sweet as honey and spits venom like a viper. Her grand ideas have cost me dear before now.'

'How so?' Florin asked, pricking up his ears, but Mimus waved the question aside. 'Come, tell me!' Florin entreated.

The jester pulled a face. 'Well, for example, at the last court festivity she loudly declared that it was time I learnt to ride. Theodo never denies his beloved daughter anything, so I was promptly tied to the back of a wild boar. And away we went!' Mimus rubbed his backside reminiscently. 'They hunted the boar with horses and hounds, this way and that, across ditches and through bramble patches. By the time the king thrust his spear into the monster's throat I was more dead than alive.'

Florin shook his head in disbelief. 'You exaggerate,' he said. 'I've seen village lads race astride young wild pigs. It was great sport, and no one ever suffered more than a graze or two.'

'We'll talk of it again when *you're* astride a boar,' said Mimus, shovelling more plums into his mouth. 'And now, Sir Know-All, no more idling.' Before Florin knew it, the jester had snatched up the last remaining plum. 'Tonight is poetry night. All the court's brightest spirits will be showing off their paces. We shall have to be well prepared if we don't wish to make fools of ourselves.'

Florin rolled his eyes.

'Rhyming on the spur of the moment,' Mimus went on implacably. 'I give you a word, and you have to devise a poem about it at the drop of a hat, understand?'

'I understand well enough, but I'm no poet.'

'Even a cat has to learn how to mouse,' Mimus rejoined. 'Come, put me to the test. Well, go on!'

'Hm,' said Florin. 'What about "gingerbread"?' The very word made his mouth water.

'My poor, ever hungry little Mimus,' mocked the jester. 'Forget your vile stomach and regale yourself with the divine food of poetry. Very well, a hymn to gingerbread:

> *O product of the baker's craft*
> *whose scents into my nostrils waft.*
> *Come not too near my greedy mouth*
> *or you'll be gobbled up, forsooth.'*

Florin chuckled. 'That could well happen.'

'He laughed!' Mimus clutched his heart. 'Let trumpets ring out! His Royal Highness laughed!'

'Idiot,' said Florin. 'Will you make up another rhyme? About roast goose, perhaps?'

Mimus rose. 'That will be your task. Wield your stick of charcoal well. By the time I return the goose must be nice and crisp.'

Florin's good mood evaporated almost as soon as he was poring over the parchment. Why had he settled on roast goose? How on earth could he write a poem about it?

> *Of all the dishes on this earth*
> *roast goose conduces most to mirth . . .*

he scribbled listlessly, knowing full well that Mimus would pronounce himself dissatisfied with it.

'Where have you been?' he demanded when the jester returned to the stable a good while later.

Mimus abruptly rounded on him. 'Are you my wife, that I have to account to you for my whereabouts? You're becoming altogether too familiar!'

Offended, Florin bent over his parchment again. Not a trace of the afternoon's cheerful atmosphere remained.

'Well, how goes it?' Mimus asked in a rather more conciliatory tone, reaching for Florin's parchment. 'What poetic gem have you produced?'

He looks weary, Florin thought, as he watched the jester perusing his verses.

'The beginning is weak,' was Mimus's verdict, 'and the end is weaker, but these few lines in the middle bear reading aloud:

> *Wife, if your husband's mood is sour*
> *and he berates you every hour,*
> *feed him roast goose, and you will see*
> *his gloomy face light up with glee.*
> *His heart will leap within his breast*
> *because roast goose of all tastes best.'*

'It doesn't sound at all bad,' Florin said proudly.

'Not bad,' said Mimus, 'is far from good.'

Casually, he tossed Florin's poem on the floor and handed him a scroll. 'Here's what we'll recite later. You'll take alternate verses, so memorise them well. And make haste—it'll soon be nightfall.'

———

MIMUS'S poem was a terribly vulgar ditty in which two dumplings vied for the affections of a pork sausage, and Florin's cheeks burned as he recited it turn and turn about. However, it certainly amused the assembled courtiers—including the bishops, who slapped their thighs with merriment. King Theodo rewarded his jesters by tossing them a hard-boiled pigeon's egg apiece.

Leaning against the pillar, they watched the next item on the program. A tall man with the beginnings of a paunch and a mane of flowing grey hair struck a pose in front of the throne.

> *'His sails all swollen with the whistling wind,*
> *the king set forth from Vinland's sacred shore*
> *and steered for distant lands beyond the seas.'*

'The grey-haired giant is Theodo's court poet,' Mimus whispered. 'His name is Perkin Godbold, but he calls himself Haedus Venerabilis.'

Florin almost choked on his precious pigeon's egg. 'Haedus Venerabilis? Do you know what that means?'

'No, what?'

'Venerable Goat.'

'Truly?' Mimus's eyes gleamed. No longer was he the weary, ill-tempered man Florin had seen shortly before. Haedus Venerabilis was in for a hard time, no doubt about it.

For the moment, however, the poet was still in his element:

> *'Aboard the royal barque were maidens fair*
> *who raised their snow-white arms and sweetly sang:*
> *"Return in triumph, noblest king of all!"'*

Tense in every muscle, Mimus seemed to have imbibed the poet's verses like a mug of ale. While Haedus Venerabilis was acknowledging the applause with many a sweeping bow, he tiptoed up behind him, spread his arms, shook his ass's ears just as the court poet had shaken his flowing locks, and loudly declaimed:

> *'His belly swollen with much whistling wind,*
> *the poet left a steaming stool behind*
> *and swiftly to the nearest privy ran . . .'*

The mood of solemnity was dispelled at once. Scarlet-faced, Haedus

Venerabilis was compelled to listen to the jester's garbled version of his poem.

> *'Some hairy goats accompanied him there.*
> *With cloven hoofs upraised, they bleated: "Baa!*
> *The privy is your rightful place, so stay!"'*

A roar of laughter greeted the jester's recital, but King Theodo laughed loudest of all. He didn't spare his affronted court poet another glance.

Theodo, thought Florin as he watched him—Theodo, Gift of God. No name could have been less appropriate.

Having concluded his performance with a hilarious imitation of a lovesick billygoat, Mimus returned to his place beside the pillar. He was clearly delighted with himself.

'That was malicious of you,' Florin said reproachfully. 'Look at the poor man.'

Haedus Venerabilis, official poet to the court of Vinland, had subsided onto his chair like a mountain of misery, not daring to raise his eyes.

'The bungler! The simpleton!' Mimus hissed the words like an angry goose. 'That bloated booby lolls on a chair, sleeps in a feather bed, eats pies and capons—and you feel sorry for him?'

'If you'd also become a poet,' jeered Florin, 'you wouldn't be in the king's menagerie now. Everyone forges his own destiny.'

'You, of all people, say that?' Mimus regarded him with narrowed eyes. 'I don't see any forging hammer in your hand. All I can see is a miserable piece of iron being hammered into the shape Theodo desires.'

Taken aback, Florin fell silent.

Just then a young woman took her place in front of the throne. Her features were disfigured by pockmarks and her hands rough and workworn, but Florin forgot her appearance as soon as she began to sing. In a voice as sweet as a blackbird's, she sang of Galand, the young hero who sailed the seven seas, discovered unknown lands and defeated Orkan, the savage, red-eyed, boundlessly evil Lord of the Storms . . .

Florin closed his eyes. Back home in Montfield Castle it was a red-letter day when a minstrel joined them for the evening meal. The boys could never have their fill of ballads that told of adventures and heroic deeds. In their imagination, it was always they themselves who went out into the world, swam raging rivers, roamed snowy wastes and scorching deserts, fought dragons and demons, braved any danger or exertion, and ended by triumphing over their devilish foes.

The song and the strains of the harp died away. Opening his eyes, Florin saw the singer's face light up with pride and happiness when Theodo presented her with a gold ring and addressed some friendly words to her.

That the devilish foe was a handsome, gracious monarch loved and revered by his subjects, and that Florin was utterly at his mercy and could do nothing about it—no minstrel had ever recounted such a story . . .

– AUDIENCE DAY –

'GET UP, YOU idle sluggards!' Rollo called the next morning. 'Do something for your daily bread. It's audience day!'

Florin crawled sleepily out of his nest of straw. 'Anyone would think I was at home,' he muttered.

By the time they entered the audience chamber shortly afterwards, King Theodo was already seated on his throne and conversing in a low voice with his chancellor. Like Chancellor Artold at Montfield, Vinland's Chancellor Benedict was ensconced behind a massive oak desk strewn with scrolls of parchment. Clerks standing at lecterns against the walls were busily wielding their quills. The chamberlain and the master of ceremonies were shooing their footmen and pages around, neither of them missing any opportunity to jostle the other or tread on his toes.

'Those two fight like cat and dog,' Florin whispered to Mimus.

'Are you surprised?' the jester replied. 'When two bloated bladders collide, there's always an explosion!'

At that moment the chamberlain caught sight of them.

'To your places, jesters!' He clapped his hands peremptorily. 'Quickly, quickly!'

'Choose one,' Mimus said softly as they made for the throne.

'Choose one what?' asked Florin.

'A royal foot,' Mimus told him. 'Right or left—I leave the choice to you.'

'Then I'll take the one in the middle,' said Florin, '—the devil's cloven hoof.'

King Theodo took no notice of them as they sat down at his feet on the lowest of the steps leading up to the throne.

'This isn't a bad spot,' Mimus whispered in Florin's ear. 'You can pursue your own thoughts in peace, but you mustn't miss your moment.'

The master of ceremonies rapped on the floor with his staff and the first of the petitioners was conducted before the throne. The man's breeches and leather boots were at eye level, and Florin had to crane his neck to see his face.

'I'll let you into a great secret,' Mimus whispered. 'A petitioner's footwear will disclose his request and—'

'—and his opening words. Yes, I know,' Florin said drily. 'I used to practise the same form of divination with headgear.'

Surprised, Mimus fell silent for a moment. Then he grinned appreciatively. 'You're right: whether seen from above or below, everything remains the same.'

'And audiences—whether witnessed from above or below—are always tedious in the extreme,' Florin added, pulling a face.

Petitioners came and went in an endless stream. Florin was almost lulled into a trance by the same words droning away overhead, but he couldn't afford to doze off. If the king scraped his feet, that was their signal to intervene.

The first to evoke such a reaction was a very dignified delegate

from the bakers guild. After uttering the customary compliments and
courtesies, the man bluntly complained that the royal baker was selling
his bread in the city as well. While he was painting a drastic picture of
the plight of the city's bakers—'Our wives and children are starving,
Your Majesty! Our pigs and cattle are famished—even our cats and
dogs are fading away!'—Theodo started to shuffle his feet impatiently
and Mimus's keen eyes gleamed.

'Our municipal rights take precedence, Your Majesty,' the master
baker protested in a quavering voice. 'If your court baker continues
to—'

Mimus bobbed up in front of him like a jack-in-the-box.

'Do you always bake your head as well as your loaves?' he
demanded, rapping the man's bald pate with his knuckles.

His flow of words abruptly cut short, the master baker stared at
Mimus's ass's ears with an uncertain smile. 'Your Majesty's jester, I
assume? I've heard tell of him.'

'I know of a remedy for baldness,' said Mimus. He carefully
extracted a little bone vial from his pocket. 'Hair-growing tincture—as
precious as liquid gold.'

Holding the vial up to the candlelight, he let fall a drop of cloudy
yellow fluid. 'Personally concocted by the court magician of Perseus,
King of Persia. I shall now demonstrate its miraculous properties. Little
Mimus,' he said to Florin, beckoning him imperiously, 'come here!'

He rubbed a few drops of the tincture on the back of Florin's
hand, chanting in a low, mysterious voice. 'Somi, omi, romi . . .'

'It stinks like bear's piss,' Florin whispered.

'What a sensitive little nose you possess,' the jester whispered back.
'Zito, mito, rito,' he continued to chant, rubbing away with circular
movements. 'And now, lo and behold!'

Florin had distinctly felt Mimus, with lightning dexterity, stick a
piece of hare's fur to the back of his hand. To the onlookers' applause,
he proudly displayed his hairy paw.

'Surely that's just a cheap conjurer's trick?' the baker murmured doubtfully.

Mimus turned to King Theodo. 'Most beloved king, will you, whose grace and favour surpasses human understanding, permit me to test this precious essence on our worthy baker?'

'Proceed,' said Theodo, containing his mirth with difficulty.

The baker could hardly reject this mark of royal favour. With a suspicious air, he suffered the jester to anoint his bald head with the stinking substance and rub it in vigorously.

'Somi, omi, romi . . . Zito, mito, rito . . .' Even as Mimus continued to chant, the baker's bald pate turned bright red before the spectators' marvelling eyes.

'Lackaday!' the jester cried in mock horror. He swiftly took a mirror from his pocket and held it up in front of his victim. 'What a misfortune! The Persian magician spoke of two kinds of hairless men on whom the elixir has this particular effect: murderers—'

'I'm not one, as God is my witness!' the baker protested.

'—and rogues who have the effrontery to pester His Majesty with their miserable, avaricious requests.' Mimus clicked his tongue and sighed deeply. 'Dear, dear, I fear you'll keep that crimson noddle to the end of your days.'

The baker stared at his reflection, frozen with dismay. 'But . . . How can I ever show myself in public?'

'I'll give you my ears if you like,' Mimus said obligingly. 'I know of a magic spell that will cause them to take root in your skull.' He made to remove his fool's cap. 'Ezli, mezli, rezli . . .'

The baker shrank away in superstitious dread.

'No, no,' he stammered, 'by all means keep them!'

Having hurriedly bowed to the king, he dashed headlong from the room amid roars of laughter from all present. 'Farewell, Master Toadstool!' the jester called after him.

Mimus and Florin resumed their places at the king's feet and the audience continued in a sedate, serious manner as if nothing had happened.

Florin watched Mimus out of the corner of his eye. For a moment he pictured himself seated on the throne with a court jester at his feet—one of his own age. Whenever the proceedings became tedious, the jester would jump up and—

'The envoy from Moltovia!' Florin was jolted out of his reverie.

A man approached the throne. His boots were dusty and the hem of his cloak was bespattered with mud. Florin cautiously peered up at him. To his relief, the man's face was unfamiliar. A Vinlander, no doubt.

Theodo turned to him. 'Your report, Count Maren. How does the country look?'

The envoy came straight to the point. 'Your Majesty, Moltovia has lost its head in the truest sense of that phrase. The throne is empty, the armies are leaderless, the Privy Council is incapable of effective action.'

'And no wonder,' Chancellor Benedict put in, 'with Moltovia's king, generals and Privy Councillors imprisoned in our dungeons.'

'The king's capture has thrown the inhabitants into a panic,' Count Maren reported. 'Many believe that Almighty God is punishing them for their sins, and that the end of the world is nigh. You can exploit this hopeless confusion, my king. All depends on whether you do the right thing.'

'And the right thing is?' asked Theodo.

'Dispatch a large army without delay,' the envoy advised. 'If you strike hard and swiftly, Moltovia will be yours at last.'

The king nodded. 'Go on.'

'Your next step must be to seize the throne. For that you will need the support of the Moltovian nobility. All have sworn an oath of allegiance to King Philip, and most will be reluctant to break it. In order to win them over notwithstanding, certain concessions will be necessary.'

'What manner of concessions?'

The count's reply was brief and to the point. 'Gifts and favours.'

'Gifts and favours,' Theodo repeated. 'To what do you refer?'

'To the Moltovians' possessions,' Count Maren replied swiftly. 'King Philip and his son are in your power. That means you have free access to their towns, villages, castles, mills, farms and landed estates. Share them out among the nobles—generously so—and they'll pledge themselves to you.'

'Generosity is a royal virtue,' Mimus broke in from below. 'Toss some morsels to the slavering pack and they'll lick your boots in return.'

Theodo preserved a thoughtful silence. 'You forget, Count Maren,' he said at length, 'that the King of Vinland can also find a good use for towns, farms and landed estates. Am I heedlessly to disperse the wealth that has fallen to my lot by the grace of God?'

He stroked Florin's ass's ears while speaking—absently, so it seemed.

They're dismembering my country and it selling off, thought Florin, and I let myself be fondled like a lapdog.

But he didn't move, anxious not to miss a word.

'Doesn't the royal crown weigh more than a castle?' asked the count. 'Aren't the silver mines of Argentia worth more than a few acres of ploughland? My king, act wisely now and by spring you'll be Moltovia's new liege lord.'

'Your advice is sound,' Theodo said, nodding. 'I shall need an inventory of that pestilential family's possessions.'

'I've already had one drawn up, Your Majesty.' Count Maren handed him a parchment scroll. 'You'll see, a large number of King Philip's nobles will prove susceptible to bribery. They'll soon transfer their allegiance to you.'

'Should I buttress my claim to the throne of Moltovia by touring the country on horseback?' Theodo asked thoughtfully.

'Under no circumstances,' the count replied. 'Moltovia is in utter chaos—you would be in mortal danger. Leave it to intermediaries like me to arrange matters. As for yourself, spend the winter within Bellingar's walls and wait until the dust has settled. With the prisoners as hostages, your enemies will remain idle willy-nilly, whereas your friends will gather strength. Time is on your side, King of Vinland.'

Theodo considered this advice, then nodded.

'You are one of my most able advisers, Count Maren. Chancellor Benedict will escort you to the treasury to reward you.'

The count chuckled. 'No need, Your Majesty.' He turned and beckoned to a manservant, who handed him a silver casket. 'A little foretaste of Moltovia's treasures,' he said. 'Reward me from this.'

Florin heard the lid of the casket open with a click and craned his neck. At the same instant, the king's hand roughly gripped his head and forced it downwards.

'Truly a sight to rejoice the heart,' Theodo said gaily, without relaxing his grip. 'Take your pick, Count Maren.'

'With your permission, Majesty, the medallion adorned with roses. It will suit my daughter admirably.'

Florin couldn't restrain the tears of rage that sprang to his eyes. The rose medallion had belonged to his mother. Chancellor Artold would never have willingly surrendered his father's sacred keepsake. What could have happened at Montfield Castle?

'Envoys from Arelia request a hearing!' the master of ceremonies announced from the doorway. The malice in his voice was unmistakable.

'Send them away,' Theodo commanded. 'If need be, set the dogs on them!'

As if nothing had happened, three more petitioners were admitted. Then Theodo rose, nodded to Chancellor Benedict, and left the audience chamber without further explanation.

'Remain in your places, everyone, His Majesty will be returning shortly,' said the chancellor. 'It's the queen,' Florin heard him tell the chamberlain in a low voice. 'She's confined to her bed again.'

Pages bustled around, refilling the dignitaries' goblets with wine. The clerks laid aside their quills and flexed their fingers. Florin, too, found it impossible to sit still. He got up off the steps and stretched his stiff legs. At once, the chamberlain's scathing voice rang out. 'Return to your place, you useless little fool!'

Before Florin could comply, Mimus had faced up to the chamberlain and was strutting to and fro in front of him.

'Nobody pays you any heed, you pompous ass,' he said. 'The worshipful master of ceremonies: yes, everyone makes way for him in awe. The most that ever makes way for you is the wind from your backside!'

The chamberlain's face turned purple. 'How dare you!' he yelled, hoarse with rage. 'Wait till I inform His Majesty! Your impudent words will stick in your craw. He'll have you . . .'

Florin stopped listening to the altercation. He had caught sight of Chancellor Benedict and Count Maren deep in conversation beside the fireplace.

Without thinking, he slid off the steps to the throne and crawled toward them inch by inch until, hidden behind a pillar, he could overhear their subdued voices.

They were speaking to each other in Latin.

'. . . those envoys,' Chancellor Benedict was saying. 'That's the tenth time already. Who would have thought that proud King Guido of Arelia would knuckle under so easily?'

'Have a care, Benedict,' Count Maren rejoined. 'I've heard he's mustering troops along our borders.'

'We know that.' Chancellor Benedict gave a casual shrug. 'An empty threat, nothing more. Guido of Arelia will not intervene—not unless he wishes to see the heads of his brother-in-law and nephew looking over the battlements on the end of a pike.'

'Do you think he'll remain compliant indefinitely, like Ludvik of Frankenland?'

'He would be well-advised to do so.' A sarcastic smile appeared on the chancellor's ratlike face. 'After all, King Ludvik is still at liberty to strut around in silk and velvet like Theodo's lackey. Compared to Philip's dungeon rags, that's the better choice!'

Carefully, Benedict fished a smouldering branch from the fire and extinguished its glowing end on the flagstones.

'See here, Maren.' He proceeded to draw on the floor with the charred end. 'Here is Vinland . . . with Moltovia in the east and Frankenland between them . . .'

Florin gazed at the drawing in fascination. Little Frankenland sat perched on top of the two large kingdoms of Vinland and Moltovia like the head of an eagle with two big wings.

'By uniting Vinland with Moltovia, Theodo will make himself the most powerful monarch far and wide,' said Chancellor Benedict. 'And the lion of Vinland is still hungry. It will swallow Frankenland ere long, no matter how studiously King Ludvik pats it on the head. Also on its menu—' he started drawing again, 'are Arelia in the south, and beside it Angelland.'

It now looked as if the eagle had pulled on two bulky boots, the left one, Arelia, being twice the size of the right, Angelland.

'But Arelia would be no easy meat for the lion of Vinland,' Count Maren pointed out. 'Ten thousand Arelian cavalrymen would have to be defeated first.'

Chancellor Benedict shrugged again. 'Once Theodo rules the united kingdoms of Vinland and Moltovia, who can stand against him? The king's calculation is simple: five countries for five healthy sons. Moltovia is only the beginning.'

Count Maren nodded. 'And for a very good reason. Seldom have the chill hunger for power and the burning thirst for revenge gone so closely hand in hand.'

Benedict laughed. 'Maren, when you speak Latin you sound like our court poet. You're right, for all that.'

He beckoned to a page to replenish his goblet and drank deep. 'Throughout all these years,' he went on, 'the king has preserved his hatred for Philip in a leather shroud. Now he has opened it, and he'll savour his triumph to the full, believe me.'

Florin, listening from behind his pillar, blinked in bewilderment. *In a leather shroud* . . . What did the chancellor mean? Had he misunderstood the Latin phrases?

'The king cannot be blamed for enjoying his belated revenge,' Count Maren agreed.

Hatred, revenge . . . The words re-echoed in Florin's ears. But hatred and revenge for what? His knees hurt, he hugged them so tight.

'It gives King Theodo the greatest pleasure to see his archenemy in chains,' said Benedict. 'He visits him in his rat-hole almost daily.'

'But he'll have to dispense with that pleasure sooner or later,' Count Maren rejoined. 'Once his dominion over Moltovia is assured, the hostages will be needless ballast.'

'And he won't hesitate to have them torn limb from limb, one after another,' said the chancellor. 'What's your opinion, Maren? How soon can matters in Moltovia be settled?'

The count wagged his head with a pensive expression. 'The country is still in considerable turmoil. If the king follows my advice, by the spring. Possibly even earlier.'

'Let's drink a toast to that.' Chancellor Benedict raised his goblet. 'May God be with us and all end well!'

'And badly for Philip!' Count Maren added sarcastically, taking a swig of wine. 'But what of the young prince?' he asked. 'If he defies expectations and survives imprisonment in the dungeons, Theodo won't hesitate to . . . Well, look at that,' he said suddenly. 'See how the little jester pricks up his ears!' Breathlessly, without realising it, Florin had sidled out from behind the pillar and edged closer to the count's chair. He lowered his gaze too late. 'Anyone would think he understands every word.'

'But he does,' the chancellor said calmly.

'Of course.' Count Maren laughed. 'How could it have slipped my mind? At the court of Vinland, the warhorses speak Greek and the jesters Latin.'

'At the court of Vinland, my dear Maren,' the chancellor replied, 'things happen of which you would never dream. Even the donkeys may be of royal blood.' He prodded Florin with his foot. 'Isn't that so, little Mimus?'

– KITCHEN AND CELLAR –

'PEOPLE ARE STRANGE,' Florin said to himself. As usual in the afternoon, he was sitting all alone in the jesters' stable with a yard-long sheet of parchment in front of him. 'I've every reason to weep and gnash my teeth, but instead I blithely go on living. I breathe, eat and sleep. Yes,' he added, smiting the parchment with the flat of his hand, 'I even learn ridiculous rhymes. *Daddle, deddle, diddle, duddle,*' he read grimly, '*my poor wits are in a muddle.*' He massaged his forehead in despair. 'And I'm too miserable to give up.'

Ten days had gone by since the audience, each as wearisome as the next. In the mornings Mimus put him through acrobatic contortions; in the afternoons, when the jester disappeared to wherever he went, Florin had to learn interminable rhymes and proverbs by heart; and in the evenings, after Mimus had tested him, he had to appear before Theodo and the entire court in the role of model pupil.

Mimus was unmoved by Florin's complaints. 'Be grateful to me,' the jester told him 'Each of the king's chuckles earns you another day of life.'

Much as Florin wanted to prolong his own life by participating in this wretched charade, he couldn't stop worrying about his father. He had been more anxious about him than ever since eavesdropping on the conversation between Chancellor Benedict and Count Maren. His father's execution, he now knew, was a foregone conclusion. Theodo simply found it enjoyable to torment him in the dungeons for a while. But for how much longer would he keep his archenemy alive?

While roaming the castle Florin often lingered on the steps that led down to Bellingar's gloomy cellars, listening for sounds from below. Although he never managed to penetrate the dungeons themselves, it consoled him to be a little nearer his father. However, this consolation was becoming ever rarer now that Marsus summoned him to the royal family's lunch table every other day.

'The fault is yours alone,' Mimus told him scornfully. 'You shouldn't have started telling those stories.'

It occurred to Florin that Mimus was jealous rather than pleased to be left in peace. '*You* tell some stories, then,' he thought.

But the little princes wanted to hear Florin, and it was his good fortune to be able to draw on Tanko's store of tales like someone drawing water from an inexhaustible well. However many he recounted, the princes could never have their fill of stupid giants and cunning dwarfs, flying dragons and enchanted caves filled with treasure, magic steeds and evil sorcerers.

As if to demonstrate what clumsy nonsense his stories were, Mimus set Florin ever harder tasks each day. Somersaults were succeeded by handstands, handstands by handsprings, handsprings by double somersaults. It was no longer enough for Florin to recite rhymes; he now had to sing them in time to the tambourine, which he heartily detested. He learnt to play the flute, imitate animal cries, and—last but not least—train the monkeys.

'Teach them to form a pyramid,' the jester commanded when he returned to the stable that evening. 'You can have five days. Then you must get them to perform their trick before the king.'

So Florin climbed the stairs to the monkeys' quarters every afternoon for the next five days. The door of Zito's den on the first floor was always open, and he regularly prayed to heaven that Rollo hadn't forgotten to chain him up. Just as regularly, he paused on the second floor and spoke softly to Brother the wolf. He would have liked to fondle the animal, but it always slunk into a corner as before.

The monkeys, on the other hand, soon became attached to him. When he entered their chamber they rushed at him and caressed him so fervently that he would have needed four arms to hug them all at the same time. They had no names, and Florin would have liked to give them some, but Mimus forbade it. 'Like "Dance, Mimus!", "Jump, monkey!" is all that's required.'

Getting them to form a pyramid was a tricky business. Although the three larger monkeys soon did what Florin asked of them, the smallest stubbornly refused to clamber on top of the other three.

Florin coaxed, flattered and stroked it for five successive afternoons. On the night of the fifth day, when his pupils performed their trick before the court and the smallest monkey took its place on top of the pyramid as if it had never done anything else, he felt genuinely happy and proud—until the king tossed him and the monkeys their edible rewards.

You've long been a trained monkey yourself, he thought, filled with shame. How much lower do you propose to sink, Florin of Moltovia? But hunger overcame him, and he greedily pounced on his tidbit.

———————

THE morning after the monkeys' performance, Mimus told him: 'Today your training program will be devoted to one of the more advanced jester's arts: that of pulling faces.'

He made Florin knit his brow, blow out his cheeks, wrinkle his nose and stick out his tongue in turn.

'Stay like that!' he ordered, producing a mirror from his pocket. 'Now look at yourself.'

Florin had hardly glanced at his reflection when he started back in horror. Although he had gained a mercifully vague impression of his appearance from the surface of the water in his bucket and the shiny silver ewers and chandeliers in the banqueting hall, his reflection in the mirror was a thousand times worse. This revolting, greenish-yellow froglike creature with lop ears and a pallid face—surely it couldn't be him!

Shaking his head, Mimus took the glass from Florin's hand. When he looked at himself in it, his face assumed a radiant expression: his eyes shone, and he admiringly stroked his cheeks and ass's ears.

'We jesters,' he warbled in a high-pitched voice, 'dote on our own reflections and consider them lovelier than the fairest damsel. That, little Mimus, is another jester's rule!'

'Jester's rules are the figments of a diseased imagination!' Florin snapped. 'Who lays them down?'

'Don't be like that,' said Mimus, reverting to his normal voice. 'If I can put up with the sight of you all day long, surely you can do so for a minute or two. Look in the mirror!'

'No.' Florin couldn't have endured a second glance. When Mimus held the mirror in front of his face again, he snatched it from his hand and hurled it into a corner, where it shattered into a thousand pieces.

The jester didn't turn a hair. 'As Your Highness pleases,' he said. 'No pulling faces, then. Instead, three more tasks: first, you'll pick every last one of those splinters out of the straw; secondly, you'll badger Rollo until he procures me another mirror; and thirdly, you'll spend tomorrow in the castle kitchen. Let's see if we can't rid you of these princely moods.'

MIMUS was as good as his word. Immediately after their morning gruel the next day, he delivered Florin to the kitchen like a sack of turnips—except that turnips would probably have been more to the kitchen-master's taste.

'What am I to do with this little donkey?' asked the man, who wore a huge ladle in his belt as a badge of office. 'Fresh cream would turn sour at the sight of him.'

'Not at all, worshipful kitchen-master,' Mimus said humbly. 'Little Mimus has come to sweeten your life by gladly performing all the dirty, menial tasks that no one else cares to do.'

'If that's the case,' the kitchen-master said with a shrug, 'leave him here until nightfall.'

Mimus turned on his heel and walked off without another word.

The kitchen-master led Florin over to the two huge fireplaces that occupied one whole side of the kitchen. At this early hour of the morning, the massive spits and gridirons were black with soot and burnt fat.

'Rake out the ashes,' he ordered, 'and polish those spits and gridirons until I can see my face in them.' He beckoned to one of the kitchen lads. 'Benzo, bring little Mimus some sand and a hank of tow.'

The scullion gave Florin a wink as he deposited a tub of sand in front of him, and Florin recognised him as the red-haired boy who had watched the fight between himself and the pages a fortnight—no, three weeks before. Benzo thrust a bunch of hemp fibres into Florin's hand and looked at him expectantly, as if expecting a word of thanks or a friendly nod. When nothing of the kind was forthcoming, he walked off with a shrug and returned to his post at the huge stone mortar in which he'd been pounding spices.

Florin kneaded the tow irresolutely in his hand. Beside him, an assistant cook was stirring some copper saucepans that gave off an alluring scent of almonds and cream. Across the way, a butcher was gutting the gory carcass of a deer while a scullion stood ready with a bowl to catch the offal. Scullery maids in coarse linen smocks were cleaning and polishing gold platters and goblets from the royal table, which looked curiously out of place in these gloomy surroundings. More than two dozen people were at work in the spacious vaulted chamber, as many as the guests who shared the king's table on a normal night. They all seemed to know exactly what they had to do. Florin alone had no idea how to set about removing grime with sand and a handful of shredded hemp.

Sullenly, he reached for one of the encrusted grills with his fingertips and gave it a half-hearted rub. That thrice accursed jester and his nine times accursed mirror!

The kitchen-master peered over his shoulder. 'Where did the king dig *you* up?' he demanded, wagging his head. 'Anyone would think you'd never done a hand's turn all your life.'

'Nor have I,' said Florin. He brushed his ass's ears aside with the back of his hand. 'I was bedded on silk cushions and fed with gold spoons at birth.'

The kitchen-master laughed. 'The jester's no bad teacher, it seems. You already know how to crack a joke.'

'I do, don't I?' Florin said grimly.

'Benzo,' the man called, 'show little Mimus how to polish a grid-iron. After all, we can't wait to stoke the fire until the king is seated at table.'

Benzo shuffled over to Florin and gave him a look of commiseration. 'Look, here's the water, here's the tow, and here's the sand.' He pointed to each in turn, speaking slowly and distinctly as if addressing a deaf-mute. 'You dip the tow in the water, like this, and then in the sand. Have you got that?'

Florin simply couldn't resist the temptation. 'Eh?' he said helplessly, like a village idiot.

Benzo gave him another patient demonstration. 'The tow in the water first, then in the sand. Understand?'

'Eh?' Florin said again. It was all he could do not to laugh.

The scullion sighed. 'Blessed are the poor in spirit,' he grumbled, 'but I have aniseed and nutmeg to pound up small, or the assistant kitchen-master will scold me.'

Shrugging, he picked up a gridiron. 'Why should a jester know how to do this, too?' Much to Florin's amazement, his practised hands soon had the spits and gridirons gleaming.

A scullery maid plunked a pail of water down in front of Florin and thrust a coarse scrubbing brush into his hand. 'If you're capable of nothing else,' she said, 'scrub the floor!'

This time, feigning stupidity availed Florin nothing. He cursed Mimus long and heartily as he scraped his knees raw on the flagstones. The scoundrel was bound to be laughing up his sleeve at him, comfortably stretched out on the straw!

Meantime the fires had been kindled and the kitchen was becoming unbearably hot. The door was open, and Florin spent a long time scrubbing the flagstones on the threshold.

'Have a care the draft doesn't give you a stiff neck, little Mimus!' called the kitchen-master. 'Come over here by the fire and turn this spit nice and steadily, so the meat doesn't catch!'

The sweat was streaming down Florin's cheeks in no time, and he felt like one of the ducks on the spit. Perhaps I'll be lucky, he thought, and my confounded bells will melt in the heat. But nothing of the kind happened. Instead, he blistered himself on the scorching hot metal. Almost more tormenting than the heat was the aroma of roast fowl. He was already wrestling with his pangs of hunger when a new scent assailed his nose. It was rising from a copper pan being stirred by a skinny young cook who was blowing incessantly on a tin whistle.

'What is he making?' Florin asked the scullery maid.

She looked at him disdainfully. 'Who, the confectioner? Sweetmeats, of course. That's why he has to keep whistling, so the head cook knows he isn't dipping his fingers in the pan.'

When the ducks were brown and crisp, Florin scrubbed the gruel saucepans, after which he turned the whetstone for the butcher to sharpen his knives on, and swept out the great stone ovens.

Afternoon came, then twilight began to gather. Florin had blisters on all ten fingers and every bone in his body ached. His hopes of at least getting a meal in return for this drudgery had faded swiftly. Nobody made a move to give him anything. Even Benzo the scullion, who was standing behind a mountain of apples and pears in conversation with a young cook, seemed to have forgotten all about him.

That evening, when some baker's boys carried in baskets filled with fresh, fragrant bread, Florin couldn't tear his eyes away. Dared he break off a piece? He looked round surreptitiously: no one was watching him. It wouldn't be stealing, he told himself. After all, he'd slaved away all day long. Abruptly making up his mind, he reached for a loaf—and simultaneously received a stinging blow across the knuckles that made him gasp with pain and alarm.

'I was waiting for that.' The kitchen-master gave a contented nod and stuck the ladle back in his belt. 'Never dare to lay your grubby jester's hands on the king's bread again! Benzo, go on peeling those apples, but keep a sharp eye on this little donkey!'

The scullion came and stood beside Florin with a bucketful of apples on his arm. 'It's strictly forbidden to help yourself to our gracious king's victuals,' he whispered, peeling an apple without having to lay the knife aside for an instant. 'But how was a poor devil like you to know that?'

Florin's knuckles were smarting as if he'd plunged them in a nettle patch. At the same time he was infuriated by his own loss of self-control. A kitchen lad's pity was the last thing he could endure at this moment.

'Your gracious king can choke on his pie and capons, for all I care!' he hissed. 'Together with all his cooks and courtiers!'

Benzo lowered his knife with an air of perplexity. 'You played a trick on me,' he said. 'You're no fool.'

'No, I'm not!' Florin growled. 'But what business is it of yours?'

His churlishness seemed to bounce off Benzo. 'Even if you aren't a fool,' he said, 'I expect you're hungry, aren't you?'

Florin wrestled with his pride for a moment, then nodded. An instant later he felt something firm in his hand.

'Quickly, put it in your pocket. Don't eat it until you're out of the kitchen!'

'WELL, your majesty, was the work to your liking?' the jester inquired when he came to fetch Florin at nightfall. 'There are better chores yet: next time I'll put you to scouring the privies.'

In the stable Florin sank down on the straw with a sigh of relief. Back, arms, legs—every part of him felt as if it had been belaboured with a cudgel. It was a weight off his mind when Mimus growled, 'Stay here. I'd welcome an evening without you for once.'

The door had scarcely closed behind him when Florin groped in his pocket for the treasure Benzo had given him. It was a big apple, crisp and sweet, and he devoured it slowly and with relish. The day might have been wretched drudgery, but tonight was the best for a long time. The apple left a pleasantly warm sensation in his stomach, and he grinned in the darkness at the memory of how he had duped Benzo. It had done him good to speak with someone other than Mimus, be it only a simple scullion. For all that, he thought, already half asleep, he would never set foot in the kitchen again . . .

He was roughly shaken awake. 'On your feet, little Mimus,' said the jester's voice, 'the king wishes to see you. Quick, get dressed!'

Florin struggled into a sitting position. 'What's the matter?' he asked dazedly, raising one arm to shield his eyes from the torch Mimus was holding above his face.

'Get a move on!' Mimus said impatiently, and thrust his costume at him. Florin started to put it on with his eyes closed. He became hopelessly entangled in the garment's tight-fitting arms and legs, so he welcomed it when Mimus came to his aid. For one pleasurable moment he imagined that he was at home in Montfield Castle, and that Ramon was helping him to dress.

'Where are we going?' he asked, shivering, as he followed Mimus up the stairs.

'To Theodo's bedchamber. The king has called for entertainment. He cannot sleep.'

'Then he might at least let others do so,' Florin muttered sullenly. He ached in every limb, and his eyes were smarting with fatigue.

A janitor held the carved oak door open and gestured to them to be quiet. They tiptoed along the passage to another door, where Mimus discreetly knocked and a young manservant admitted them.

Florin was met by unaccustomed warmth. Crackling on the hearth in an alcove was a fire to which a second manservant kept adding more logs.

'My king . . .' Mimus cautiously approached the bed in which Theodo, propped up against countless pillows, half sat, half lay with his eyes closed. The manservant who had opened the door knelt down beside the bed, dipped a silk cloth in a bowl in which rose petals were floating, and dabbed the king's brow and temples with it. Florin couldn't tear his eyes away: Ramon had done the very same thing to him when he was unable to sleep at night.

'So the jesters have deigned to appear at last,' Theodo growled without opening his eyes. 'Very well, entertain me!'

Florin saw Mimus's eyes roam round the room for a moment. Then they lighted on the chamber pot beneath the king's bed and a smile flitted across his face.

'The Song of the Chamber Pot, my weary king:

A king possessed a chamber pot
he held in great affection.
This gave the vain, presumptuous pot

> *ideas above its station.*
> *"A pot like me does not belong,"*
> *it said, "beneath a bed."*
> *"Too true," the king replied, and so*
> *he put it on his head.'*

'On his head . . . very droll,' Theodo murmured as the manservant continued to dab his brow with the silken cloth. 'Continue!'

Mimus surveyed the bedchamber once more. For want of any better source of inspiration, he took his cue from the king's discontented face.

> *'Master and Mistress Crosspatch*
> *with snow were covered over.*
> *"Alas," sighed he, "were summer here*
> *we two would be in clover."*
> *His wife replied: "You grumble more*
> *than any man I know.*
> *Were summer here, without a doubt*
> *you'd wish us deep in snow!"'*

King Theodo lay motionless beneath his silk sheets, submitting to the manservant's gentle touch.

The warmth of the open fire enfolded Florin like a cosy blanket. If only he could shut his eyes for a spell! Might he be permitted to lean against the bedpost? He stood beside Mimus, swaying with exhaustion and fervently hoping that Theodo had fallen asleep at last—until he heard the king say: 'Now you, little Mimus!'

Startled, he opened his eyes wide. Beside him, Mimus indicated the silk canopy above Theodo's head. What did the jester mean? One moment—was he alluding to one of the umpteen humorous poems about the mouse who dwelt in a royal bed canopy and fell out of it into the sleeping monarch's open mouth?

'Hearken, my friends, to the terrible plight
that befell a proud king in the course of the night,'

Florin began—and stopped short.

'The mouse was curled up in its comfortable nest . . .'

His head felt as hollow and bloated as the pig's bladder dangling from his belt. It was a superhuman struggle to keep his eyes open.

'. . . in its comfortable nest . . .'

'I know that one,' Theodo snapped ill-humouredly.

'Then say the rest yourself!'

Florin knew he'd made a blunder the moment the words escaped his lips, but he didn't care; he'd had his fill of reciting rhymes. He wanted to sleep, just sleep!

Mimus strove to salvage the situation. 'A weary jester jests but poorly, my king. Send this sleepyhead off to bed and permit me to recount the tale of the—'

'Hold your tongue, Mimus!' snapped the king, reaching for the bell beside his bed. Its shrill reverberations went echoing through the silent castle.

'You rang, Your Majesty?' As if by magic, Marsus appeared at the king's bedside, immaculately attired as usual.

That popinjay never sleeps! Florin thought indignantly. Just then he heard King Theodo say, 'Take little Mimus downstairs to Master Antonius. Twenty goodnight caresses will sweeten his slumbers.'

'Certainly, Your Majesty.' Marsus bowed.

Florin felt strangely light, almost airborne, as he followed the valet down the stairs. It was as if a tingling draught of sweet wine had gone to his head. In one corner of his mind he knew that something was far from right, but his brain refused to register that knowledge. Marsus conducted him through a veritable labyrinth of stairways and passages, farther below ground than he would have believed possible. It was almost, he thought dreamily, as if Bellingar Castle possessed a subterranean counterpart, like a building that duplicates itself when reflected in water. Florin couldn't repress an involuntary grin at the notion that everyone in the subterranean castle walked around upside down.

'Why so merry, little Mimus?' asked the valet. 'You truly are a fool!'

Marsus threw open a heavy door, and they crossed a low, dimly-lit vault whose many stout columns resembled a stone forest. An ideal place for hide-and-seek, thought Florin. Some guards were seated round a table beside an iron door, playing cards, with their swords and spears leaning against the wall ready to hand. When they saw Marsus, one of them took a bunch of keys from the table and unlocked the iron door.

'Is the donkey to have his hide simply tanned, or flayed forthwith?' he inquired with a grin.

He's talking about me, Florin thought in dismay as he followed Marsus into a spacious chamber brightly lit by an open fire in the centre. He found the place thoroughly pleasant at first glance. It wasn't until he looked again that he really woke up and ice-cold fear pervaded his limbs.

Hanging on the walls in order of size, like tools in a smithy, were heavy pairs of tongs and pincers, leather whips and straps, and spiked iron clamps. Above the massive fireplace was a gridiron the size of a man. It was quite similar to the gridirons in a kitchen, except that leather nooses were attached to its extremities. What, in Christ's name, could their purpose be?

Several men, who had been sitting or lying on benches round the fire, got up without undue haste when they entered. All were dressed alike in leather shirts, breeches and aprons, but only one of them wore a precious golden amulet depicting St. Hadrian, the patron saint of jailers: Master Antonius, thought Florin.

The tall, broad-shouldered dungeon-master smiled at them. 'Belated visitors, eh?' he called. 'Welcome!'

Marsus ignored this friendly salutation. 'Twenty strokes of the whip for little Mimus,' he announced. 'The king wishes it.'

'I was well and truly asleep already,' said the dungeon-master. 'My charges are remarkably quiet tonight.' His gaze rested briefly on a second iron door at the far end of the chamber.

My father's in there! flashed through Florin's head. Of course, the dungeons must be down here. He stared, spellbound, at the iron door.

'If you please, Master Antonius,' Marsus insisted, clearly ill at ease. 'Give the youngster his thrashing. I have little desire to spend the rest of the night down here.'

'What a prickly fellow you are, Marsus.'

Master Antonius nodded to his assistants. One of them seized Florin by the arms and another bared his back. Then they laid him face down on a wooden bench. Although they didn't handle him roughly, or no more so than Rollo, Florin went numb with terror as they tightened leather straps round his wrists. Desperately, in defiance of all common sense, he strained against his bonds in an attempt to free himself, but the straps merely bit into his flesh.

'Don't trouble, you'll only hurt yourself to no avail!' said a voice in his ear. With an effort, Florin turned his head in its direction. Master Antonius was standing right beside him, whip in hand.

'How many did you say, Marsus?'

Florin turned his head in the opposite direction, away from Master Antonius, and found himself looking straight at the second iron door.

'Twenty.'

If he cried out now, would his father hear him?

'What did he do?'

'What's that to you?' Marsus sounded more impatient still. 'He was lazy and rebellious, much to the king's displeasure. Won't you get on with it at last?'

Master Antonius bent over Florin. 'A jester who displeases earns himself a double measure of displeasure,' he said. 'Bear that in mind!' And he raised the whip.

Florin did not cry out—for the first ten strokes. He had never been beaten before. His initial emotion was one of stupefied amazement that anything could hurt so much. Every stroke felt like a white-hot poker being thrust against his skin. He gasped, flinging his head feverishly to and fro, to and fro, from the iron door to Master Antonius's leather apron and back again. Tears ran down his cheeks. At the same time, a voice in his head relentlessly counted the strokes: 'Eight, nine, ten . . .'

At the tenth stroke his back seemed to burst open along the spine. He uttered a yell, overcome with terror. The whip would cut him in two, shatter his backbone . . . 'Fifteen, sixteen . . .' Merciful God, why didn't someone come to his aid? Master Antonius . . . the iron door . . . his father . . . Could he hear him? Whirling red sparks were dancing before his eyes. 'Nineteen . . .'

And then it was over. The men released his bonds, set him on his feet, swabbed his back with a sponge and pulled his costume over it.

'Pay me another visit sometime, young Mimus,' the dungeon-master called after Florin as Marsus led him out. 'Little jokesters are always welcome here. Down in the underworld, the days and nights are long!'

WHEN Florin returned to the king's bedside, he had to exert all of his willpower to stand up straight and hold his head erect. He had a frightfully distinct sensation that loose strips of skin were dangling down his back, and it was only with the greatest difficulty that he restrained himself from pulling down his costume and peering over his shoulder. At the same time he felt something warm running down his chin: blood from the lips he'd bitten while being whipped.

King Theodo eyed him lingeringly. Then he said: 'You learnt a lesson down there. What was it?'

Even as the king was speaking, Florin felt sick to his stomach. It serves you right, he thought with grim satisfaction. If I throw up over your bed, you can't even punish me for it. I won't survive another whipping—it would kill me, and that you don't want. Not yet . . .

'What was it?' Theodo repeated calmly.

In desperation, Florin blurted out: 'A jester who displeases earns himself a double measure of displeasure.'

'You may go,' the king said. 'Mimus, you will remain!'

Florin vomited as soon as he reached the stable. Half senseless with pain, he pulled off his jester's costume, buried himself in the straw face down and clasped his head in his hands. He continued to retch, and a burning sense of shame compounded his physical agony. He had winced like an animal in the presence of those uncouth torturers— whimpered and howled like a whipped cur. His father had been behind that iron door. He should have been strong for King Philip's sake. He should have steeled himself against the pain and endured it . . . The image of that iron door never left him, and when at last he fell asleep it accompanied him into his dreams.

———————

THE heavy iron door was ajar. Master Antonius made a gesture of invitation. 'Go in, little Mimus.'

Florin peered through the crack but couldn't see a thing. Icy darkness came wafting toward him.

'What's in there, Master Antonius?'

'See for yourself!'

Florin pushed the door open wider, and this time the darkness smote him in the face like a giant spider's web. It plastered itself over his eyes, infiltrated his nose and mouth. Blinded and gasping for breath, he staggered backward. As he desperately strove to wipe the sticky blackness off his face, he heard Master Antonius utter a low laugh. By the time he could see again, the door was shut.

ROLLO whistled through his teeth when he caught sight of the welts on Florin's back the next morning.

'Somebody seems to have made the acquaintance of Master Antonius,' he said. Having rummaged in his innumerable pockets, he produced a small jar. 'There's nothing like ox lard for curing a donkey's maltreated hide.'

Florin bit his lips, making them bleed afresh, as Rollo proceeded to rub the grease thoroughly into his weals.

'It's the only way,' the bestiarius told him, 'unless, of course, you wish to end your days with a pretty pattern of stripes on your back.' He gave Florin an encouraging pat. 'Think yourself lucky, you rascal. Master Antonius no more than stroked you. Your master here—' he nodded at Mimus, 'can sing you a different song about being whipped.'

When Rollo had gone, Florin sat up with a grimace of pain.

'Welcome to the Knightly Order of Jesters,' Mimus said sarcastically. 'You've got your dubbing safely behind you.'

'How many whippings has the king sentenced *you* to?' Florin asked when they were spooning up their morning gruel.

'Master Antonius has promised to let me off my thousandth,' the jester said gruffly, 'but it seems he won't get the chance. I've grown too cunning in the course of time.'

'A jester who displeases earns himself a double measure of displeasure,' Florin muttered darkly.

'I invented that proverb,' Mimus declared with pride.

Florin stared at him in disbelief. 'You make up rhymes about your own humiliations?'

'Do you think your back will hurt less if you mope?'

Florin moved his shoulders gingerly. 'What right has Theodo to do such things?' he demanded bitterly.

'He's the king,' Mimus replied with a shrug. 'In his exalted position he can mete out punishment like the Almighty himself.' The next moment he jumped up. 'Oh, I'd quite forgotten,' he cried in mock horror. 'You're a king yourself—or almost. Forgive me, my little king with ass's ears.' He set Florin's fool's cap on his head and gave an ironical bow. 'Have you by any chance heard the story of King Midas?'

Florin shook his head.

'But you should,' said Mimus, resuming his seat. 'That noble king could easily have been your ancestor. Like you, he wasn't the shrewdest of mortals. He angered the god Apollo, who punished him by making ass's ears sprout from his head. Poor King Midas had to go around with a cap on his head for the rest of his days. Well, does that sound familiar?'

'I'm sure King Midas didn't have to recite absurd poems in the middle of the night,' Florin grumbled.

'He would certainly have made a better fist of it than you,' said the jester, raising his eyebrows. 'You *deserved* a beating for that brilliant performance of yours. Very well, recite the poem about the mouse in the bed canopy. For every time you falter—' he gave a spiteful grin, 'you'll perform ten somersaults. Tomorrow at latest!'

FLORIN spent two afternoons lying on his stomach in the straw. On the third day he couldn't endure being cooped up in the stable any longer. He was relieved to note that the skin of his back felt tight rather than painful, as if it had been daubed with resin. He was preparing to set off on one of his usual solitary excursions when he suddenly saw the glint of Benzo's coppery hair on the stairs above him. He quickened his pace. Then, when he was three steps behind the kitchen lad, he slowed and cleared his throat.

Benzo turned round. Seeing that it was Florin, he smiled.

'I have to fetch some trout for the royal table,' he explained. Florin noticed only then that he was carrying a fishing net and a wooden club. 'If you have time enough, come with me to the fish pond. Then we can talk.'

Nothing would have pleased Florin more, but he shook his head. 'I'm not allowed to leave the castle.'

'You won't have to.' Benzo grinned mysteriously. 'Come along.'

To Florin's astonishment, Benzo led him farther up the stairs. He had never ventured so high before. The top floor was occupied by the men who would defend the castle from its roof in the event of a siege. This was where the archers ate and slept, and where the weapons of war were stored: javelins, fire arrows, sharp-toothed iron mantraps, catapults, slingshots.

None of the soldiers looked up as Benzo and Florin climbed the stairs past them. The higher they went, the lighter and colder it became, because the stairs led straight to the roof.

Once at the top, Florin felt dizzy and had to cling to the iron handrail. He was outside! The sun was shining, but it must have rained not long before because the puddles on the slabs of slate gleamed in the sunlight like molten lead. A strong wind buffeted Florin's costume and set his bells a-jingling. He drew in deep breaths of the fresh, moist air. How many days had it been since he was last outside?

The roof of the castle was entirely enclosed by a stone parapet. Archers stood motionless behind this wall like parts of the building, their vigilant gaze fixed on the surrounding countryside. Arrows lay ready to fire across their longbows, and more arrows reposed in leather quivers behind them. Other soldiers were hurling their spears at straw dummies with grim determination, over and over again. Florin had always thought that Montfield's garrison commander was a stern taskmaster, but Theodo's soldiers were evidently subjected to far more rigorous training. His spirits sank at the sight. Even if attackers managed to penetrate the castle, they would suffer heavy casualties. And by then the prisoners would long ago have been slaughtered.

Benzo's voice intruded on his thoughts. 'Hey, what is it? I don't have much time, the kitchen-master is waiting for his trout.'

Eager to discover where on earth Benzo would find trout on the castle roof, Florin followed him. Sure enough, behind a small shed used for storing weapons, he was amazed to see a fish pond. It was enclosed by a rubble wall and obviously quite deep.

'A fine thing isn't it?' said Benzo, as proudly as if the pool were all his own work. 'There are always fresh trout to be had for our gracious king's table.'

Scores of fish were swarming just beneath the surface. Florin sat down on the low parapet, dipped his hands in the water, and watched the trout scatter in all directions.

'Don't scare them away!' Benzo said behind him. And, before Florin could stop him, he had playfully slapped him on the back. Florin jumped to his feet with a yell.

'What—' Benzo began, looking astonished, but Florin quickly cut him short. 'It's nothing. I . . . You startled me, that's all.'

Benzo looked puzzled but said no more. With a practised movement, he immersed his net in the pond and scooped out half-a-dozen wriggling trout.

'Do you come from these parts?' he asked as he laid the net down in front of him and reached for his club and knife.

'No. From, er . . .' Florin gestured vaguely at the horizon. 'From a long way off.'

'My family dwells in the city,' said Benzo. 'I have eight brothers and four sisters. I seldom see them now that I work at the castle.' He grinned. 'That's one advantage, at least.'

While speaking he dealt the first trout a well-aimed blow on the head with his club, slit its belly open, removed the guts, and replaced it in the net with its live companions in misfortune. He reached at once for the next fish, chatting away as he did so.

'My father works as a carver at the royal manufactory.'

'The royal what?'

'You didn't know?' Benzo laughed at Florin's mystified expression.

'His Majesty owns a flourishing carver's workshop. It makes ivory dice, amber chessmen, table fountains of rose quartz, combs, brooches, and so on. After all, the luxuries of Bellingar Castle have to be paid for somehow, don't they?'

He tossed the next trout back into the net. 'Last week a hell-fire preacher's sermon put the fear of God into the townsfolk. Since then my father has been overwhelmed with work. Everyone turned pious overnight. Nobody wants dice or chessmen any more, so my father is busy transforming those sinful objects into rosaries and figures of saints. He's a master carver—he can turn a chess king into St. Peter in the twinkling of an eye.'

He raised the club again. 'Why don't you lodge with us in the servants' quarters?'

Florin tore his eyes away from the wriggling net. 'Because I live in the Monkey Tower with Mimus, Zito, Brother and the monkeys.'

'I know Mimus,' said Benzo. 'The bear and the monkeys, too, but who is Brother?'

'The king's wolf,' Florin told him. 'I'm not surprised you've never seen him—he never leaves his stable.'

Meanwhile, the fishes' blood-stained guts had formed a little mound at Benzo's side. Florin tried hard not to stare at them. Could one eat such things?

'Your stable can't be worse than the hovel in which we scullions live,' Benzo said firmly. 'But at least we eat well.' He took a closer look at Florin's face. 'Am I wrong, or do they keep you on short commons in the Monkey Tower?'

Ashamed to admit he was starving, Florin shrugged his shoulders.

'But you jesters are forever dancing attendance on the king,' Benzo said in surprise. 'Why doesn't he give you some of his fine fare?'

'He tosses us a morsel now and then,' Florin said bitterly. 'To reward us when we entertain him well.'

Benzo took another look at Florin's face. 'Then you'll have to work harder in the future,' he said. 'What does the jester teach you?'

'Nothing worth more than a pinch of manure,' said Florin.

Benzo laughed. 'I wouldn't care to have the jester for a master,' he confessed. 'His tongue is sharper than the kitchen-master's cleaver. Still, if you've had enough of him you can always run off and rejoin your troupe of travelling entertainers. Tell me,' he said hesitantly, 'that trick you used to give those pages a drubbing—could you possibly teach it to me?'

Florin shook his head. 'It takes years of practice.'

'I see,' said Benzo, looking impressed. 'What's your real name?'

'Florin.'

'Florin?' Benzo grinned. 'Like the coin, you mean?' He sighed. 'Ah, if only I could hold a gold florin in my hand just once. Have you ever seen one?'

Florin was involuntarily reminded of how his father had ordered a thousand gold florins to be thrown to the cheering throng on his last birthday. 'No,' he replied, 'never.'

'Nor will you.' The last trout met its end and Benzo wiped the knife on his filthy smock. He eyed Florin's striped costume with a puzzled frown.

'You're remarkably clean for someone who lives in a stable,' he said.

Florin pulled a face. 'Mimus empties a whole bucket of water over me every day.'

'Every day?' Benzo looked appalled. 'It's a wonder you haven't been washed away. The jester must be crazy.'

'He may well be,' Florin replied, but he knew this wasn't the whole truth. His morning ablutions had become an important ritual for him, too. They differentiated him from the animals in the king's menagerie, which didn't wash.

'Well,' said Benzo, 'will you be paying us another visit in the kitchen sometime?'

Florin grimaced. 'Once was enough for me, thank you.'

'You jesters want no truck with hard work, eh?' Benzo shouldered his fishing net. 'You're right, little Mimus. Take life easy!'

– A NOCTURNAL VISITOR –

'OH YES, WHAT an easy life I lead!' Florin muttered grumpily.

Before leaving the stable, Mimus had thrust the usual yard-long parchment into his hand. 'Your task for this afternoon,' he said mockingly. 'Acrobatic exercises for the clumsiest part of your anatomy: tongue-twisters, little Mimus—three hundred and sixty-five of them, one for every day of the year. Practise them carefully. The king likes people to dislocate their tongues for him.'

For over two hours now, Florin had been pacing from one end of the stable to the other as he wrestled with those confounded tongue-twisters.

'Six sleek swans swam swiftly southwards, southwards swiftly swam six sleek swans,' he murmured to himself. 'Silly sheep sleep and weep, silly sheep sleep and weep. What nonsense!' Furiously, he crumpled the parchment into a ball, then bethought himself of the castle latrines and quickly smoothed it out again. 'Two tried and tested tridents, three short sword thrusts,' he read on. 'May Theodo and his entire court die of a thousand short sword thrusts!'

'What's that I hear, you little rascal?' Rollo was standing in the doorway. 'Are you eager to sing another song for Master Antonius?'

He jerked his thumb at something behind him. 'The king's third ear,' he growled softly. Just then, Florin caught sight of Marsus's silken coat tails. He had taken an immediate dislike to the king's foppish valet, but their last encounter had left him with a profound loathing of the man.

'You're wanted, little fool,' Marsus announced haughtily.

So the king was asking for him—that was worse than any tongue-twister. In the blackest of moods, Florin attached the bauble and pig's bladder to his belt and followed the valet upstairs.

Silently, with impassive faces, the sentries stood aside and opened the carved wooden door.

'You will wait outside,' Marsus ordained. 'And don't dare move so much as an inch from the spot.'

The door closed behind him.

'Did you hear that, friend?' asked the sentry on the left.

'Yes, friend,' replied the sentry on the right. 'The little donkey is not to move, or his rump will get a taste of the whip.'

Without a flicker of expression, the left-hand sentry jabbed Florin's arm with his pike. It was only a prick, but the pain transfixed him like a wasp sting.

'How startled the little donkey looks,' the right-hand sentry said happily. 'But we, friend, are only made of wood. Isn't that so?'

'You're right, friend,' said the left-hand sentry. 'Pieces of furniture can't hurt a little donkey!' He emphasised the last word by delivering another jab with his pike, this time so hard that Florin uttered an involuntary yelp.

He retreated to the landing, but he was still far from out of range of the sentries' pikes. Should he run for it? That would only mean another visit to Master Antonius. Better to stick it out. Furiously, he stared at the ornately carved door. The king would surely appear sooner or later.

The left-hand sentry raised his pike again. 'Come, friend,' he said with a broad grin. 'Let us prick the donkey's hide together. One, two, three . . .'

The carved door opened. Quick as lightning, the sentries shouldered their weapons and bowed low. Florin breathed a sigh of relief, glad of Theodo's presence for the first time ever.

But it wasn't the king. To Florin's surprise, the princess emerged. She was wearing a finely embroidered velvet gown and a matching bonnet on her dark ringlets, and Florin was struck once more by her strong resemblance to Theodo. Following her at a respectful distance came a lady's maid bearing two racquets under her arm.

Imperiously, Princess Alix beckoned Florin closer. 'From now on you're to be my jester as well. My father has permitted it.' She gave a radiant smile. 'For your information, there's nothing he won't give me if I truly want it.'

Florin almost groaned aloud. He felt as if the ten plagues of Egypt were descending on him one after the other. First he'd been whipped, then the sentries had tormented him, and now, to crown everything, he had become the princess's plaything. It was intolerable.

'Well,' he said, not even attempting to disguise the repugnance in his voice, 'what am I to do?'

'Can you play tennis?' Without waiting for a reply, Alix made for the stairs. 'Come with me,' she commanded. 'We have a paved tennis court below the castle walls.'

Florin didn't move. 'If so, you'll have to play against yourself, princess,' he said with grim satisfaction. 'I'm not allowed to leave the castle.'

'Then we'll play in the castle courtyard.'

He shrugged his shoulders. 'I'm not allowed outside the door. The gracious and worshipful King of Vinland has forbidden it.'

She gave him a challenging look, and he noted with some annoyance that they were precisely the same height. 'Do you always do as you're told, like a good boy?'

You yourself would be more obedient if they'd whipped the skin off your back! The words were on the tip of Florin's tongue, but he controlled himself and said nothing.

'As soon as I've spoken to my father we'll play outside,' Alix announced firmly. 'Until then you'll have to help me pass the time indoors. What else is a jester for?'

'I could tell you a story,' Florin said listlessly, 'but might we go inside?' The sight of the sentries, who were once more standing there like blocks of wood, made his arm hurt.

'Oh no,' Alix said in an amiable tone, 'let's treat these good sentries to a little entertainment. You'll do your tricks out here. You can tell my little brothers stories. For me, you must think of something more amusing.'

Florin was overcome with rage. She seemed to sense just how uneasy the sentries made him feel and took pleasure in humiliating him.

'I'm waiting, little Mimus,' she said pertly. 'Somersaults, handsprings—show us what you can do. Or are you too clumsy even for jester's tricks?'

'Better clumsy than ill brought-up like you,' he retorted angrily. 'Has no one ever taught you that other people should be treated with decency and discretion?'

'Yes, indeed,' she hissed, 'but I never knew that court etiquette applied to cattle and jesters.'

She threw back her head and regarded him with narrowed eyes. 'Do you jesters in the Monkey Tower possess a mirror? You don't seem to realise what you are, or you wouldn't be so impertinent—you loathsome, warty frog!'

The lady's maid tittered behind her hand and the sentries couldn't help grinning. Florin finally lost his temper.

'That will do, princess,' he said hoarsely. 'If you wish to torment a monkey, send for one and leave me in peace!'

So saying, he turned and ran down the stairs.

'Come back!' he heard her call, but he didn't stop.

WHEN Mimus returned to the stable that evening, Florin was poring over the tongue-twisters as if nothing had occurred. The jester was monosyllabic and ill-humoured. When Florin stumbled over a tongue-twister he swore at him angrily, and Florin wondered, not for the first time, what Mimus did in the afternoons to make him so moody in the evenings. He made no mention of his altercation with the princess—he would be hauled off to Master Antonius soon enough. But nothing happened. When the time came for their evening performance, Mimus told him to fetch the monkeys from their quarters. Then they set off for the banqueting hall.

Had the princess not betrayed him after all? Florin appeared before the king with a pounding heart, but Theodo seemed to know nothing and greeted him as affably as his monkeys.

The guests at dinner tonight were few, all members of the king's inner circle. The only outsiders, seated at the lower end of the table, were strangers whose brown habits identified them as mendicant friars. The large seashells on their cowls were the badge worn by all who had undertaken a pilgrimage to Santiago de Compostela.

Mimus, sitting on the floor with two of the monkeys, eyed the friars up and down. 'Generally speaking,' he said, 'priests of all kinds give Bellingar Castle a wide berth. I myself,' he added smugly, 'bear no small responsibility for that.'

'Doubtless the pious brethren could find no other night's lodgings on their pilgrimage,' Florin hazarded, rolling a leather ball from one monkey to the other. 'Be merciful, Mimus. Keep a bridle on your blasphemous tongue. They must be weary after their long journey.'

'It's their own fault,' said Mimus, making one of the monkeys perform gymnastics on his head. 'What business have they in the outside world? They should remain within their monastery walls and fondle widows and orphans, as is their duty.'

He held the monkey's tail to one side, the better to observe the king's three guests. 'Strange,' he said. 'They've had second helpings only. As a rule, mendicant friars gorge themselves like hogs.'

Florin, too, eyed the strangers curiously. Two were elderly, bent-backed men who never looked up from their plates. The third was young, little more than twenty, and his hooked nose and keen gaze were reminiscent of a bird of prey.

When the meal ended, a page conducted the three friars before Theodo's throne, where they bowed respectfully and thanked him for his hospitality.

'Now tell us, good sirs,' he said. 'What miracles did you encounter at the tomb of St. James?'

'Now tell us, good sirs,' Mimus chimed in. 'Did St. James end by giving fish legs to walk with? Worms wings to fly with? And priests heads to think with?'

'I cannot understand,' Florin heard the young monk whisper to his companions, 'how anyone can take pleasure in such creatures.' To the king, he said: 'God, in his immeasurable wisdom and goodness, did not consider us worthy enough to witness any miracles. We are, when all is said and done, only the humblest of his servants.' And he meekly cast his eyes down.

'Does that mean you made your long pilgrimage in vain?' asked the king.

'No, on the contrary,' said one of the older friars. 'For simple monks like us, travelling is always profitable and instructive. Those who keep their eyes and ears open learn all manner of things.'

He fell silent and looked at his young companion.

'For example,' the latter went on, 'it came to our ears that you, the King of Vinland, are lodging some distinguished guests in your cellars.'

Florin, who was just lifting the smallest monkey onto his shoulder, froze in mid-movement. He scarcely felt Mimus take hold of his arm and give it a warning squeeze.

King Theodo eyed the three strangers keenly. 'You are neither pilgrims nor monks,' he said. At a signal, guards arrayed themselves menacingly in front of the table. 'Who are you? Who sent you?'

'I am Count Victor of Solutre, envoy of King Guido of Arelia.' From one moment to the next, the young man abandoned all semblance of pious humility. He pointed to the guards with a mocking air. 'You would do better to dispense with this show of force, King Theodo, and give ear to what I have to say.'

Theodo looked amused. 'It takes considerable courage to address me thus at my own table. What's the meaning of this ridiculous charade?'

'Having been refused an audience,' said Count Victor, 'we were compelled to resort to a subterfuge. Its success proves us right: we stand here before you.'

The king sat back on his throne. 'What makes you so sure I won't have you thrown out this instant?'

'Our reliance on your shrewd intelligence, Your Majesty,' said the young count. 'I am empowered to negotiate the release of your captives.'

Florin saw the king's men give him a covert glance.

'Am I a huckster to be haggled with?' Theodo asked sarcastically.

Victor of Solutre remained impassive. 'I hope so, for your sake. There's gold to be had, my king. A great deal of gold.'

'You could shower me with all the gold on earth,' Theodo said calmly. 'The captives are not for sale.'

A hand gripped Florin's neck from behind. 'Greetings from the king, little Mimus,' hissed Marsus, pretending to retrieve a napkin from the floor. 'Betray yourself, and your father will die this very night—in agony!'

Florin stared with smarting eyes at the three men before the throne. 'Here is our offer, Your Majesty,' he heard the young count say. 'Half a million gold florins for the release of King Philip and his son.'

Half a million gold florins! Until that moment, Florin hadn't known there was that much gold in the entire world. Clasping the smallest monkey to his chest, he mechanically tickled it behind the ears. Silence had descended on the table. Then Theodo burst out laughing.

'Convey my compliments to Guido of Arelia,' he said. 'Tell him to spend his money on a castle with battlements of gold and windows of diamonds—he'll not get the prisoners!' His expression hardened. 'For the last time: I do not bargain. I have made no demands and accept no offers.'

'I'm unacquainted with your motives, Your Majesty,' said Count Victor, and Florin could see that he was preserving his composure with an effort, 'but I do know the consequences of your course of action. The kingdom of Moltovia is tottering like a headless giant. Your soldiers have banded together with murderers and brigands. They roam the countryside, killing and pillaging as they please, and there's no one there to stop them. Those who refuse to surrender their property are slaughtered like cattle. Whole districts have been laid waste, villages burned, crops destroyed, inhabitants put to flight.'

Florin remembered his ride through the countryside. He had a vision of the devastated villages, the empty windows, the mutilated cats impaled on spikes, and his heart grew heavy. At the time he'd thought that he was leaving the murk of war behind, bound for a bright, peaceful future, but it was clear that Moltovia had subsided into darkness and destitution.

'Only one person can restore order,' said Victor of Solutre. 'Moltovia's rightful king!'

Theodo spread his hands in a mocking gesture. 'He sits here before you.'

Count Victor shook his head. 'Ambition has blinded you, King Theodo,' he said, 'or you would see how much the people of Moltovia hate you. They will never accept you as their sovereign.'

'So *you* say,' Theodo replied calmly.

'One last thing, King of Vinland,' said the third envoy, who had not spoken until now. 'The combined armies of Arelia and Angelland are ready for battle. If we solicit support in *your* new kingdom of Moltovia—' he stressed the word sarcastically, 'what do you think will happen then?'

King Theodo didn't bat an eyelid. 'You threaten to besiege me?' he asked quietly. 'Then this is my response: if my lookouts report seeing a single banner, a single cavalryman on the horizon, none of the prisoners in Bellingar Castle will survive. Inform your king of that!'

Throughout this exchange, Mimus had been sitting on the floor beside Florin, rolling the leather ball from one monkey to another. Suddenly he jumped to his feet.

'I, too, have a king!' he crowed loudly. 'See here, pious brethren! Allow me to present my royal family.'

He took two of the monkeys by the paw and led them up to the envoys. 'These two,' he said, making the monkeys perform a graceful bow, 'are my king and my queen. And this one—' he seized Florin's hand and gave it a tug, 'is my prince. Tell me, isn't he the spit and image of his parents?'

Florin stared at Mimus open-mouthed. What was he up to? Had he lost his wits?

The two elderly envoys paid no attention to the jester's words, but the young count drew himself up, straight as a ramrod, and looked at Florin keenly. He did not seem unduly pleased by what he saw, because he almost imperceptibly shook his head and turned back to Theodo.

'If that is your last word, King of Vinland . . .'

'It is,' Theodo said brusquely. 'And now, forgive me if I have you thrown out.' He gave a mocking laugh. 'Half a million gold florins should procure you suitable lodgings for the night, even at this late hour.'

He sounded quite unruffled, but the glance he cast at Mimus—by chance, so it seemed—made Florin's blood run cold. The jester continued to prattle blithely on about monkey princes and princesses, but Florin was undeceived by his innocent grin. Mimus must have known how gravely he'd defied the king.

The three envoys bowed with chill courtesy and followed the guards from the room.

They were scarcely out of sight when King Theodo turned to Mimus. 'Now for you, master jester,' he said quietly, 'and your royal family.'

'Would you like to meet some more of them?' asked Mimus.

He seized the smallest monkey by the tail and dragged it forwards. The little creature uttered a screech and bared its teeth in self-defence. 'Here's the youngest scion of the dynasty. Isn't he truly royal in appearance?'

'That will do, Mimus.' Theodo nodded to Marsus. 'I'm going to see to it that you receive a royal whipping such as you haven't enjoyed for years.' He gestured impatiently at Florin. 'You! Make yourself scarce! And take those monkeys back to the tower with you!'

ANXIOUS though he was, Florin fought off sleep for a long time. He wanted to wait up for Mimus, but at some stage his eyelids drooped.

Someone gently touched his hand, his cheek.

'Mimus?' he muttered, half asleep. When he opened his eyes and saw a stranger shining a candle in his face, he scrambled to his feet in alarm. 'Who are you?'

'Who are *you*?' asked the stranger. 'We need to be certain.'

He threw back his cowl, and the candlelight revealed the lean, hawklike features of Count Victor of Solutre.

Florin was taken aback. 'How did you get here?' he demanded.

'That's unimportant,' said the young count, who was still wearing his brown monastic habit. 'I ask you again: *Who are you?*'

'The jester already told you,' Florin replied curtly.

'That means nothing. Talking nonsense is a jester's trade.'

Florin felt a surge of anger. 'How dare you refuse to believe him? Do you have any idea of the price he's now paying for his audacity?'

Count Victor made a dismissive gesture. 'He's naught but a jester,' he said coldly. 'Just as you are, unless you persuade me otherwise.'

Florin glared at him. Then he thought of the previous evening and saw himself with the count's eyes: an emaciated boy dressed in jester's motley and frolicking around on the floor with some monkeys . . . A feeling of utter hopelessness overwhelmed him.

'Not that I can prove it,' he said softly, 'I'm Florin of Moltovia.'

'If that's true, I have a gift for you,' was the young count's unexpected response. 'Your Uncle Guido entrusted me with a portrait of your mother.'

A portrait of my mother, thought Florin. He swallowed hard. At Montfield Castle there were three portraits of her. One hung on the stairs and showed her in her wedding gown, whose voluminous folds almost concealed her from view. In the second painting, which his father had hung in his bedchamber, she was kneeling in prayer before St. Bridget, her patron saint. But Florin's favourite portrait was the delicate pen-and-ink drawing his father kept in an ivory casket. Whenever Florin thought of his mother, this was the likeness that appeared in his mind's eye.

'Look!' Count Victor handed him a sheet of parchment.

Florin bent over it in the candlelight. It was a line drawing of a young woman. She looked vaguely familiar, but he couldn't have put a name to her. All he knew for certain was that she wasn't his mother.

'Well,' asked the young nobleman, 'doesn't that gladden your heart?'

Florin fully realised that he was being put to the test. He held the drawing close to the candle once more. And all at once he recognised the girl, even though he had first seen her face many decades later, when she was an old woman.

'It's Muriel!' he cried in amazement. 'Muriel as a girl. I didn't know that a likeness of her existed.' Affectionately, he clasped the sheet of parchment to his chest. 'May I keep it?'

Count Victor smiled and bowed. 'It's yours, my prince. King Guido gave me this picture of your nursemaid for use in the unlikely event that I managed to reach you. Which I did, thanks be to God . . .' He shook his head incredulously. 'I was prepared for anything, but I never dreamt that circumstances would be as they are. I entreat you, Prince Florin, to pardon me for mistrusting you.'

'How can I blame you?' Florin murmured. 'There are times when I myself am uncertain who I am.'

He couldn't tear his eyes away from the drawing. Muriel, who had been his mother's nursemaid in Arelia, had accompanied her to Moltovia on her marriage. This drawing must have originated many years earlier. Ramon would be flabbergasted when he showed him Muriel as a pretty young girl, and Muriel herself would ensure that every last lady's maid and lady-in-waiting at court saw her likeness. She would probably hang it up outside her room, right beside his own bedchamber. His own bedchamber . . . Homesickness smote him like a blow from a fist. He turned away quickly so that Count Victor would not see his face.

'The king had you thrown out,' he said, when he could trust his voice again. 'How did you re-enter the castle?'

Victor of Solutre gave him a conspiratorial grin, and for a moment he looked like an overgrown boy. 'Three false friars were with the king, and three false friars left the castle,' he said. 'No one knows of the fourth false friar we posted at the entrance for safety's sake.'

'You're running a terrible risk,' said Florin. 'If you're discovered here, King Theodo will have you thrown into the dungeons.'

'Then I'd be in the best of company,' said Count Victor. 'How many men are being held with your father?'

'Nearly all of them were treacherously murdered. Only a score or so have survived until now.'

'Can you give me their names? Their families should be informed that there's still some hope.'

Florin proceeded to enumerate them. 'Duke Bonizo; Duke Quentin; my godfather, Count Etigo; Count Abram, administrator of the royal castles; Judge Hilduin; and, of my father's generals, Counts Gilbert, Bertin and Bernold . . .'

'What of Count Herman of Crahlen?' asked Victor of Solutre.

Florin well remembered the sturdy, ruddy-faced young nobleman. That spring, when he was appointed the junior member of King Philip's personal bodyguard, Count Herman had wept tears of joy.

'He's not among the captives,' he said curtly.

'Herman was my comrade in arms,' Count Victor said, controlling his voice with an effort. 'We trained together at the court of Arelia.'

He bowed his head, and Florin knew that he was silently offering up a prayer for his dead friend. He waited respectfully. Then he said: 'You'll have to make haste, Count Victor, or the rest of the prisoners will be dead before your news arrives. King Theodo will have us all killed sooner or later.'

'You think we don't know that?' Count Victor replied quietly. 'We're making every effort to rescue you from that wild beast's clutches before he does so.'

'But how?'

The young count looked searchingly into Florin's face in the candlelight. 'My prince, I'll tell you of our plans if you wish, but remember this: if the truth were extracted from you on the rack, all would be lost.'

For a moment Florin pictured the gridiron with the leather straps in Master Antonius's cellar. He shivered.

'They don't keep you under lock and key,' Count Victor said thoughtfully. 'Why are you still here?'

'No chains or bars are needed to keep me captive,' Florin said bitterly. 'My father pays for any attempt to escape in his dungeon.'

'I see.' Count Victor smiled, but it was an angry smile. 'Invisible shackles, strong as the heaviest of iron chains. For all that, it may be a fortunate dispensation of providence that you're free to move around inside the castle.'

His dark, hawklike eyes studied Florin for a moment. 'Would you feel able, my prince, to assist in your rescue from inside the castle, dependent on yourself alone?'

'Er, yes.' Florin hoped he hadn't sounded sound too hesitant.

The young count gave a satisfied nod. 'We shall find ways of getting word to you.'

'When you say "we",' Florin said, 'who do you mean?'

'Do you really wish to know?'

'Yes,' said Florin, only to shake his head immediately afterwards. 'No, you're right. One look at a pair of red-hot pincers, and I'd blurt out their names on the spot.'

Count Victor's expression conveyed a mixture of sympathy and respect. 'I know it's hard, Highness, but you must be patient. However long it takes, never abandon hope. Keep your eyes and ears open and count on us. And now, farewell.' He walked swiftly to the door, listened for a moment, and went out.

Florin lay down on the straw again, too agitated to sleep. His thoughts kept returning to Mimus. Was he still being tortured down in that frightful cellar? What were they doing to him?

Some time later, when the door burst open and Mimus staggered in, Florin leapt to his feet.

'What happened?' he asked anxiously.

The jester brushed this aside with a weary gesture. 'Help me out of my motley,' he said hoarsely.

Even in the semi-darkness Florin could make out the weals that criss-crossed Mimus's back and chest like writhing black serpents, the deep wounds and lacerations from which blood was oozing. He hurriedly pushed some straw into a heap, then helped the groaning jester to lie down. Trying to find some way of helping him, he moistened one sleeve of his jester's costume in the bucket, to at least wipe off the blood. But Mimus yelled with pain at his very first touch, so he limited himself to dabbing the jester's brow.

There could be no more thought of sleep that night. Standing at the window, Florin spent a long time watching the dark silhouettes of the sentries patrolling the battlements above the castle courtyard, which resembled a pool of molten lead in the moonlight. Dawn broke at last, and Rollo's familiar cursing and clattering could be heard outside the door.

'By all the saints!' The bestiarius inspected Mimus's back and chest with a connoisseur's eye. 'Master Antonius has wrought another of his masterpieces. It's many a day since I saw your hide so well and truly tanned.'

'Yes,' croaked Mimus, grinning feebly. 'The good man laid it on with a will. He had no wish to disappoint his old acquaintance.'

'I'll wager you'd crack a joke with your dying breath,' Rollo growled admiringly. He took the jar of ox lard from his pocket. 'But now you can yell to your heart's content.'

When Rollo had left the stable, Mimus lay back on the straw looking pinched and very pale.

Florin pulled the bowls of gruel toward him. 'Do you want some?' he asked hesitantly.

'Do fish swim? Do birds fly?' The jester smacked his lips with his eyes shut. 'You need only put the spoon in my mouth.'

'Why did you do it?' Florin asked as he fed Mimus with millet gruel. Mimus didn't answer until the bowl was empty. Then he said:

'It's not until he's in the soup that the rooster knows he shouldn't have crowed so loudly.'

'You tried to help me.' The words slipped out before Florin could stop them.

The jester gave an indifferent shrug—and went white to the lips with pain. 'Those so-called friars wouldn't have recognised you in any case,' he said through gritted teeth. 'They couldn't see over their mountain of gold. And now let me sleep.'

For a moment Florin was tempted to tell Mimus everything, but he decided against it. The jester was unpredictable. Yesterday he had betrayed Florin's true origins; tomorrow he might tell King Theodo about the nocturnal visitor. For all that, Florin was infinitely grateful to him for what he had done. He felt a flicker of hope deep inside. There was still a chance that his father would escape death, and that he himself would be able to remove his jester's motley.

At noon—Mimus was snoring, exhausted, on the straw—Florin went up to the castle roof. None of the soldiers took any notice of him, so he climbed on top of the shed beside the trout pool and looked in all directions with a pounding heart. Although he knew it was pointless, he scanned the countryside for signs of impending rescue. He saw nothing, of course, but before returning to the stable he once more ran his eyes over the harvested fields, the forest, the ships on the river. They seemed but a stone's throw away, yet they were all as unattainable as the stars in the sky.

– THE EXCURSION –

FLORIN HAD SECRETLY hoped that his bruised and bleeding master would refrain from giving him any lessons for a while, but Mimus struggled to his feet the very next morning. Although hobbling and grimacing with pain, he doggedly issued his instructions:

'To warm you up, a hundred quick forward and backward somersaults! I'm counting!'

'Toss the pig's bladder in the air and catch it on your nose! And again—until even a clumsy oaf like you can manage it!'

'Ten handstands followed by a forward roll! Faster, faster!'

'Now for the real test,' said Mimus while Florin was still gasping for breath. 'You'll walk on your toes until the clock strikes noon.'

'*What!* What's the point?'

'If you want to control your body, you must control every last little part of it,' Mimus declared. 'We've already taken the tip of your tongue in hand, now it's the turn of the tips of your toes.'

On any other day Florin would have protested loudly, but today he obediently rose on tiptoe. He found the exercise easy, having been walking on air since Count Victor's visit. Had the jester ordered him to turn a triple somersault without touching the ground, he would have done that, too.

Mimus eyed him keenly. 'There's something amiss with you today,' he said.

Involuntarily, Florin checked his costume. The ass's ears were correctly aligned, the bauble and pig's bladder neatly attached to his belt. 'What?'

'I miss your *Oh-God-not-that-again-I-can't-I-won't!*' Mimus said gruffly. 'I miss your eternal grumbling. Is Your Highness feeling quite well?'

'Perfectly well,' Florin assured him with a smile. 'I enjoy walking on my toes, that's all.'

'We'll see,' the jester said dryly.

It wasn't long before Florin's cheerful mood evaporated. He gritted his teeth and tried to take his mind off his aching calves by tiptoeing along the narrow strip of sunlight that was slanting in through the barred window. The strip gradually lengthened until he could no longer suppress his groans. At last, when it had reached the opposite wall, he resorted to entreaties. 'Is that enough?' he pleaded. 'My toes hurt.'

'Of course they do,' Mimus said inexorably. 'When you've walked around on them for a hundred days, *then* they'll cease to hurt. Just wait until it's the turn of your fingertips!'

An eternity later—Florin's feet had become lumps of lead and his legs were stiff as sticks—the clock struck noon. He subsided onto his heels with a sigh of relief.

'Don't rejoice too soon,' Mimus told him, pointing to the doorway. Marsus was already waiting for him.

Florin had completely forgotten about his set-to with the princess until he was telling the young princes a story and felt her eyes boring into him like needles. No, Alix had not, as he'd hoped, forgotten. On the contrary, she seemed to be gloating—saving up her revenge until later. Just like her father, Florin reflected, on his way back to the stable. Then he thrust the thought of Alix aside. There was no point in meeting his troubles halfway—better to think of his nocturnal visitor. He remembered every last word the young count had uttered. He'd been able to say little enough, but how comforting that little had been: *Count on us!*

Florin entered the stable with a smile on his face.

'Why do you keep grinning today? Are the fleas tickling you?' Mimus demanded brusquely. He attached the bauble and pig's bladder to his belt, then handed Florin a sheet of parchment. 'Your task for this afternoon.'

Florin stared at the handwritten scrawl. 'What's this, more tongue-twisters?'

'Certainly not,' Mimus retorted. 'Something far more delightful: twenty charming love songs, all to be sung to the same melody.'

Florin's sunny mood darkened abruptly.

'I'm supposed to be a jester,' he said with a frown. 'Why must I be able to sing love songs?'

'Because, my little ignoramus,' Mimus told him, 'love songs are always sung by jesters.' He turned to go. 'Adieu, young minstrel!'

'You don't even have a sweetheart!' Florin called after him.

On the other hand, he reflected immediately afterward, who knows what Mimus gets up to on all these afternoons when I'm left alone in this stable? Perhaps he spends them taking his ease in the chamber of some maidservant who fondles his ass's ears. He couldn't help laughing at the notion.

He took a closer look at the parchment—and the grin died on his lips. He had never liked singing in front of other people, but ever since last summer when his vocal cords had developed a peculiar life of their own, he had positively hated doing so. From one moment to the next, his high, clear treble voice of old became a raucous bass.

That was precisely why Mimus made him sing all the time. 'When they hear you,' he said, 'they'll split their sides laughing. What more do we want?'

Glad of the stable's seclusion, Florin proceeded to sing to himself in a loud voice:

> *'Roses red beyond compare*
> *sweetly scent my lady's hair,*
> *violets plucked this very morn*
> *do her lissom waist adorn,*
> *and the dainty columbine*
> *decorates her gown so fine . . .'*

When he came to the closing lines his voice gave a mighty squawk and he had to start again:

> *'If you ask me which of those,*
> *violet, columbine or rose,*
> *I would rather be, say I:*
> *"None of them" is my reply.*
> *Flax supplied the linen thread*
> *which her little bodice made.*
> *Were I but that humble flower,*
> *I would nestle every hour,*
> *blithesomely and free from care,*
> *'gainst her snow-white bosom fair . . .'*

Thank goodness nobody's listening, he thought—only to spin round abruptly at the sound of someone clearing his throat. Marsus was standing in the doorway.

'The princess is waiting for you, little Mimus,' he announced. 'And I strongly advise you not to sing her that song.'

––––––––

TO the extent that Florin was acquainted with them, the royal family's apartments were all light and spacious, but Alix's chamber was especially pretty, with three big round-arched windows, comfortably upholstered window seats, a thick wool carpet, and a ceiling painted all over with festoons of flowers.

Alix, who was sitting beside one of the windows, waited until Marsus had shut the door behind him. Florin had butterflies in his stomach. What form of revenge had she devised for him? One thing was certain: he refused to apologise or ask for mercy.

'You're no longer a prince,' she began without preamble. 'You're a court jester, and you have to do whatever I tell you. You deserve the whip for having run off like that, but—' she paused for a moment, 'I'll let it pass, just this once. You shall learn that the King of Vinland's daughter is capable of magnanimity.'

Florin stared at her in astonishment. The haughty princess had actually taken his words to heart!

'Well, say something,' she demanded impatiently. 'I graciously forgive you, and you stare at me with eyes like saucers. You're no court jester, you're a lame duck. Mimus would long ago have hurled a suitable response at my head.'

'I'm still learning,' he said sheepishly.

She indicated the cushioned window seat beside her. 'Sit down.'

The soft upholstery felt strange. Florin hadn't sat on a chair since his first night in Bellingar Castle.

'Er . . . You live in comfort, princess,' he said to bridge the awkward silence.

'But my chamber's true adornment isn't here.' Alix pointed to a big four-poster ranged against the opposite wall. 'That's where my governess, the virtuous Countess Wogrim, sleeps,' she explained. 'She smells of mothballs, embroiders like a woman possessed, dozes off over the chessboard, and is universally known as Wogrim the Warhorse.'

Florin grinned despite himself. 'I believe I've seen her.' He thought of the horse-faced lady-in-waiting he'd noticed at the royal lunch table. 'Where is she? And where is your lady's maid?'

'My worthy governess has gone to stay with her sister for a week—to recoup her energies!' Alix laughed. 'As for my two maids, I sent them into the garden to air my winter clothes and furs.' She pointed out of the window. 'Down there, look!'

Florin did as he was told, but he paid no heed to the two little figures, dwarfed by distance, that were busying themselves in the castle garden. He gazed at the sky, which looked as high and as limpidly blue as only an autumn sky could look, and at the forest, whose golden foliage was gleaming in the sunlight.

'Beautiful, don't you think?' said Alix.

Embarrassed, Florin withdrew his hands. Without realising it, he had leant against the window frame.

'Do you miss it all?' She made a gesture that encompassed the forest and the sky.

He could only nod.

'I spoke to my father,' she said, 'but he wouldn't budge. You're not permitted to leave the castle.'

Florin had expected nothing else.

'On the other hand,' Alix went on with a faint smile, 'no one would prevent me from going for a stroll escorted by a page.'

Florin's heart suddenly beat faster. 'What of it?' he said.

'The page will be you. I shall provide you with the necessary clothes.'

He was on his guard at once. Was it a trap? Was this the form her revenge would take?

She looked at him. 'What do you think of the idea?'

'What proof have I that I would survive the excursion unscathed?'

Alix shrugged her shoulders. 'I won't repeat my offer,' she said. 'Whether you accept or reject it is up to you.'

Florin couldn't tear his eyes away from the window. He yearned with every fibre of his being for the open air, for field and forest, for a world that wasn't enclosed by stone walls. Even if Alix had set a trap for him, the bait was irresistible. 'I accept,' he said.

'Then wait here.' She left the chamber and returned in a trice laden with boots, hose, feathered cap, and the brown doublet worn by all the pages at court. She modestly averted her eyes while Florin was getting changed.

'Well, well,' she said admiringly, when he was ready, 'you look quite human.'

'No longer like a loathsome frog?'

She grinned. 'Only like an ugly toad. Here . . .' She thrust her cloak into his hands. 'It will look more convincing if you carry something for me.'

Florin couldn't help thinking of the last carnival at Montfield, and how much he'd disliked it when commanded by his father to exchange clothes with a page. He had felt shabby and ridiculous for the rest of the evening. Now, as he followed the princess downstairs in page's attire, he felt positively regal.

You were wrong, Mimus, he thought to himself. Things look far from the same when seen from above and below.

The sentries guarding the portal, who respectfully presented arms to Alix, did not spare Florin a glance. His pulses raced as he followed her across the sunlit courtyard and over to the inner gateway: it would now become apparent if the princess had played a trick on him. He could almost feel the guards' rough hands fasten on him and hear her mocking laughter—but nothing happened. They bowed to Alix in silence and let them pass without more ado.

The princess hurried on ahead, taking the familiar path that led past the servants' quarters, stables and horse pastures. Florin dared not look to right or left. At the outer gate, too, the sentries merely bowed. Then they were outside! In a wholly unprincesslike way, Alix hitched up her skirt and broke into a run with Florin at her heels. They raced down the castle hill and across a harvested field, startling a flock of cawing rooks, then ran on to the nearby forest.

Once on the edge of the trees, Florin flopped down on the ground and breathed deeply. The air was heavy with the sweet, spicy scent of resin, of mushrooms and the few remaining blackberries that clung to the brambles. The grass was warm and dry. Pleasurably, Florin stretched his legs, pillowed his head on some sun-warmed moss, and closed his eyes.

'Hey, little Mimus,' he heard Alix say, 'there was no talk of idling. You're still on duty, even without your jester's motley.'

He propped his chin on his hand. 'What would you say, princess, if I quit your service this minute and ran off? This is a favourable opportunity, you must admit.'

'You don't mean it.' She stared at him in alarm, and it was clear that the possibility had never entered her head. 'If you ran away now, father would scold me terribly.'

Florin shook his head. 'The gracious and worshipful King of Vinland has seen to it that I will never do such a thing.'

'I guessed as much,' Alix said contentedly. 'You cannot run off for as long as your father is imprisoned in our dungeons.' She indicated the spot beside Florin. 'Spread out my cloak. Come, be quick.'

Florin complied, and she sat down on the grass beside him. They didn't speak for a while. He felt the sunbeams on his face and listened to the birds: a chaffinch singing in a bush nearby, a jay's strident call, a falcon uttering its piercing cry high above the trees. And there—wasn't that a distant cuckoo? It should long ago have flown south to the lands where the rivers were molten gold and the people as black as burnt toast—or so Tanko claimed, at least. The poor cuckoo had probably been misled by the dazzling autumn sunshine, the deceptive warmth. Now there were some icy months in store for it.

Cuckoo, cuckoo . . . Florin counted. For how many years would he remain Theodo's jester?

As ill luck would have it, the cuckoo was an exceptionally vociferous bird. Florin gave up when he reached ninety and reached for some half-shrivelled blueberries.

'Tell me something,' Alix said beside him.

He popped a berry into his mouth. 'What would you like to hear?' he asked. 'The story of Reynard the fox? Or would you like to know why the sea is salty?'

'How do you come to know so many stories?'

'I got them from Tanko,' said Florin. 'He was a squire at Montfield Castle and a friend of mine—that's to say, he still is.' Tanko might be sitting in their hideaway at this very moment, spinning yarns to the other boys . . .

'What is Montfield Castle like?' asked Alix.

Florin shrugged. 'Much the same as Bellingar. A trifle smaller, perhaps. It certainly doesn't have as many dungeons.'

She pulled a face. 'How do you know, have you counted them? When I was little I pictured your castle as an atrocious place full of snakes and spiders—dark and hellish, with severed heads impaled on pikes above its battlements. Your father was rumoured to be savage King Shaggy-Beard, a devourer of little children.'

No, princess, thought Florin. It isn't *my* father who's a fiend in human guise. Aloud he said: 'Where appearances are concerned, I imagined your own father quite differently.'

'I'm cold.' Alix jumped up. 'Help me on with my cloak.'

Florin frowned. He wasn't a lady's maid! Even so, he picked up the cloak and draped it round her shoulders.

Alix didn't move. 'The clasp.'

She regarded him intently while he fiddled with the clasp. Then she said casually: 'You may be up to your neck in a morass, but at least you're at Bellingar, the finest castle in the world.'

He stepped back a pace. 'You speak as if I fell into the morass out of stupidity,' he said angrily. 'It's your father who is the author of our misfortunes.'

He had expected her to fly off the handle, but she merely shrugged her shoulders. 'He hates you,' she said. 'More than anything in the world.'

'Why?' asked Florin.

'How should I know?' She sat down again and gestured to him to do likewise. 'For as far back as I can remember, my father has never spoken of Moltovia without cursing you and your family.'

'Even if he has some reason to hate us,' Florin retorted, 'he's breaking the commandments. Treachery and deceit are never pleasing in the sight of God.'

With a jerk, Alix sat bolt upright. 'Who are you to judge?' she demanded. 'Moltovia and Vinland were at war, and now that you wolves have lost, you howl and whimper! If my father or my mother or one of us royal children was imprisoned in Montfield Castle, any Vinlander would lay down his life to rescue us. Are your vassals really such a cowardly bunch? Or is it,' she added with an angelic smile, 'that they're glad to be rid of you?'

That shaft struck Florin in his most vulnerable spot. 'So glad that your father dares not cross the frontier,' he blurted out, 'because he wouldn't survive the Moltovians' gratitude!' Angrily, he struggled to preserve his composure. 'Our men will come, princess, rely on it—and then you'll all rue the day!'

'Warn me in good time,' Alix said sarcastically, 'so that I can take my puppy and my songthrush to a place of safety.'

Florin abruptly turned away, fuming. Why should he have to endure the jibes of this conceited little goose? To calm his nerves he plucked some blades of grass and tore them to shreds. Suddenly, he heard Alix's voice behind him: 'Why didn't you heed the old woman who leapt in front of your horse when you were on your way here?'

Florin spun round. 'How did *you* know that?'

'The house beside the bridge belongs to my maidservant's uncle,' Alix explained. 'Old Margret is her aunt. The bridge is the only means of crossing the river—you had to pass that way . . . *Woe unto thee!*' she cried, imitating the old woman's sepulchral voice. '*Woe unto thee! Turn back, my prince!*' She twisted a blade of grass round her forefinger, lost in thought. 'Riccardo and I had it all planned so carefully.'

Florin couldn't have been more astonished had Alix turned into a rosebush before his very eyes.

'You and your brother?' he said incredulously. 'Why should you have done that?'

She looked at him as if he were terribly slow on the uptake. 'To help you, of course. We knew that you were coming. Two days earlier, when your father and his retinue arrived at Bellingar, we were not allowed to leave our quarters. The next morning we heard that all our enemies were either dead or in chains, and we danced for joy in the castle court-yard. But then Father Anselm preached us children a sermon. It was a sin to rejoice at the death of others, he said. We should love our enemies and not wish ill upon any of them, however vile.'

Had Father Anselm really uttered those words? The man who had driven him from the chapel like a soulless animal?

'He spoke so earnestly, so beautifully, that I couldn't help but weep,' Alix went on. 'Riccardo comforted me. Then he hit upon a way of doing a vile enemy—you, in other words!—a good turn.' Her eyes shone. 'You should have seen how excited we were the next day, and how carefully we laid our plans. But alas,' she wound up, grimacing with disappointment, 'you were far too intent on hurrying to your doom.'

Florin thought of the black-clad figure on the bridge.

'The old woman sounded as if she was raving in a delirium,' he said dejectedly.

Alix shook her head. 'You were surrounded by royal guards, so Margret was wise to feign madness. But it didn't work.' She shrugged. 'Well, now you're our court jester and can consider yourself lucky if nothing worse befalls you.'

'So Riccardo wanted to protect me.' Florin still couldn't take it in. 'He has never exchanged a word with me.'

'Nor will he,' Alix said tersely. 'He's the crown prince—he has better things to do than concern himself with our father's new fool.'

'So why are you doing so?'

'Because I'm bored,' she admitted frankly. 'I spend most of my days listening to lessons in etiquette from Wogrim the Warhorse or homilies from Father Anselm. You can help me to while away the time.'

A dark ringlet had strayed across her face. She brushed it aside. 'So now tell me, why is the sea salty? No, wait!' Her eyes sparkled mischievously. 'I think I know: *Once upon a time a king's son was imprisoned in a castle overlooking the sea. As he stood weeping at the window day after day, night after night, his ceaseless tears rained down on the waves until the honey-sweet water of the sea turned salty . . .*'

Florin behaved as if he hadn't heard.

'*Once upon a time,*' he began, '*a mariner rescued a mermaid whose hair had become entangled in some waterweed. In token of her gratitude she gave him a mill that could grind whatever his heart desired. That night, while preparing his supper, he commanded the mill: "Grind me some salt!" The mill did so. When he had enough he cried: "Stop!" But the mill went grinding on. No matter what the good man tried—"As you were!" or "Never again!"—the mill continued to grind, and so . . .*'

IT was late when they ran up the steps. The courtyard was already deep in shadow, and the last rays of the setting sun were illumining a big stone relief over the portal, which Florin had completely failed to notice in his excitement the evening he arrived. Skilfully carved, it showed a lion crushing a wolf beneath its paw.

Theodo has even had his hatred engraved in stone, he thought.

When they dashed into the princess's chamber, panting, the maidservants eyed them curiously from behind the wardrobe door.

'Don't worry,' said Alix. 'Those two would sooner have their hair torn out by the roots than betray me.'

Florin found it thoroughly embarrassing to put on his jester's motley in the presence of the three girls, and the maidservants' titters and covert glances made it no easier. The princess had sat down in front of the mirror with her back to him. One of the maidservants handed her a silver goblet, the other laid out a fresh gown.

'Er, princess . . .' Florin said irresolutely. He wanted to thank Alix for the afternoon in some way. An extempore poem, perhaps?

> *A thousand thanks, princess. This happy day*
> *has driven all my cares and woes away!*

Out of the question. He would never bring himself to say it.

> *The memory of fields and sunshine bright*
> *will sweeten all my lonely dreams tonight.*

No. Impossible.

'Thank you,' he muttered at the door. Alix gave no sign that she had heard him.

———

IN the stable Mimus was waiting for him with a grim expression. 'You didn't practise your songs,' he said sternly. 'Where have you been?'

'I could ask you the same thing,' Florin retorted. Cupping his hand, he scooped some water out of the bucket and drank it thirstily. 'What do you get up to in the afternoons, when you leave me toiling away in here?'

'None of your business,' growled the jester.

'Then it's none of *your* business where I've been,' Florin snapped.

'Very well,' Mimus said curtly, 'sing them to me tomorrow night—after you've ladled out the latrines.'

Florin flew into a rage. 'I've been entertaining Princess Alix on the king's orders. Ask *him* if you don't believe me!'

A look of genuine commiseration appeared on Mimus's face. 'So you've been through the mill like me, my boy. It's a miracle you're still in one piece.'

Florin had ceased to be surprised by anything. 'It could have been worse,' he said. 'Just because she once gave you riding lessons . . . If you want to know, I'd also have liked to see you astride a wild boar.'

'I'm sure you would.' Mimus's eyes narrowed. 'Yes, it's amusing when other people have to play the fool. I myself will be hugely amused tonight, when you sing "The Rooster's Wedding".'

Florin's spirits sank. 'No more animal impressions, please!' he entreated.

The jester remained unmoved. 'You'll bark like a dog, grunt like a hog and neigh like a horse. But don't fret: no one will be able to tell the difference between that and your love songs. Come, it's time to go.'

- THE MESSAGE -

ALL SAINTS' DAY came and went, and Florin was unable even to light a candle for his dead mother. Two days later, when King Theodo held another grand hunting party on the Feast of St. Hubert, all that the occupants of the Monkey Tower heard of it was the clatter of hoofs and the blare of horns. Florin's days and nights, jester's lessons and duties succeeded one another like the ever-recurring steps of a tread-mill. The bright hopes he had cherished after Count Victor's visit grad-ually faded, becoming as feeble as the sun that so seldom appeared in the bleak November sky. As time went by, that nocturnal encounter seemed more and more like a dream. Had the young count really appeared in the stable dressed as a mendicant friar? Had he really bade him be of good cheer and promised to rescue him, or was that memory just a figment of his despairing imagination?

Again and again Florin climbed to the castle roof and scanned the countryside. Although he had no idea what he was looking for, he hoped to discover some clue, some indication that help was at hand.

But no matter how hard he stared in all directions, nothing stirred except the sluggishly flowing river and the omnipresent rooks, whose cawing rang in his ears like derisive laughter.

The soldiers on the roof had long grown used to the sight of him. They laughed when he braved the wind and rain in his thin costume and teased him good-naturedly, but they tolerated his presence.

'Why shouldn't the little fool be foolish?' he heard one of them say to another.

At night the Monkey Tower was beset by howling autumn gales. The wind penetrated its unglazed windows with merciless severity and went whistling through the interior. It was only when Florin developed a cough that Rollo deigned to block up the stable window with some calfskin stretched on a wooden frame.

'Ah, you jesters,' he growled as he did so. 'More sensitive than peacocks, you are. You ought to be housed in a heated aviary.'

'I wouldn't object.' Florin rubbed his hands together, shivering uncontrollably.

'You should be more like my Zito,' the bestiarius said with paternal pride. 'That bear is never ill.'

The next morning he brought Florin a mug of herb syrup as bitter as wormwood.

'Rollo's miraculous elixir,' jeered Mimus. 'It cures horses of colic, bears of diarrhoea, dogs of earache, peacocks of the moult—'

'And malingering jesters of their imaginary ailments!' Rollo put in swiftly.

'It's true.' Mimus rolled his eyes. 'One mug three times a day and you're well again—or dead!'

Florin survived the fearsome beverage—and went on coughing.

With mounting anxiety, he calculated that his father had now been languishing in Theodo's dungeons for upwards of two months. He had no idea what conditions were like in those underground cellars—at Montfield Castle prisoners were held on the upper floor of a watchtower. How long could a person survive down there? What if his father had long ago been stricken by some mortal disease and was lying there alone, deprived of solace and assistance?

Florin's nights were haunted by his dream of the iron dungeon door. It always stood wide open, tempting him to enter and set eyes on his father. But always behind the door lurked an amorphous blackness that draped itself over his face, robbing him of sight and breath and threatening to suffocate him. He awoke from these dreams with a cry, his face wet with tears and his heart racing. Sometimes, as he made the transition from dreaming to wakefulness, he would feel Mimus's hand on his brow. When that happened he refrained from opening his eyes so as not to drive the jester away.

He spent his free afternoons roaming the castle as before. On lucky days he would encounter Benzo. The scullion always had some task to perform—fishing trout out of the pond, fetching clean linen from the washerwomen, replenishing the salt cellars on the royal banqueting table—and he chatted to Florin while going about his work. To Florin those afternoons were like friendly islands in a cold, dark sea. Benzo was no adventurer like Senna, no storyteller like Tanko, and certainly no bosom friend like Radbod, but he was a straightforward, good-natured youngster who didn't care a fig about Florin's cap and bells. Like Florin himself, he seemed glad to have found a friend in the castle.

While looking for Benzo one afternoon, Florin stuck his head round the door of the banqueting hall and saw that the boy wasn't alone. A page was standing beside him, hands on hips in a self-important pose.

'Oh no!' Florin groaned when he recognised Raoul. Slowly and carefully, so that the bells wouldn't betray his presence, he stole nearer.

'So you've no idea who he is, scullion?' he heard Raoul say. 'What has he told you?'

'What should he have told me?' Benzo rejoined. 'I know the king purchased him from a troupe of entertainers, that's why he gave you all such a drubbing.' He grinned delightedly at the recollection.

'You've nothing but pea soup for brains,' said Raoul. 'But perhaps even you soup-stirrers have heard it said that some prisoners from Moltovia are confined in Bellingar's dungeons. The greatest of the great are assembled down there: dukes, counts, barons—even the king himself.'

Florin had heard enough.

'Be silent,' he said sharply, stepping between Raoul and Benzo. 'Your stories are of no interest to anyone.'

'Ah, our young jester,' Raoul scoffed, but he quickly took several paces to the rear before readdressing himself to Benzo. 'Now, kitchen lad, guess who's the son of one of those prisoners?'

In desperation, Florin said: 'The king has forbidden—' and could have bitten his tongue off.

Benzo stared at him wide-eyed. 'So it's true? You're the son of some Moltovian baron?'

'A *baron's* son?' Raoul said with a smirk. 'No, no, Donkey-Ears is a far more exalted creature!'

Florin was within an ace of driving his fist into Raoul's pale, grinning face.

The page could evidently gauge his fury from his expression. 'Farewell then, *Prince* Donkey-Ears,' he said maliciously. He bowed to Florin with exaggerated deference and sauntered off.

Benzo had overturned his sack of salt. The precious grains were trickling out and forming a white mound on the table, but he didn't notice. He had involuntarily retreated a step.

'*Prince* Donkey-Ears?' he repeated. 'Which of the prisoners is your father?'

It was too late now. 'King Philip of Moltovia.'

'I see.' Benzo nodded with a face like stone. 'Of course.' He nodded again. 'A king's son. And I, soup-stirrer that I am, imagined that we two could be friends.' He laughed abruptly. 'I hope you've at least been amused by my simple ways, Your Highness.'

'By all the saints, Benzo, look at me!' Florin gripped the boy's shoulders and shook him. 'Look at me,' he repeated a trifle more calmly. 'Can *you* see any prince?'

Benzo slowly released himself. 'Why didn't you tell me the truth?'

'Because . . .' Florin broke off. Because you're the only person I can talk to, he thought. Because I'd die of loneliness but for you. Because I was afraid you'd turn on your heel. Because I need a friend . . . He shrugged his shoulders mutely.

'For a prince,' Benzo said suddenly, his face breaking into a smile, 'your attire is hardly suitable, is it?'

'No,' said Florin. He could have wept with relief.

'Florin of Moltovia . . .' Benzo spoke the words slowly, as if he had to get used to them. 'And your royal father is really imprisoned in the dungeons here?'

Florin nodded.

Vigorously, Benzo proceeded to shovel the salt back into the sack. 'Don't tell anyone, but my own father went to jail once,' he said. 'He thought he could outwit the tax inspector. After ten days in the debtors' prison he gladly paid his taxes and donated the same sum to the poor.'

He stopped shovelling and looked at Florin. 'Have you any idea what our king intends to do with you?'

'Theodo is holding my father hostage until his dominion over Moltovia is secure.'

'And then?'

'Then he'll have him executed.' Florin was surprised at his calm tone of voice. 'I shall remain his court jester until he tires of me and has me killed, too.' In his head he added bitterly: because no dream hero will come to our rescue.

Pensively, Benzo weighed a little heap of salt in his hand. 'Our gracious king can be quite a snake, eh? I'd salt his soup good and proper if I could, but seasoning dishes is the kitchen-master's prerogative.'

———————

WHEN the message came after all, it did so in a wholly unexpected way. Its bearer was a petitioner at an audience, and in hindsight Florin couldn't even have said what the man looked like. He remembered him only by his footwear: laced-up boots of deerskin.

When the man bowed to Theodo after presenting his request, an odd-looking ball of thread fell from his pocket. He quickly stooped as if to retrieve it, then deliberately brushed it toward Florin with the hem of his cloak.

Having seen this from his place at the king's feet, Florin didn't hesitate for an instant. Even before he'd had a chance to examine the tangled ball of thread more closely, he stuffed it into his pocket.

Mimus raised his eyebrows. 'What do you want with that?' he whispered. 'Have you taken to eating wool?'

Florin didn't look up. His heart beat a furious tattoo in his chest. Had anyone apart from Mimus spotted him? He didn't breathe more easily until the next petitioner, a young woman in white stockings and dainty buckled shoes, bowed to Theodo and began to speak.

The audience followed its usual course. Was it Florin's imagination, or was King Theodo especially impatient today? He shuffled his feet three times in quick succession: the signal for his jesters to jump up and amuse him with all manner of antics. To Florin's relief, Mimus was at his best that day—brimming with ingenious ideas. When a priest came to remind the king that his annual contribution to the upkeep of his church was due, he stealthily severed the stitches in the worthy cleric's breeches, with the result that he displayed his bare backside every time he bowed. As if that were not enough, Mimus turned the head of an honest farmer's wife by paying her compliments and kissing her hand so ardently that she sat down hard on her basketful of eggs.

When he followed this up by cracking the eggs that were still intact and a live mouse emerged from each, the poor woman swooned with fright. Unfeelingly, the jester tipped a pitcher of water over her head, then juggled with all the mice at once. Florin had only to recapture the mice whenever they tried to escape.

The mysterious ball of thread was burning a hole in his pocket throughout this time, but he dared not even touch it. Many hours later, when Theodo dismissed his jesters at last and an exhausted Florin flopped down on the straw, it was so dark that he could only examine his treasure by touch. His fingers encountered twine, knots and beads. What could it be?

Tomorrow, he told himself.

───────────

BY daylight the ball of thread proved to be a single string long enough to go twice across the stable when laid out on the floor. Threaded on it was an assortment of wooden beads: white and black, small, medium-sized and large. Florin walked slowly along the string, completely at a loss. The beads appeared to be located at random intervals. With the best will in the world, he couldn't make head nor tail of their arrangement.

'What are you up to?' asked Mimus, who was busy at the bucket with his sleeves rolled up. Beside him was a bucket of slimy fish bladders.

'Nothing of importance,' Florin replied quickly.

Mimus glanced over his shoulder. 'You picked that up during the audience yesterday,' he said. 'What is it, a necklace for your sweetheart?'

'I don't know,' Florin answered truthfully.

'It looks like a rosary—,' said Mimus, 'a rosary made by a nun who has just tipped three chalices of Communion wine down her pious throat.'

Meditatively, Florin allowed his gaze to roam the length of the string. A rosary . . . Then every large bead would represent a Paternoster and every small one an Ave Maria. But where was the sense in that?

'Leave it.' Mimus kicked the string of beads aside. 'Concentrate on the important things of life.' He thrust a fish bladder into Florin's hand. 'Fill that with water.'

'What for?'

'Can it be that my pious pupil doesn't know what day this is? The most important day in the year—second only to the Feast of St. Anthony, that admirable saint who, as everyone knows, is the friend of all donkeys.'

Florin thought for a moment. The ninth day in All Souls month was sacred to the memory of St. Aurelius of Milan and St. Theodo the Recruit.

'The king is honouring his patron saint, you mean?'

'Yes, and to mark the occasion he has invited all the foremost bishops and abbots in Vinland to a banquet.' Mimus grinned in gleeful anticipation. 'Quite by chance, each of them will have a water-filled bladder under the cushion on his chair.'

Florin gingerly squeezed an empty fish bladder between his fingers. 'Not a drop will penetrate their thick brocaded vestments,' he said. 'I know of a better idea.'

'Hark, hark!' said Mimus. 'Sir Greenhorn knows of a better idea.'

But he watched closely as Florin spat on his hand three times and rubbed the saliva on the fish bladder. 'Now for a straw,' he muttered, stooping to pick one up from the floor. He thrust it carefully into the bladder. 'Now to blow the whole thing up and secure it. Hand me a piece of twine, Mimus.'

Having tied the bladder up tight, Florin deposited it on the floor. 'Sit down,' he said with a gesture of invitation.

Mimus sat down, whereupon the air escaped with a loud farting noise.

The jester was clearly taken with Florin's idea. 'My prince,' he said, 'you amaze me sometimes. Did you ever place such an object on the chair of one of your father's Privy Councillors?'

'I? The Crown Prince of Moltovia? Never!' Florin said with an air of innocence. 'I was always a shining example to all!'

'Even so,' Mimus said gruffly as he watched Florin at work, 'you display remarkable dexterity.'

THAT afternoon, by which time the fish bladders were lying ready in the bucket and Mimus was snoring on the straw, Florin laid out the string once more and pored over it.

In a rosary, each bead represented a prayer. What did these beads represent? Why were some white and some black? Why the different sizes and intervals?

He crouched down and measured the gaps between the beads with his finger. The smallest intervals corresponded to a finger joint, or about an inch; the largest were four times as big. On the ends of the string were two strange objects: threaded on one end was a piece of eggshell, on the other a chicken bone. When Florin examined the eggshell more closely, he saw something scratched into the surface: 'No X.' His bewilderment grew when he made out 'No Z' on the chicken bone.

No X, no Z . . . What of it?

'This message can't be read by its recipient,' he muttered in annoyance. 'How secret can you get?' It was like dangling a honeycomb in front of Zito's muzzle—inside a locked casket. How could he get at the key?

Mimus turned over with a thunderous snore. Their afternoon repose would soon be at an end. Then it would be tomorrow before he got another chance to plumb the mystery of the beads.

Think, Florin, he commanded himself. *Think!* Or have you turned into a donkey already?

He stared intently at the beads until they swam before his eyes—

until he suddenly got the impression that they were moving, forming patterns of black and white . . .

On threads of seaweed we arrange
pearls that each denote a change.

Florin realised only then that these lines had been running through his head the whole time. They were from a song that came into one of Tanko's stories. Far below on the ocean bed, water sprites wove carpets of pearls, and each time they added another pearl the course of history changed, kingdoms arose or declined and sank forever into the abyss. The carpets of pearls were like pages in God's everlasting chronicle of the world, but the writing in which they were inscribed . . .

The realisation transfixed Florin like a shaft of lightning. No X, no Z, but letters! White and black, small, middling and large, the beads were threaded on at different intervals. Could they be a form of writing? How many letters were there in the alphabet?

Holding his breath, Florin reached for his stick of charcoal and proceeded to jot them down on a scrap of parchment: A, B, C, D, E, F . . .

Discounting X and Z, there were twenty-four letters.

Then he started on the beads. Two different colours, three different sizes, four different intervals. Two times three times four . . .

White before black, small before large—the small white beads came first.

Feverishly, he whispered to himself: 'Small white bead one inch apart: A. Small white bead two inches apart: B. Small white bead three inches apart: C. Small white bead four inches apart: D. Medium-sized white bead one inch apart: E. Medium-sized white bead two inches apart: F . . .'

From M onwards the unknown writer of the message must have switched to the black beads—if he were right!

'Large black bead three inches apart: W,' Florin muttered. 'Large black bead four inches apart: X—no, wait, no X or Z, so large black bead four inches apart: Y.'

That gave him the whole alphabet minus X and Z—once again, if he were right!

With a pounding heart he crouched beside the string of beads and began to measure them from the chicken bone end. 'Medium-sized black bead three inches apart: S. Small white bead four inches apart: D . . .'

A little later he was staring at the parchment in disappointment. DRAWTSAE GNIRAOS TI . . . It made no sense at all.

The next moment he smote his brow. 'What a fool I am! Eggshell at the beginning, chicken bone at the end!'

In feverish haste he started on the string from the other end. After twenty-two beads he sat back with a sigh of relief.

'By all the saints,' he whispered, 'how clever I am!' The parchment read:

FLORIN PRINCE OF MOLTOVIA.

'Just imagine,' he said to himself, beaming with delight, 'I've actually done it!'

'Well, hark at the puffed-up cockerel!' Mimus said sleepily from his bed of straw. 'Crowing just because he's found a grain of corn in the straw. Woe betide you if your fish bladders don't fart as they should tonight!'

FLORIN PRINCE OF MOLTOVIA BE OF GOOD CHEER MAKE AN ACCURATE DRAWING OF EVERYTHING BELOW GROUND AND SEND IT SOARING EASTWARD

Everything below ground . . . That could only mean the maze of stair-cases and passages, cellars and dungeons in Bellingar Castle. The sender of the message wanted an accurate representation of them—why? No matter, it was idle to speculate on the purpose of his task; carrying it out would be difficult enough. Whatever happened, he could use an assistant.

The next afternoon Florin marched straight into the kitchen. Before he could attract Benzo's attention, the kitchen-master barred his path.

'What are you doing here?' he grumbled. 'Has the jester sent you here for another dose of punishment?'

'No,' Florin said quickly. 'I'd like a word with Benzo the scullion.'

'So you'd like a word with Benzo the scullion, eh?' the kitchen-master mimicked scornfully. 'Do you imagine scullions have time to chat? Benzo is no sprig of the nobility!' With that, he made to turn on his heel, but Benzo appeared at his side.

'Grant me one hour, master,' he said humbly, wiping his hands on his smock. 'I promise I'll do the early morning shift tomorrow.'

The kitchen-master gave an ill-humoured shrug.

'God help you if you don't get out of bed,' he growled. 'You have to work for your daily bread, unlike this buffoon here. No roast pigeons fly into *your* mouth at the drop of a hat!'

Florin indignantly opened his mouth to protest, but Benzo tugged at his sleeve.

'Come with me,' he said quietly, 'I know of a place where we can talk in peace.'

Not far from the kitchen, he led the way into a small, dark chamber filled from floor to ceiling with junk.

Florin stared open-mouthed. 'What *is* this place, by all the saints?' he asked.

'We call it the kitchen sepulchre,' Benzo told him. 'Nobody needs this old rubbish now that our gracious monarch has had the new kitchen built, but the chamberlain would rather give away one of his children than discard what belongs to the king.'

Florin's eyes roamed over the pitted copper cauldrons, crack-ed wooden troughs, rusty spits and gridirons. The place really did resemble a tomb for discarded objects.

'Now listen, Benzo,' he said, coming straight to the point. 'I have a mission to accomplish here in the castle. It's not easy and not without danger. Will you help me?'

'No,' Benzo said bluntly.

Florin tried again. 'I'm appointing you my squire, my ally, my comrade in arms. That's a great honour.'

'I'm sure it is,' Benzo said drily. 'An honour for a donkey. I've no wish to be a hero.'

'Benzo,' Florin said coaxingly, 'I'll teach you to fence. Anyone who picks a fight with you will get the shock of his life.'

'What am I to fence with?' Benzo said irresolutely, but the fish was already wriggling on the hook. 'I have no sword—not even a jester's bauble.'

With a grin, Florin pointed to the heaps of rusty junk around them. 'But you've any number of spits.'

'When would we start these fencing lessons?' Benzo asked casually. Florin was secretly amused by the unmistakable eagerness in his voice.

'As soon as you've helped me to reconnoitre the castle cellars.'

Benzo looked genuinely horrified. 'What for?'

'I'm sure you've always wanted to see the treasures and wonders they contain, haven't you?'

'No, by the Holy Virgin!' Benzo had turned pale. 'I've had a fear of dark cellars,' he said plaintively, 'ever since I fell into an open grave as a little boy. I was down there for one whole day and a night. A person remembers such things for the rest of his days.'

Florin made no comment. He picked up a spit, tested the tip with his finger, and launched into a lightning display of swordsmanship. Benzo watched him with shining eyes.

'We'll go down there tomorrow afternoon,' he said firmly. 'And the day after that we'll do some fencing.'

MIMUS had only just left the stable the next afternoon, leaving Florin to memorise ninety-nine wise proverbs, when he hurled the parchment scroll into a corner and hurried to the kitchen sepulchre.

Benzo was already waiting. Florin had to suppress a grin at the sight of him. Over his grubby smock the kitchen lad was wearing a kind of breastplate which he had obviously woven from willow shoots. At his side, carefully sharpened and polished, hung a spit.

'How did you escape the kitchen-master?' Florin asked.

'The early morning shift,' Benzo replied with a shrug. 'One of us has to start work at midnight—fetch water, sharpen the knives, stoke the bread ovens so they're ready for baking in the morning . . . If I volunteer for that job I get the afternoon off. Mark you,' he added with a long, cavernous yawn, 'it leaves me mighty weary.'

'Let's go, then,' Florin urged him, 'before you fall asleep.'

Benzo plucked at Florin's costume. 'How do you propose to sneak along the passages sounding like a tambourine?'

Florin stared at him, thunderstruck. He hadn't thought of that.

'Wait,' Benzo said suddenly, and ran off in the direction of the kitchen. He returned carrying a small wooden keg. 'Old mutton fat,' he explained. 'No one'll miss it. We'll silence your bells with that.'

While they were smearing the bells with fat, Florin couldn't resist sticking a fingerful in his mouth. Benzo watched him with a mixture of horror and admiration.

'You should pray to St. Agatha,' he said. 'She's the patron saint of the starving.' He gave a satisfied nod: Florin's bells no longer made the smallest sound. 'Where's your lamp?'

'Er . . . There isn't one in the Monkey Tower,' Florin said sheepishly.

'It's lucky *I* have one, then.' Benzo fished a small tallow lamp out of his smock pocket and lit it with a tinderbox.

They set off down the stairs to the cellars. It grew darker with every step, until, on reaching the bottom, they found themselves in pitch blackness.

'And now,' Benzo said in a strained voice, 'what are we doing down here in the bowels of the earth?' Lit from below by the tallow lamp's flickering light, his face looked ghostly pale.

Florin, too, had an uneasy sensation in the pit of his stomach. They couldn't afford to run into Master Antonius or the guards, not at any price. Besides, he thought, how was he to produce an accurate representation of Bellingar's cellars? That time when Chancellor Benedict made a drawing of the five kingdoms, it was as if he'd had a bird's eye view of Frankenland, Vinland, Moltovia, Arelia and Angelland. Florin would now have to do the same with the cellars. He wondered briefly how Benedict had known the respective sizes and shapes of the five kingdoms. After all, you couldn't pace the length and breadth of an entire country as you would a room.

He produced a sheet of parchment and a stick of charcoal from his pocket.

'Listen, Benzo,' he said in a low voice. 'Can you light the walls and floor of every cellar with your lamp?'

'If that's all I have to do,' Benzo said gruffly. 'You need only haul me back if I run off screaming.'

It proved a wearisome task. Bellingar's innumerable underground passages and vaulted chambers branched off in all directions like the roots of an ancient tree. The castle garrison used most of the cellars as storerooms, so Benzo and Florin had to climb over mountains of stone cannon balls and barrels of pitch, creep on their bellies beneath wooden catapults and battering rams, and squeeze with bated breath past sharp-toothed iron mantraps.

Every bend, every closed door sent icy fingers of terror down Florin's spine. He expected to come upon the torture chamber or the dungeons at any moment. At his heels, Benzo mumbled a monotonous litany of saints that seemed to give him courage.

The doors of many of the cellars bore heavy padlocks. Peering through the bars, they made out barrels, baskets, stone jars and wooden chests.

Benzo identified them at a glance. 'Storerooms,' he said. 'The chamberlain keeps them as securely locked as our gracious king keeps his treasure chambers.'

Florin paced out each cellar in turn and faithfully recorded its dimensions on the parchment, together with a note of its contents and special features.

'Small, round, vaulted chamber. Empty save for rat droppings.'

'Large vaulted chamber containing some three dozen wine casks. Three ventilation holes in the wall.'

'Small, low-ceilinged chamber filled with pikes and spears.'

He was also careful to put in all the staircases, doors and connecting passages.

Benzo held the lamp for him to draw by, trying in vain to warm his hands at it. 'I'll freeze to death if you don't make haste,' he complained. 'It's as cold down here as it was that time in the grave.'

His words pierced Florin like a dagger. He and Benzo had been at work for an hour at most, but already the cold was agonising. King Philip and his men had been buried alive in this icy tomb for over two months. How much cold and darkness could a person endure?

It was as if Florin's thoughts had guided his steps. Stealing down a flight of stairs, he found the passage ahead of him lit by sconces. Warned by some sinister premonition, he cautiously opened a door—and gulped at the sight of the spacious vaulted chamber with its stone forest of columns.

'What's the matter?' Benzo whispered behind him. 'Why not go in?'

As slowly and cautiously as his jangling nerves permitted, Florin shut the door again.

'Two dozen guards, Master Antonius and his torturer's assistants, and beyond them the dungeons,' Florin enumerated softly. 'All behind this door. Do you still want to enter?'

Instead of replying, Benzo resumed his litany of saints at twice the speed.

Florin strove to reassure himself as they tiptoed on. Perhaps the prisoners had been given coats or blankets. Perhaps the iron door admitted some warmth from Master Antonius's fire. After all, Theodo had no wish to let King Philip freeze to death and deprive himself of the pleasure of an execution.

Concern for his father was bound up with another worry: the dungeons formed part of the castle's cellars, but how was he to draw them on his plan if he couldn't get near them?

Deep in thought, he suddenly heard voices and footsteps approaching.

'Quick, Benzo, blow out the lamp,' he hissed. 'We must hide—go on, in there!' Swiftly, he hustled Benzo down a side passage. They waited with pounding hearts and bated breath for the detachment of guards to go past.

'I don't think we've been here before,' Benzo said when he'd rekindled his lamp.

Florin consulted his plan. Then he nodded. 'We must have overlooked this passage on our way downstairs.'

The passage was flanked to left and right by four doors. Wooden tables and benches were stacked in the first cellar, nets and bales of cloth in the second. The third contained nothing but cobwebs and rats' nests. When Florin opened the last door, however, he froze in astonishment.

Before him lay a large vaulted chamber brightly illuminated by a dozen huge candles. These were arranged on either side of a block of black granite on which lay something that Florin mistook at first glance for a tree trunk: a leather sack fastened with cord, the brown hide cracked and mildewed. Not until he had plucked up the courage to go nearer did he perceive that the sack wasn't empty. Clearly visible beneath the leather were the outlines of a human figure: skull, rib cage, pelvis, arm and thigh bones. As he stared at it, a memory surfaced in his mind: *In a leather shroud* . . . Where had he heard those words before?

He looked round, shivering. On the end wall was a large red tapestry of Vinland's heraldic lion. Behind the granite block was a marble altar bearing a sumptuous bejewelled cross of solid gold. It was clear that prayers were often said here, for the red velvet of the prie-dieu was badly worn, but the floor round the granite block was adorned with flowers—fresh white lilies! How on earth did anyone procure flowering lilies in the everlasting month of November?

Florin turned to Benzo. By the light of the candles he saw that his friend was pale as death and his hair stood on end.

'This . . . is a tomb,' Benzo stammered.

Florin pointed to the leather sack. 'Complete with a dead body.'

Benzo shrank back in terror. 'Let us go, Florin,' he pleaded.

'Wait,' Florin said absently. Drawing a heavy velvet curtain aside, he discovered a narrow spiral staircase behind it. He crept up the stairs on tiptoe—and found himself back in the castle chapel, just beside the stairs leading to the gallery. Father Anselm was reading his prayer book in front of the altar.

Florin withdrew as silently as he could.

———————

'WELCOME, you grimy imp,' said Mimus.

Startled, Florin looked down at himself. In his excitement, he'd completely forgotten to wash on returning from the underworld— he'd dashed back into the stable without thinking. His jester's motley was thick with dust and soot, and mutton fat was oozing from the bells.

'No, don't tell me,' Mimus went on. 'Let me guess: the king's little daughter dipped you in a barrel of fat and then made you dance in the fireplace. Am I right?'

'Er . . . something of the kind,' Florin mumbled. He was so relieved, he could have jumped for joy.

The jester pointed to the bucket of water. 'You have one hourglass in which to turn yourself from a wild boar into a spruce little donkey. The king is entertaining some guests tonight, and you're to show off your monkey pyramid.'

While Florin was toiling away with a scrubbing brush and ice-cold water, he said pensively: 'What are they like, I wonder, the dungeons beyond Master Antonius's iron door?'

'They're the height of comfort,' Mimus replied promptly. 'A number of cosy little chambers on either side of a central passage.'

Florin was astonished. 'How do you know?'

'Because my magical eyes can see through walls and doors,' Mimus whispered mysteriously. 'Look!'

He pressed both thumbs into his eye sockets. When he removed them his eyeballs had turned inward so far that only the whites were visible. He was a weird sight.

'Doesn't that hurt?' Florin asked.

'You'll see,' the jester replied cheerfully. 'I'll teach you how to do it tomorrow morning.'

THE next afternoon Florin crouched down behind the firewood shed on the castle roof and drew in the dungeons on his plan just as Mimus had described them.

Then he ran a critical eye over his finished handiwork. Some of the chambers were too big, others too small. Many passages were either too wide or too narrow, nearly all the lines were skewed and crooked, and his hurriedly scribbled notes were almost illegible. He shrugged his shoulders. It would have to suffice.

Very carefully, he folded the stiff parchment into a dart. How fortunate that Sturmius, his efficient but oft-derided bodyguard, was a master of the art of fashioning darts out of parchment!

When he launched his dart over the battlements and sent it soaring eastward, it was caught by a gust of wind and carried far out across the fields. He could only just see it when it landed, a tiny speck that stood out white against the dark surrounding soil.

What if it rained tonight? If so, the charcoal drawing would simply be washed off. What if a badger used the parchment to line its burrow?

He shook his head reprovingly. FLORIN, PRINCE OF MOLTOVIA, BE OF GOOD CHEER—that was how the encoded message had begun. All he could do now was to put his faith in God. And in his unknown saviour.

– THE RENEGADES –

WHEN NEXT THEY met in the kitchen sepulchre, Benzo's cheeks had regained their normal colour.

'And now,' he said happily, 'I'm going to learn how to fence.'

With an expression which conveyed that he was presenting Florin with a suit of glittering gold armour, he produced a second basket-work breastplate from behind his back. 'I made this last night.' He beamed at Florin. 'It's for you!'

'Thank you,' said Florin, buckling on the breastplate, which made him feel like a human birdcage.

'Can you count?' he asked.

Benzo nodded proudly. 'On all my fingers and toes.'

'Then pay attention.' Florin selected a rusty spit from the pile and took up his position. 'On the count of one, you take a step forward. On two, you extend your arm. On three, you lunge. On four, you recover. All clear? Very well: One . . . two . . . three . . . Hey!'

He retreated just in time to prevent Benzo from thrusting his spit through the basketwork at chest level.

'Am I doing it right?'

'Er, wait,' Florin said quickly. 'Let's use wooden spoons to start with. It's customary,' he added, seeing the look of disappointment on Benzo's face. 'We only fenced with sticks, even at the royal school of knighthood.'

He was thoroughly grateful for this white lie by the end of the lesson, because Benzo was so impetuous that he would more than once have skewered him with the spit despite his basketwork breast-plate.

'When I think—' Benzo said dreamily as he gathered up the splin-tered remains of his wooden spoon, 'when I think that I shall one day be able to do what you can do . . . Everyone will knuckle under to me. I'll be the king of the scullions!'

Before returning to the jesters' stable Florin ran quickly upstairs to Brother's chamber, where he had hidden the string of beads behind a loose stone in the wall. He took it out and ran it through his fingers.

'You see, Brother, it's true,' he said to the wolf, which had slunk into a corner as usual. 'I didn't dream it.'

Mimus had just finished his afternoon nap when Florin returned to their stable and was bending over the bucket of water. 'By the way,' he said casually, sluicing his face, 'tonight's guests will be to your taste.'

Something in his voice aroused Florin's suspicions. 'Who are they?'

'Some noblemen from your country. They're eager to pay homage to Theodo as their new king. *Gifts and favours*, remember?'

'The miserable traitors,' Florin muttered.

'How harsh of you, my prince,' Mimus said in a tone of mild reproof. 'Rather call them men who have learnt to wave their little flags with the wind, not against it. You might consider doing like-wise.' He gave Florin a searching stare. 'The king desires you to be a truly model fool tonight. He wishes his guests to laugh heartily at you.'

Florin had turned pale. 'So I'm to make an ass of myself in front of a bunch of traitors?'

'That's precisely what Theodo has in mind,' the jester told him cheerfully. At the thought of appearing in cap and bells in front of those renegades, Florin succumbed to a bout of despair. Whoever they were, they would recognise him—they would jeer at him in company with their treacherous, lying host . . .

'What will you give me,' Mimus asked suddenly, 'if I help you to make the laughter stick in their throats?'

Involuntarily, Florin looked down at himself. 'What *could* I give you?' he asked with a shrug. 'I've nothing to give.'

'The next three tidbits Theodo throws you,' the jester said bluntly.

Florin hesitated. He thought of the evenings when the jesters received not a crumb from the king's table, and of the nights thereafter, when hunger gnawed at his vitals like a ravenous beast. But tormenting though those nights were, it was far more tormenting to be the helpless butt of mockery and derision. He gave a resolute nod.

'A wise decision indeed,' Mimus said approvingly. With a conspiratorial air, as if divulging a highly effective magic spell, he handed Florin a sheet of parchment. 'You must learn this by heart before tonight,' he whispered.

'You've duped me,' said Florin. 'You'd have given me this parchment in any case.'

The jester grinned sardonically. 'And behold, the child grew and waxed strong in spirit, filled with wisdom. My lessons are already bearing fruit. Your fellow countrymen will be awestruck at your sagacity.'

THEY'LL laugh me to scorn, Florin thought as they waited to make their entrance in the lee of the pillar. They'll scoff and jeer and run their hands over their newfound riches. Will one of them be the new master of Montfield Castle?

The king was seated with his usual circle of close advisers round

him. A second table set with golden plates and goblets was still unoc-
cupied. Riccardo was sitting, proud and erect, beside his royal father.
The sight of him filled Florin with sadness. He could guess exactly how
the crown prince was feeling from the few times when he himself had
been privileged to attend an important banquet with his own father.
Since then he had come to abominate all banquets.

'The same thing seen from above or below is far from the same,'
he murmured.

'How true,' Mimus whispered beside him. 'Take Marsus: from
above a silver decanter; from below a chamberpot.'

Stationed in the doorway, the master of ceremonies solemnly
rapped the floor with his staff of office. 'Princes and noblemen of
Moltovia!' he announced.

'By all means let them enter,' King Theodo called in high good
humour.

Florin had firmly resolved to feel nothing but chill disdain at the
sight of the renegades, but he couldn't help it: every name the master
of ceremonies called out pierced him like a needle. He knew them all:
Duke Markward, whose huge estate lay in the north of Moltovia;
Counts Odo and Ivo, two quarrelsome brothers who had often come
before the royal court of arbitration; powerful Duke Vibert and his
two grown-up sons; white-haired Baron Valbland, a fearsome warrior
despite his one eye . . .

Just as they now approached the throne in their costly, fur-
trimmed robes and humbly bowed to Theodo, so they had once sworn
loyalty and allegiance to Florin's father.

'Count Tillo,' the master of ceremonies announced.

Florin's self-control nearly snapped. He hadn't thought of
the count for many a day, but now, as he looked at that scarred,
well-remembered face, he began to seethe with fury. How friendly
Count Tillo had seemed, and how coldly, smilingly, he had betrayed
him!

'Judas,' Florin hissed, and his bells tinkled loudly. 'Did Theodo at least pay you thirty pieces of—'

'Hush!' Mimus nudged him. 'Or do you wish to visit Master Antonius?'

Florin leant against the pillar, trembling with rage. To regain his composure he shut his eyes and breathed deeply. What a bunch of villains! And in a few moments Theodo would mockingly introduce him to them as Prince Donkey-Ears. It didn't bear thinking of!

He was so agitated, he paid no further attention to what was happening in the banqueting hall—until, all at once, some words came loudly and distinctly to his ears above the general hum of conversation.

'My king, your invitation honours us greatly.'

At the sound of that voice Florin felt as if boiling pitch had been poured down his throat. Opening his eyes, he saw a man and a youth bowing respectfully to Theodo.

'Count Essrin,' Theodo said with an engaging smile, 'welcome to Bellingar Castle. Your visit gives me particular pleasure.'

Count Essrin bowed still lower, thrusting the boy beside him forward. 'My son Radbod.'

'Excellent.' The king nodded. 'The crown prince—' he pointed to Riccardo with unmistakable pride, 'is of the same age. Your son could become his equerry. Kindly take your places and be my guests.'

As if in a bad dream, Florin watched father and son being conducted to the guests' table by a page. It was Radbod beyond a doubt—Radbod with his tousled fair hair and thin, earnest face. How sorely he had missed his friend, and now he was a guest of honour at Theodo's table!

The banquet was carried in by an endless procession of maidservants and footmen. The tables positively groaned under expensive gold platters, glass decanters set with precious stones, and an abundance of choice dishes that would have satisfied several times the number of guests.

Florin knew that the court of Vinland usually dined off pewter plates and drank from plain silver goblets. An elaborate display like tonight's banquet sent an unmistakable message to the renegades from Moltovia: you have done right to side with mighty King Theodo, a monarch who enjoys God's favour for all the world to see.

One of the bishops said grace. Then Chancellor Benedict rose, contorting his sharp-featured, ratlike face into a gracious smile. 'In token of His Majesty's favour, the crown prince will now distribute gifts among his guests.'

As Riccardo went from guest to guest bearing a velvet cushion, the wealthy Moltovians' eyes glittered with greed. Florin felt ashamed of his countrymen. Then he looked more closely at the velvet cushion and gave a gasp.

'Do you know what he's doing?' He nudged Mimus in the ribs, beside himself with fury. 'He's presenting our hunting knives to those vultures! Look at the wolf engraved on the hilts!'

'Hush!' Mimus hissed.

When Riccardo had returned to his father's side, King Theodo raised his goblet. 'A toast, honoured guests from Moltovia!' he cried amiably.

Duke Vibert rose to his feet. 'Let us drink to our future king,' he said. 'Our salvation, our blessing, our rising sun—our harbinger of a new age.'

'By the holy quill,' Mimus whispered in disgust, 'he sounds for all the world like Haedus Venerabilis. Do all Moltovians speak in such a fashion?'

'Only the braggarts and windbags among them,' Florin said bitterly.

Count Tillo rose in his turn. 'Let us drink to peace,' he said, and the scar writhed along his cheek. 'To peace between Vinland and Moltovia. Under your unifying dominion, my king, both kingdoms will enjoy good fortune and prosperity. God's blessing will be with us all!'

The words pierced Florin to the quick. How fine they sounded, and how final! *It will be as if your pestilential family had never existed!* Why did his rescuers remain invisible, while these traitors sat before him in person?

'I've had enough of this hot air,' Mimus said beside him. 'Come, my prince, into the fray!' So saying, he seized Florin's arm and dragged him over to the throne.

'My sweet king,' he called to Theodo, 'have a care! Honey trickling into your ear lures wasps and bumblebees into your head!'

He bowed to Duke Vibert and Count Tillo with mock reverence.

'Welcome, thrice noble honey-tricklers!' he lisped, then broke into song:

> *'A glorious place is the king's backside,*
> *where many a nobleman likes to reside.*
> *A royal backside is the finest of all,*
> *so into its depths would I willingly crawl!'*

The guests from Moltovia were unfamiliar with court jesters. Florin saw their faces register the same mixture of disgust and fascination that he himself had felt on first seeing Mimus. No one had yet recognised him in his cap and bells.

'Well, little Mimus,' Theodo said amiably, 'won't you, too, welcome the gentlemen from Moltovia? Come closer!'

'Prince Florin!' No, they didn't laugh him to scorn. Instead, they gazed at him with undisguised horror. 'This is barbarous!' he heard Duke Vibert whisper. Count Tillo had bowed his head, but Radbod, white as a sheet, was staring at Florin as if he'd seen a ghost.

'What ails you, my noble guests?' King Theodo inquired, watching them intently. 'Doesn't my little jester find favour with you? He still requires a good deal of training, it's true, but he's a thoroughly talented little fellow.' He clicked his fingers. 'Come, little Mimus, show the gentlemen what you can do!'

Florin felt the blood rush to his cheeks as he trembled all over with suppressed fury. He didn't regain his self-control until Mimus suddenly croaked like a frog beside him—indeed, he even managed to grin faintly. The jester had selected an apt fable for him to recount.

'Hearken to my story, good sirs,' he began. So as not to have to look at Radbod or Count Tillo, he fastened his gaze on portly Duke Vibert.

'Once upon a time, the frogs in a pond had a king. He ruled over his subjects just as other frog kings did, neither better nor worse, until, one night, a handful of them began to murmur loudly.

"What a wretched life we lead in this pond!" they croaked. "Let us leave here and find a better one!"

Their croaking was overheard by a snake in the pond next door. "Make me your king," it hissed coaxingly, "and I will show you something you've never seen before!"

The frogs were foolish enough to yield to the snake's whispered entreaties. They promptly drowned their old king and set the snake on his throne the very same day. The snake began its reign just as promptly—by devouring its subjects one after another.

"Alas!" the frogs lamented. "We allowed ourselves to be deceived!"

"Why complain?" the snake retorted with a struggling frog's leg dangling from its jaws. "Your wish was fulfilled. Had any of you ever before seen a serpent's mouth from the inside?"'

Florin bowed low before the Moltovians' table. 'Rejoice, good sirs! You are not like those foolish frogs, for you know all too well what a serpent's mouth looks like, with its forked tongue and poisonous fangs. Never will a greedy, sneaking serpent succeed in luring *you* to your doom with *gifts and favours*!'

'Now tell me,' King Theodo asked his guests, 'doesn't my little jester have some droll tales to tell?' His expression was serene, but Florin involuntarily wondered if the fable would cost him dearly.

Still smiling, the king held out a leg of roast chicken. 'Here,' he said coaxingly, as he would to a dog, 'come and get it!'

Florin stood rooted to the spot. In the silence that fell he heard someone at the Moltovians' table—was it Radbod?—utter a faint groan.

'What's the matter, little Mimus?' Theodo demanded in a mocking tone. 'As a rule, you pounce on every morsel.'

'Your Majesty,' said Duke Vibert, rising ponderously to his feet, 'this morning I swore allegiance to you. I now venture to ask a favour of you.'

'Your request is as good as granted,' King Theodo said graciously.

'Set the prince free.'

Florin couldn't believe his ears. Duke Vibert glanced at him, betraying an emotion he found hard to interpret. Was it pity? Affection?

'Let me take the boy home with me,' the duke went on. 'He will never prove an obstacle to your dominion over Moltovia, I'll stake my life on it.'

Looking at him, Florin felt a faint flicker of hope. Then he turned to the king, and the spark was instantly extinguished.

Theodo looked from Duke Vibert to Florin with feigned astonishment. 'I see no prince here, noble duke, do you? You waste your request on a empty-headed donkey.' He turned to Mimus. 'Or am I wrong, old fool? Has a prince been dwelling in your stable of late?'

'Well . . .' Mimus pretended to have to consider the question. 'It's said that, if treated appropriately, frogs have turned into princes before now.' He shook his long ears. 'But I've never heard the same thing said of donkeys.'

Theodo turned back to Duke Vibert. 'You heard that, worthy duke?' His face hardened. 'No prince, no favour!'

The duke had bowed his head. 'Very well, my king.'

'But wait, noble sirs,' cried Mimus. 'I'll box my young assistant's ears a few times. If by some miracle he turns into a prince, I'll inform you without delay.'

So saying, he hauled Florin into the lee of the pillar and cuffed him hard.

'That was my chicken leg by rights!' he growled angrily.

Florin flushed—he'd completely forgotten about their bargain. 'Surely you understand,' he said quickly. 'I couldn't, not in front of those—'

'What do I care about your stupid princely pride?' Mimus interrupted brusquely. 'You've deprived me of a chicken leg, you conceited dunderhead! Do you know when I last had such a delicacy between my teeth? This will cost you an extra tidbit!'

Florin almost lost his temper but thought better of it. The magnitude of the jester's disappointment was only too clear to him.

'Mimus,' Theodo called from his throne, 'come here—sing us a merry song.'

'Don't budge an inch!' the jester hissed to Florin. He bounded out in front of the banqueting tables and broke into song, accompanying himself on the tambourine:

> 'Two hungry carp lived in a mere,
> a husband and a wife.
> Said she to him, "I love you, dear,
> far better than my life."
> Said he to her, "That's good to know,
> because I long to sup
> on tender, tasty carp." And so
> he swiftly ate her up.'

Several of those present joined in the song or clapped in time to it. Everyone's attention was focused on the jester. Florin leant back against the pillar with a sigh of relief. Almost simultaneously he felt a hand on his shoulder.

'Florin,' Radbod whispered. Florin shook his hand off with an indignant jerk.

'Florin,' Radbod repeated. 'Speak to me, please!'

Florin's throat was so tight he could hardly breathe. He had yearned to see his friends all these long, comfortless weeks, and now Radbod was standing behind him. He would have liked to turn and give his friend a hug. Instead, he concentrated on keeping his confounded bells quiet.

'Do you imagine I enjoy sitting at Theodo's table in the role of a traitor's son?' Radbod asked sadly. 'I'm so ashamed, I'm at my wits' end. How can I ever look you in the face again?'

Florin slowly turned round. 'You'll doubtless be spared that embarrassment again,' he said coldly. 'Is your father the new master of Montfield Castle?'

He experienced an almost physical pain when Radbod leant against the pillar close beside him. His friend was so near, he had only to stretch out his hand to touch him. At the same time, he was as far away as if an ocean lay between them.

'You haven't heard, then?' Radbod said in a strangely unsteady voice. 'Montfield Castle no longer exists. It was razed to the ground at Theodo's behest.'

Florin forgot himself and seized Radbod's hand. 'And our forest? The hideaway?'

'Everything has been burnt to ashes for five miles around.'

Florin was appalled to feel tears spring to his eyes. Desperate for any way of venting his emotions, he threw caution to the winds and started to berate Radbod.

'Go away! Out of my sight!' he snapped. 'I want nothing to do with traitors like you and your fine father!'

Radbod cringed as if his face had been slapped, but Florin didn't care. Wild, vengeful rage coursed through him.

'You called yourselves our friends!' he said loudly and distinctly. 'Leeches would have been a better name for you—leeches fattening yourselves on our royal blood. Vile, blood-sucking parasites who—'

Theodo's voice broke in like a whiplash: 'Come here, little Mimus!'

Florin cast a last contemptuous glance at Radbod before he approached the throne with his head held high.

'How dare you insult my guests!' Theodo barked. 'Down on your knees this minute and beg their forgiveness!'

'Never!' Florin retorted, wild with rage.

The next instant Mimus had appeared beside him and was relentlessly forcing him to his knees. 'Noble lords of Moltovia, I most humbly beg your pardon,' he said in Florin's boyish voice, gripping his chin with steely fingers and opening and shutting his mouth as if Florin himself were speaking. 'It will never happen again.' Then he forcibly swivelled Florin's head in Theodo's direction. 'I beg *your* pardon too, dearest king,' he lisped. 'I'll be an obedient little donkey from this day forth.'

Theodo's black scowl persisted for a moment longer. Then he threw back his head and roared with laughter. Florin heard Mimus sigh with relief.

'That's more to my liking, little Mimus,' the king said. 'I wish all disobedient servants could be brought to heel as easily.'

'Alas, my king, the trick only succeeds with donkeys,' said Mimus, releasing Florin. 'With wolves it fails.'

'What does the jester mean?' Florin heard Duke Vibert whisper.

'Droll guests you have at your table, my king,' said Mimus. 'They take pity on little donkeys. Wolves, on the other hand, they allow to perish with a heartless smile.' Abruptly, he broke into song again:

> 'My purse is empty, lackaday!
> Ah, would that I could fill it.
> My honour is worth little, but
> right willingly I'd sell it.'

'Well, noble sirs from Moltovia, how say you? If your royal wolf is slain, will you not dice for his hide?'

'What is all this nonsense?' Count Essrin demanded angrily.

Mimus promptly changed the subject. 'Now hearken, honoured sirs,' he cried, 'to the highly dramatic tale of the stork, clack-clack, and the frog, croak-croak. There once was a stork, clack-clack, that went strutting along a riverbank. It caught sight of a frog, croak-croak, and lunged at it, but its beak stuck fast in the mud.'

He lapsed into silence.

'Well,' said Theodo, 'what happened next?'

'That I cannot tell you,' Mimus replied sadly, 'until the stork has extricated its beak from the mud.'

AGAIN and again the Vinlanders and their Moltovian guests drained their goblets to a glorious future and toasted Theodo as monarch of them all. It was long past midnight when he finally signalled the end of the banquet by turning his goblet upside down.

While the guests were taking their leave of him with many a tipsy compliment, Radbod stole back to the pillar.

'Florin,' he whispered hurriedly, 'I know you won't believe me, but listen. Something big is underway: a secret alliance against Theodo. Your uncle Guido, many Moltovian and Arelian noblemen, Senna and his father—they all belong to it. They're sparing no effort to get you out of here, but for heaven's sake mention it to no one, it could cost them their heads.' He glanced at his father with loathing. 'Not every Moltovian is a traitor,' he said bitterly. 'Many have remained steadfastly loyal to you and your father at the risk of their property, their freedom or their lives. By God,' he said, clenching his fists and gritting his teeth, 'if only I were a few years older!'

'Radbod!' Count Essrin called sharply from the doorway.

'I'm coming, father!'

Although Radbod's unhappy, despairing farewell glance wrung Florin's heart, he turned his back on him without a word.

They returned to the stable in silence. It wasn't until Mimus had stretched out on the straw with a contented grunt that Florin asked: 'Are you still vexed with me on account of that chicken leg?'

'Prick up your ears,' said the jester. 'The source of those growls is neither Zito nor Brother, but my poor betrayed stomach!'

'I wish I could serve you a whole roast capon,' Florin said remorsefully. 'You truly deserve one. But for you, the night would have ended badly for me.'

'No doubt,' Mimus replied in a sleepy voice. 'Your reckless, scatterbrained behaviour will send us both to the devil's kitchen yet.' The straw rustled as he turned to look at Florin. 'That sprig of the nobility was a friend of yours, wasn't he?'

'So I thought until today,' Florin said bitterly.

'At all events,' Mimus remarked in a self-congratulatory tone, 'the fable of the frogs and the snake was well chosen. Did you see the look on the guests' faces?'

Florin uttered his secret fear aloud: 'Will the king send me to Master Antonius for it?'

'No,' Mimus said firmly. 'It was your right as a court jester to speak as you did.'

'I don't understand,' said Florin. 'I break a ridiculous jester's rule and forget some stupid ditty, and I'm punished. I'm impertinent to the king's face, and nothing happens.'

'Little Mimus, you've still a lot to learn.' The jester yawned. 'Now go to sleep.'

– IN THE DUNGEONS –

THERE SEEMED TO be a point beyond which the human spirit simply rejects an overabundance of misfortune, just as the surface of a frozen pond refuses to absorb a shower of rain. Florin knew that Montfield Castle and his friendship with Radbod lay in ruins, but the knowledge failed to break his heart, which was protected by a thick layer of ice. In some strange way he was even relieved not to have to picture his home occupied by strangers.

To his surprise, moreover, something was stirring within him: a resurgence of courage. Count Victor's visit had not been a dream; Radbod's words and the string of beads proved it. They had not been forgotten. Something was happening out there—something of which Theodo, that royal oath-breaker, knew nothing.

Florin's newfound hopes revived his spirit of initiative. The image of the iron dungeon door still tormented him at night, but in one of his next dreams he saw, for the very first time, a glimmer of light beyond it. He sat up with a start, he was so surprised, but soon went back to sleep. How comforting that chink of light had been! When he awoke at dawn, even before Rollo had come to rouse them, he lay quite still and turned the dream over in his mind. He now knew what he had to do.

'Pay me another visit sometime,' Master Antonius had called after him that terrible night. 'Little jokesters are always welcome here.'

Antonius had still been holding the whip with which he'd thrashed him like a dog—no wonder the words had sounded to Florin like sheer mockery. Now, however, the invitation had taken on a new significance. If he wanted to see his father, Master Antonius would provide the key.

That afternoon, when Mimus left him to his own devices, Florin resolutely made for the cellars. Although he had no lamp with him, his feet seemed to find their own way down the stairs and along the gloomy passages until he was confronted by the well-remembered chamber containing the forest of stone columns. He drew a deep breath, then marched boldly across it.

The guards on duty outside the first iron door barred his path.

'Master Antonius is expecting me,' he said hurriedly. 'He wishes me to amuse him.'

'Tell me another,' said one of the guards, shaking his head. 'Little Mimus come to pay Master Antonius a visit? Since when does a mouse throw itself into the jaws of a snake?'

'He's expecting me,' Florin repeated, only just suppressing an urge to panic. 'Ask him yourself!'

The guard growled something and disappeared inside.

'Very well,' he said when he returned, 'in you go. I trust you've said your prayers to the Holy Virgin and all the saints.'

Once more Florin saw the blazing fire, the gridiron with the leather straps, the bench on which he'd been whipped. Once more he saw the tongs and pincers arrayed on the wall and inhaled the pungent smell of iron and leather.

This is madness! cried a voice in his head. *Turn round!*

But Master Antonius was already coming toward him.

'Welcome, little Mimus,' he called, as he had the first time. 'What brings you to the underworld?'

Florin gazed fixedly at the inner door. It looked different from the one in his dreams, paler and equipped with iron fittings of another kind. 'You invited me to help you while away the time. Well, here I am.'

If Master Antonius was surprised, he didn't show it. 'Then show us what you can do,' he said, beckoning to his assistants. Silently, with arms folded, the men took their places on a wooden bench.

Show us what you can do . . . Now was the time to demonstrate what he had learnt, Florin thought grimly. Why else had Mimus been schooling him day after day? Like his tutor, he unobtrusively scanned the chamber in search of inspiration for an amusing rhyme. His gaze fell on the blazing fire.

> *'If the truth you wish to find,*
> *singe your victim's bare behind,'*

he chanted loudly like a fairground barker, already surveying the instruments of torture on the wall. The words seemed to gush from his lips of their own accord:

> *'But do not, with your cruel tongs,*
> *tweak your sweetheart's dainty nose.*
> *Prick her not with iron prongs,*
> *or her tender flesh you'll bruise,*
> *and bind her not with leather thongs,*
> *or her love you'll surely lose.'*

Florin felt genuinely proud of himself—until he saw the look on Master Antonius's face. The dungeon-master's dark eyebrows had contracted into an ominous line. 'No one jests about my trade!' he growled.

'Very well, er . . . a love song, then,' said Florin, hastily changing his tune.

> *'He kissed her on her lips so red*
> *and fondly held her hand.*
> *"Thou art beyond a doubt," he said,*
> *"the fairest in the land."'*

This seemed more to the taste of Master Antonius and his assistants—at least, Florin decided to interpret their occasional grunts as signs of approval.

They've locked their laughter away, it occurred to him. Like their prisoners.

He did his utmost. He danced, he cracked jokes, he turned several somersaults in midair—a trick he'd learnt only in the last few days—but stopped when he landed with an almighty crash on one of the wooden benches. And throughout this time he never for one moment forgot why he had come.

It was far from easy to act the fool and spy out the torture chamber at the same time. Nevertheless, he did spot a big bunch of keys hanging on a hook beside the inner door. It was all he could do not to stare at it constantly. If only he could lay his hands on it!

Even as he was singing his last song—it told of 'The doughty warrior Ethelred, who iron filings ate like bread'—a plan took shape in his head.

'Was that to your liking?' he asked expectantly.

Master Antonius nodded with a face like stone. 'It makes a change to hear one of you sing instead of bellow.'

'I thought screams of agony sounded sweeter to your ears than the most dulcet melody,' said Florin. Instantly appalled by his own audacity, he was relieved to see the big man's lips twitch in the semblance of a smile.

'Will you come again?' Master Antonius asked.

'If I may,' Florin said, secretly overjoyed. He'd done it! He'd cleared the first hurdle!

He dashed back up the stairs two at a time. The midday break was not quite over. If he was in luck, Benzo would be waiting for him in the kitchen sepulchre.

'Benzo,' he said, performing an exultant little dance around his friend, 'you must learn to do some card tricks!'

'Stand still, I can't hear a word above those bells of yours,' said Benzo. He had passed the time by punching holes in a battered old saucepan with his spit. He now inverted the saucepan over the tallow lamp—and transformed the little cubbyhole into a place of enchantment. 'Come, let's do some fencing!' he urged. 'There's still time for a quick bout.'

But Florin wasn't listening. 'Listen,' he blurted out, 'I've just paid Master Antonius a visit. The keys to the dungeon—'

'You paid *who* a visit?' Benzo broke in, staring at him in disbelief. 'Have you lost your wits?'

Florin dismissed this with an impatient wave of the hand. 'I wish to see my father,' he said, his tone conveying that this was the most natural thing in the world and Benzo a trifle slow on the uptake. 'While you distract Master Antonius and his men with some card tricks, I'll purloin his bunch of keys and be back before anyone notices.'

'I've never touched a playing card in my life,' Benzo said bluntly.

Florin was already standing in the doorway—it was high time he returned to the stable. 'I'll teach you all the tricks I've learnt from Mimus,' he promised. 'Magic Riffle, Ace in the Hole, Flick of the Finger—it's just as easy as fencing. Think how amazed the other scullions will be when you pick the king of hearts out of a whole pack lying face down on the table!'

Benzo knitted his brow. 'So be it,' he said. 'Teach me these card tricks of yours. But after that we'll go back to fencing.'

THE very same night, while Mimus lay snoring beside him, Florin stole the pack of playing cards from his pocket—not without saying a precautionary prayer to Balthazar, the patron saint of card players, that they wouldn't be called upon to show the king any card tricks in the immediate future.

Marsus summoned him to attend the royal family's midday meal the next day, but the day after that he hurried down to the cellars again. The more he ingratiated himself with Master Antonius, the more likely his plan would be to succeed.

'You again?' the guard asked, wagging his head. 'Wasn't one visit enough for you?'

'No,' Florin replied. 'I like it here far better than in the king's dining room.'

The soldier tapped his forehead meaningfully, but he opened the door and Florin hurried into the torture chamber.

'Hello,' he felt like shouting, 'I'm back again!'—but the words stuck in his throat. His bells jingled for a moment longer. Then he froze and the sound died away.

A half-naked man was kneeling beside the fire with a filthy loincloth round his waist and his hands bound behind his back. Florin recognised him at once despite his blindfold and shaven head: it was his godfather, Count Etigo, one of King Philip's most faithful friends. The man beside him was holding an iron ring in the flames with a long-handled pair of tongs. Another man was stirring the coals into a blaze with a poker.

'You won't lay hands on any of us again, my friend,' snarled the man with the poker, whose cheek was scratched and bleeding. 'This collar will tame you.'

Master Antonius came over. 'Is all in readiness?'

Florin emitted an involuntary gasp. Master Antonius and his henchmen were engaged in forging the count a heavy iron collar! He retreated into the farthest corner of the chamber, trying desperately to regain his composure. Count Etigo, his godfather . . . Last Easter he had presented Florin with a ball of some soft, golden-yellow substance that could soak up a whole pail of water, solemnly assuring him that balls of that kind grew deep down on the ocean floor and were harvested by little mermaids! Florin had looked in vain for a surreptitious smile on his face . . . What in the world could have induced him to attack one of his jailers?

Florin turned his face to the wall—on no account must Master Antonius see that he knew the prisoner—but he couldn't stop his ears. He heard the collar being placed round Count Etigo's neck—heard his groans, the hiss of the cooling metal and the vile jeers of his tormentors. The sounds wrung his heart.

At the same time, he was overcome with paralysing fear. Had he really believed that getting to his father would be child's play? This place was hell on earth, and Master Antonius was its ruler. And he himself, Florin, was very close to that hell. All that stood between it and him were a few jester's tricks . . .

He started violently at the touch of a hand on his shoulder.

'Get on with it!' said Master Antonius.

Florin nodded and followed him over to the fire. Count Etigo had disappeared and the bunch of keys on the wall was still swinging gently. With all the determination at his command, Florin forbade his knees to tremble. If he failed now, he might as well abandon hope. Then, like the others, he would end up amid the nameless horrors behind the iron door.

'Which is the most talkative of birds?' he cried overloudly, to disguise the tremor in his voice. 'No, not the parrot: the whinchat, because it *chats*!' Without drawing breath, he went on: 'Which is the most irresolute of birds? The hawfinch, because it hums and *haws*! Which is the most inexperienced of birds? The *green*finch! Which is the most amorous of birds? The p*lover*! Which is the windiest of birds? The nightin*gale*!' And so on and so forth . . .

THE next day Florin began to teach Benzo card tricks in the kitchen sepulchre. It was a laborious business.

'Can't I do something else?' Benzo asked when the whole pack of cards lay strewn around him yet again. 'Couldn't I bake Master Antonius an apple pie, for instance? I can bake fine, juicy apple pies, but this—' he tapped the knave of clubs despondently, 'I shall never master.'

Florin felt like agreeing with him. Instead, he gathered up the cards and replaced them on the upturned cauldron that served them as a table. 'You'll do it,' he said firmly. 'You're far better than you were when we started. Pick up your cards—hold them quite loosely . . .'

Benzo's perseverance stood them in good stead. He not only repeated the tricks tirelessly but managed to borrow a pack of cards from the stable lads so that he could continue practising in his room. During the second week he slowly developed a certain dexterity. Florin showed him how to fan out the cards with a single movement, how to conjure an ace from his sleeve or substitute one card for another unobserved and at lightning speed. They practised like maniacs, so zealously that they forgot about everything else. The third time Florin came dashing into the stable far too late, Mimus told him: 'Birds that flutter too far must have their wings clipped. From now on, you'll leave this cosy nest only when duty calls.'

Florin turned pale. 'You can't do that,' he said. 'Send me to the kitchen again by all means, but don't shut me up in here. I'd explode!'

'Then you'd at last do something I can't do,' the jester said drily.

Let him say what he likes, thought Florin. The next afternoon, while Mimus lay snoring amid the straw, he stole to the door on tiptoe—and gave a violent start when the jester materialised in front of him like a jack-in-the box.

'It seems we must resort to other measures, my princely pupil,' Mimus said brusquely. 'Up into a headstand with you—that ought to correct your topsy-turvy view of things! And woe betide you if you wobble!'

So Florin spent his next few free afternoons standing on his head with the blood pounding in his ears. Although he sensed that precious time was trickling away like sand from a broken hourglass, he offered no further resistance. In the mornings he worked his legs off doing acrobatics; in the afternoons he memorised his lessons like a man possessed. In short, he became a model pupil—all in the desperate hope of changing the jester's mind.

His calculations proved correct. On the afternoon of the tenth day—he had already gone up into a headstand without being asked— Mimus growled: 'Enough is enough. Be off with you!'

Florin positively sprinted to the kitchen sepulchre, only to discover that Benzo wasn't there. Poised on top of the upturned cauldron, however, was a house of cards so intricate and delicate that it threatened to collapse under his gaze. Florin stood marvelling at it. Could Benzo's rough hands really have created such an architectural masterpiece? It seemed so. After all, his father the bone-carver was famed for his manual dexterity.

Suddenly he heard Benzo's voice behind him. 'Where have you been all this time?'

'In the stable,' he replied tersely. 'Come, let's go on.'

But he didn't have the heart to destroy the house of cards. Benzo himself brought it tumbling down by removing the lowest card.

To Florin's delight, Benzo had made the most of the time and continued to practise diligently. Not only did the cards he'd palmed no longer fall out of his sleeve, but he unerringly found any given card concealed in the pack and could pluck the knave of clubs from Florin's ear.

'Benzo, you're a hero,' Florin told him at the end of an hour, and his pupil grinned proudly. 'That will have to do. Tomorrow I'll tell Master Antonius about you.'

Benzo's grin vanished. He had turned pale beneath his freckles.

'Er, Florin,' he said hesitantly, 'you know what trade Master Antonius follows. What happens if your plan misfires?'

That was the possibility Florin dared not dwell on.

'It won't,' he said, trying hard to believe his own words.

IT'S *bound* to misfire, he thought angrily the next day, while enacting the sad tale of the frog and the stork in front of Master Antonius and his assistants. Whether he was hopping around as the frog or strutting majestically along as the stork, the same thought went round and round in his head. His plan couldn't help but fail! Even if Benzo distracted the men with his card tricks—even if he, Florin, got hold of the bunch of keys and managed to slip through the iron door—for how long would Benzo be able to retain the dungeon-master's attention? When he returned from the dungeons he would find the torturers waiting for him. Then they would lay him down on the whipping bench with poor, innocent Benzo alongside. He had no right to expose his friend to such danger.

He resolved to abandon the wretched scheme, yet he heard himself saying, as he took his leave of Master Antonius: 'Might I bring a friend with me the next time? He's a veritable wizard with the cards and cannot fail to entertain you.'

'Bring him, by all means.' Master Antonius rose from the bench and accompanied Florin to the outer door. 'But not the next time,' he said in a low voice, when they were out of earshot of his assistants. 'The next time I shall give you your reward.'

Florin was on his guard at once. 'I expect no reward from you,' he said.

'But of course you do,' said Master Antonius. 'Do you really believe I don't know why you visit me?'

Florin swallowed hard. Master Antonius had known all the time who he was! What was this reward he spoke of? Neatly arrayed on the opposite wall, directly in Florin's line of vision, were the whips and scourges.

Master Antonius noted his glance. 'Reward,' he said, 'not punishment. The next time,' he went on, indicating the iron door, 'it will be open for the space of one hourglass.'

'What if the king learns of it?' Florin asked breathlessly.

'Don't concern yourself on that score.' The dungeon-master chuckled. 'The world above is far away. Down here, I am king.'

'Remember,' he called after Florin. 'One hourglass, no longer. Be prepared.'

BENZO was immensely relieved. 'I would have done it for you, but my belly was already tying itself in knots with fear,' he confessed. 'Just imagine what would have happened had things gone wrong! Besides, my hard work hasn't been in vain. The next time I burn the porridge I'll produce the knave of clubs from the kitchen-master's ear. His eyes will pop out of his head!'

The next morning dragged on interminably. Already with his father in spirit, Florin was anxious and preoccupied. While performing a handstand on Mimus's shoulders he overbalanced and measured his length on the floor—something he hadn't done for a long time.

'What elegance!' the jester remarked sarcastically as Florin rubbed his aching shoulder. 'How inimitably graceful! You look like a squashed dung beetle.'

The chapel bell struck punctually at noon, but just as Florin was about to dash off, Marsus appeared in the doorway. Florin cursed him bitterly under his breath.

Pompous windbag! Titivated nitwit! Perfumed cockroach! He could have driven his fist into the valet's rouged and powdered face. It would now be another whole day and a night before he could get to Master Antonius.

The fairy tale he told at the royal lunch table degenerated into a horror story in which a monstrous hound guarded a cave filled with gold and bit off the head of each courageous treasure-hunter in turn. By the end the little princes were sitting there pale-faced and terrified, and it was Florin's good fortune that King Theodo and Queen Elina had been too deep in conversation to overhear him.

The afternoon, night and following morning crawled by unbearably slowly. Then, at long last, the noontide bell struck once more. Florin's hurried prayer was heard—Marsus did not appear—and he dashed downstairs helter-skelter.

When he came panting into the torture chamber, heart thudding, he found Master Antonius on his own.

'It's lucky you came,' the big man said. 'I wouldn't have been able to send my men away again.' He draped a cloak round his shoulders. 'This concerns you and me alone.'

Before reaching for the bunch of keys he thrust a tallow lamp into Florin's hand. 'Take care it doesn't go out.'

The handle of the lamp was hot, but Florin paid it no heed. He had eyes only for the iron door, which swung open surprisingly easily. No, there was no yawning chasm ahead, no amorphous blackness. Instead, he was confronted by a narrow vaulted passage dimly illuminated by a single torch in a bracket.

Not until the door closed behind them did Florin feel the cold that pierced him to the marrow and made him shiver. The walls gleamed, black with mould, and the floor resembled a path across a marsh, so deep was the slime that instantly soaked through Florin's thin cloth shoes. The air was filled with a stench of decay and rat droppings.

On either side of the passage, doors were let into the walls at regular intervals. They were so small and low, one might almost have imagined that cosy little chambers for dwarfs lay behind them—had it not been for the heavy iron bolts with which they were secured.

As he passed them, Florin mentally assigned each door to a different prisoner. 'Count Gilbert, Count Bernold, Duke Quentin, Count

Etigo, Duke Bonizo, Judge Hilduin, Count Abram, Count Bertin . . .'

Worst of all was the silence. Apart from their footsteps, which re-echoed from the vaulted ceiling, not a sound could be heard. The silence of the grave, thought Florin. Was anyone still alive behind those doors?

Master Antonius halted outside the last door.

'One hourglass, no longer,' he said. 'Make the most of your time.'

He slid back the heavy iron bolt, opened the door a few inches and pushed Florin inside.

The lamp made little impression on the darkness of the cell. Florin heard the bolt slide home with a crash behind him. Abruptly, he was overcome with panic. Master Antonius has duped me, he thought. It was all a ruse concocted with Theodo. I'm doomed to remain in here forevermore . . .

Then he heard his father's voice.

'For pity's sake, hold that lamp behind your back. The light pricks my eyes like red-hot needles.' And, after a pause: 'Who are you?'

Florin opened his mouth to speak but couldn't utter a word. He heard a rattle of chains as his father stood up. He could now make him out in the gloom: a tall, gaunt figure swathed in rags, his shorn head bowed to keep it clear of the low ceiling. Involuntarily, Florin raised the lamp a little to see his father's familiar features—and recoiled at the look of undisguised revulsion on his face.

'Another jester,' said King Philip. 'How many of you monsters does Theodo keep? Have you come to mock me in my miserable cell like the other?'

'No,' Florin said quietly. 'I have come in token of my love and respect for you.' There was a momentary hush. Then King Philip said in a tense voice: 'Hold the lamp near your face, quickly!'

Florin silently complied. His father raised a hand and gingerly, as if afraid of doing so, brushed Florin's cheek with his fingertips.

'Florin!' he exclaimed, aghast. 'God in heaven, you're alive! But what have they done to you?'

'Don't be concerned, father,' Florin said quickly. 'I manage. I'd be far worse off in a dungeon. Nothing will happen to me as long as I play their game, and Mimus, the jester, means me no h—'

He suddenly remembered what his father had said first of all. 'Mimus was here?' he asked incredulously.

'Almost every day,' said his father. 'He lends spice to Theodo's visits.'

King Philip spoke in a calm voice, but his eyes roved restlessly over Florin as if seeking something concealed about his person. When Florin bent down to put the lamp on the floor he was shocked to see his father grimace with disgust at the sound of his bells.

'How are you, father?' he asked, at a loss for something to say. He could have bitten his tongue off. What a ridiculous question!

His father regarded him in silence, like one stranger eyeing another.

'It's only a costume,' Florin murmured unhappily.

'Take it off,' King Philip said suddenly. 'Now, this minute. I'd sooner see you naked than . . . like that!' He uttered the last word through clenched teeth.

Florin nodded, overcome with shame. He stripped off the motley, removed his cap, and faced his father, stark naked and shivering.

'You've grown thin, my son,' said King Philip. 'Is Theodo's fare so meagre?'

'He has given me a cook of my own,' Florin replied. 'His name is Pinch-Belly.'

'Then he cooks for us both,' said the king. 'His pastries and puddings are quite excellent, don't you agree?'

Florin looked down, first at himself, then at his pale, emaciated father, and suddenly he couldn't help it: he shook with laughter. King Philip, too, began to laugh. At the same time, he reached out and clasped Florin to him. They hugged each other and laughed till the tears ran down their cheeks.

It's lucky only his feet are chained, Florin thought. It's lucky he can hold me in his arms . . .

'My boy!' said King Philip. 'And I thought I'd never see you again.' He held Florin at arm's length and gazed into his eyes. 'But they haven't consigned you to the dungeons, have they? You don't have to remain down here in this hell on earth, do you? Tell me quickly!'

Florin shook his head. 'I struck a bargain with Master Antonius,' he explained. 'I entertained him; that's why he let me see you.'

'This is insane,' said King Philip, clasping Florin to him once more. 'Insane and wonderful at the same time. Down here, we all live in constant dread of the grim dungeon-master, yet he succumbs to your jester's antics!'

Florin ventured to look round the dungeon from the shelter of his father's arms. It was a cramped little cell some six feet high, wide and long—too small to enable its tall occupant to stand erect or lie at full length. On the floor reposed a heap of rotting straw, and embedded in the rear wall was the heavy iron ring to which King Philip's leg-irons were chained. Behind the mound of straw Florin discerned a dark hole in the stamped mud floor with a grating over it. Even as he watched, a shadowy form flitted from the rustling straw and disappeared head first down the grating, followed by two or three more.

Startled, Florin pointed to the spot. 'What's that?'

'My greatest luxury here below,' his father explained. 'A privy. Bellingar's architect was an ingenious man.'

Another shadowy form emerged, paused for a moment, then disappeared down the grating in its turn. A chorus of ferocious squeaks and snarls came drifting up from below.

'He didn't allow for the rats, alas,' King Philip went on. 'A veritable dynasty of them dwells down there, from the oldest great-grandfather to the youngest sprig. We dwell peacefully together most of the time. They grow troublesome only when there's bread to be had.'

With a shudder, Florin tried to imagine his father having to fight off rats with his bare hands in this gloomy dungeon. 'Do you never have any light?'

'I'm granted the favour of a candle-end from time to time—whenever Theodo lays the document proclaiming my abdication before me and urges me to sign it.'

Florin tore his eyes away from the rat-hole and turned to his father. 'How can that madman believe that Moltovia's hereditary king would ever renounce the throne of his own free will?'

King Philip gave a bitter laugh. 'He has promised me honourable treatment and living quarters befitting my station: daylight, life and fresh air in exchange for my crown. The bargain has its attractions, I cannot deny.'

'Don't trust him,' Florin said quickly. 'If you sign, he'll . . .' Appalled, he broke off.

'He'll have me beheaded,' King Philip amplified. 'Has he made that threat to you?'

Florin nodded silently.

'It isn't my life alone that's at stake,' his father went on. 'If I consent to abdicate, Theodo will spare you and the other prisoners as well.'

'Don't believe him,' Florin insisted. 'It's a lie. As soon as he's king of Moltovia he'll have us executed—all of us without exception.'

'No one knows that better than I,' King Philip replied. 'Yet there are many days when the lie strikes me as more merciful than the truth.'

He smiled, but that smile seemed to drain the last of his energy. Florin's heart bled for him. How must his father feel after so many days and nights in this rat's nest, cold, hungry and devoid of hope?

As if he had read Florin's thoughts, King Philip said loudly: 'God has forsaken us, my son. All hope is gone.'

'No, father,' Florin said quickly. 'You're mistaken.'

And he proceeded to tell him about the enormous sum of money

King Guido had offered in return for their freedom; about Count Victor's nocturnal visit; about his own mysterious mission, the string of beads, and the airborne message he had sent their unknown rescuers.

'Pray God the miracle occurs,' said King Philip, 'and they get here in time.'

A shadow crossed his face when Florin went on to tell him about the renegades' visit.

'Essrin, my friend,' he muttered. 'What can have possessed you?'

'Some are traitors, to be sure,' said Florin, 'among them Count Essrin, Duke Vibert and scar-faced Count Tillo, who delivered me into Theodo's hands, but most of our retainers have remained loyal—loyal unto death, father. Radbod spoke of a widespread conspiracy against Theodo.'

He gripped his father's hand. 'That is why you must not yield to him! If you consent to abdicate, all our friends' exertions and sacrifices will have been in vain. All will be lost.'

King Philip nodded. 'I've rejected his offers hitherto, and I'll continue to do so,' he said. 'If only I weren't so deprived of news in this rat-hole! It's not for nothing that Theodo keeps me cut off from everything and everyone—he knows how uncertainty wears a man down. But now'— he squeezed Florin's hand—'God has played a trick on him and sent you to me, my son. And, because nothing is beyond the power of our heavenly father, why shouldn't he also send rescuers to lead us out of this dark and terrifying forest?'

Florin had heard his father speak of a dark forest before, he recalled. It was in the dream he'd had immediately after his attempt to escape. He thought with a shudder of the misshapen figure on the white horse. But, God be praised, his father was standing here before him, wretched and exhausted, it was true, but all in one piece. He decided to ask the question that had been haunting him.

'Father, cast your mind back to your first few days in this dungeon.

Can you remember what happened five nights after you were brought here?'

What a foolish question, he thought at the same moment. How could he expect his father to remember one particular night in an endless succession?

'You mean the night of the day you tried to escape,' King Philip said quietly.

Florin couldn't repress a start. 'What did King Theodo do to you?' he asked in a low voice.

His father drew the tattered remains of his coat around his shoulders as if they could lend him some warmth.

'I was taken to Master Antonius's torture chamber and made to watch them put out Duke Bonizo's eyes with a red-hot dagger. Then they placed my hands on the gridiron and compelled me to say which of the prisoners should be blinded the next time you tried to escape.'

'Well?' Florin whispered. 'Whom did you choose?'

'Myself,' his father replied. 'Fortunately for me, you never tried again.'

Seeing the look on Florin's face, he clasped him tightly. 'You weren't to blame, Florin. It was Theodo's revenge for Bonizo's attack on that repulsive jester of his.'

Horrified though he was, it distressed Florin to hear his father speak of Mimus so contemptuously.

King Philip seemed to sense this. 'Given that they've made you wear that attire,' he said cautiously, 'I assume you've had a fair amount to do with the jester?'

'Mimus is my tutor,' said Florin. 'He's . . . he doesn't treat me badly.'

'And Theodo?'

Florin had firmly resolved to say nothing about his cares and woes, but the question seemed to fling open a door inside him. The words gushed from his lips. Hurriedly, breathlessly, he told his father about

Father Anselm's denial that he possessed a soul, about the stable where he dwelt like an animal, about his lessons in jesterdom, about his hunger and the morsels he hated to accept, about the mockery and blows to which he had been subjected.

King Philip listened in silence, but Florin could tell from his expression how saddened he was to hear of his son's lot. The more he told him, however, the lighter the iron ring round his heart became.

He fell silent when he was done, ashamed of his outburst. He had filled his father's ears with lamentations like a foolish little boy. What were his hardships compared to the cold and darkness here below? What was the jesters' stable compared to this dismal dungeon?

'What of the other prisoners?' he asked. 'Do you know anything about their fate?'

King Philip nodded. 'Duke Bonizo is blind, Count Abram suffers from bouts of vomiting, Duke Quentin has a deep wound in his leg that refuses to heal, Count Etigo wears an iron collar. The rest are as well as can be expected.'

Florin thought of the bolted doors, the deathly hush. 'How did you learn all those things?' he asked.

King Philip smiled. 'By doing what prisoners have always done: we tap on the walls at night, when Master Antonius and his assistants are asleep.'

Florin glanced at his father's bruised and bleeding knuckles.

'A small price to pay to relieve the solitude within these walls,' said King Philip.

At that moment Florin remembered something he'd forgotten until now, incredible though it seemed. 'But you didn't know,' he said dejectedly, 'that Theodo has had Montfield Castle razed to the ground.'

'I guessed as much,' his father replied. 'Ever since that accursed jester sang a song about the walls of Jericho and addressed Theodo as King Joshua.' Again he drew the rags round his shoulders. 'It was only to be expected that Theodo, in his hatred, would not spare our ancestral abode.'

'But why does he hate us so much?' Florin asked very quietly.

'Because he's an evil man, Florin.'

'Yes,' said Florin, 'he's harsh and overbearing. At same time, he's respectful and affectionate to the queen, a fond father to his children, and a monarch whom his vassals love and honour with all their hearts. No, I don't mean that,' he said, desperately searching for the right words. 'I mean the boundless, bitter loathing that prompts him to treat us as he does. Us, father, no one else!'

He looked his father straight in the eye. 'Why does he hate us so?' he asked again.

King Philip merely shook his head in silence.

'Do you really believe, father, that there is still something I must not be told? Something from which you must shield me, even now?'

With an infinitely weary gesture that cut Florin to the quick, King Philip drew a hand across his brow.

'You're right,' he said at length. 'You're at Theodo's mercy every day and must know the truth: I killed his brother. That is why he hates me and all who are dear to me.'

'What!' Florin said, stunned.

'It happened three years before you were born,' his father went on hurriedly, as if seeking to escape from his own memories. 'At the court of Arelia lived a young and beautiful princess who was courted by two princes. One was Morvan of Vinland, the other was myself.'

'Morvan of Vinland?' Florin had never heard the name before.

'Morvan, Theodo's elder brother, Crown Prince of Vinland. His betrothal to the princess had long been an accomplished fact when I was introduced to her at a court function.'

A reminiscent smile flitted across King Philip's face. 'I fell in love with her on sight, and she with me. To cut a long story short, she went to her father and asked him to dissolve the betrothal, but Morvan refused to renounce his claim and challenged me to a duel. So we fought for her.'

He paused. 'Up to this point, Florin, it sounds like one of those heroic ballads minstrels sing to the harp. But there was nothing heroic about our duel. We cut and thrust at each other from sunrise to sunset, until neither of us could do more than crawl in the dust like a worm, bereft of dignity and reason. In the end I drove my dagger into Morvan's throat. God alone knows why it wasn't the other way round . . .'

'But you were the victor in an honourable fight,' Florin protested.

'The victor, yes,' King Philip said bitterly, 'but assuredly not an honourable one. If I had paused for thought at that moment, Florin, the worst could still have been avoided. Theodo was a young hothead, but upright and God-fearing. Vinland and Moltovia were not yet at war. It behoved me to make amends and humbly beg pardon of God and the Vinlanders for doing what I did: I had Morvan's corpse sewn up in a leather sack and transported back to Vinland on a donkey cart.'

'A leather sack . . .' Florin repeated slowly.

His father nodded. 'My mean-spirited revenge for the mortal fear I'd endured in the course of that duel.' He fidgeted restlessly, and his leg-irons rattled. 'The body spent a fortnight under the sweltering August sun—today I know what that must have meant to his family. But I was young and bedazzled by my supposed triumph. Morvan had not yet reached Vinland when we married at Montfield Castle. As if nothing had happened.'

'You . . . and my mother,' Florin said haltingly.

'Yes. As you know, God did not bestow his blessing on our love . . . No,' he amended quickly, 'that's not true, God has blessed me a thousandfold. I have you, my son.'

'What happened in Vinland?' Florin asked.

'The old king never recovered from the shock and died of grief.

Theodo succeeded him on the throne. Vinland invaded Moltovia less than six months later. The rest, you know.'

Florin said nothing, he was so absorbed in trying to grasp what he had heard. Then something occurred to him. 'If you knew all this, father, how could you ever have trusted Theodo? You accepted his invitation and followed him here to the castle. Had you forgotten what had happened?'

'No.' King Philip kneaded his grazed knuckles. 'How can I explain it to you? I think I simply wished to believe that Theodo had forgiven me. It was all so many years ago, and our two kingdoms had suffered so grievously from a senseless war born of arrogance and hatred . . .' He fell silent, lost in thought. 'No one could have guessed that King Ludvik would allow himself to be bought like an unscrupulous mercenary. And Theodo proved a masterly actor—until he dropped the pretence in his lion's den.'

He raised his head suddenly. 'Footsteps,' he whispered. 'Master Antonius.'

Florin hurriedly dressed in his costume. 'The hour must be up.'

'Listen, my son,' said King Philip. 'If Theodo has me killed—no,' he cut in, when Florin opened his mouth to protest, 'we both know that he'll do so. But when I am no more, Florin, you must go on living.' He spoke with great insistence. 'Who knows, perhaps this costume will protect you. Play the buffoon and bide your time. Whatever happens, and however long it takes, you must never forget who you are: Florin, the last scion of the royal house of Moltovia. All our people's hopes depend on you.'

The footsteps drew nearer and the bolt was withdrawn with a crash. Florin's eyes remained glued to his father's face. That smile, those familiar features, would be deeply, indelibly imprinted on his memory forevermore.

'It's time, little Mimus,' said Master Antonius. 'Bring the lamp with you.'

'Little Mimus—is that what they call you?' King Philip asked as he gave Florin a final hug. 'Farewell, then, little Mimus. Never forget how proud of you I am.' He made the sign of the cross on Florin's forehead, just below the fool's cap. 'God bless you, Prince of Moltovia!'

– CHRISTMAS –

MIMUS MADE NO attempt to deny his visits to the dungeon.

'My compliments,' he said when Florin took him to task. 'It can't have been easy to get into the dungeons, still less to get out again. What did you do, dance a jig with Master Antonius and his men?'

Florin was trembling with anger. 'Even that would be better than humiliating a helpless prisoner!' he snapped. 'What do *you* do down there: tweak my father's nose?'

'I do as Theodo asks,' Mimus replied calmly. 'How often does one get an opportunity to make a real, live king jump through a hoop?'

'You did *that*?!' Florin hissed, white to the lips.

'I do but jest,' said Mimus. It was impossible to tell from his expressionless face whether he was telling the truth. 'What ought I to do, in your opinion? Refuse to obey and die a hero's death?'

'Spare me your pleasantries!' snarled Florin. 'Just run to the king and tell him I visited my father. He's bound to reward you with some plump morsel!'

'Don't tempt me,' the jester retorted.

'You're even more despicable than those renegades,' Florin said contemptuously. 'They've sold us for gold and land; you'd do it for a chicken leg!'

'My mouth is watering already,' Mimus rejoined, quite unmoved. 'However, my banquet would come to nothing, more's the pity. If I went to the king, I'd only earn myself a whipping—for failing to keep my disobedient foal on a tighter rein.' He stared at Florin with a puzzled frown. 'What am I to do with you: tether you to the wall by your ass's ears?'

'Do as you please,' said Florin. 'Only promise me you'll never torment my father again.'

'Willingly.' Mimus's eyes twinkled. 'As long as you promise me never to draw another breath.'

Florin's anger boiled over again. 'Oh, you poor, poor creature,' he jeered. 'You're like the wooden head on a jester's bauble—you have to dance in the king's hand?' He gave a mocking laugh. 'It's not as simple as that. You could refuse.'

'No,' Mimus said flatly.

The next day, when Florin, still seething with anger, told Benzo about the jester's visits to the dungeon, Benzo couldn't understand his indignation.

'The thing is as clear as chicken broth,' he said. 'When the kitchen-master tells me "Make soup!" I make soup. "Make porridge!" I make porridge. When the king tells the jester "Mock the prisoner!" he does so. It's his trade.'

'If Mimus had an ounce of pride he'd refuse,' Florin said bitterly. 'But he's a trained monkey who jumps whenever his master clicks his fingers.'

'He's our gracious king's jester,' Benzo insisted. 'If he helped you, he'd get a whipping. Why should he make life more difficult for himself?'

Why indeed? Mimus had never disguised the fact that Florin was as welcome to him as a ball and chain. How could he ever have believed otherwise? Just because he himself yearned so desperately for a friend and ally, it didn't mean the jester was on his side—far from it. Mimus was Theodo's puppet and would remain so.

Florin was bitterly disillusioned. At night he lay down on the straw as far away from Mimus as possible. He sullenly followed the jester's instructions during lessons and their evening performances. The rest of the time he turned his face to the wall—not that Mimus seemed to care.

A week went by in this manner. Florin grew more miserable every day, distressed by his self-imposed silence and the poisonous atmosphere in the stable. At the same time, he was eaten up with longing for his father. The hour had passed so terribly quickly, and there were so many things he could still have told him . . .

Every afternoon became a torment. He now knew that while he was sitting alone in the stable, Mimus was playing spiteful pranks on his father. When the jester returned at nightfall, unspoken questions hovered on the tip of his tongue. What had his father done and said? Was he well or sick, despondent or in good heart? But, hard though he found it, he resolutely kept his questions to himself.

Until Mimus himself broached the subject.

Florin had recited his afternoon's lesson as usual—thirty-three animal fables—and was silently awaiting his orders for the evening when Mimus suddenly fished a crumpled scrap of parchment from his pocket. 'Take a look at that!'

The charcoal drawing had been roughly, hurriedly done, but Florin recognised what it was at first glance: the five-country eagle Chancellor Benedict had drawn for Count Maren in the audience chamber. But in place of the eagle's left wing, where Vinland should have been, was a revolting monster with a lion's body and the head of a pig. The pig's head, its greedy jaws agape, was busy devouring the rest of the eagle, and beside it was written: 'The gallant King of Vinland bestows the kiss of peace on his neighbours.'

'Your father,' said Mimus, 'drew that on the deed of abdication instead of signing it.' He smiled faintly. 'Our gracious king was not best pleased.'

'Well?' asked Florin. 'How did you repay him?'

'Not as generously as his defiance merited,' Mimus replied. 'Your father is stronger than you think.'

You're mistaken, Florin thought. The man down there in that rat-hole is only the shadow of my father, and that hate-maddened king of yours will never rest until he has destroyed him utterly. Aloud, he asked: 'Have you ever heard tell of Morvan of Vinland?'

'Of course. Theodo had an elder brother by that name.'

'It was my father who killed him in a duel.'

Mimus nodded without undue surprise. 'No one speaks of Morvan at court,' he said. 'They should have buried him deeper. Then he would no longer haunt the living.'

'His remains lie beneath the chapel,' Florin said. 'Not that a godless jester like you has ever set foot there.'

'How could I?' Mimus demanded. 'That sacred temple is guarded by Father Anselm, the most pugnacious of all castle chaplains. But now that Your Highness has deigned to address a word to me at last, I'll make a bargain with you. Look at me.'

He came and stood in front of Florin. Then he bowed his head and, shivering as if with cold, drew his jester's motley more tightly around his shoulders. The gesture was so like his father's that Florin stared at him open-mouthed.

'From time to time,' said Mimus, 'I'll bring you some word, some image or gesture of your father's. That's the most I can do. In return, you'll cease to be a tight-lipped crosspatch and become a talkative little donkey again. Well, what do you say to my offer?'

Florin gulped, then nodded without a word.

IT was a good thing that Mimus had broken the ice between them, because the weather now turned truly icy cold. Winter arrived almost overnight—a season of rock-hard frosts such as Florin had never known at Montfield. Ice glittered on the stable walls and the straw froze to the floor; a thick layer formed on the water in the buckets, and Florin's morning wash became an ordeal that made his teeth chatter for hours afterward. It never occurred to anyone to give him a coat or a blanket. When he finally swallowed his pride and asked Rollo for one, the bestiarius merely laughed.

'The cold is healthy, my lad,' he said. 'Grow a donkey's winter coat!'

It's all very well for you to talk, Florin thought, as he watched Rollo stomp out of the stable in his hareskin jacket and fur-lined boots.

The cold was worst at night, when it seeped from the damp straw and permeated Florin's every limb until his arms and legs were completely numb. Alarmed to find some bluish, discoloured patches on his hands and forearms one morning, he showed them to Mimus.

'Chilblains,' the jester told him with a shrug. 'They're as much a part of winter as beads of sweat in summer.'

Mockery, hunger, cold—the old fool accepts them all! thought Florin.

The other inmates of the menagerie were also suffering from the cold. Whenever Florin went upstairs to visit the monkeys, he would see Zito the bear lying motionless, like a big brown boulder, in the huge mound of straw that Rollo had raked together for him. Brother the wolf, by contrast, prowled restlessly to and fro. Even the monkeys were less lively than usual. They sat huddled together in a corner, chattering quietly to themselves.

'At least you can warm each other,' Florin muttered enviously.

He himself behaved like Brother the wolf. To keep the cold at bay he paced to and fro, hopped on the spot while learning his lessons by heart, flapped his arms, turned handsprings and somersaults. Even the huge open fire in the banqueting hall warmed him only superficially. The cold, which had crept deep into his marrow, governed all his thoughts and emotions.

One night, when some young maidservants crowned with lighted candles in honour of St. Lucia filed into the banqueting hall, Florin became aware for the first time that Christmas was approaching.

We're on the threshold of a new year, he told himself, and with it will come our deliverance.

But he didn't truly believe this. Gone was the spirit of initiative that had swept him along and engineered the meeting with his father. His hopes had congealed in the cold. They had withered like the rose-bushes he could see from the roof, which resembled fleshless skeletons. Late roses had still been blooming in the castle garden on the day he launched his parchment dart. When had that been: a thousand years ago?

In the next few days a word went the rounds of the castle's passages. Florin overheard it on one of his afternoon jaunts: a word that had always held a magical appeal for him.

'You heard aright,' Alix told him. 'Father means to hold a Christmas tournament at Bellingar—the first in five years.' Her eyes shone. 'I can hardly wait. Oh, how wonderful it will be!'

They were sitting in Alix's window alcove, playing chess. The world outside was a flurry of grey, whirling snowflakes. Although it was early afternoon, a footman had already lit the sconces and was now distributing wax candles with noiseless tread. He placed one beside the chessboard, another beside Countess Wogrim, who was embroidering an altar cloth next to the tiled stove, and a third between the two lady's maids, who were seated on stools side by side, adorning one of the princess's bonnets with colourful ribbons.

Alix sent for Florin at least once a week, so he was well acquainted with the scene in her chamber by now. 'Pincushion afternoons,' Mimus called them—an apt name, Florin reflected with a sigh. Soft though the cushion in the window alcove was, he had to be constantly on his guard against Alix's needle-sharp tongue.

But one thing more than made up for all her jibes: the big green tiled stove in the corner. Whenever she permitted him to, Florin stood beside it and warmed himself. He would have crawled inside it if he could.

He gazed at it yearningly, but they hadn't finished their game of chess, and it was his move.

'A Christmas tournament,' he repeated, successfully repelling Alix's latest attack on his king. 'I suppose your father intends it to celebrate his splendid victory over Moltovia.'

'It would surprise me if he still remembers that,' Alix replied haughtily. 'After all, who cares about a few half-decayed prisoners and a little jester?'

Florin bit his tongue. Coping with Alix's taunts was quite as hard as walking on his toes for hours, but he'd learnt to do both. He awaited her next move in silence.

'It will be a splendid affair,' she said enthusiastically. 'King Ludvik of Frankenland is to be our guest of honour. Also in attendance will be countless dignitaries from Vinland and Frankenland. From Moltovia, too,' she added triumphantly.

'They all jousted at our own Christmas tournament last year,' Florin retorted. 'You may be truly proud of guests such as those!'

She thrust out her lower lip. Then she made a move he had failed to foresee, being too preoccupied with what she had told him. 'Checkmate,' she said. 'By the by,' she went on casually, 'there may even be a betrothal to celebrate this Christmas.'

Florin raised his eyebrows. 'Yours, princess?'

'Mind your own business,' she said pertly.

'Why mention it then?' He spoke more heatedly than he'd meant to, and it irked him. There was no need to make it plain to Princess Prickle-Tongue what was going on inside the head of a prince who might, under other circumstances, have been her betrothed.

To change the subject, he whispered: 'Shall I spur your beloved Warhorse into a gallop? I know just the thing.'

Countess Wogrim glanced at Florin suspiciously from her place beside the stove. When first they met she had stared at him as if he were a particularly loathsome insect, and even now she addressed him only when absolutely necessary. These cases of absolute necessity arose whenever Florin recounted one of Mimus's indecent stories. Then the countess would cock a bony forefinger and say, with righteous indignation: 'Keep a bridle on your tongue, little jester. That filth is not fit for a princess's ears!'

Alix, however, had her own notions of what was fit for her ears. 'Go on,' she said with a grin.

'*Once upon a time,*' Florin began, '*a nobleman married a beautiful young woman of whom he was deeply enamoured. He was doubly distressed, therefore, when she fell ill with a mysterious disease. Her hips lost their shapely curves and her rosy cheeks grew pale, until, in the end, she was even unable to share the marriage bed with her unhappy spouse.*

The nobleman urged his ailing wife to tell him what he could do to make her better. At this, her almond eyes regained a little of their lustre. Sighing feebly, she said: "I have but one desire, dearest husband. I yearn to smell the sweet scent of an apple and sink my teeth in its flesh. Methinks that might restore me fully to health."

The winter was a severe one, however, and there were no apples to be had. So the solicitous husband rode across hill and dale for many a day, until, on reaching warmer climes, he purchased three apples. But when, filled with joy, he brought them home to his wife, she turned her lovely face to the wall and left the apples unheeded.

Her husband fretted for three long days, but on the fourth he went to market. In the street he encountered a man who was toying with an apple in his hand. "Good man," *he asked,* "where did you get that apple?"

"From my lady-love," *the stranger replied.* "Her cuckolded husband *has been away on a long journey . . .*"'

'What does "cuckolded" mean?' Alix asked innocently.

'Well . . .' Florin flushed to the roots of his hair and cursed himself for doing so. Did she really not know? 'Well, er . . .'

He was saved by the countess's upraised forefinger. 'Keep a bridle on your tongue, little jester! This is—'

'—not fit for a princess's ears,' Alix broke in. 'Continue!'

'"*. . .to buy her three apples. Meanwhile, however, I have called on her every day. This morning she presented me not only with the fruit of her body, as is her usual custom, but also with this apple.*"'

'The cure is working,' Alix whispered. 'Look, the Warhorse has flattened her ears and is pawing the ground!'

As if the stove had become too hot for her, the countess was shuffling uneasily to and fro. She bent over her embroidery with ears aflame.

Florin almost burst out laughing at the sight, but he pulled himself together and went calmly on with his story.

'*Mightily enraged by these words, the nobleman hurried home to call his wife to account. On the way, however, he met another man in the street with an apple in his hand. And, when he stormed into the bedchamber, a third man was lying in his wife's snow-white arms. He was holding the third apple in his hand, but his teeth were nibbling fruit of another kind.*'

Alix winked at Florin. 'Spare me the rest,' she said loudly. 'I know how the story ends.'

Countess Wogrim looked up from her embroidery. 'But I do not,' she said. The disappointment in her voice was unmistakable.

On his way back to the stable, Florin thought again of the forthcoming Christmas tournament. Did the court of Vinland, too, hold contests for adolescent boys? Last year, at home in Moltovia, they had competed at ring-sticking, archery and fighting with the quarterstaff.

The pupils at the royal school of knighthood, who looked forward to the occasion for weeks, had practised their spear-throwing and swordsmanship under Count Ursio's supervision. As usual, Senna had won all the prizes except the one for deportment, which he left to Florin, but no one resented his victories; the tournament had been far too enjoyable . . .

'A Christmas tournament, eh?' said Mimus when Florin told him the news. He looked as if he had bitten into a crabapple. 'That means visitors.'

'What else?' Florin asked in surprise. 'Hundreds of guests took part in our tournament last year. It's the same at Bellingar, surely?'

'You misunderstand me,' said Mimus. '*We'll* be receiving visitors. Some of the noble lords bring their court jesters with them, and they make themselves at home in our stable.'

His bells tinkled as he shook himself involuntarily. 'We'll have trouble with the drivelling idiots all day long, and at night, when the king's exalted guests are as full as wineskins after their jousting, they'll set us on each other like gamecocks. Hallelujah, that's the nature of *our* Christmas tournament!' He spat contemptuously.

Florin gazed at the floor. His elation had evaporated. When would he stop dreaming at last? For a jester like him there were jesters' tournaments, nothing more.

Preparations for the Christmas gathering were in full swing. Labourers toiled for days to clear the jousting yard and paddock of ice and snow. Carpenters constructed stands and erected colourful pavilions from which fluttered the armourial pennants of the invited guests.

Inside the castle, the passages rang from dawn to dusk with the nagging voices of the chamberlain and the master of ceremonies. Servants gave the walls and ceilings a fresh coat of whitewash; chambermaids beat the carpets and wall hangings outside in the snow. Every corner of the castle was tidied and swept; every article of gold and silver polished anew. Even at dawn Florin heard oxen bellowing in the courtyard and porters cursing under their heavy burdens. Wagonloads of wine casks arrived, together with baskets of fruit and delicacies from distant lands: venison and poultry, crabs and fish. Brewing, boiling and roasting went on unceasingly, and the most delicious smells came wafting along the passages. Like all the kitchen staff, Benzo never had a moment to spare.

In the universal turmoil, Florin often fancied himself back home. Montfield Castle, too, was regularly swept from top to bottom before Christmas, and Muriel and Count Marrod kept the servants fully occupied until, when the winter solstice came, everything shone like new. But that was a thing of the past. Never again would they all assemble in the festively bedecked banqueting hall; never again would jousting take place in the great royal meadow beyond the forest.

The atmosphere at Bellingar Castle became merrier and more expectant—and Mimus's face longer—with every passing day. Florin, on the other hand, allowed himself to become infected by the festive spirit prevailing everywhere. In vain he warned himself that Christmas could not but be a sad occasion without his nearest and dearest; secretly, he began to look forward to it.

Two days before Christmas even the Monkey Tower was invaded by festive activity. In the morning Rollo brought them and the monkeys some new costumes—striped red and gold, but otherwise no different from the old ones. A little later, grousing and grumbling, the bestiarius swept the jesters' stable. While doing so he had to endure Mimus's sarcastic jibes. Comfortably lolling on a heap of straw with his legs crossed, the jester pointed out every grain of dust Rollo had missed until the bestiarius lost his temper and tipped a bucket of dirty water over his head.

'Well done, Rollo!' Soaked to the skin, Mimus leapt to his feet and spread his arms like a goose with an injured wing. 'I hope you realise what the king will do to you and me if I fail to appear before him in my new motley tonight!'

'You always go too far, you miserable blabbermouth!' cried Rollo, but a decidedly anxious expression had appeared on his moon face. 'My wife can remedy matters,' he ordained. 'There's time enough.'

Rollo's wife appeared. Even shorter and fatter than her husband, she surveyed the stable with distaste. Then, without a word, she pulled Mimus's sodden costume over his head and marched out again.

'My compliments, Rollo,' quipped Mimus, sitting on the straw in his sackcloth smock. 'Your lady wife is a paragon of grace and loveliness.'

'How true!' The bestiarius beamed all over his spherical face. 'I couldn't have put it better. She's not only as beautiful as the morning sun but a damned fine cook into the bargain.' He licked his lips. 'Her roast cow's udder, her stuffed pig's trotters, her sheep's eyes in aspic are all beyond compare . . . But what would you gruel-eaters know about *that?*'

With a shrug, he seized his broom and proceeded to sweep up the filthy straw so ferociously that Florin took shelter behind Mimus's back.

'Why don't *you* have a wife?' he asked, but Mimus merely scowled and shook his head.

'Our exalted jester is too high and mighty to wed,' Rollo answered for him. 'The king has long wished to marry him off. Maidservants, laundresses, chambermaids—he has offered him any wife his heart desires, but our lord jester plays coy like a shrinking violet.'

'The devil I'll marry,' Mimus growled.

The bestiarius gave a meaningful grin. 'You know full well what the king wants of you.'

'What?' Florin asked, his curiosity aroused.

'Little jesters, that's what,' said Rollo. 'A whole litter of them, like organ pipes!'

For a moment Florin saw the scene in his mind's eye: the entire stable filled with baby jesters. In cradles, in little wooden handcarts, on the floor—and all in cap and bells.

'But how would that profit the king?' he asked in surprise.

'He'd sell them,' the bestiarius explained, 'sell them to other courts as soon as they could walk. A healthy little jester is worth his weight in gold.'

'That's enough,' Mimus said sharply.

But Florin couldn't help asking one more question. 'A jester's children are jesters from birth?'

Mimus nodded. 'They grow ass's ears in their mother's womb,' he said, straight-faced. 'Does it surprise you that I'll have nothing to do with a woman?' Before Florin could say anything more, he added: 'It's quite the same with princes, by the way. They come into the world with crowns on their heads.'

'And Vinland has five of them,' the bestiarius exclaimed. 'The poor queen!'

THEY were roused at dawn the next day by a succession of fanfares. Mimus's spirits hit rock bottom.

'Why can't they postpone their caterwauling until I've something in my belly?' he grumbled.

Florin thought of his father. How would those fanfares make him feel? Did any sounds reach him down there? At least, he reflected thankfully, the festive hurly-burly would certainly leave Theodo no time to visit his father.

'The guests arrive today,' he said, his stomach tingling expectantly. He well remembered driving Ramon to despair last year because he'd been too excited to sleep for three nights before the tournament.

Mimus emitted a contemptuous snort. 'The sooner Rollo brings our gruel the better. That's the main thing. No one can rob you of what's already in your belly.'

A little while later he was staring out of one of the tower windows at Florin's side, still with a face like thunder. Florin grinned surreptitiously. The jester couldn't be in such an ill humour if he didn't want to miss the spectacle.

It was a cold, clear winter's day. A strong west wind was buffeting the colourful pavilions on the jousting field, causing the banners and pennants to flutter festively. The entire court had assembled to greet the guests in order of rank and status, from Theodo's Privy Councillors down to the flunkeys and pages. The latter were shivering in their new silk doublets, and Florin was maliciously pleased to see Raoul and his companions shuffling from foot to foot.

The common folk were herded together behind wooden barriers. In addition to Bellingar's servants, many farmhands and workmen from the surrounding district had gathered to cheer the guests as they arrived—and regale themselves on loaves and ale at the king's expense.

'Hurrah!' the crowd kept shouting. 'Long live King Theodo!'

'Just look at them,' Mimus said disdainfully. 'Feed that bleating flock on bread and beer, and they'd cheer the monkeys if we dressed them up in armour.'

Another fanfare rang out. The inner gates swung open and soldiers formed a guard of honour on either side with their pikes high.

'Open wide the gates!' Mimus cried loudly, although no one but Florin could hear him. 'Here comes our royal lord and master!'

Florin, who was seeing Theodo in armour for the first time, had to concede that he cut a splendid figure. He wore thighplates made of finely woven gold chainmail, a gold breastplate, and over it a sumptuous surcoat of crimson velvet embroidered in gold with a lion rampant. Riccardo, likewise attired in a crimson surcoat, was riding at his side. When they trotted across the tournament field and took their places at the head of the receiving line, deafening cheers rent the air.

'Long live our king! Long live the prince! Long live the valiant Lions of Vinland!'

'Don't you agree with me,' Mimus asked over the applause, 'that our beloved king has chosen the wrong heraldic beast?'

Florin looked down at the coat of arms on his right thigh. Seen upside down, the lion did not look half as impressive as it did on

Theodo's velvet surcoat. 'Why do you say that?' he asked.

'He bears no resemblance to a lion,' said Mimus. 'Another kind of beast would suit his face far better. A sneaking, lurking, cunning . . .'

Cheers were still ringing out over the tournament field. 'Long live Theodo, the victorious lion!'

'A stoat, perhaps?' Florin suggested.

'A viper,' Mimus put in spitefully.

'A weasel.'

'A polecat.'

'A scorpion.'

'A spider.'

Florin chuckled at the thought of a fat golden spider on Theodo's royal surcoat.

Theodo had now been joined by Queen Elina and Alix. The queen wore a snow-white ermine cloak that made her look like a statue carved in ice. Alix, on the other hand, with her cape of green velvet and her cheeks aglow with excitement and the cold, resembled a fresh, vigorous sapling in springtime . . .

'Ouch!' Florin said angrily. Mimus had grabbed him roughly by the nose and turned his head toward the castle gates.

'Just look,' he warbled. 'The guests are coming!'

With all due pomp and ceremony, the invited guests approached on their gorgeously caparisoned chargers. Riding up to King Theodo and Queen Elina one by one, they dismounted and bowed low. Then they and their retinues were conducted to the pavilions that bore their coats of arms.

Florin closely scrutinised each new arrival, but failed to discover any familiar faces from Moltovia. Alix had probably been exaggerating to annoy him.

All eyes turned to a particularly splendid mounted procession. The retainers were attired in silver and emerald green, but the horseman at their head wore glittering silver armour.

'King Ludvik,' said Mimus.

Theodo paid tribute to his exalted guest by riding to meet him. To wild applause, the two kings dismounted and exchanged kisses on the cheek before climbing back into the saddle.

'The gallant King of Vinland bestows the kiss of peace upon his neighbour,' Florin said sarcastically.

'A kiss of peace that has often proved more lethal than a scorpion's sting,' Mimus added.

Just behind King Ludvik rode a youth some three years older than Florin, and so fat that his massive rump completely overflowed the saddle. His horse, the biggest charger Florin had ever seen, looked as if it might crumple under his weight at any moment. His face set in an expression of arrogant disdain, the boy spared not a glance for the cheering throng.

'Who's that?' Florin asked.

'I knew you'd take to the youngster on sight,' Mimus said. 'That's Cedrik of Frankenland, King Ludvik's younger brother. An utter nincompoop, but next in succession to the throne. In short, a much-coveted candidate for marriage.' He paused, then added with relish: 'There's talk of a betrothal.'

Florin swung round. 'Alix, you mean?'

'Who else?' Mimus grinned at his look of dismay. 'King Ludvik is childless. Should our princess be widowed early—and that noble youth gives every hope of such an eventuality—Frankenland would fall to Theodo without fight. Besides,' he said with a contented nod, 'he's just the husband she deserves.'

'That's not true!' Florin exclaimed. 'You're being unjust!'

Mimus regarded him indulgently. 'You mean that the Crown Prince of Moltovia would make her a better match?' A spiteful grin appeared on his face. 'What a couple: King Donkey-Ears and Queen Prickle-Tongue!'

'Oh, be silent,' Florin muttered sheepishly.

He watched as Cedrik of Frankenland manoeuvred his unfortunate steed into position beside Alix and turned to her with a supercilious smile. Even from the tower he could see Alix's face darken. After a moment's hesitation she whispered something in Cedrik's ear that made him turn red and bite his lip in annoyance.

'Unless I'm much mistaken,' said Mimus, 'the gallant youth has just received a foretaste of the joys of matrimony.'

Alix marry that mountain of flesh? Out of the question! Florin knew for certain that Alix would never be compelled to take a husband against her will. King Theodo loved his daughter far too dearly for that.

'Enough of this gorgeous spectacle.' Mimus pulled Florin away from the window. 'Off to the stable. We shall be just in time to welcome our guests.'

'Why, has someone brought a jester with him?' Florin asked in surprise. He had concentrated his attention on the notables, not their respective retinues.

'A jester?' Mimus said grimly. 'There are eight of them!'

ALTHOUGH it was not attended by any pomp and fanfare like that of their masters, the jesters' entrance was no less impressive.

The first to appear was a veritable giant so tall that he had to duck to negotiate the stable doorway. He glanced at Mimus and Florin and blew out his cheeks contemptuously. 'You poor creatures are as thin as Lenten herrings—you'd fall over if I so much as blew on you!' He made Florin feel his biceps. 'I,' he bragged, 'am the Mighty Margon, wrestler and jester to King Ludvik!'

He was still speaking when the next jester, a spindle-shanked bean-pole of a man, came shuffling in. He said nothing, unlike Mighty Margon, but he craned his scrawny neck until it threatened to snap, and his bulging eyes roamed this way and that.

Where physique and intelligence were concerned, the next arrival bore a remarkable resemblance to Zito the bear. His name was Iron Jan, from the iron bar he always carried and could effortlessly tie into a bow.

Like monstrosities in a fairground showman's tent, jester after jester entered. Each was stranger in appearance than the one before, but the most remarkable of all was the eighth and last. A female jester, she was a thickset dwarf whose sensational attributes included a luxuriant moustache and a phenomenal ability to belch. This she did whenever she opened her mouth.

That very same evening Florin caught himself thinking how pleasant a place their stable used to be—without guests. It was now terribly crowded thanks to its eight additional occupants, who kept tripping over each other's feet, squabbling and coming to blows.

When he surveyed the mixed bunch of jesters, Florin congratulated himself on having ended up with Mimus. The only one capable of uttering an intelligible sentence was Mighty Margon, King Ludvik's court jester. Iron Jan and the tall, goggle-eyed one—aptly named Ben Beanpole—could just about say their names, but the female dwarf could only belch. Like Mimus, they all wore fools' caps and garish jesters' costumes, but unlike him they weren't in disguise: they were simply fools, nothing more.

That night, in honour of their visitors, and perhaps because it would soon be Christmas, Rollo brought a hunk of black bread and a mug of ale for each. Florin was just savouring this unexpected luxury when Iron Jan snatched the bread from his hand and crammed it into his enormous mouth.

Enraged, Florin turned to Mimus. 'This fat hog stole my bread!'

Mimus had stuffed the whole of his bread into his mouth at once. He serenely finished chewing it, then said: 'Another time, be quicker!'

THE following day was the twenty-fifth of the winter solstice month, Our Lord's birthday and the first day of the new year. All the bells in the city had been ringing since dawn. At the same time, a thoroughly unholy din broke out in the jesters' stable. No sooner had Rollo carried in the morning gruel than a fight broke out over who should have the fullest bowl. The guests continued to growl, grunt and snarl until the moustachioed dwarf smashed her bowl on Iron Jan's bald head, at which the latter didn't even blink.

Rollo watched this pandemonium from the doorway. 'By three-tailed Beelzebub,' he groaned, 'what have I done to deserve such an affliction? And on Our Lord's sacred birthday, too! If I were your master, I'd drive you all to the nearest cattle market!' So saying, he stomped out of the stable.

Mimus had pulled Florin into a corner, where they hurriedly spooned up their gruel unheeded by the others.

'Didn't I tell you?' the jester demanded, patting his stomach. 'Once it's in there, no one can rob you of it.'

Florin watched Iron Jan scooping the gruel off his bald pate and into his mouth.

'What on earth are we to do with them?' he asked despondently.

'You now have eight new tutors in jesterdom,' Mimus said with a malicious grin.

He insisted on keeping Florin in the stable all morning and did not let him go until the afternoon.

While roaming the castle in his usual way, Florin peeked into the banqueting hall, where final preparations were in progress for the grand Christmas banquet to be held that night. The walls were hung with richly embroidered tapestries that depicted the birth of Jesus, the angel appearing to the shepherds, and the adoration of the magi, all on a blue background. The tables, which glittered with exquisite pieces of gold tableware, were lavishly adorned with sprigs of fir and silken ribbons. All manner of sweetmeats filled the air with a beguiling scent of honey, cinnamon and cloves. Florin marvelled at the sight of a crystalline tree whose twigs and foliage were spun from pure sugar.

Flautists and lutenists were practising their melodies, dancers rehearsing their steps. As he listened to the music and sniffed the scented air, Florin found himself looking forward to the banquet for the first time. It oughtn't to be too strenuous, not with so many performers and eight additional jesters. King Theodo would be bound to distribute some lavish tidbits. He, Florin, might even be granted a morsel of gingerbread . . .

The master of ceremonies came over to him. 'Shoo!' he said, as if addressing a stray tomcat. 'You've no business in here. Be off with you!'

Florin returned to the stable, but his agreeable sense of anticipation remained with him all afternoon. Unlike Mimus, who was sitting grim-faced in a corner, he tried to be friendly to their guests. He questioned Margon about his wrestling bouts and evoked roars of laughter from Iron Jan by vainly trying to bend his iron bar. He even made the moustachioed dwarf laugh by rolling a leather ball toward her and then, as soon as she made a grab for it, snatching it away.

He was in such high spirits, he eventually hurled the ball at Mimus's head.

'Hey, Master Sourpuss,' he called teasingly, 'it'll soon be dark.' He pointed to the other jesters. 'What happens, exactly? Do we all go to the banquet together?'

Mimus looked into his shining, expectant eyes for a moment.

'What makes you think that?' he asked brusquely. 'Priests are sent for on Christmas Eve, not jesters and monkeys.'

'But . . .' Florin felt his throat tighten with disappointment.

'But nothing,' Mimus retorted. 'We're permitted to celebrate the occasion in here. After all, wasn't dear little Jesus born in a stable? Wasn't his father an ox and his mother a donkey?'

'Stop it, Mimus,' Florin told him, 'that's blasphemy. But surely they'll let me hear Christmas Mass in the chapel?' he added in a mournful voice.

'Try it,' Mimus said quietly.

Rollo came in and distributed some bread and ale. Before taking his leave of them he brought the monkeys downstairs and put a lantern on the window sill.

'A merry Christmas Eve to you jesters,' he said gruffly. 'But don't become too lively.'

Florin sat in a corner with his legs drawn up, eating his hunk of bread and watching the goings-on in the stable. Mimus, too, had withdrawn to his corner and was sitting with his back to everyone. Lanky Ben Beanpole cavorted from person to person, shrieking in such a horribly strident voice that it eventually became too much for Margon. The muscular wrestler didn't hesitate: he seized Ben by his scrawny neck and shook him until his bones rattled ominously. Meanwhile, Iron Jan kept tying his iron bar in knots. As for the moustachioed dwarf, she sat on the straw with the smallest monkey on her lap, crooning to herself and beaming with contentment.

Florin couldn't stand it any more. Hugging the wall, he stole out of the stable and up the dark stairs to Brother's quarters.

'No, stay,' he said, when a rustling sound told him that the wolf was slinking into a corner. 'I won't harm you.'

So as not to alarm Brother, he slowly and cautiously lay down on the straw. Stretched out on his back with his eyes shut, he tried to summon up memories of his last Christmas. It had been a grand and glorious occasion attended not only by his uncle, King Guido, who came accompanied by his wife and a large retinue, but by many noble families from Moltovia and Arelia. Florin recalled some splendid days of jousting, mounted excursions and boar hunts in the wintry forest, sleigh rides and snowball fights, sumptuous banquets, boisterous games, music and dancing at nights. But it was odd: the scenes in his mind's eye remained dim and blurred, almost like the recollections of a stranger. Other, more powerful images overlaid them: King Theodo in his golden armour, the festively decorated banqueting hall, the jesters squabbling in the stable, Iron Jan with his iron bar, the dwarf cradling the monkey in her arms like a parody of the Virgin Mary and Child . . .

I'm losing my identity, thought Florin, and fear flared up inside him.

'From this day forth, it will be as if your pestilential family had never existed!' Theodo's words.

Those people downstairs were jesters, cripples, idiots—and he was one of them. Perhaps that was a particularly effective method of destroying someone: keeping him among the insane until he himself lost his reason. It was like condemning a healthy person to live among lepers until he inevitably became a leper himself . . .

'Never forget who you are. All our people's hopes depend on you.' His father's words.

'I am Florin,' he said aloud. 'Prince of Moltovia. Florin of Moltovia. I am Florin, Prince of Moltovia . . .' He said his name again and again, repeating it like a magic spell. 'Florin, Prince of Moltovia. Florin . . .' He gave a start: something warm and alive had brushed against him.

'There you are, Brother,' he said in a low voice. He gingerly put out his hand, but the wolf shrank back a few inches.

'You're just like Mimus,' Florin murmured. 'You trust no one, but I would be your friend if only you'd let me.'

He clasped his hands behind his head and lay quite still, and the wolf stole warily closer again—so close that he could smell it. As familiar as that of the dogs at home, its scent was at the same time unfamiliar, acrid and bitter.

It even smells unhappy, he thought.

He edged nearer, inch by inch, and this time the wolf didn't move when he rested his hand on its flank. As he nestled against Brother and took comfort from the animal's warmth, he pictured the banquet now in progress.

The whole court would have assembled—men, women and children who had spent the day longing for nightfall and decking themselves out in their finery to celebrate the Saviour's birth in a fitting manner. The festivities had begun in the castle chapel, which was lit by hundreds of candles. Christmas Mass had been held beneath the stained-glass window that showed Mary bending over the crib in her blue cloak, and the thoughts of everyone present had been centred on the little child who, though naked and defenceless, was possessed of divine power.

On the way from the chapel to the banqueting hall, the choir had sung the hymn of the angels: '*Nunc angelorum gloria* . . .' Singing as they walked in procession behind King Theodo and Queen Elina, everyone would have filed into the banqueting hall, the little princes clinging to their nursemaids' hands in wide-eyed anticipation of the wondrous things that awaited them . . .

Was Alix wearing the gown he'd seen hanging in her chamber the last time he visited it—the one of green silk embroidered with pearls? It couldn't fail to go well with her dark eyes and ringlets . . .

Already half dreaming, Florin shook his head in self-reproof. What were Alix's gown and the colour of her eyes to him? Better to visualise the platters filled with sweetmeats and imagine the taste of cinnamon and honey on his tongue . . .

He felt someone stroke his forehead in his sleep.

'Your hand is always far gentler than your tongue,' he murmured drowsily.

'Hush, little donkey,' said Mimus's voice. 'You're dreaming.'

Without opening his eyes, Florin felt the jester pick him up and carry him downstairs.

- DUEL WITH A GIANT -

NOTHING REMAINED OF the scents and splendour of the previous day's festivities when Florin entered the banqueting hall with the
other jesters. Nothing, that is to say, except the golden table fountain
from which, judging by their glassy eyes and flushed cheeks, the
gentlemen present had been helping themselves to wine for a considerable time.

King Ludvik, swathed in a sumptuous sable cloak, occupied the
place of honour at Theodo's side. Including his large retinue and the
other tournament guests, twice as many men as usual were seated
round the table.

Mimus surveyed the drunken company. 'Tonight is *our* Christmas
Eve,' he said. 'Men only, I see. This evening's entertainment won't be
suitable for sensitive souls.'

The ten jesters were lined up in front of the table and subjected to
inspection like oxen at market. Meanwhile, the tipsy noblemen plied
them with amiable compliments.

'The carpenter who nailed that rickety bag of bones together should be hanged!'

'That monstrosity with the toothbrush on its lip—can it really be a wench?'

'What do they give that colossus to eat? Acorns, like a hog?'

'That pair of hideous frogs must surely feed on flies!'

Florin vainly tried to ignore these cheap jibes, but his cheeks burned with shame. Unlike him, the other jesters revelled in everyone's attention. Mighty Margon flexed his muscles, the dwarf produced an exceptionally loud belch and winked at the men coquettishly, Iron Jan tied his bar into a double bow. And Mimus . . . Mimus strutted up and down cockerel fashion, flapping his arms like wings and regarding the company with a defiant air.

'Cock-a-doodle-do, you iron-bound jousters in your soft armchairs!' he cried mockingly. 'Will you not strap spurs to our ankles for the cockfight?'

'That's an impudent rooster of yours, Theodo,' said King Ludvik. He cast a complacent glance at his wrestler. 'Mighty Margon will pluck out his tail feathers one by one. How say you? Will you venture a wager?'

'Five hundred gold florins say my jester wins,' Theodo replied without hesitation.

'God's blood!' King Ludvik eyed Mimus's slight build disdainfully. 'What's his secret?'

'Discover that for yourself,' said Theodo, depositing a bulging leather purse on the table in front of him.

'I shall.' King Ludvik likewise produced a purse from his pocket. 'Let us drain a goblet to our wager. May the better gamecock win!'

While the men at table raised their goblets and toasted each other, footmen stripped Mimus and Margon naked save for a loincloth. Then they smeared them from head to foot with hog fat and dipped their faces and hands in ash.

When the two jesters took up their positions with baubles raised, ready for the fray, they resembled the savages in Tanko's stories: menacing and belligerent, half man, half beast.

Involuntarily, Florin gripped his own bauble tighter. Margon was an experienced wrestler, and far superior to Mimus in strength. What would the outcome be?

The bout began. Margon promptly leapt at Mimus and hurled him to the floor. Kneeling on his chest with all his weight, he battered him with his bauble. Mimus groaned under the hail of blows, writhing and wriggling like an eel. When he managed to extricate himself from Margon's murderous grip, the grand gentlemen round the table set up a yell worthy of cobblers' apprentices. With a deafening roar, the wrestler renewed his attack, but Mimus slipped through his fingers with incredible agility. He danced round Margon, in front of him one moment, behind him the next, and redoubled the wrestler's fury by tapping him on the shoulder or tweaking his earlobe. No matter how Margon twisted and turned, flailing his arms like windmill sails and snarling with rage, he simply couldn't catch his opponent.

The noble spectators were unsparing with their sarcastic comments:

'Since when do you wrestle with thin air, Mighty Margon?'

'I'll wager you'd be quicker to grab a buxom wench!'

'Be honest, King Theodo, you feed this frog of yours on worms and snakes!'

The momentum of Margon's attacks gradually waned. His ferocious roars became rarer, his movements more sluggish. This was the moment Mimus had been waiting for. Without warning, he smote Margon from behind. One swinging blow with the bauble caught him between the shoulder blades and knocked him down. The mighty wrestler collapsed and failed to rise.

To triumphant yells from the Vinlanders, Mimus planted his foot on the nape of Margon's neck. He was breathing heavily and bleeding from the nose but seemed otherwise unscathed.

'Well done, old fool!' said Theodo, contentedly weighing the gold he'd won in his hand.

Flunkeys helped Margon to his feet and propped the dazed wrestler against a pillar.

Mimus wiped the blood from his nose. 'The king could build a new castle with the gold I've already won him as a gamecock,' he growled.

From his place farther along the table rose a corpulent man with a red goatee and a magnificent jewelled pendant on his chest. 'A heavy-weight contest, Your Majesty!' he called in a drunken voice. 'Your Master Bruin versus my Iron Jan. What say you to a bear fight?'

Theodo nodded. 'Tell the bestiarius to fetch the animal from its stable.' He picked up his goblet and drained it at a gulp. A page stepped forward and promptly refilled it.

Giddy with wine and excited by the previous bout, one of King Ludvik's young vassals jumped to his feet. 'To give us something to laugh at in the meantime, Your Majesty,' he called to Theodo, 'let us set your little jester on Iron Jan.'

A roar of laughter greeted this suggestion.

'That would be a sight worth seeing!' someone cried. 'The pygmy versus the giant!'

'The flea versus the elephant!'

'Give your consent, King Theodo,' the bearded man said with a laugh. 'If victory went to your little jester, it would make you rich!'

'Except that the little fellow would be strewn all over the floor,' quipped someone else.

King Theodo raised his goblet once more and drained it at a gulp. 'How much?' he asked.

The bearded man looked at him inquiringly. 'Your meaning escapes me.'

'How much would you wager on your Iron Jan?'

'Well . . .' The man looked from Florin to Iron Jan as if weighing the odds. 'Against so dangerous an opponent,' he chuckled, 'I think I might risk a thousand gold florins.'

Theodo pointed to the two leather purses in front of him and nodded. 'A thousand gold florins it is. Let them fight.'

The bearded man, who had been laughing only a moment ago, stared at the purses with sudden sobriety. 'You can't be serious, Your Majesty,' he said. 'My Iron Jan would tear your jester to pieces.'

'I did not jest,' Theodo said calmly.

His guests exchanged incredulous glances.

'I'll make you an offer, Theodo,' King Ludvik said soothingly. 'I'll buy the little jester from you for a thousand gold pieces. There's room for a second donkey-ears at the court of Frankenland.'

Theodo laughed and shook his head. 'Ludvik, my friend, I wouldn't sell you that treasure even for a hundred times a thousand gold pieces.'

'And no wonder!' Mimus cried loudly. 'Little Mimus is far too clever a donkey. He can count up to three and beat his drum. No one would sell so well-behaved a little beast, far less feed it to a great big hog!'

Theodo ignored him. 'Little Mimus is not for sale,' he declared. 'But fight he will.'

Margon was still leaning against the pillar. 'They call us fools,' Florin heard him whisper, 'but all the fools are sitting at table!'

Florin stood there clutching his bauble. He had yet to feel genuinely frightened. Any moment now, Theodo would clap his hands and put an end to these insane proceedings. But a quick glance at the throne convinced him of two things: that the king was very drunk, and that he need not hope for mercy. Theodo was undisguisedly gloating over his hopeless predicament. He had watched Duke Bonizo fly at Mimus's throat with the same look of pleasure.

The flunkeys stripped Florin of his costume, smeared him with hog fat and dipped his face and hands in ashes. Then they planted him in front of the table facing Iron Jan.

It was the same Iron Jan who had laughed like a child at Florin's futile attempts to bend his iron bar, so delighted that he had hugged and patted him again and again. Now he was facing Florin with his weapon poised to strike, uttering hoarse, inarticulate battle cries.

'Jan?' Florin called softly, but there was no sign of recognition in the brute's narrowed eyes, which were glittering with bloodlust.

He'll kill me, thought Florin. Fear throbbed in his veins like a flurry of short, sharp drumbeats. This brainless colossus will squash me like a flea, he told himself, and everyone will watch without pity. They'll bury me in some filthy hole in the ground, without a prayer or a headstone. Are you doing this for your slain brother's sake, vengeful king? Do you think he will find peace in his leather shroud if you sacrifice me? I promised my father that I would survive, and now I shall die before him. God in heaven, what a miserable end . . .

'David versus Goliath,' said King Theodo. 'Cudgel your brains, little Mimus, or the world will be one jester the fewer—and I,' he added with a laugh, 'a thousand florins the poorer!'

In spite of his fear, Florin burned with rage. This drunken, perjured king thought he could torment and trample him like a cockroach. He was Florin, Florin of Moltovia, and he wanted to live to see the day when Theodo was painfully reminded of that fact. He would survive!

Without taking his eyes off Iron Jan, he gripped his bauble tighter. In his head he heard Count Ursio's voice: 'Always remain calm in battle. Even the strongest foe has a weak point. Your task is to discover it.'

The colossus confronting him had precisely two weak points: he was brainless and ponderous.

Slowly, with the iron bar raised in his huge paws, Jan advanced on him. For one perilous moment Florin felt paralysed, unable to think of anything save the absurd spectacle they must have presented: a giant matched against a dwarf less than half his height. Then he recovered his wits, and before Iron Jan could seize him he dived between his legs.

That was the prelude to a singular form of dance. Taking a leaf out of Mimus's book, Florin never stood still for an instant. Forever leaping in front of the giant or dodging behind him, he drove the bauble into his flanks.

'Well, man mountain, are you enjoying yourself?' he panted.

Iron Jan grunted, turned ponderously on the spot, and tried to swat Florin with his bar like a bothersome fly.

Florin nimbly dodged the blow, switching from foot to foot and prancing in a circle. As he did so, he was nonsensically reminded of the man who had given dancing lessons at Montfield Castle. A desiccated little hunchback, he had taught Florin and his friends the courtly dances with great solemnity. 'Place your feet daintily, gentlemen! Be mindful of your steps!' The boys had regularly driven him to distraction by cavorting around like billygoats in a meadow. It had been amusing. Well, this dance wasn't amusing. Florin was streaming with sweat. How much longer could he keep it up? As soon as he tired, Iron Jan would grab him with his shovel-like hands and crush him to death.

He would have to put him out of action in some way.

But how? Perhaps he could set his bauble ablaze and fend Jan off with it. To roars of derisive laughter from the spectators, he made a headlong dash for one of the great fireplaces and thrust his bauble into the flames. But the giant returned to the attack, his outstretched hands reaching for Florin's throat even before the wooden bauble had started to smoulder.

That was when Florin broke into song. Gazing resolutely into Iron Jan's dull, staring eyes, he began to sing the first love song that came into his head—and a miracle occurred. The man's eyes took on a soft, dreamy look, only to regain their murderous glint whenever Florin drew breath. And so, while waiting for his bauble to catch fire, he continued to sing unceasingly of fair maidens and lovesick swains, lily-white cheeks and rose-red lips, and the colossus swayed in time to his singing.

But this was not at all the fight the noble spectators had envisioned.

'That dwarf is singing the giant to sleep!' someone yelled. Another hurled his goblet at Iron Jan. 'Don't be lulled by his warbling, Master Bear-Hug!'

Their loud cries jolted Jan out of his trance. No love song availed Florin now. Slowly and surely, the huge man came closer. In desperation Florin withdrew his bauble from the flames and held it out in front of him. Instead of making the wooden head blaze like a torch, however, the fire had merely ignited the tip of its nose. When Florin brandished it menacingly, Iron Jan bellowed with laughter and spread his arms wide.

Frozen with fear, Florin could imagine Jan's lethal embrace. What now? Behind him was the blazing fire. He looked up in panic. The mantelpiece! It was wide and solid enough to offer a means of escape.

Although the ledge was some two arms' lengths above his head, mortal fear seemed to lend him superhuman strength. With gritted teeth he clawed his way up the stonework like a fly, toes and fingers scrabbling for a hold, until he was looking down at Iron Jan's bald head with his back to the wall.

His relief was short-lived. Iron Jan's hands seized his ankles in a vicelike grip. Panic-stricken, Florin battered them with his bauble, heedless of how much pain he was inflicting on himself, until at last— at last!—Iron Jan let go. But a moment later the giant seized him again, and again Florin brought the fool's sceptre down with all his might. After the third blow Jan managed to grab the wooden bauble and wrest it away, almost tugging Florin off the mantelpiece.

A murmur ran round the banqueting hall as the giant snapped Florin's makeshift weapon like a dry twig and hurled the pieces aside. Then with a broad, contented grin he approached the mantelpiece again.

'Let us end this fight,' Florin heard the bearded man call out. 'The little fool has acquitted himself bravely. I propose we call it a draw.'

'No,' said Theodo. 'Let Iron Jan pluck his apple!'

Florin felt himself grabbed by the ankles and jerked off the ledge. He landed plumb in Iron Jan's arms like a ripe fruit. With a bellow of triumph, the giant lifted Florin above his head and hurled him to the floor, then almost lovingly encircled his neck with both hands. Florin kicked and struggled, pounded Jan's chest with his fists and heeled him in the ribs, but the more he resisted the tighter his opponent squeezed. His gullet burned as if he were swallowing liquid fire, his eyes threatened to pop out of his head at any moment. In the end he abandoned all resistance and simply lay there with the breath rattling in his throat.

Without relaxing his grip, Iron Jan stared down at him. His furrowed brow clearly conveyed disappointment that this amusing game would be over so soon. Abruptly releasing Florin's throat, he seized him by the ankles and dragged him all round the banqueting hall. Florin noticed none of this; he was too busy getting some air back into his burning lungs.

Lifting him high in the air once more, Iron Jan flung him like a rag doll straight into the midst of the jesters. This time Florin lost consciousness. When he regained his senses he saw, through a blood-red mist, Ben Beanpole and the dwarf bending over him with an air of curiosity. Distant cries came to his ears: 'Stand away from him, you jesters! The fight has yet to run its course!'

Florin no longer felt frightened. His sole emotion was one of vague surprise. Was he dead? If so, angels would very soon take him by the hand and bear him off into the world to come . . . But instead of angelic hands, he suddenly felt something round and hard between his fingers. At the same time, Mimus's voice whispered in his ear: 'Aim for his eye! You've only three peas—aim well!'

Florin saw the huge, shadowy figure of Iron Jan bearing down on him. As his fingers gripped the peashooter, several images passed before his mind's eye in quick succession: Rollo burying his remains with a surly scowl; Theodo laughingly complaining that he'd lost one jester and a thousand florins; and his father's earnest face—'You, Florin, must survive.'

Survive! With his last remaining ounce of strength, Florin put the peashooter to his lips. Iron Jan's grinning countenance loomed over him like an immense target, and before the giant could strike he'd fired off three peas. For one endless moment Iron Jan stood motionless. Then he clutched his face in both huge hands, staggered backward, and began to roar like a wounded beast.

Florin remained lying on his back, incapable of moving a muscle. He saw faces contorted with excitement at the banqueting table, heard a chorus of yells, glimpsed Iron Jan rolling around on the floor out of the corner of his eye. He lay there panting, gazing up at the star-spangled ceiling and hearing the blood pound in his ears.

I'm alive, he thought. Father, I'm still alive.

But he was far too exhausted to feel exultant.

Two strong hands seized him under the arms from behind and hauled him to his feet.

'You came within an ace of missing that huge full moon,' Mimus growled, giving him a quick hug. 'I'd have rejoiced to be rid of you.'

'That's your misfortune,' Florin tried to say, but all that issued from his smarting throat was an unintelligible croak. It hurt him unbearably to move, so he was grateful just to lean against Mimus and watch the bearded man push his purse of gold across to Theodo.

'The stronger they are, the more they whimper,' he said with a shrug, looking at Iron Jan. 'Victory is yours, Your Majesty.'

- THE GAME OF CHESS -

THE TOURNAMENT CONTINUED for ten glorious days, but all that Florin perceived of its pomp and splendour was the sound of cheering and fanfares. He spent the whole time lying on the straw, sick and battered. When the festivities finally ended, he didn't know what pleased him more: that he could regain his feet and hobble around, or that the departing guests had remembered to take their jesters with them.

Everyone in the stable had timidly kept their distance from him after his victory. The simple-minded jesters believed him to be a demon who had defeated their giant companion by means of magic. Iron Jan howled and covered his eyes if Florin so much as moved his little finger. He would have been amused by this superstitious dread, had he not felt as if he'd been pulverised by a miller's grindstones.

The jesters vanished like lemurs and ghostly apparitions, and the next day Zito died. In the course of the contest that did, after all, take place a few days after Florin's victory, the bear had sustained a terrible blow from Iron Jan's bar and collapsed with its muzzle bleeding profusely. Although it managed to scramble up once more, and although Rollo poured buckets of his magic elixir down its throat, the strength steadily drained from its mighty body until, on the morning of the day after the tournament, Zito was found lying stiff and lifeless in his stable.

Rollo was sick with grief. Pale and unshaven, he shuffled in every morning, deposited the bowls and bucket on the floor and shuffled out again.

'Come now, Rollo,' Mimus said encouragingly. 'While you're moping away down here, Zito is dancing round the heavenly beehive with a beautiful she-bear in his arms.'

'Dancing be damned,' the bestiarius retorted sadly. 'My poor Zito doesn't even have a head any more!'

This was an indisputable fact, now that a skilled taxidermist had transformed the bear's skull into a receptacle for the carving knives used at the king's table.

Mimus sighed. 'Won't you utter one tiny little oath, Rollo?' he entreated. 'Just one, for my sake?'

But the bestiarius merely shook his head with an expression of boundless sorrow and shuffled out of the stable.

The next day, when Florin made a tour of the castle on his still shaky legs, he was surprised to find that Rollo wasn't alone in his dejection. The festive mood had changed overnight. No one laughed or sang in the passages, the chamberlain looked grumpier than ever, the chambermaids whispered together with pallid, tearful faces. Even the ubiquitous hounds had tucked their tails between their legs.

On returning to the stable Florin asked Mimus the reason. 'What ails them all? They can't be mourning the bear, surely?'

'It's enough that Rollo sheds tears for him by the bucketful,' said Mimus. 'The rest are all afraid for the queen, who has been stricken with the ague. Father Anselm and the court physician are tending her turn and turn about: one confesses her and the other bleeds her.' He shrugged. 'It remains to be seen which treatment sends her to her grave the quicker.'

'No wonder they all look so glum,' Florin said quietly.

'Glum?' said Mimus. 'Wait until you see the king. A saucepanful of boiling gall is nothing beside his embittered face!'

Although his anxiety about the queen accounted for the king's black mood, it rendered him no more tolerant. The banqueting hall remained deserted for several nights in succession. The scullions were left to their own devices, the pages loitered idly in the passages. Only the jesters had the unenjoyable task of cheering the melancholy monarch.

'This door,' Mimus whispered on the threshold of Theodo's private chamber, 'is our direct route to Master Antonius. If not today, then tomorrow.'

The king was seated in a comfortable armchair near the hearth with a silver goblet of wine beside him, staring intently into the fire. Flunkeys were slinking around him on tiptoe—a sight that made Florin long to turn tail in the doorway.

'Dearest king,' Mimus cried loudly, 'what's this dismal weather I espy on your royal countenance? Clouds of woe, showers of melancholy, mists of tedium? I know of a proven remedy for them!'

Quick as a flash, he produced a pair of scissors from his pocket, grabbed the hem of a flunkey's doublet and severed it with a single snip.

'Damnation!' the man said angrily. 'Are you mad!'

> *Your face is as long*
> *as your doublet is short.*
> *I'll sing me a song*
> *as I trim it for sport!'*

sang Mimus, swiftly cutting off the flunkey's cuff as well. 'There, perhaps that will amuse my sweet king.'

On any other night Theodo would have laughed heartily at his servant's furious face. Tonight he merely looked daggers at Mimus.

'Careful, Mimus,' Florin whispered.

The jester tried again. 'Scowling faces ne'er won races. Gloomy thoughts put you out of sorts. Moans and tears redouble your fears. Smiles and laughter—'

'Stop it!' Theodo grimaced with disgust. 'I've had enough of your inane chatter. Out of my sight, both of you!'

But before Mimus and Florin could reach the door, he called after them: 'Come back!'

They exchanged a glance. Mimus cast his eyes up to heaven and whispered: 'O Goddess of Fortune, let it be spring and grant our king another enjoyable campaign!'

Then they went back to Theodo.

Tilting his head back, he regarded Florin through half-closed eyes.

'You play chess, little Mimus.' It was a statement, not a question.

So you haven't forgotten yet who I am, thought Florin. 'Yes, Your Majesty,' he replied.

Theodo picked up a small handbell and rang it. 'Marsus, the chessboard,' he commanded when the valet entered.

Florin couldn't but marvel at the chessmen Marsus set out between them. Carved in amber, they were black with shimmering veins of red and gold on Theodo's side, and, on his own side, white streaked with golden-yellow like honey poured into milk. He wondered whether this magnificent set was the handiwork of Benzo's father.

'Proceed,' Theodo growled. 'And keep still, or those confounded bells of yours will distract me.'

Sitting back comfortably in his armchair, he propped his chin on his hand. Florin stood bent over the board in front of him. At first he paid more attention to his bells than to the game, but gradually, with each successive move, he experienced a surge of pure delight.

King Theodo was an abysmal chess player. Seemingly unaware that Florin had quickly gained control of all the strategically important central squares, he moved his pawns and knights up the margins of the board, placing himself in a hopeless position from the outset.

What a laugh! thought Florin. To think that a royal trickster like Theodo can't play chess!

He knew of only one player as poor as Theodo: his own father. It was all he could do not to grin. The sad lot of kings! All the courtiers at Montfield had been loath to play the king. If they did so, they lost deliberately rather than humiliate their royal lord and master. That was why King Philip had never really learnt how to play—as he laughingly admitted whenever Florin swept his pieces off the board for the umpteenth time. Florin, on the other hand, had not only attended the same Latin lessons as his fellow pupils at the royal school of knighthood; he had also undergone rigorous tuition in chess. It would never for a moment have occurred to Senna, Tanko or Radbod to let him win deliberately . . . *Radbod* . . . Distressed by the thought of his friend, Florin redirected his attention to the chessboard. Mimus, who had watched in silence until now, began to sing softly:

'The king becomes a beggar man,
the beggar man a king.
Today one wears a silken shirt,
tomorrow not a thing.
Thus does the wheel of fortune spin—'

'Hush, Mimus!' Theodo snapped ill-humouredly. 'Your babbling disturbs me.'

But Florin had understood just what Mimus was getting at, and it annoyed him. How simple-minded did the jester think he was? He realised, even without any shrewd advice, that he couldn't afford to win the game at any price—not unless he wanted to visit Master Antonius quicker than he could say 'checkmate'.

However, he savoured his superiority for a while longer. He lured Theodo into a pawn trap, captured a bishop and—in passing, so to speak—wiped one of Theodo's knights off the board with his own bishop a moment later.

Mimus broke into song again:

> 'Said the fly to itself:
> "What a sumptuous repast!
> I'll feast on that honey!"
> And then it stuck fast.'

Theodo gave the board such a thump with his fist that the chessmen jumped in the air. 'Will you be silent, or shall Master Antonius shut your mouth for you?'

But Mimus was right. It was high time for Florin to initiate his own defeat. A faint sensation of uneasiness stole over him as he stared at the board, lost in thought. Was it possible for the king to win with the pieces he had left? He would have to sacrifice both his bishops to Theodo's queen as soon as possible—and hope that the king didn't notice anything untoward.

Theodo captured the first bishop with a triumphant smile. The second aroused his suspicion. He eyed Florin keenly. 'What are you doing? That was a blunder—take it back.'

They played the game to a finish. Florin won as inevitably as a stone, once dislodged, rolls down a hillside.

King Theodo gave him a beaming smile, but Florin detected a look in his eyes that boded no good. 'My thanks for the game, little Mimus,' he said. 'We'll play again 'ere long. And now, out of my sight, you jesters!'

'Enjoy your victory while you can,' Mimus said gruffly on their way back to the stable. 'It'll cost you dear.'

'Let me worry about that,' Florin snapped. He was determined not to show how horrified he had been by his victory. 'At least the game didn't go according to Theodo's rules for once.'

'You're mistaken,' said the jester. 'The game went exactly according to his rules—and it has only just begun.'

———————

THE next morning Rollo brought in two buckets and two bowls in the usual way. Mimus picked up his bowl and scowled.

'Wonderful,' he muttered. 'Look.' He handed the bowl to Florin. It was empty.

Florin peered quickly into the other bowl: empty likewise.

'Theodo's retribution,' Mimus growled. 'Simple but effective.'

'Why should he punish you because I defeated him?'

Mimus shrugged. 'I'm your tutor. The stupidities you commit in your princely arrogance reflect on me.' He turned to the door with a sigh. 'Let's persuade the monkeys to give us their breakfast.'

When he tried to leave the stable, two guards barred his path with their pikes. 'Stay where you are,' one of them told him. 'The king advises you to instruct your pupil more carefully in future.'

Mimus made no comment, but he spent the rest of the day putting Florin through his paces with merciless severity. Somersaults, flying splits, handsprings, headsprings, upstarts, pirouettes—he rapped out his orders in quick succession. Florin was allowed no rest, not even a moment to catch his breath.

He submitted to this bullying without protest. By the time Mimus was through with him that evening, fiery circles were dancing before his eyes and his knees felt like jelly. Panting, he flopped down on the straw.

'Mimus, I'm sorry,' he said hurriedly, when he'd got his breath back. 'The mistake was mine. I should have—'

'Spare me the rest,' Mimus said brusquely. 'If I know the king, you'll have more than enough time to rue your mistake.'

The next morning their bowls were empty again.

'Rollo, wait!' Mimus caught hold of the bestiarius by his woollen smock. 'How long are we to go hungry?'

Rollo shook his hand off. 'Why ask me? I only do as the king commands.' In the doorway he added: 'You jesters must really have run riot. Your starvation diet will last a while yet, I reckon.'

If Florin thought that Bellingar Castle had already taught him the meaning of hunger, he learnt better in the days that followed. Hunger wasn't the long familiar companion that had made his stomach rumble at nights and aroused wistful dreams of gingerbread and roast goose; it had become a savage, sharp-toothed beast that ravaged his innards and tore at his flesh until he rolled around, whimpering, on the straw.

Impassively, the guards continued to bar the door. Impassively, Rollo continued to set the empty porringers before them until, on the morning of the sixth day, he paused in the doorway and gave his head a thoughtful scratch.

'What is it, bestiarius?' Mimus growled. 'Shall we invite you to our banquet, or are you already measuring us for our graves?'

'You'll survive for a long time yet, you tough old donkey,' Rollo growled back at him. 'It's the youngster that concerns me.'

As if it had finally accepted its lot, however, Florin's stomach was surprisingly peaceful that morning. He managed to get up and even— with the trembling legs of someone recovering from a long, wasting fever—practised some juggling under Mimus's supervision. But this respite was deceptive: by the afternoon he felt wretched again. Silently, he pored over the sheet of parchment Mimus had set before him. He read letters, syllables, words, but none of them made sense. His temples were hammering away like a score of blacksmiths. Why on earth should an empty belly give such a headache?

'Shall I tell you something, king among chess players?' Mimus said suddenly. 'It's time we gave some thought to your father's execution.'

Florin raised his head and stared at him.

'It won't be too long now,' the jester went on. 'Remember Theodo's order to you: you must crack jokes on the day in question.' His eyes sparkled. 'Far be it from me to blow my own trumpet, but the king owes me several very successful executions.'

'Stop it,' Florin said wearily.

Undeterred, Mimus prattled on. 'My execution ditties are the undisputed highlight of such occasions.

> *'A dozen mighty blows you've struck,*
> *and still the head's attached?*
> *My little penknife would, with luck,*
> *your axe have far outmatched.'*

'Or how about this?

> *'The blade cuts short his cries of dread,*
> *and from his neck flows lifeblood red.'*

'Stop it!' Florin repeated.

Mimus's eyes became narrow slits. 'A king's head on the block is something very special, of course. How does this appeal to you?

> *I yearn to buy a headsman's axe*
> *besmirched with royal blood.*
> *A pig that's been cut up therewith*
> *yields sausage twice as good.'*

Florin clenched his fists until the knuckles stood out white. 'Stop it, please! You're distressing me.'

'Defend yourself, then.' Mimus laughed harshly. 'What ails you? No stomach for a little duel? It's swordplay of the highest quality. You cut and thrust, except that you do so with your tongue.'

Mimus thought for a moment. 'How about this?' he asked.

'King Philip's lying in his cell,
hark, hark, I hear him knock!
"How soon," he cries, "will I get out?
Prithee the door unlock!"

"Be patient, king," the jailer says,
"those words were best unsaid.
The day you see the sun once more,
you'll headless go to bed."'

'Enough!' Florin cried. 'I'll not hear my father's name on your vile, accursed jester's lips!'

'That's better.' Mimus gave a contented nod. 'Anger revives the spirits.' He thought some more. 'A lavish banquet will be served before the execution. Not for the luckless protagonist—no, for the guests invited to witness his spectacular demise. The kitchen and cellar will give of their best: roast fowl stuffed with grapes and plums, pike stewed in wine . . .' Mimus had closed his eyes. 'Spiced pancakes, sweet lardy cakes, little pastries studded with almonds and cloves . . .'

Florin was listening with helpless fascination. 'What else?' he asked softly.

'Wait, I'll show you.'

The jester bowed low to Florin and tied an imaginary napkin round his neck. Then he proceeded to serve.

'Here, young sir, if it please you, is a bowl of fortifying chicken broth. To follow, a roast partridge with crispy skin. Next, a ragout of venison in sweet gingerbread sauce. Then, to tickle your palate, a little bowl of raspberry syllabub served with thick sour cream . . .'

As Mimus approached him again and again, tottering under the weight of brimming dishes, inhaling their aroma with gusto, smacking his lips and rolling his eyes, dipping his finger in sauceboats and licking it with every sign of delectation, Florin felt his anger dwindle away to nothing, and his heart went out to the jester. And when Mimus solemnly approached bearing a blancmange so enormous that he had to steady it with his hands, feet and chin—only to tip that culinary showpiece into his lap, Florin laughed until he developed hiccups. With a conspiratorial air, the jester handed him a spoon, and they scooped up the blancmange together. Florin's tongue detected the taste of almonds, vanilla and cinnamon—until a sudden sharp, gnawing pain in his belly brought him down to earth with a bump.

His fingers still curled round an imaginary spoon, he asked: 'How much longer will the king leave us to starve?'

'Not much longer,' Mimus replied. 'He means to torment us, not kill us.'

'Speak for yourself,' said Florin. 'Don't forget my fight with Iron Jan. Theodo will starve me to death if he wishes. If not, I'll die at the next opportunity. He's playing cat and mouse with me.'

'Then join in the game,' Mimus told him. 'Let the king laugh at you. The longer the cat enjoys itself, the longer the mouse survives. Ah me!' He rubbed his stomach wistfully. 'What wouldn't I give for a nice succulent little mouse!'

———————

THE king sent for them on the evening of their seventh day without food. He was sitting beside the fire with the chessboard in front of him, as before.

'Let's play, little Mimus,' he said without more ado.

Florin drew a deep breath. Don't be a fool this time, he admonished himself. It's only a game. Lose and think no more about it.

But it was strange: although he was so weak he had to cling to the edge of the table, he found it immensely hard to lose on purpose under Theodo's mocking gaze. As if all his pride, anger and hatred were spilling over onto the chessboard, his white pieces continually threatened the king's black ones, and he needed all his willpower not

to win yet again. Mimus's pale, grave face was a help. The jester said
not a word. He watched the game intently until Theodo knocked
Florin's king over with a flick of the finger.

'Checkmate, little Mimus.' Theodo sat back contentedly. 'I see,' he
said, turning to Mimus, 'that your pupil has added to his store of
knowledge in the past week. You're an excellent tutor, Master Jokester.'

'Master Jokester?' said Mimus. 'It was Master Famine who taught
little Mimus how to play chess properly. You can send him away now;
his tutor's severity has had the desired effect.'

Theodo laughed.

_____

THE brimming bowl of millet gruel Rollo brought Florin the next
morning was the most delicious fare he had ever tasted. Unlike Mimus,
who wolfed his gruel in a trice, he made his own breakfast last, enjoying the wonderful sensation that pervaded his stomach.

'So,' said Rollo, who had lingered in the doorway and was watching them, 'you jesters have learnt at last which side your bread is
buttered on.'

Although the time of empty porringers was over, hunger again
became the daily torment with which Florin had learnt to live. His
lessons and duties followed their accustomed course, and one day, to
his great surprise, he found Queen Elina seated at the lunch table once
more. Whatever had accomplished this miracle, Father Anselm's prayers
or the court physician's medicaments, she partook of some soup and a
little almond puree. Although still very pale and with bluish shadows
beneath her eyes, she smiled and took a lively part in the general
conversation. Theodo seemed overjoyed at her recovery. He never once
let go of her hand throughout the meal, not even when casually tossing
Florin a dried fig at the conclusion of his lunchtime story.

As the queen recovered her strength, so the atmosphere in
the castle improved. Theodo took to holding banquets again—

interminable, arduous occasions where the jesters were concerned, but infinitely preferable to the nights they had spent with the king in his sad and solitary state.

It was long since Florin had had to think twice about his jester's tricks. A click of the fingers, and he leapt on to Mimus's shoulders. A tap of the foot, and he turned handsprings across the banqueting hall. A whispered instruction, and he reeled off the requisite riddles and rhymes. Bereft of all shame, he blithely cracked coarse jokes, called forth roars of laughter by mimicking his master's indecent gestures, and, like him, was forever craving tidbits. If Theodo let him live much longer, he reflected bitterly, he really would become a fully-trained court jester.

ON the last day of February, Florin paid his first visit to the castle roof for a considerable time. Purely out of habit, and without really counting on it, he looked for some sign that deliverance was at hand. Although the keen east wind made him shiver, the afternoon sunlight was bright and balmy. The first streaks of brown were showing through the mantle of snow on the fields.

'It won't be too long now . . .'

Florin couldn't get Mimus's words out of his head. Had the jester meant them as a warning, or were they just a product of his annoyance at their starvation diet? Whatever the truth, time was running out. Disaster was approaching as inevitably as Florin had occasioned his own undoing in that game of chess. His father would die, and he himself, if he survived, would become a jester for good and all—which was just another form of death. He would then be Mimus the fool for the rest of his days, just as Mimus had predicted. No, there was little time left and no salvation in sight. No help, nothing.

He was jolted out of his reverie by loud voices and the clash of steel. The soldiers on the castle roof were engaged in a mock battle. They were being hard pressed by the attackers, who had come storming up from the battlements with their blades at the ready. All the combatants were excellent swordsmen, Florin noted admiringly. They feinted and parried with skill, chose the right moment to advance, and never forgot to keep their guard up. At the same time, archers fired their arrows into the thick of the fray and hit the straw dummies with breathtaking accuracy.

The fighters up here weren't a wretched rabble like Theodo's chessboard army. They would resolutely defend the castle and their king to the last man, with all the resources at their command. As he watched the defenders drive the attackers back with a flurry of sword strokes, Florin couldn't help envisioning the battle to come as a game of chess: the dark lions of Vinland versus the pale wolves of Moltovia.

Which side would Mimus be on? He had helped him during the visit of the false friars and had even saved his life during the fight with Iron Jan. Against this, he never missed an opportunity to torment him—and, worse still, he tormented and mocked his father day after day. As on the chessboard, so in reality, Mimus would doubtless be black and white at one and the same time, a cross between a lion and a wolf. But how could one play with a chessman that might change sides from one move to the next?

The mock battle was at an end. Armour-bearers collected up the swords and replaced them in the weapon store. An absurd idea occurred to Florin as he watched them: if no help came from outside, what was to prevent him from undertaking his father's rescue himself? He had managed to wheedle Master Antonius once; why shouldn't he do so again? Except that this time he would be carrying a well-concealed dagger—one he could hold to the dungeon-master's throat. Before the others noticed that anything was amiss, he would release all the captives from their cells. Dangerous it might be, but anything was better than bowing to the inevitable . . .

Florin spent most of the following day persuading himself that his plan could work—until he told Benzo about it. His friend listened in silence. Then he said: 'The sooner you forget this nonsense the better.'

'I might have guessed,' said Florin. 'What does a scullion know about valour?'

'As much as a king's son about making soup,' Benzo said drily. 'But even a lily-livered soup-stirrer knows when someone is rushing headlong to his doom out of sheer desperation.' He gave Florin a consoling hug. 'Don't lose your head. They'll get you out.'

Florin nodded bitterly. 'Without a head.'

THE TAVERN

IT HAPPENED QUITE unexpectedly, as before.

This time it was a woman, a baron's young widow. In audience with King Theodo she tearfully entreated him for protection against her evil brother-in-law, who was seeking to evict her and her little daughter from her castle. When the string of beads fell from her petticoats, Florin stared at it for a moment, thoroughly disconcerted. Before he could recover his wits, it had disappeared into Mimus's pouch.

'Give it here!' Florin hissed.

'I'm no fool,' Mimus retorted in a whisper. 'I'd like a handsome necklace, too.'

'Give it here at once!' But the jester spread his arms apologetically and pointed to his ears as deaf men do.

The audience lasted well into the evening, as usual. They had scarcely left the chamber when Florin tried again. 'Give me that string of beads!'

'The charming young lady intended it for me,' Mimus declared.
'Didn't you see the languishing glances she gave me?'

'Don't talk nonsense!' Florin said angrily. 'Give it to me!'

'Patience is a royal virtue.' The jester grinned and patted his
pouch. 'Tomorrow, perhaps.'

Florin waited until Mimus was snoring with the pouch beside him,
then stole over to it on tiptoe. He rummaged through its contents—
sheets of parchment, a mirror, a pair of scissors, quills, playing cards, a
lump of something sticky he preferred not to examine too closely—
until he finally came, right at the bottom, to the string of beads.

After a brief pause for thought, Florin wound the string tightly
round his arm and secured it with a dozen knots. It now belonged to
him. He would decipher the message in the morning. Happily stroking
the wooden beads, he drifted off to sleep.

WHEN he opened his eyes the next morning, the first thing his bleary
gaze lighted on was Mimus. Sitting cross-legged on the straw, the
jester was about to cut up the string of beads with his scissors.

'Don't!' yelled Florin. He reached Mimus's side in a single bound
and wrested the scissors from his hand.

'Heavens, what agility!' cried Mimus. 'Why gallop around like a
lame carthorse?'

'How could you . . . ? How did you . . . ?' Tears of rage and disappointment welled up in Florin's eyes. 'Give it here!'

'Come and get it!' Mimus jumped up and dangled the string of
beads teasingly above his head. 'Well, come and get it!'

Florin snatched at the beads again and again, but the jester skilfully
eluded him every time. 'Tell me,' he asked with a gleam in his eye,
'what's so special about this rosary that you should strain your legs
leaping for it?'

'I . . . I need it for my prayers,' Florin blurted out, vainly trying to
pull the jester's arm down.

'And I've been invited to a banquet by the devil's grandmother,' Mimus retorted sarcastically. 'If you don't let the cat out of the bag this minute, I'll toss these beads into the privy!'

Florin deliberated. 'In that case, I suppose I'll have to tell you the truth,' he said with feigned resignation. 'They're a magic amulet—a love charm,' he added with a conspiratorial air. 'Whenever I take a fancy to a beautiful damsel, I cut off a bead and she falls desperately in love with me. But the magic only works with me.' He pointed to the string in Mimus's hand. 'The white beads stand for fair-haired maidens, the black ones for dark-haired, the small ones—'

'—for dwarfs and the big ones for ogresses,' Mimus amplified with a grin. 'Not a bad yarn, my princely pupil. Very well, you win.' He held out the beads on the flat of his hand.

The morning seemed to drag on interminably until the noontide bell rang. Mimus stretched out on the straw and Florin hurriedly unwound the string of beads. He deciphered the message in no time— only to spend the rest of the afternoon staring in disbelief at the parchment on which he'd written it down. But its meaning was plain enough:

FLORIN PRINCE OF MOLTOVIA AT THE THIRD HOUR ON SAINT JEREMIAHS DAY COME TO THE LION BESIDE THE WATER IN THE CITY

The next day Florin waited for Benzo in the kitchen sepulchre. Seated on the upturned copper cauldron with his legs dangling, he scanned the message for what was probably the hundredth time.

So it involved a meeting. But who would be waiting for him in the city, and how could he leave the castle without being recognised? St. Jeremiah's was the day after tomorrow. He would have to think of something by then.

What if the message was just another evil trick on Theodo's part? What if the king was looking forward to hunting him down like a wild boar? What if he intended to have him summarily hanged in the marketplace? But, even if it weren't a trap, King Philip would pay a terrible price if his son were captured outside. Theodo wouldn't hesitate to have him mutilated. Did the sender of the string of beads realise how dangerous a request it was?

'But go I must,' Florin said quietly to himself. 'It's our only hope.'

'Go where?' Benzo had come in, accompanied by a gust of air laden with the scent of roast pork.

'Do you know *The Lion Beside the Water?*' Florin asked.

'If you mean the tavern of that name in the city, yes,' said Benzo. 'It stands beside the river below St. Andrew's Hospital.'

'Could you take me there?'

'One moment.' Benzo scratched his neck as if a flea had just bitten him. 'I thought you jesters were forbidden to leave the castle—you especially?'

'I have to be in the city at three o'clock on the afternoon of St. Jeremiah's Day,' Florin said firmly. 'Do you own a horse, Benzo?'

The scullion's expression suggested that Florin had lost his reason. 'My mother keeps a pig, that's all.'

'Then I'll take a horse from the stables,' Florin said resolutely.

'Do that, and you'll never even get past the stable gates,' Benzo predicted. 'The grooms are only waiting for a horse thief like you. No, out of the question. But wait,' he said thoughtfully. 'The donkey that brings firewood for the kitchen—no one would think twice if I fetched it from the stable . . . Yes, that ought to work.' He nodded. 'Stick a thistle under its tail and it gallops like a courser. What's more, it's sturdy enough to carry the two of us.'

'So you'll take me?' Florin asked tensely.

'If you're really set on going.' Benzo shrugged. 'The tavern is easy enough to get to. But you—how will you manage it?' He gave the ears on Florin's cap a playful tug. 'A whole flock of birds would be after you in no time, hoping to peck the grain out of your dung!'

'I shall have to disguise myself,' said Florin. 'Is there anything of yours I could wear?'

'Well . . .' Benzo squirmed a little. 'You, er . . . you could borrow my Sunday smock,' he said reluctantly. It was plain how loath he was to make the offer. 'But you must take good care of it. I only washed and mended it at Christmastime.'

'What about my lack of hair?' asked Florin. Mimus had shorn his head afresh the day before. 'You kitchen lads wear no caps.'

'I'll think of something,' Benzo promised. 'Rely on me.'

STANDING in the kitchen sepulchre two days later, Florin looked down at himself. Benzo's Sunday smock flapped round his body like a hundredweight sack and his feet would easily have fitted into the wooden clogs twice over.

'What do you think? Will I pass muster?'

'Hm.' Benzo regarded him with furrowed brow. 'You bear a passing resemblance to the scarecrow in the castle garden. Wait, though, you still lack some hair.' He groped in his pocket. Then, filled with pride, he presented Florin with a wig woven from the fur of a hare—a mangy one, from the look of it.

Florin eyed it distastefully. 'Couldn't you have found something else?'

'What's amiss with it?' Benzo demanded. 'Many women wear such things when their hair falls out. This wig is our old scullery maid's pride and joy. Don't lose it, whatever you do!'

With a sigh, Florin pulled the wig over his bald pate. 'We can only pray that the sentries don't take too close a look at a pair of dirty scullions.'

'Not so much of the dirty!' Benzo said indignantly as he followed Florin to the door. 'Speak for yourself.'

In the event, no one showed any interest in them, neither the two doorkeepers, nor the sentries playing dice beside the castle gate, nor the stable boy who dragged the stubbornly resisting donkey out of its stall for them.

Once past the outer gate, Florin had to lean against the wall for a moment. They had cleared the first hurdle, but a thousand butter-flies were fluttering in his stomach at the thought of what might await him in the city. Resolutely, he straddled the donkey's bare back. A jolt, a violent lurch, and Benzo was sitting astride behind him.

'I'll guide the beast,' he said with a sly grin, showing Florin a thistle on the end of a cord. 'Hang on tight!'

No sooner had Benzo tied the thistle beneath the donkey's tail than it set off as if pursued by a whole pack of wolves. He hadn't exag-gerated its speed, but neither had he mentioned that the obstinate beast followed a route of its own without the least regard for those on its back: up hill and down dale, across ditches and bramble patches, and through the densest undergrowth in the forest. Clinging to the halter and the donkey's neck in turn, Florin was shaken about like a pebble on a sieve.

The donkey came crashing out of the bushes and thundered on across ploughed fields and pasture. Florin breathed a sigh of relief when the city walls came in sight.

'Well, what did I tell you?' Benzo asked proudly. 'With a little encouragement, it goes like the wind.' He removed the thistle from the donkey's tail and it instantly slowed to a comfortable jogtrot.

———————

THEY entered the city by the same gate through which Florin had unwittingly ridden to his doom a thousand years before. While the donkey trotted leisurely through the streets, Florin stared wide-eyed at the hustle and bustle around him: stallholders crying their wares, girls filling their pitchers at a fountain, a monk bent over his prayer book as he paced up and down in a monastery garden, a gaggle of little boys propelling a hoop along with sticks . . . People everywhere, in every

square, on every street corner—carefree people at liberty to come and
go as they pleased.

Florin's head spun as if he were seeing such activities for the first
time. These things had been going on all the time, he reflected. He
alone had been buried alive in a stone tomb.

Behind him, Benzo said: 'Take that street just ahead on the right,
then turn left at the next fork and make for the river.'

'Is that it?' Florin asked excitedly. He had sighted a tavern with a
bronze lion's head outside.

Benzo shook his head. 'All the taverns in the city are called The
Lion's Head,' he said. 'I'd wager my kitchen ladle you won't find a
tavern by any other name in the whole of Vinland.'

Bordering the riverbank was a row of narrow houses with steep
gables. Wooden skiffs and oars were leaning against the walls beside
their doors, and fishing nets had been hung up to dry. One of the
buildings was painted a conspicuous shade of rust red, and carved on
its weather-worn inn sign was an animal which a charitable beholder
might just have recognised as a lion.

'That's it,' said Benzo.

They watered the donkey at the river, then tethered it to an iron
ring beside the entrance. Issuing from the open doorway were drunken
cries unmelodiously interspersed with loud belches and vile oaths.

Benzo craned his neck mistrustfully like a hound scenting danger.
'Are you quite sure you want to go in?'

'You can wait for me outside,' Florin suggested, sounding far
braver than he felt.

'But what shall I do if you don't come out again?' Benzo asked. 'I
could stand here till doomsday. No, I'd sooner come, too.' He screwed
up his courage and crossed the threshold first.

The dark, narrow passage stank of stale beer and cat's piss. The
door to the taproom was shut, but a loud babble of voices indicated
that the place was full to bursting. Florin noticed that his knees were

knocking with suspense. He felt for the latch with trembling fingers, opened the door—and promptly stepped back in alarm.

The low, smoke-blackened room was thronged with Vinlandian soldiers, all of whom bore Theodo's heraldic lion on their leather helmets. They had propped their swords and pikes against the walls and were seated over tankards of ale and pewter plates of salt beef, dicing or playing cards.

'By all the saints!' hissed Benzo. 'What business have you with these soldiers?'

Florin shrank back against the wall of the passage, struggling to collect his thoughts. A whole taproom thronged with Theodo's soldiers . . . It was like one of his worst nightmares, yet something told him that they weren't there by the king's command. It was probable that they were merely members of the city garrison who were drinking away their pay. If he ran off now, he would never meet the sender of the message. No, he had nothing to lose. Resolutely, he made for the door again.

'That fool's cap of yours has rubbed off on you,' Benzo grumbled as he followed Florin into the taproom. 'You're an utter fool!'

Under the landlord's suspicious gaze they brushed some crumbs and mouse dirt off a small table and sat down on two rickety stools. Florin had had the impression that the men gave an almost imperceptible start when he walked in, but now they were drinking and dicing as before. Some of them had started to bawl a soldiers' song: '*The Lion of Vinland's men are we, no prouder army you will see . . .*'

The landlord hurried out from behind his counter. 'Either you lads order something,' he said gruffly, 'or out you go. Beggars and starvelings have no business here.' To emphasise the point, he rolled up the sleeves of his filthy smock. 'Well?'

'Wait,' Florin said quickly, turning to Benzo. 'Have you any money?'

Benzo looked as if he'd been held up by highwaymen.

'Two copper pennies,' he said unhappily, fishing out the coins. 'The whole of my worldly wealth.'

Florin readdressed himself to the landlord. 'Will that suffice to buy something?'

The man took the money with a contemptuous expression. 'Two small beers,' he grunted. He went behind his counter and returned a moment later with two small tankards.

While sipping his ale, Florin covertly watched the men at the next table passing the dice cup from hand to hand. They were Vinlandian soldiers beyond a doubt; they looked just like the sentries at Bellingar Castle in their leather helmets and tunics of brown wool. Yet there was something odd about them. What the devil was it?

Florin nearly fell off his chair when the truth dawned on him.

'The lion—' he whispered in astonishment, 'the lion is wrong!'

The right thigh of his jester's motley was adorned with Theodo's heraldic emblem. He'd looked at it countless times—he'd absently traced its outlines with his finger again and again during Theodo's interminable audiences. Vinland's heraldic beast had five toes on each foot, not three like the one on these soldiers' helmets!

With bated breath, Florin looked round the taproom. Not one of the soldiers present was wearing the correct emblem. What did it mean?

'Why are you staring at them like that?' Benzo asked anxiously. 'Much more of it and you'll land yourself in trouble.'

As if his prediction had come true even sooner than they would have wished, one of the soldiers at the next table got up and confronted Florin with a menacing air. 'Why gawp at me like that, you idle monkey?' He seized Florin roughly by the collar and hauled him to his feet. 'Send the Vinlander out,' he hissed in Florin's ear. 'Get him to keep the landlord busy outside.'

He pretended to shake Florin violently. 'Go and twiddle your thumbs elsewhere!' he growled. Then he thrust Florin back onto his chair and rejoined his companions, cursing volubly.

'Benzo,' Florin whispered as soon as he had recovered from his surprise, 'take the landlord outside with you. Keep him occupied for as long as possible.'

'What for?' Benzo protested.

'Just do it,' Florin entreated. 'For my sake.'

Benzo gave a resigned nod. 'But how, pray, am I to distract him?'

'The donkey,' Florin said hurriedly, for want of any better idea. 'Pretend you want to sell it. Haggle with him.'

'I'm no horse trader,' Benzo hissed, but he reluctantly stood up and went over to the counter.

'Good man,' Florin heard him say half-heartedly, 'would you by any chance like to purchase a donkey? You could take a look at the animal—it's just outside.'

The landlord came out from behind the counter, wiping his hands on his grimy apron. 'My mule died on me last week, and I need a beast of burden to carry the ale casks.' It was clear from his crafty grin that he hoped to strike a favourable bargain. 'But just so you know right away,' he said as he made for the door, 'I won't pay a penny more than five shillings.'

'My donkey is worth at least ten times that,' Benzo declared. 'Meek as a lamb, strong as an ox, fleet-footed as the wind . . .'

They were scarcely out of sight when two soldiers shut the door and stationed themselves in front of it with their pikes crossed. The rest rose and turned to face Florin.

'Who . . . who are you?' he asked hesitantly, in a voice he didn't recognise. His heart was beating fit to burst.

'By the living God,' bellowed one of the soldiers, 'have you been so blinded by this mangy lion on your helmets that you fail to recognise your own kind? I vow that, by tomorrow night, the wolf of Moltovia will have taken its place! Welcome, my prince—welcome home!' So saying, the tall, broad-shouldered man removed his leather helmet and bowed low. It was as if the scales had fallen from

Florin's eyes: the man was Baron Henried, Senna's father!

A moment later, when another figure stepped out from behind the baron, as tall and broad-shouldered but far younger, Florin knew that he had never been so glad to see anyone in his life.

'Greetings, Florin!' With a beaming smile, Senna too bowed low. 'You're more of a little prince than ever, but the finest sight I've seen these six months past.' He opened his arms and hugged Florin as tightly as if he meant to squeeze him to death.

'Senna, er . . . that lion of yours,' Florin said feebly, trying hard not to weep with joy and relief. 'Theodo's heraldic beast has five toes on each foot, not three.'

Baron Henried gave a bellow of laughter. 'That proves what dolts these Vinlanders are!' he cried. 'You're the first to notice it, my prince.'

Meanwhile, the others had also removed their helmets. In addition to Moltovian noblemen and army commanders, Florin recognised members of his Uncle Guido's bodyguard from Arelia.

'Remember me, my prince?' someone asked, smiling. He was a dark-complexioned young man with a face like a hawk.

'Count Victor!' Florin nodded. 'And I was on the point of dismissing you as a dream.'

'I fear we had to try your patience sorely,' said the young count, 'but now the time is at hand.' He spoke with barely suppressed excitement. 'Tomorrow night, Prince Florin, we storm Bellingar Castle.'

Florin's head was seething with questions. 'Tomorrow night?' he repeated in dismay. 'But how? Where's your army? Besides, have you forgotten Theodo's threat? As soon as armed men appear outside the castle walls, he'll have all the prisoners killed!' He gave Baron Henried an almost imploring look. 'For God's sake, don't do anything rash!'

'Fear not, Your Highness,' said Count Victor, and he and Baron Henried launched into a hurried explanation. Little by little, a picture took shape in Florin's head

As soon as word of Theodo's craven treachery reached Moltovia,

King Philip's surviving retainers had rallied to Chancellor Artold and Baron Henried. Although Theodo had rapidly infiltrated Moltovia with his spies and henchmen and reduced a dozen or more castles to rubble and ashes, more and more Moltovian noblemen, together with their knights and squires, had joined the 'Wolf Pack', as the loyalists proudly and defiantly styled themselves. At the same time, Guido of Arelia and Alan of Angelland had mobilised their armies and placed a vast sum in gold at the loyalists' disposal. But the crucial question remained unsolved: how were they to proceed without endangering the hostages?

'Ten thousand men and enough gold to purchase half the earth,' said Baron Henried, 'but no possibility of taking even one step into that confounded castle!'

It was Chancellor Artold who'd had the idea that eventually clinched matters. As a young soldier he had witnessed the outcome of a feud between a mercantile city and its liege lord. The ingenious townsfolk had undermined the walls of their hated master's castle and brought them crashing down. On the strength of Artold's recollection, the loyalists had evolved a daring plan: they would dig a tunnel beneath Bellingar Castle and undermine it.

'God ordained that the accursed Vinlanders should build their royal castle on soil, not rock,' Baron Henried declared. 'A hundred Argentian miners have been toiling away for the last three months. Yesterday the tunnel reached Bellingar's foundations. Tomorrow, when the men set fire to their pit props, the walls will collapse like a house of cards. We shall be in the midst of the lion's den even before the sentries can sound the alarm!'

Florin was dumbfounded. He simply couldn't take it in: while he had been straining his eyes on the roof of the castle, his rescuers had been there all the time, deep in the earth. If only he'd had an inkling of it!

'We shall storm Bellingar with five hundred men,' said Count Victor, 'the finest soldiers Arelia and Moltovia can muster.'

'But where are you hiding them?' Florin asked in astonishment.

'They moved into the city and the neighbouring villages months ago—in twos and threes, so as not to attract unwelcome attention. Since yesterday they have been deployed in the woods surrounding the castle.' Count Victor looked at Florin. 'My prince, we know how dangerous to you and your father this meeting could be, but we need the answers to a few last questions.'

Florin nodded. 'Ask away.'

'Our scouts report that Bellingar's permanent garrison numbers two hundred men. Can you confirm that?'

Florin conducted a mental survey of the guards in the cellars, on the roof and the battlements. 'That's correct. They're all excellent fighting men.'

'How many are archers?'

'About a third of them.'

'On which side of the inner courtyard will we find the best cover?'

'The west side. The timber arches there would offer protection from arrows.'

'At what points is the main staircase guarded?'

Count Victor's questions came thick and fast. Florin did his best to answer them concisely and accurately, but he couldn't help it: his gaze was magnetically drawn to the loaves and salt beef on the tables.

'At what hour does the king leave the banqueting hall?'

'Around midnight, as a rule. Tomorrow being Shrove Tuesday, possibly later.'

'Will any guests from outside be present?'

'I know nothing of that, but it's quite possible,' Florin said absently. Confronted by a whole table laden with food, he simply couldn't restrain himself any longer. 'Forgive me, but . . .'

The next moment his left hand was holding a morsel of meat, his right a hunk of bread. He crammed his mouth so full he could scarcely chew, aware that he was behaving like an animal in front of everyone. He didn't care, though.

The men glanced at each other in dismay. Nobody said a word until Senna put his arm round Florin's shoulders.

'One thing I promise you, my prince,' he said, and Florin had never known him to speak so earnestly, 'I shall make it my lifelong endeavour to see that you never go hungry again.'

Count Victor walked quickly over to the table and filled a pewter platter with bread and meat.

'Time presses,' he said, as he put the brimming plate down in front of Florin. 'Eat your fill, my prince, but hear me out. How many men are assigned to guard the dungeons?'

'Counting the dungeon-master and his assistants, three dozen or so.'

'Is there any possibility of informing your father and the other prisoners?'

Florin, his mouth full of bread, thought hard. The only person able to enter the dungeons was Mimus. Could he confide in him? No, the jester was too unpredictable. What if he hurried straight to Theodo?

He shook his head firmly.

Count Victor accepted this without demur. 'Tomorrow night, as soon as you hear a dull rumble and feel the earth shake, you'll know that the time has come. Then, if you can, hasten to your father's side. We shall do our utmost to get you out unscathed. And now,' he said, looking from Florin to Senna with a smile, 'make the most of whatever time remains while your young Vinlander holds the landlord in check . . .'

'They shall pay,' said Senna, as soon as Count Victor had stepped aside. 'They shall pay for the hunger and humiliation to which you've been subjected in that hellhole. Count Victor has told us about it. The Devil himself will hang jester's bells on those stinking Vinlanders, and I pray that I shall be able to send a few of them on their way to him!'

Florin gulped in surprise. 'Will you be joining the assault?'

'Yes,' Senna replied, his eyes shining, 'as my father's shield-bearer, and with Count Ursio's personal blessing. The old birddog has finally admitted that he can teach me no more.'

For a moment Florin was back on the roof of Bellingar Castle, watching Theodo's soldiers fight their mock battle, seeing the perfect coordination between swordsmen and archers, hearing the whistle of arrows and the dull clang of blade on blade. He stared at Senna in silence.

'Have no fear on my account,' Senna told him. 'I'm only a shield-bearer. My father has a broad shield and an even broader back.'

Baron Henried had overheard the last few words. 'But God's shield is broader still,' he said. 'Victory will be ours.'

As father and son stood there, two sturdy, smiling figures abrim with confidence, Florin felt a sudden upsurge of boundless joy. The thing of which he had dreamt all these dismal months—the thing in which he had ceased to believe—was about to happen! This long nightmare would truly end!

Once again, Senna hugged Florin as if he would never let him go. 'It's quite absurd,' he said, half laughing, half weeping. 'We move heaven and earth to get you out unscathed, and here you are before my very eyes, hale and hearty. If only you could simply stay here!'

'It's no use,' Florin said wearily. 'I must go back. No one must suspect anything, especially now.'

'Look out!' called the guards on the door.

When the landlord re-entered the taproom with Benzo at his heels, the soldiers were seated round the tables, cursing, drinking and dicing as if nothing had happened.

With his ill-concealed grin, the landlord resembled a fox that has just run off with a plump goose. Benzo, by contrast, was looking thoroughly dejected.

'That cutthroat wheedled it out of me for six shillings,' he grumbled.

Florin was appalled. 'You mean you sold him the donkey? You were only meant to pretend to.'

'I'm no horse trader,' Benzo retorted angrily. 'All that haggling made my head spin. When he held out his hand, I slapped it.'

Florin, who had caught sight of Count Victor surreptitiously beckoning him over to the door, got to his feet. 'Let's go.'

Outside, Benzo stared sadly at the untenanted iron ring. 'He took the beast straight to his stable,' he mumbled. 'It's all my fault. What are we to do now?'

'What's amiss?' asked Count Victor, who had followed them out.

'Er, in the heat of battle, Benzo sold our donkey to the landlord,' Florin explained.

'Wait here.' Count Victor disappeared into the tavern. 'You can fetch the donkey from the stable,' he said when he returned. 'I ransomed it.'

Benzo seemed unconcerned by the fact that a complete stranger, or so he thought, had bought the animal back for them. 'How much did you pay him?'

'Twenty shillings. Why do you ask?'

'Because that landlord is the biggest cutthroat I've ever met,' Benzo grumbled before disappearing into the stable.

Florin looked at the count. 'The tunnel—,' he said, 'may I see it before I return to the castle?'

After so many weeks of fruitless waiting, after all his hopes and fears, he simply had to satisfy himself that deliverance was at hand.

Count Victor hesitated for a moment, then nodded. 'Wait here, I'll fetch my horse.'

———————

MOUNTED on their donkey, Florin and Benzo followed the young count to the royal forest. After they had ridden along the paved road for about a mile, he told them to dismount.

'From here we must proceed on foot,' he explained.

Florin deliberated. 'Benzo,' he said discreetly, 'this soldier has promised to take me to a hermit in the forest who will pray for my father and me. The old man can perform miracles, but he dwells in a hole in the ground . . .' He glanced at Count Victor. 'That's true, isn't it?'

The young nobleman understood at once. 'A dark, cramped hole,' he confirmed, looking solemn, 'deep in the bowels of the earth.'

'I'll stay here then,' Benzo said hastily. 'After all, someone has to mind the beasts.'

The farther they went, the more impassable the undergrowth became. Florin found it hard to keep up with Count Victor, his wooden clogs forever getting stuck in the marshy ground. He brushed the hazel bushes and young willows with his fingers as he trudged past. Still bare and dead in appearance, they would soon be putting out their first green shoots.

In the midst of the forest, to Florin's surprise, they came to a small river. It wasn't wide—he could have cleared it with one determined leap—but it looked deep. The water, which was almost black, could scarcely be distinguished from the forest floor and the roots of the trees on its bank.

'This river is an important ally of ours,' said Count Victor. 'We use it to transport timber beams by night, and it also carries away the earth from the tunnel. Now don't be alarmed,' he said abruptly.

'What at?' Florin asked, only to give a terrible start as the forest around them suddenly came to life. Men in brown leather jerkins, their faces black with soot and grime, emerged from the shelter of the trees or slid down ropes to the ground.

'What brings you to us, noble sir?' asked a thickset captain who had camouflaged his iron helmet with sprigs of foliage. 'Do you have some new orders for tomorrow?'

'No, our plans are unchanged.' Count Victor indicated Florin. 'I merely wish you to conduct this boy along the tunnel for me.'

'I see,' the man said gruffly. Although clearly put out, he didn't venture to argue the point. Grim-faced, he helped the other soldiers to haul some branches and brushwood aside, revealing a dark hole and the rungs of a ladder.

As the captain set off down the ladder, Florin heard him muttering to himself. 'On the eve of the assault, too . . . as if I hadn't anything better to do . . .'

At the bottom of the shaft the captain picked up one of the torches that were lying ready to hand and lit it. 'Come on, then,' he growled. 'Let us get this over quickly.'

The tunnel was so low that even Florin could only proceed at a crouch. Every four or five feet the roof was supported by stout lengths of timber. The farther they went from the entry shaft, the harder Florin found it to breathe in the stale, oppressive air.

The captain's mood improved with every step, however. 'This tunnel is almost a mile long, my lad,' he said proudly, 'and it's taken us less than three months. The men have been toiling day and night. Not any old farmhands and day labourers—no, miners from Argentia. They know their trade better than anyone else in the world.'

While Florin followed him with his head bowed, he tried vainly to imagine what it must be like to toil away in this dark and airless world with twenty feet of soil overhead. He was already feeling like an earthworm.

'You should have seen us four weeks ago, youngster,' the captain said gaily, 'when the ground was frozen as hard as granite. The miners had to hack away at it with their picks. We all lost our fingernails in the godforsaken cold!' He held up his hands to prove it.

'I'm sorry it has been such a difficult and dangerous task,' Florin said unhappily.

The captain smiled, his teeth glinting white in his grimy face.

'I'll say it's difficult and dangerous,' he said. 'A lad like you won't understand this, but we perform it gladly. Whether soldiers or miners, all of us down here hail from Moltovia. We do it for the sake of King Philip and our crown prince.'

As they proceeded farther, the tunnel suddenly became higher and wider until it resembled an elongated underground chamber. Feverish activity prevailed at the far end, where miners armed with pickaxes were exposing massive oak tree trunks black with age.

'There you see the buried treasure for which we're digging,' said the captain, 'Bellingar's foundations. Those tree trunks have supported the weight of that Satan's stronghold for two hundred years. They would probably have done so for another thousand, but tomorrow their time will be up.'

He pointed to some men who were busy ladling pitch out of buckets and pouring it over the foundations. 'Well daubed with pitch, those beams will burn like tinder . . . Out of the way, lad!'

Florin leapt aside just in time to miss being run down by a handcart filled with soil, which was being pushed toward the mouth of the tunnel by three miners.

'The next to last of ten thousand barrowloads,' the captain said contentedly. 'We've reached our goal. The castle's inner wall is immediately overhead.'

He bent to pick up a pebble and tossed it at the roof of the tunnel. 'From here, if we wished, we could ram our pikes up the Vinlanders' stinking backsides. By tonight we'll have reached the rear of the foundations, then to hell with Bellingar!'

Glorious conquerors crawling to victory on their bellies, like earthworms . . . No poet would immortalise the battle to come, yet this tunnel was the shrewdest strategy imaginable. Barricaded behind his walls, King Theodo was about to be felled like a tree unaware that the axe was already descending on its trunk.

Florin paused at a turning off the tunnel. By the light of the captain's torch he made out a small side passage whose walls were faced with massive slabs of stone. The roof, too, was faced with similar slabs supported by thick timbers embedded in the ground.

Hauling those immensely heavy slabs the length of the tunnel must have been a back-breaking task.

Florin stared at them in surprise. 'What is their purpose?' he asked.

'Wait, I'll show you.' The captain fished a crumpled scrap of parchment from his pocket. Florin recognised it at a glance: it was his own drawing of Bellingar's nether regions.

'The dungeons run parallel to this shaft,' the captain explained, '— here, here and here. The purpose of the slabs of stone is to shield them from the flames. But for them, the prisoners would be roasted alive in their cells. They'll be warm enough as it is.'

Florin stared at the plan, dry-mouthed. What if he had drawn the dungeons in the wrong place? He could never have guessed that the prisoners' survival would depend on his rough scrawl. Did the dungeons really lie behind those stone slabs? What wouldn't he have given now to possess the magical eyes with which Mimus claimed to be able to see through doors and walls!

The captain conducted him along the last stretch of tunnel. All round them, miners were laying bare the foundations in feverish haste. The shaft ended abruptly in a solid wall of earth, except where a narrow fissure seemed to penetrate still deeper.

Florin pointed to it. 'What's that?'

'That, my lad,' the captain declared, 'is the most dangerous place imaginable. Before we can widen the tunnel and insert the supports, someone has to dig on ahead. That task is performed by our human mole. He's about your size,' he went on, glancing at Florin, 'or he wouldn't go through. That boy risks his life every day. One cave-in or rockfall, and he'd be flatter than a tortoise beneath a horse's hoof.' He illustrated this by holding up his finger and thumb a bare inch apart. 'But our mole is a brave lad, and God is with him . . . Ah, here he comes!'

As Florin watched, a skinny boy crawled out of the crack. He was encrusted with mud from head to foot, and his sluggish movements bespoke his exhaustion. He was towing a big net filled with soil and stones.

Involuntarily, Florin stepped forward. His heart was overflowing—

he wanted to say something nice to the boy, wanted to thank him. Then his mouth and eyes opened wide.

The human mole was Radbod.

And his expression was as disconcerted as Florin's.

'It's fortunate,' he said feebly, 'that I'm too weary to be frightened, or I'd mistake you for a ghost and run off yelling.' He leant against the damp wall of the tunnel, smiling shyly. 'It really is you, isn't it? Did you contrive to escape?'

Florin shook his head. 'I must go back.' He couldn't take his eyes off Radbod. His old friend's grimy face looked pinched with exhaustion. 'Radbod, how in the world do you come to be here?'

'I couldn't . . .' One of the men set a pitcher of water in front of Radbod, and he drank thirstily before continuing. 'I couldn't just wait until I was old enough to fight, so halfway home to Moltovia I gave my father the slip and rode back here.'

The captain stared at them both and scratched his head. 'Let me roast in purgatory for a thousand years longer if I understand so much as a word of what you're saying to each other,' he said.

Radbod paid no heed to what the captain had said. 'It's almost finished. Tomorrow the castle will be stormed.'

Florin nodded. 'I already spoke with Senna and his father, and—'

'Senna's here?' Radbod looked astonished.

'You mean the pair of you knew nothing of each other?' Florin exclaimed. 'You were down here all the time, am I right?'

'Dig, eat, sleep and dig some more,' Radbod said with a faint grin.

Florin grasped his hand. 'Just tell me how I can ever thank you.'

'Forget it, Florin,' said Radbod. 'Let's talk when all this is over.'

'Florin?' the captain repeated, eyeing Florin in amazement. 'You aren't . . . You can't be . . . But that's impossible . . .'

'Quite impossible,' Florin said quickly. He gave Radbod a hug. 'Promise me you'll be outside when the castle falls.'

'Gladly,' said Radbod. 'As soon as my work down here is finished,

I shall hide in the woods until the excitement is over. You can come and look for me afterward.' He grinned, but Florin knew that they were both haunted by the same fear: what would happen when Bellingar's walls collapsed?

The captain, who had become noticeably monosyllabic, conducted Florin back to the mouth of the tunnel. Florin's foot was already on the first rung of the ladder when the man caught him by the arm.

'I don't know who you are,' he said, 'but one thing I do know for certain. In our mole, you have a friend worthy of a king.'

'And retainers of equal merit in you and your men,' Florin replied. 'My thanks to you all.'

Count Victor, who had been waiting for him at the entrance, guided him back through the forest. When they emerged into the little clearing where Benzo was guarding the horse and the donkey, his friend stared at him in surprise.

'That hermit must truly be a miracle worker,' he said. 'Your face is glowing as if he'd shown you the treasure of the elves!'

Count Victor bowed to Florin before mounting his horse. 'You have only to endure your lot for one day more,' he said in a low voice.

'It will pass,' Florin replied, doing his best to sound confident.

'You are very courageous. Farewell!' The count vaulted into the saddle and raised his hand in salute. 'If God will, we shall soon see each other again.'

PEERING through the leafless trees, Florin could make out Bellingar Castle in the distance. The first evening mists were rising from the fields at its foot. It seemed to him, in the vaporous light, that the castle's reddish walls were rising and falling like the flanks of a living, breathing creature. Bellingar crouched on top of its hill like some great, fleshy beast lying in wait for him—patient and motionless, sure of its prey.

If only he could strike a bargain with it! Having had a whiff of freedom, he felt like the cook who could only whistle, however tempt-ing the scent that rose from his pans. He dearly longed to be able to remain outside the castle walls . . .

Until he found himself unable to enter them!

The sentries at the gate had cast only a cursory glance at the two scullions and a stable lad took charge of the donkey without a word. When they were walking across the courtyard to the door, however, Florin gave a sudden groan. 'No, Benzo, tell me it isn't true.'

As usual, two doorkeepers were standing on either side of the portal. One was a middle-aged man and quite unknown to Florin, but the other was a tall youth with a haughty face.

'It's Raoul,' Florin whispered. 'Why should he be there?'

'He must have dropped a platter while serving,' Benzo suggested, 'and this is his punishment.'

'He'll recognise me at once,' Florin said in despair, panic-stricken at the sight of the sky, which was already darkening ominously in the east. 'I must get in somehow.'

'First, let's beat a retreat before that ape sounds the alarm!' said Benzo. He took Florin's arm and drew him into the shadow of the wall.

Florin thought hard and feverishly. There were no doors other than the portal. The windows on the ground floor were barred and the big round-arched windows on the floor above were out of reach. How could he get into the castle without turning into a bird? If only he had one of the tall ladders used by besiegers, or a catapult with which Benzo could project him onto the battlements! Tanko had told of a knight who transformed himself into a missile and landed in a wicked governor's soup just as he was about to take a spoonful. But that tale was surely a figment of Tanko's imagination, like the hair-raising story of the besiegers who stormed a castle by way of the privy shaft . . .

'What is it?' asked Benzo, startled by Florin's sharp intake of breath. 'Have you had an idea?'

'Possibly,' Florin whispered. 'Let's go and see.'

They stole along the wall at a crouch. As soon as the portal and doorkeepers were out of sight, Florin headed resolutely for one of the privy shafts. Several stories high, it clung to the wall like a huge wooden worm and ended in a cesspit at the foot.

'No, Florin,' Benzo said in alarm, 'you can't be thinking what I'm thinking!'

Florin's gaze travelled upward to where, at a dizzy height, the projecting stone privy sat perched atop the timber shaft like a bird's nest. 'I happen to know,' he said, 'that a castle was once captured by that route.'

'And how many of the besiegers perished in the attempt?' Benzo asked dubiously. 'Just think: if you get stuck in there, you'll drown in excrement!'

Undeterred, Florin clambered onto the thickly encrusted iron grating over the cesspit, crouched below the mouth of the shaft and peered up its dark interior.

'I think I'm thin enough,' he muttered as he vainly strove to make out some details.

'Even if you get to the top,' said Benzo, 'what will you do if you run into someone dressed as a scullion?'

Florin went hot and cold—he hadn't thought of that.

'You must fetch my jester's motley from the kitchen sepulchre, Benzo,' he said. 'This minute!'

Benzo had already set off at a run. 'Wait there!' he called over his shoulder, as if Florin had a choice.

Florin reinserted his head into the evil-smelling shaft. When his eyes accustomed themselves to the gloom he made out some cross-pieces nailed to the sides at regular intervals. They were only a few inches wide. Could he really use them to hoist himself up?

Benzo was back sooner than Florin had thought possible. 'Don't do it,' he said, producing the costume from under his smock.

'Can you think of a better idea?' Florin demanded as he hurriedly changed out of Benzo's Sunday best.

'No,' Benzo conceded.

'Then pray that no one takes it into his head to use the privy while I'm inside there.'

'I will,' said Benzo, devoutly folding his hands.

'Can you pray and give me a leg up at the same time?'

'Pray while you work—that's what my father taught me.' Benzo bent down so that Florin could climb on his clasped hands.

Florin reached for the first crosspiece and pulled his feet up after him. The shaft was too cramped for him to turn round, the stench suffocating. Painfully slowly, like a caterpillar inside a reed, Florin used his hands and feet to haul himself from crosspiece to crosspiece. His fingers kept slipping on the slimy timber, and he had to wedge himself between the walls with his knees and elbows. Twice he got stuck, and for a few terrifying moments he was unable to advance or retreat. To conquer his rising panic he thought of Radbod: compared to his friend's ordeal in the tunnel, this was a mere stroll. He simply had to make it!

For the first time, he was grateful to Count Ursio for having chased them up steep crags again and again, heedless of their oaths as they clung to the rock by their fingers and toes. 'Keep your eyes on the sky!' the old fencing master used to call. 'If you wish to reach the top, never look down!'

Here, too, Florin carefully avoided looking down. Instead, he focused his gaze on the pale opening that continued to beckon high overhead.

'I . . . will . . . get . . . there!' he panted, and climbed on.

Good fortune was with him. No one entered the privy until he was close beneath the seat with the circular hole in it. He had just summoned up his last reserves of energy and started to haul himself through it when the door of the privy opened and in came . . . Riccardo!

At the sight of a head and shoulders protruding from the seat he gave a startled cry and crossed himself as if Florin were a ghost arisen from hell itself. 'W-what are you doing here, little Mimus?'

'W-what everyone does,' Florin stammered, quite as startled as the king's eldest son. Panting with exertion, he clambered out of the privy as fast as he could.

Riccardo regarded him with a profoundly suspicious air. 'Do you always climb into the privy to relieve yourself?'

'Always,' said Florin, striving hard to look innocent. 'Is there . . . any other way of doing it?'

Still gasping for breath, he tried to squeeze past Riccardo as unobtrusively as possible. 'I'm sure you have important business to attend to,' he said, pointing to the seat. 'Don't let me disturb you.' With a hurried bow, he darted outside.

'Phew!' he exclaimed.

But his sense of relief disappeared in a flash when he realised which privy shaft he had chosen to climb. The door facing him was only too familiar: it was the door to King Theodo's bedchamber. He was standing, covered with filth and giving off a foul stench, in the midst of the royal apartments.

On tiptoe, he stole along the passage toward the carved portal that gave entry to the apartments.

'Stay shut,' he entreated the doors to left and right of him. He was still racking his brains for some way of getting past the sentries unscathed when he heard Riccardo's voice behind him. 'Wait, little Mimus! You don't mean to tell me you always . . .'

Florin instantly abandoned all hope of concocting a plan. He made a dash for the portal—and bumped into Countess Wogrim, who had just emerged from Alix's chamber. So violently did he collide with the bony old woman that he fell to the floor, his ears ringing like a bell, but he quickly scrambled to his feet and tried to dodge past her.

'Stand still!'

The Warhorse seized his collar in a vicelike grip, while holding him as far away from her gown as possible. 'What's your business here? And why in Christ's name—' she sniffed with distaste, 'do you stink like a polecat?'

'I was in the privy,' Florin said truthfully.

'What were you doing in there?' Alix had appeared in the doorway.

Florin just managed to suppress a ripe oath at the sight of her. Everything seemed to be conspiring against him.

At that moment they were joined by Riccardo. 'The jester was in the privy!' he exclaimed.

'We already know that.' Alix surveyed Florin's filthy costume, wrinkling her nose. 'Ugh! Did you fall in, you clumsy dolt?'

'No,' Florin mumbled, staring at the floor. 'I was hiding, that's all. I simply had to know.'

Alix's dark eyes twinkled. 'Know what?'

'If it's true what they say about exalted personages such as your-self,' Florin replied innocently. 'That you all pee rosewater and orange juice.'

Alix burst out laughing, and Riccardo grumbled: 'You must know the truth of that perfectly well.' However, they were drowned by Countess Wogrim's indignant voice: 'Keep a bridle on your tongue, little jester! That filth is not fit for a princess's ears!'

'There you have it, straight from the horse's mouth,' Alix said with a grin. 'Nevertheless, because you told the truth so nicely, we shall have mercy on you yet again. You may go.'

Florin gazed at her for a moment. She looked so clean and pretty in her white silk gown, he surely deserved a little revenge for all the nasty jibes he'd endured at her hands.

'Oh, thank you!' he exclaimed. And before Alix could resist, he clasped her to him in a tight embrace. 'A thousand thanks!'

– SHROVE TUESDAY –

BEFORE REJOINING MIMUS, Florin made a detour via the laundry. Although the washerwomen called him a number of unflattering nicknames, they permitted him to climb into one of their big tubs and give himself a thorough scrub with ash lye.

Back in the stable once more, he glowed with elation to such an extent that he found it hard to keep a straight face. His heart was singing. Tomorrow night was the night! Their rescuers would pull Theodo's throne from under him with a crash like thunder. Then he could sit on the bare floor and croak like a frog . . .

Florin had a mental picture of his father and the other captives. Released from their rat-holes, they would make the ascent to daylight and fresh air—they would see the sun once more. Life would begin anew for all—and this time, Florin reflected happily, it was not just wishful thinking. It was really going to happen . . .

He listened intently. Was that a rumble he could hear far below? Had the ground shaken a trifle? At the thought that their rescuers might, at that very moment, be applying their axes to the foundations immediately beneath the stable, he emitted a sudden, joyous laugh.

Mimus glanced at him sharply. 'Where were you this afternoon?'

'With the princess,' Florin replied as casually as he could. 'Playing hide and seek.'

'Hide and seek, indeed,' said the jester. 'Well, today isn't a good day for playing little games of your own. The king has signalled a new form of entertainment.'

'I can guess, I've heard that one before,' Florin retorted angrily. 'Obey the rules,' he mimicked. 'You're the mouse. Play the cat's game, then nothing will happen to you . . .' He was feeling so boundlessly triumphant, he simply couldn't restrain himself. 'But what if your perjured king has miscalculated? What if he has already lost—or will do so sooner than he dreams?'

'Then he'll win notwithstanding,' Mimus replied calmly. 'For by then the white king will be checkmate.'

The white king . . . An icy hand gripped Florin's heart. He had been white both times. 'What do you know, Mimus?'

'What would a jester like me know?' Suddenly, Mimus broke into song:

> *'God sits enthroned above us,*
> *the Devil dwells below,*
> *and we poor sinners all must die,*
> *that everyone doth know.'*

'The time has come, hasn't it?' Florin said quietly.

As if he hadn't heard, Mimus sang on:

> *'No matter what we are on earth,*
> *whatever our estate,*
> *monarch or jester, king or fool,*
> *we all must meet our fate.'*

'When is my father to die?'

'Tomorrow night.'

Florin's head seemed to burst, scattering his thoughts like startled birds. The time has come, he told himself. Tomorrow night, the night of Shrove Tuesday . . . an execution on Shrove Tuesday for everyone's delight . . . That's Theodo for you . . . It mustn't happen, not with deliverance so near at hand . . . Tomorrow night . . . God help us . . . They'll come tomorrow night, but too late . . . It's all too late . . .

And then, in a moment of total clarity, he knew that help could come from one quarter only.

'Mimus,' he said, 'you must help me.'

When the jester turned to look at him, Florin detected compassion in his eyes. 'Help you?' he asked.

'Yes, to save my father.'

'Your father is to die tomorrow night,' Mimus said quietly. 'I cannot bring the dead back to life.'

'Bellingar will fall tomorrow night,' Florin said resolutely. 'And now, run and tell the king for all I care, but do so at once!'

Mimus stared at him in silence, so Florin went on: 'Our rescuers have undermined the castle. Tomorrow they will set fire to the foundations, then Bellingar's walls will collapse.'

Slowly, as if the information had trickled into his head drop by drop, like sticky sap, the jester nodded.

Florin jumped up excitedly. 'Don't you understand? A few hours' delay, and my father will be saved!'

He made to seize Mimus's arm, but the jester roughly thrust his hand aside and turned away.

Florin stared at his back. It was a mistake, he thought in despair. I shouldn't have told him.

Acting on a sudden flash of inspiration, he drew the fool's sceptre from his belt. 'How dare you pester your venerable master in this way, little Mimus!' he demanded shrilly, as if the wooden head itself were speaking.

'I most humbly beg your pardon, worthy Sir Blockhead,' he replied in his own voice, 'but I know of no one else who can help me.'

'You expect your venerable master to risk his neck on your account?' snarled the bauble. 'He must go and tell the king this instant!'

'Pardon me for contradicting you, Your Wooden Worship, but he won't.'

'And why not, pray?'

'Because I'm his friend,' said Florin, 'and he is mine.'

'Your friend? Fiddlesticks!' the wooden head said angrily. '*I* am his only friend. You are a troublesome little fool from Moltovia, where they can't tell apples from pears.'

Out of the corner of his eye, Florin saw a smile flit across Mimus's face. Then the jester said abruptly: 'No harm must come to the king.'

'What else have I just been speaking of?' Florin said, looking puzzled. 'My father must be . . .' He broke off and stared at Mimus. 'Theodo, you mean?'

'Yes. If you promise me that no harm will come to him, I'll help you.'

No harm? Florin's throat went dry. But I *mean* him harm, he thought. I want them to reduce his castle to rubble before his eyes, then put a sword to his throat. I want him to whimper for mercy like a dog, like a . . .

'How can I make such a promise?' he said quickly. 'You've no idea of the tumult that will—'

Mimus brushed his objection aside with a single gesture. 'You're the king's son. They'll listen to you.'

The eyes beneath the fool's cap glowed darkly as he looked at Florin. 'Promise it, then I'll help you.'

'I promise,' Florin vowed solemnly. 'But how will you help me?' he blurted out. 'What do we do now?'

'We betake ourselves to the banqueting hall and appear before the king, what else?' Mimus replied drily. 'And tonight you'll be an amusing, unwitting little donkey, unless you wish the sky to fall in on us right away.'

FLORIN got through the evening in a kind of delirium. He did what had to be done—he hopped, skipped and sang—but in reality he was far away, either with his rescuers in the tunnel or with his father in the dungeons. King Theodo, who was in the best of spirits, more than once rewarded his jesters with tidbits that stuck in Florin's craw.

He was firmly convinced that he wouldn't be able to shut his eyes all night, but no sooner had he lain down on the straw than he glided into sleep—and into a dream.

HE was riding through the birch forest at his father's side. Although the chill morning air made him shiver, the sun was shining brightly through the treetops, causing the dewy leaves beside the track to sparkle like slivers of crystal. Their horses left deep, dark hoofprints in the young grass.

Florin heard a faint tinkling sound close by. He turned to look and gave a start: Mimus, not King Philip, was riding beside him.

'What are you doing here?' he demanded.

'Don't you remember?' Mimus replied. 'The two of us are heroes, and we're setting forth to conquer the evil Lord of the Flies.'

Florin looked at him and couldn't help laughing aloud. Heroes? With his ass's ears nodding in time to his horse's footsteps, the jester cut a comical figure in the saddle.

'I thought you couldn't ride?'

'I can't,' Mimus replied. 'They tied me on.'

Florin caught sight of a heavy iron chain encircling the jester's body.

'I've never learnt how to ride, don't forget,' Mimus went on calmly. 'But for this chain, I would be bound to fall off and land head first in a midden.'

The notion made Florin giggle, but he felt profoundly sympathetic at the same time.

'Make haste,' the jester urged. 'The Lord of the Flies wreaks death and destruction. It behoves us to seal his fate. Time is short!'

AS if he really had encountered the Lord of the Flies during the night, Florin awoke feeling as if he had a swarm of insects in the pit of his stomach. He couldn't keep still for a moment. What did Mimus have in mind? He was ready for anything. If the jester asked him, he would cut himself into little pieces . . .

First, however, Rollo entered, bearing their buckets of water and bowls of gruel, and Florin knew from experience that Mimus was best not disturbed during breakfast.

'Well,' he said hoarsely as soon as the jester had laid his empty porringer aside, 'give me your instructions. What am I to do?'

Mimus cast a brief glance at Florin's burning eyes and flushed cheeks. 'An entirely new and extremely difficult trick,' he decreed. 'It will require all your strength and skill.'

He set a bucket of water in front of Florin. 'Take up your position five feet away . . .' He gauged the distance, screwing up his eyes. 'A little farther away. No, nearer. Yes, that's right.'

He marked the spot on the floor with a stick of charcoal. Then he handed Florin a peashooter and a pea. 'Aim for the bucket. If the pea lands in the water, retrieve it with your teeth and start again. Repeat the process until noon.'

'What!' Florin was dumbfounded. 'Why?'

'Don't ask, just do it,' said Mimus. 'Much depends on our performance tonight. It must be well-rehearsed.'

The jester sat down cross-legged on the straw and watched his pupil aim at the bucket, plunge his head in the water and fish out the pea. Florin did this precisely three times, then he'd had enough. His collar was sodden with icy water and his teeth were chattering.

He rounded on Mimus angrily. 'What's the purpose of this idiotic rigmarole?'

'It's a sovereign exercise,' Mimus muttered absently with his eyes shut, 'and admirably suited to cooling exuberant hotheads.'

Florin flew into a rage. 'My father is to die tonight,' he protested, 'and you have me imitate a duck?' Furiously, he hurled the peashooter at Mimus's head. 'This comes of hoping for help from a jester!'

'Do you imagine I can help someone who skitters around like a cat with its tail on fire?' Mimus said gruffly. 'Keep calm—you can do no more.'

Reluctantly, Florin fell silent and sat down in a corner, but the hours until noon were sheer torture. His feverish imagination devised a hundred different versions of the coming night's events. One moment a vanquished Theodo was kneeling humbly before his father; the next, he was laughing triumphantly as the axe fell. One moment the attackers took Bellingar Castle by storm; the next, Count Victor, Baron Henried and Senna were lying dead in their own blood. Hope and despair continued to dance a fandango in Florin's head until he could stand no more and dunked it in the bucket of his own free will, just to banish the turbulent visions.

When the noontide bell sounded, Mimus rose, stretched and yawned.

'Are you ready?' Florin asked.

'Yes.'

'Well, what shall we do?'

'Wait and see.'

'Will you be paying my father a visit this afternoon?'

When Mimus merely nodded without a word, Florin asked quietly: 'Does he know?'

Mimus looked at him. 'Your father requested spiritual consolation. Theodo has denied him a priest.'

Florin closed his eyes. No priest, no confession, no absolution, no

means of making his peace with God. Would Theodo stop at nothing
in his thirst for revenge?

'Have you already sung him your executioner's songs?' he asked
bitterly.

'Yes, I have, damn it!' Mimus shouted suddenly. Florin recoiled.
He had never seen the jester lose his composure before.

Mimus paced angrily up and down. 'If only you would understand!' He came to an abrupt halt. 'Come, look at me. Look at me
closely.' He plucked at his costume. 'What do you see? Well, tell me!'

'A jester's motley.'

'Wrong,' said Mimus. 'These are dragon's scales, layer after layer
of them grown for fifteen long years. They're impenetrable as a suit of
armour.'

But his face, which looked unusually pale and vulnerable, belied his
words. A moment later the mask descended once more.

'Be silent now and let me sleep.'

'Answer me one thing more,' Florin said quickly. 'Are the other
prisoners also doomed to die?'

Mimus nodded. 'One after another. By Easter none will be left
alive.'

When Florin looked at him mutely, he snapped: 'Nothing has yet
been said about you. So kindly grant me my afternoon repose, or I'll
fall asleep tonight and not awaken until Bellingar has been reduced to
rubble and the moon is shining on my face.'

———————

ON that lonely afternoon Florin learnt how the poor souls in purgatory must feel. Relentlessly harried from one corner of the stable to
another by agonising fear and breathless hope, he paced up and down
without rest or respite until, utterly exhausted, he went down on his
knees and began to pray. He prayed to Jesus and the Virgin Mary, to
St Florin and all the other saints he knew; he prayed to his mother in
heaven to intercede with God on his own and his father's behalf.

Mimus, who returned from the dungeons to find him still on his knees in the straw, refrained from grinning sardonically at Florin's devotions for the first time ever. Neither of them spoke until it was time to go.

The night of Shrove Tuesday awaited them.

AT the entrance to the banqueting hall they were greeted by wild, outlandish music. To the muffled beat of a drum, bagpipers marched the length of the great chamber producing shrill, high-pitched notes from their instruments. It was the kind of music played at annual fairs, ceremonial processions, public entertainments—and executions.

The Shrove Tuesday banquet was already in full swing. The king's companions were feasting and carousing as if they could store enough in their bellies to last them for the forty days of Lent to come.

Erected in front of the banqueting table was a low platform bearing some object swathed in black. What could it be? A wine cask? A tree stump? Part of a pillar, perhaps? No: *the executioner's block!*

Florin's blood turned to ice at this realisation, and his horror almost overcame him when he saw that one of the revellers at the table was Master Antonius. The dungeon-master had been allotted a place of honour within earshot of the king. He wasn't wearing his usual leather jerkin tonight, but a sumptuous, brand-new martenskin doublet.

A reward for loyal service, Florin thought bitterly. He was still staring at Master Antonius when the latter raised his head and beckoned him over.

'Enjoy the banquet while you can, little Mimus,' he said in a low voice. 'One dungeon will soon be empty, and the king likes empty dungeons as little as I.'

Florin's thoughts raced. So Theodo was going to have him imprisoned this very night. Once down there he would cease to be the king's little jester; he would be the heir to the Moltovian throne, whom it was necessary to eliminate. He would lie in chains in that dark rat-hole, listening for footsteps just as his father must be doing at this moment . . .

'Pay attention, my boy,' Mimus whispered beside him. 'Look at the king.'

Theodo had just ended his meal and was washing his hands in a silver basin, the sign for all his guests to lay their gold knives aside.

'No mean feast, you lions of Vinland,' he cried, surveying their empty plates with satisfaction. 'That is just as it should be on the night of Shrove Tuesday!'

'And on execution night, too!' Mimus chimed in. He took Florin by the arm and towed him over to the block. 'Tomorrow you can weep and gnash your teeth, but tonight let joy be unconfined! Eat and drink and be merry—carouse to your hearts' content. Your bellies are full, so now let's play a game!'

With a jerk, he whipped the black cloth off the block. Then he rummaged in his pocket and brought out three copper cups, which he placed on the block upside down.

Florin couldn't believe his eyes. Thimblerigging! The sordid little trick with which unscrupulous fairground hustlers coaxed copper coins out of gullible peasants' pockets! 'Is that what you've been thinking about all day?' he whispered in dismay.

Mimus paid him no heed. 'Most beloved king,' he entreated, 'lend me a gold piece. If you do not receive it back a hundredfold, you may wear my jester's cap for the rest of the night.'

Theodo raised his eyebrows, but he tossed Mimus a coin that landed at his feet.

'A thousand thanks, most munificent of all monarchs!' Mimus bowed low. 'And now, good sirs,' he went on, looking from guest to guest with a challenging air, 'which of you will venture to wager a sovereign against me?'

After a moment's hesitation, one of the bishops held up a gold piece. 'May God forgive me for the sin of gambling on Shrove Tuesday,' he said with a laugh. 'I'll bet against you, jester.'

'Little Mimus, bring me the sovereign wagered by our doughty man of God,' Mimus commanded. He treated the bishop to an obsequious bow. 'Your Grace, if you can tell me under which cup this ball is hidden—' he held up a glass marble, 'you'll get your sovereign back—and His Majesty's sovereign into the bargain.'

'But then the game will be over,' whispered Florin.

'Wait and see,' the jester said tersely.

Clearly visible to all present, Mimus inserted the marble under one of the cups. He flexed his fingers briefly as if to render them more supple, then switched the cups around the block so fast that they became a blur of copper-coloured light.

But the bishop had been watching closely. 'You're out of luck, jester!' he cried triumphantly when Mimus took his hands away. 'The marble is under the cup on the left!'

'Is Your Grace quite sure?' asked Mimus. He tapped the cup in the centre, then the one on the right. 'Not under either of these?'

'It's under the one on the left, I tell you!' the bishop cried impatiently. 'Let's see it!'

'As Your Grace wishes.' Mimus removed the cup—and the bishop stared incredulously at the little brown blob that came to light.

Mimus sniffed it. 'Well, well,' he said in mock surprise, 'pigeon dung. Can it be that the Holy Ghost was at work here, warning his pious servant to abstain from the sin of gambling?'

Everyone laughed except the bishop, who compressed his lips in annoyance.

The next to hold up a gold piece was Chancellor Benedict. 'Let me try my luck, jester!'

'You're a shrewd man, Chancellor, I can tell,' Mimus said unctuously. 'For now, you stand to win no less than three sovereigns, including your own. Watch closely!' His hands skimmed across the block once more.

Chancellor Benedict chose the cup in the middle. When Mimus removed it, all that came to light was a copper penny.

'How did that little fellow get there?' Mimus exclaimed in surprise. 'You donated it only yesterday to the municipal hospital. That's what I call well-gauged generosity, Chancellor. Too much bread isn't good for ailing bellies.'

'You cheated, jester,' Benedict said sulkily. 'There's no marble under any of the cups!'

'No?' said Mimus. He removed the cup on the left—and a chick ran off across the block, cheeping loudly. 'It isn't there, true,' he said. 'Ah,' he went on, removing the right-hand cup to reveal the marble, 'there it is!'

One of Theodo's judges produced a gold piece. 'I wish to see the trick once more.'

Wager followed wager. Florin hurried to and fro between Mimus and the men at the table, collecting gold coins and piling them up on the block while striving desperately to ignore the dark stains that discoloured its surface. The cups slid this way and that under the jester's hands, swift as startled birds. The guests discovered the most peculiar things under them—birds' eggs, caterpillars, frogs, mice—but never the marble, which Mimus was always able to uncover in the end. Although Florin was closer to him than anyone else, the jester's movements were far too rapid even for him to follow them. The pile of gold on the block grew ever higher, the guests' faces ever more avaricious, and King Theodo's manner ever merrier.

'Do my eagle-eyed courtiers wish it to be said that they can be deceived by a charlatan's trick?' he asked challengingly.

'Don't watch the cups, watch the jester's fingers!' cried someone. 'We'll catch him out sooner or later!'

'You see?' Mimus whispered to Florin. 'Take advantage of their greed and stupidity, and you've as good as won.'

Florin watched the men staring at Mimus's flying fingers with flushed faces and glittering eyes. The jester was right; nothing but stupidity and avarice would have enabled him to hold the court in thrall.

'Who's next?' Florin called.

'I am.' Master Antonius proffered a gold coin.

When Florin made to take it, the dungeon-master caught hold of his arm. 'Bring this unworthy charade to an end,' he said in a low voice. 'Your father is ready and waiting. You only prolong his ordeal.'

Florin gulped. He had momentarily forgotten his father in the heat of the game.

'Faster, little Mimus!' came a chorus of voices.

'You hear that?' Florin said hurriedly. 'They wish to play on.'

'What do you hope to gain, you and the jester?' asked Master Antonius

Florin shook his hand off. 'Another wager!' he called loudly. 'Who'll play?'

The game went on and on. Mimus's hands danced across the executioner's block. The men laughed, marvelled, grew vexed . . . Another wager . . . They would play to all eternity . . . Another wager, and another . . . Coins fell, jingling, into Florin's hands . . . Another wager . . .

All at once Mimus said: 'That's it. It's over.'

'What?' Florin spun round.

'I can't go on,' the jester said quietly. Florin hadn't noticed until now that his face was ashen, his forehead beaded with sweat.

'Rest for a little while,' Florin whispered urgently, 'and then continue.' He indicated the men's greedily glittering eyes, the coins in their hands. 'We can delay matters the whole night long, and—'

He broke off abruptly, for the king was beckoning to him.

'My winnings, little Mimus!' With a satisfied smile, Theodo watched Florin stack the gold coins in front of him.

'You've eaten, drunk and made merry,' he told his guests, recalling Mimus's words. 'But now it's time to open the last page in our Shrove Tuesday book. Bring in our guest of honour!'

'What now?' Florin turned to Mimus for help. 'How are we to . . . ?'

But . . . where had the jester gone? He was no longer at Florin's side, nor in his place beside the pillar.

'No, Mimus,' Florin muttered, desperately scanning the great chamber. 'Don't do this to me—don't desert me now!'

God in heaven, if only their rescuers would come!

Instead, he heard the master of ceremonies make a loud announcement: 'Our esteemed guest, Philip of Moltovia!'

Standing motionless beside the pillar, Florin saw his father led in. He wore a clean doublet in place of his dungeon rags and his leg-irons had been removed, but his hands were tied behind his back. His eyes were shut against the light and his footsteps hesitant, as if the unaccustomed act of walking hurt him. Two guards supported him, but he held himself erect in their grasp as he approached Theodo's throne.

'You are truly tonight's guest of honour,' said Theodo, 'albeit not for long. I bid you welcome, Philip—for the last time.'

Flanked by his guards, King Philip stood in silence.

'It seems you've lost your voice on the way here,' Theodo said mockingly.

King Philip still said nothing. Then Florin saw that his father had been gagged as before. To prevent him from cursing his murderer, he thought grimly. Everyone, whether king or beggar, was afraid of being cursed by a man about to die. Such curses could not be warded off by means of prayer and good works.

'A pity, Philip, that you would not renounce the throne of your own free will,' said Theodo. He gave the pile of coins in front of him a playful flick, and the gold pieces went rolling across the table. 'You will not, therefore, live to see Easter or my first audience at the court of Moltovia, when all the dignitaries in the land—all of them without exception—will pay homage to me as their new king.'

'He's lying, father!' Florin would have liked to shout the words, but he only whispered them. He could not afford to arouse that accursed, perjured king's suspicions on any account.

'When you die, Wolf of Moltovia, you will die a forgotten man,' said Theodo. 'But first, I propose to show you the last of your glorious royal line.' He clicked his fingers. 'Come here, little Mimus.'

That shaft went astray, Florin thought triumphantly. My father has long known the truth! After a quick glance at Master Antonius, who was watching the scene impassively, he stepped between Theodo and his father.

'Before you, Philip,' Theodo said spitefully, 'stands the last scion of the royal house of Moltovia, a jingling jester in cap and bells!'

Florin's father looked at him seemingly unmoved, but to Florin it felt as if he was about to enfold him in his arms. For a moment he had the wonderfully comforting sensation that all would yet end well.

'Come, little Mimus,' said Theodo. 'Show your father what a good little jester you've become.'

Gain time! Play along, little Mimus! Florin told himself. I'll play, yes, but not your accursed game of cat and mouse. My own game is one of which you have no inkling!

Without thinking twice, he went up into a handstand and walked several times round his father on his hands; reached blindly for Theodo's gold coins and juggled with them; sang a love song and beat time with his pig's bladder; turned cartwheels and performed handsprings, singing obscene Shrove Tuesday ditties as he did so. He could have prolonged his performance indefinitely, had not Theodo cut it short with a gesture.

'You see, Philip?' he said complacently. 'Not only has the world forgotten you, but your own brat has long ago forgotten who he is. The little donkey has talent; I shall be sorry to lose him in the near future. But first,' he went on quietly, almost casually, 'it's your turn. Summon the executioner!'

The master of ceremonies tapped on the floor with his staff. 'The royal executioner!' he called.

'Here I am!' cried a voice that carried to the farthest corners of the banqueting hall with ease. The guards stepped back respectfully as a tall black figure with a cowl over its head and the headsman's axe on its shoulder marched up to the block. Florin saw his father shudder involuntarily at the sight.

'Where's the jester?' cried one of the men at the table. 'It'll be half as much sport without a song or two!'

King Theodo seemed to notice only now that Mimus had disappeared. 'Bring him here, the neglectful donkey,' he told the guards. 'Little Mimus can entertain us in the meantime.'

But he didn't look at Florin as he spoke. Like everyone else in the chamber, he too was staring spellbound at the executioner, who had deposited his axe on the block and was slowly turning his head in all directions. His eyes were concealed behind the slits in his black hood, but one could sense that he was closely scrutinising all present.

'You there,' he called suddenly in a cavernous voice, pointing to one of the pages. The boy went as white as a sheet. 'You strike me as having a nice, pretty little white neck. Will you be the sample that precedes the masterpiece?'

An incredible suspicion took shape in Florin's mind. It was impossible: the executioner who, stationed behind the block with his legs astraddle, raised the axe on high and brought it whistling down on the solid oak with a crack that made everyone wince, was a giant seven feet tall and as broad across the chest as a linen press. He had a neck like an ox and a voice like thunder, and yet . . .

'Why stand there gawping?' the executioner growled at the trembling page. 'Bring me a draft of cool wine and a couple of chicken legs. Beheading people is a hungry, thirsty business!'

When the boy made no move to carry out his order, the headsman turned to the king: 'What is this place,' he demanded reproachfully, 'a royal banqueting hall or the city jail? If my strength fails me, that poor devil—' he pointed to King Philip with a gloved hand, 'will end up with a hinged neck!'

Before Theodo could reply, there was a commotion at the entrance. 'Let us pass,' cried a voice, 'we have important news for the king!'

News for the king? Florin's heart stood still. Had the time come? Were the walls already shaking?

But who should come panting in, woollen cloak flapping and boots caked with dung and straw, but Rollo. The bestiarius was towing along a man who was three heads taller than himself and obviously bewildered. Stripped to the buff, he was more or less covering his nakedness with a scrap of cloth.

'Most gracious king,' said Rollo, 'I found this fellow in the empty bear's stable, trussed up like a chicken. He stubbornly insists he's your royal executioner.'

'I was waylaid while coming here, Your Majesty,' the man gasped excitedly. 'My assailants overpowered me from behind on the stairs—how many I don't know, but they must have numbered at least a dozen!'

Like the hum from a beehive, an agitated murmur ran round the banqueting hall. All eyes turned to the hooded figure standing motionless beside the executioner's block.

'Very well.' Theodo raised his hand. 'Mimus, you can remove your disguise.'

Cool as a cucumber, the jester threw back his cowl and shook out his ass's ears. Then he untied the thongs with which he had attached big blocks of wood to his feet and pulled the cloak over his head. As he did so, the bundles of straw he'd used to pad out his slight frame tumbled to the floor. 'What are you goggling at?' he demanded of all and sundry. 'People often exchange clothes on Shrove Tuesday, it's a fine old carnival custom. However,' he went on, carefully brushing the straw from his costume, 'my jester's motley was too good for this uncouth lout.'

With a defiant grin, Mimus planted himself in front of the naked giant, whose shoulder he barely came up to.

'Overpowered from behind by a dozen assailants?' King Theodo said scathingly. 'Let us hope, executioner, that you're strong enough to wield your axe.'

Everyone laughed approvingly except the executioner, who turned crimson with shame. But the laughter died when he donned his cloak and pulled the cowl over his head. The menacing black figure behind the block bore no resemblance to the naked, humiliated oaf of a minute before.

'Executioner,' Theodo commanded, 'do your duty.'

Dead silence reigned in the banqueting hall as King Philip was led to the block.

Florin's heart beat a rapid tattoo whose rhythm was taken up by a foolish couplet that came into his head unbidden: Too late, too late, they'll be too late. Too late, too late, it's all too late . . .

The executioner favoured his victim with a ceremonious bow and made a gesture of invitation. King Philip gave a little nod, then knelt down and laid his head on the block.

Obedient as a sacrificial lamb, thought Florin. He now knew that this was the end, and the turmoil inside him subsided. Silently, he began to recite the prayer for the dead. *Almighty God, with whom do live the spirits of them that depart hence . . .*

The executioner took up his position, legs apart for balance, and raised the axe above his head.

'Heavens alive!' Mimus exclaimed suddenly. 'I've forgotten something!'

King Theodo exploded. 'What is it now, you old fool? Don't try my patience too far!'

No, Mimus, Florin thought tormentedly as the executioner lowered his axe. Enough, it's too late.

The whole thing was pointless. This was the end, and any further delay would merely prolong the agony.

'My execution ditties,' Mimus said with a self-satisfied grin. 'No one may be sent on his way unaccompanied by some suitable rhymes.'

Florin resolutely prayed on. *Thou returnest to thy Creator. Mayest thou be greeted, when thou departest this life, by the angels and all the saints . . .*

The jester's discordant voice broke in:

*'You think an angel has flown down
to bear you off at speed?
You err, my friend: a vulture craves
your flesh its chicks to feed.'*

Florin gazed steadfastly at his kneeling father and tried to ignore the roar of laughter that followed. *May the choir of angels receive thee and conduct thee to Paradise. Mayest thou have eternal rest . . .*

Everything within him recoiled when Mimus began to sing once more.

*'King Philip knocks at heaven's gate,
his head beneath his arm.
Angels and saints come swiftly forth,
their welcome is right warm.
They quickly spread the joyous news
throughout the Lord's abode.
"Thank God," they cry, "who on us all
a new ball hath bestowed."'*

'No, Mimus!' Florin shouted. 'Stop it! Stop it!'

Casting self-control to the winds, he dashed toward the jester, yelling at the top of his voice. 'Stop that! I can't endure it any more!'

But his cries were drowned by a loud commotion outside the banqueting hall. Hurried footsteps and agitated cries could be heard. Simultaneously, a muffled concussion shook the floor and walls and set the goblets on the table jingling. Even as the guests were exchanging dumbfounded glances, a captain came rushing in and fell on his knees before Theodo.

'Your Majesty, the castle is collapsing!' he said breathlessly. 'The outer walls have already fallen, the inner walls are tottering!'

Theodo sat as if turned to stone. All the blood seemed to have left his cheeks.

'What a fool!' he whispered. 'What an utter fool I am!'

Florin, standing at Mimus's side, saw him gazing raptly at the king. His face was glowing with triumph.

– THE JESTER'S PEACE –

AS ONE MAN, the guests in the banqueting hall leapt to their feet and surrounded the king, who awoke from his trance with a jerk.

'Triple the guards on the dungeons,' he commanded. 'Count Fulco, take your men and secure the staircases. The swordsmen are to take up their positions in the courtyard and entrance hall. Assign a quiver-bearer to every archer. And bring swords enough for every man present.'

Although his voice was repeatedly drowned by thunderous detonations, Theodo issued his orders with calm authority. After each one, men left the banqueting hall at a run.

Theodo beckoned two captains. 'Assign your best men to guard the royal apartments,' he said. 'Each of them will answer with his head for the safety of my family. Kill all intruders instantly and without mercy.'

A babble of cries rang out from the direction of the staircase. 'Stand to! Enemy within the gates! Fire! Fetch water, quickly!'

A soldier who came dashing into the banqueting hall with his arms full of swords knocked over a candelabrum by accident. A page quenched the flames with trembling hands.

'Those mangy wolves will now learn how we greet uninvited guests at Bellingar,' growled Theodo, as a captain girded on his sword for him. He caught sight of King Philip, who had removed his head from the block and was rising to his feet—slowly, with the faraway expression of one who has just returned from a distant land.

Theodo seemed of two minds for a moment. He looked at the executioner, who was still standing behind the block, axe in hand.

'If I may venture a suggestion, Your Majesty,' said Chancellor Benedict, whose ratlike face was as yellow as beeswax. 'Let Philip live for the time being. If the worst comes to the worst, he and his son will make valuable bargaining counters.'

Theodo deliberated briefly, then beckoned three soldiers. 'Take the hostages upstairs to the royal apartments,' he commanded. 'Guard them like the apple of your eye.'

Surrounded by the rest of his men, he strode toward the door. 'And put that dog of a jester in chains!' he called over his shoulder.

Anxiously, Florin turned to look at Mimus, but the jester was beside him no longer. He had once more disappeared without trace.

Two of the soldiers seized King Philip by the arms; the third prodded Florin in the back with his pike. 'Forward march, the pair of you! Look sharp!'

As the troopers hurried them upstairs, half carrying his father between them, Florin saw sulfurous yellow clouds of smoke drifting up from below. At the same time, an acrid stench brought tears to his eyes. The staircase rang with bellowed orders and the clatter of weapons, accompanied by a low, menacing rumble that shook the whole castle to its foundations.

Swordsmen were drawn up four deep outside the carved wooden door. 'Let us pass!' called Florin's captor. 'Orders from the king!'

Florin saw tension on the men's faces as he was hustled through their ranks. This was no ordinary siege, for which the garrison was always prepared. '*Enemy within the gates!*'—to be awakened by that direst of all warning cries was enough to unnerve the most hardened veteran.

As if severed with a knife, the din of battle ceased as the door closed behind them. All that still pierced them through and through, even here, was the rumble of collapsing masonry.

'Where are you going with that miserable pair?' a captain inquired disdainfully.

'Orders from the king,' Florin's escort said again. 'The two prisoners are to be held under guard up here.'

In the anteroom, in the passageway—soldiers armed to the teeth were everywhere. The captain jerked his thumb at a door. 'Better put them in there with the rest. At present, it's the safest place in all of Bellingar.'

Although Florin had never before entered the queen's chamber, he recognised it at once by the scent of lilies and roses, the sumptuous silk bed curtains and the picture of St. Elina on the wall. It was a lofty, spacious room whose big round-arched windows could not have failed to illuminate it brightly by day. The ceiling, like Alix's, was covered all over with festoons of painted flowers.

Discounting the king himself, the whole of the royal family had gathered round the fireplace: Queen Elina, Alix, Riccardo and the four younger princes, together with ladies-in-waiting and nursemaids. Wogrim the Warhorse had seated herself on a chest with her obligatory piece of embroidery, but she wasn't plying her needle; she was patting Alix's arm reassuringly.

'I beg Your Majesty's pardon,' Florin's escort said respectfully. 'Your royal husband has given orders that these hostages are to be held in here.'

The queen's gaze rested on Florin for a moment, but she seemed to look straight through him. Alix, on the other hand, nodded to him before regarding King Philip with curiosity. It occurred to Florin that she had never seen his father before.

'Over there!' The guards thrust their two captives into the corner farthest from the fireplace. Utterly exhausted, King Philip sank to the floor. His face was paler than the whitewashed wall.

'It's our friends, father,' Florin said in a hurried whisper. 'Molto-vians and Arelians have undermined the—'

'Silence!' his escort bellowed. When he made to remove his father's gag, the man prodded him in the chest with his pike. 'Let him be!'

Florin watched out of the corner of his eye as Alix got up and went over to the table, where she filled a cup. Kneeling down beside his father, she removed his gag and put the cup to his lips. 'Here, drink.'

The soldier grimaced with annoyance, but he dared not object.

King Philip drained the cup in a few gulps. 'Thank you,' he said faintly.

Alix inclined her head. She glanced quickly at Florin, then returned to the fire without another word and resumed her place beside her mother.

From time to time one of the little princes whispered to his nurse-maid or gave a noisy sniff. That apart, total silence reigned. The rumbling had ceased; the room no longer shook. The destruction of the castle walls appeared to be complete. So as not to invite further harassment, Florin moved away from his father and sat down on the floor with his back against the wall. King Philip smiled at him, then closed his eyes, overcome with fatigue.

Florin looked toward the fireplace. Alix had her back to him, like the others, but one of the princes waved to him shyly and he returned the little boy's smile. With the best will in the world, he couldn't have told him a story tonight.

How were they feeling? The womenfolk, and the queen first and foremost, showed no outward emotion. Riccardo, by contrast, seemed to be almost bursting with impatience. He kept fidgeting on his chair as if it were a red-hot gridiron.

Florin understood him too well. While the battle was raging outside, they were sitting here as helpless as hares in a trap—all of them, without exception. They could only wait and pray.

However, the Almighty had already performed one miracle: his father was still alive and at his side! And Mimus had provided God with an effective helpmate. Where was the jester now? Far from the fray, beyond a doubt. In the Monkey Tower or a maidservant's bedchamber, or perhaps he had seized the opportunity and escaped, to dwell elsewhere in the world as a man, no longer a donkey in cap and bells . . .

The next moment Florin shook his head in self-reproof. Count Victor, Baron Henried and the others were fighting for his own and his father's freedom outside. Senna was risking his life for them while he sat here and thought about Mimus. But was it so surprising that he should have become foolish after being forced to live for so long as a fool?

He studied his father's face in profile. It was thin and waxen, with deeply incised furrows round the mouth and nose, yet it did not look like the face of a man who had just come so close to death. Even in his sleep King Philip made a vital, hopeful impression, like someone who, after a long and wasting illness, was at last on the road to recovery.

Shouted orders and the tramp of many boots in the passage broke in on Florin's thoughts. Their rescuers were coming! Or was it just that the guards outside the door had been reinforced? He jumped up, only to be roughly thrust to the floor again.

'Don't move from the spot, boy!' snapped the guard.

King Philip had opened his eyes and was listening intently. Queen Elina, Alix and Riccardo had risen to their feet in alarm. Instinctively, the nursemaids drew the little princes into the shelter of their arms.

Ferocious fighting had broken out beyond the door. Steel clattered against steel; bodies collided with muffled thuds; groans, yells and battle cries rent the air. Was it Vinlanders or Moltovians who were shouting? Once, Florin thought he recognised Baron Henried's booming voice. Then the din subsided and nothing could be heard but hoarse gasps and grunts, as if the exhausted combatants had called a truce. A moment later the din of battle began again.

The longer the fighting went on, the more unendurable the suspense became. The three soldiers in the bedchamber gripped their pikes until their knuckles went white. Riccardo paced restlessly up and down in front of the fireplace; the little princes clung to their nursemaids' skirts. Alix's face was pale and pinched with fear. Florin would gladly have comforted her, but apart from the fact that he couldn't budge an inch from the spot, what could he have said to her? He longed for precisely what she dreaded: the fall of Bellingar Castle.

Again they heard a babble of angry yells, the clash of steel on steel, the thud of falling bodies. Then the door burst open and soldiers stormed in with upraised swords—soldiers with the wolf of Moltovia on their helmets! More and more crowded in at their heels. They surrounded the women and children beside the fireplace and menacingly advanced on the three guards, who, hopelessly outnumbered, lowered their pikes.

'That's wise of you, indeed,' growled one of the attackers. 'What are the sick man and the jester doing here?'

Another soldier swung round at his words. Under his helmet Florin recognised the lean, hawklike face of Count Victor of Solutre.

'We've found you, God be praised!' the young nobleman exclaimed. 'Bow, man!' he barked at the soldier. 'You're in the presence of Moltovia's king and crown prince!'

The soldier's jaw dropped. While he was bowing low, Count Victor severed King Philip's bonds with a single swordstroke. Florin saw that his left sleeve was dark and discoloured with blood. His own?

'What of my men in the dungeons?' asked King Philip, chafing his wrists.

'They're safe, Your Majesty,' Count Victor replied. 'We contrived to get them out of the castle.'

King Philip shut his eyes for a moment. 'God in heaven,' he whispered, 'how great are your mercies!'

'Most of the Vinlanders are dead or put to flight,' the young count reported, 'but the fighting is not yet over. Theodo and his retainers are resisting like devils incarnate, and their archers are maintaining a truly murderous fire.' He involuntarily touched his arm and winced. 'It's as if Beelzebub himself is guiding their arrows.' He eyed King Philip closely. 'We must get you out of this diabolical place as quickly as possible. Can you walk unaided?'

'Well enough,' King Philip said calmly.

'What of Baron Henried and his son?' asked Florin. 'Will they join us on the way?'

'You know Baron Henried,' Count Victor replied with a grim smile. 'For him the battle won't be over until Theodo's head is on the end of a pike.'

A terrible, piercing scream made them all start. It wasn't until Florin saw Alix drop to her knees beside her mother that he realised the queen herself had uttered it.

Count Victor's dark, hawklike eyes gleamed. 'Thank you, madam,' he said with a little bow. 'You could not have done us a greater favour. Attracted by your birdcall, your husband will now do his utmost to reach you.'

At a gesture from him, four swordsmen posted themselves on either side of the door with their blades at the ready. 'As soon as the king appears,' he ordered, 'strike him down!'

Queen Elina gave a muffled cry and clapped her hand to her mouth. Alix and Riccardo stared in horror at the upraised swords.

'No.' Florin walked resolutely up to Count Victor. 'No harm must come to King Theodo.'

For one interminable moment he stood there, braving the Moltovians' bewildered glances. Count Victor tugged at his ear as if unable to trust his senses. His father's face looked suddenly grey and sunken.

'I . . . I vowed it,' Florin muttered.

'Your Highness,' Count Victor said angrily, 'you know not what you ask. That treacherous swine will appear at any moment. Think of your father, of all the Moltovians who have been slain, of your own humiliation. He deserves to die!'

'No harm must come to him!' Florin insisted. As he spoke, he stepped in front of the door to prevent the men from wielding their swords.

'To whom in the world did you make this vow?' Count Victor demanded hoarsely.

Conscious of his father's piercing gaze, Florin was briefly tempted to lie. 'To the jester,' he said.

'Then the vow is null and void,' cried one of the soldiers. 'The jester isn't a man!'

Florin stood his ground. 'To me, he's—'

He broke off abruptly as the door burst open and men rushed past him: Vinlanders with King Theodo in their midst. They hurled themselves at the Moltovians like blood-crazed lions. Florin saw milling bodies and blades flashing in the candlelight, heard the men's heavy breathing . . .

'Stand back, or the prince dies!'

Count Victor had seized Riccardo and put a dagger to his throat.

'Harm a hair of Prince Riccardo's head and I'll sever this lad's gullet!'

Before Florin could move, Chancellor Benedict had grabbed him and was likewise holding a blade to his throat.

The din abruptly ceased. As if the sight of the imperilled princes had cast a spell over the room, the Vinlanders and Moltovians froze. The two kings stared at their sons with horror.

Quite suddenly the silence was broken by a strange noise: a muffled scratching sound that seemed to come from the chest at the foot of the queen's bed.

'It's . . . it's the devil,' stammered Countess Wogrim, who was still clutching her embroidery. 'He's come for us all!'

Everyone in the room stared at the chest, from which definite sounds of movement were now issuing. The carved wooden lid gave a lurch and was raised a few inches. Then, like something out of a fairground puppet show, a cap adorned with ass's ears appeared above the edge of the chest.

'Ooh!' said Mimus, looking round. The next moment his head disappeared and the lid snapped shut. 'Knock three times when the butchery is done,' they heard him say in a muffled voice.

'Get him out of there!' Theodo ordered.

Mimus, looking like an oversized frog, was hauled out of the chest by two of his men.

'Mercy, dearest king!' he wailed. 'Give me leave to return to my chest! I cannot endure the sight of blood!'

'No, you don't!' barked Theodo. 'You're in this with the rest of them!' He never took his eyes off Riccardo as he spoke. The young prince stood quietly in Count Victor's grasp, his darting eyes the only sign of the mortal fear he felt. Alix, standing close beside him, had clutched her cheeks in agitation.

'Look at me!' screeched Mimus. 'I'm naught but a peace-loving jester. Take pity on me, you hard-hearted warriors! Spare my miserable life!'

Florin almost laughed at his woebegone expression, but he dared not move with the blade against his throat.

'I was quicker than all the rest and went in search of a quiet little nook,' the jester whined. 'There wasn't a soul to be seen when I hid up here. How could I have known that your gory battle would extend to the queen's bedchamber, of all places? Spare me, good sirs! No poet will sing your praises if you slay a jester.' His voice suddenly acquired a razor-sharp edge. 'Rather slay those for whom the devil is already waiting impatiently!'

From one moment to the next, Mimus's face transformed itself into the mask Florin knew so well, with its glittering, predatory eyes and the corners of its mouth turned down in scorn. His forlorn demeanour and whining voice had been nothing more than a charade, Florin realised in a flash.

'What is this,' the jester scoffed, 'the battle of the stuffed dummies? Surely you aren't deterred by fears for the princes' tender little throats?' He slunk up to Theodo. 'It's unlike you, my sweet king, to be so squeamish about slitting throats.'

'Your own throat will be in jeopardy if you don't shut your mouth this instant!'

'Did you say something, Your Majesty?' Mimus inquired amiably.

'I told you to shut your confounded mouth!'

'Speak louder, I can't understand you.' Mimus cupped a hand to one of his ass's ears. 'You've addressed me too softly for fifteen years— my poor ears have had enough. Speak louder! Let your voice be heard!'

Florin saw Theodo bite his lip with anger.

Loud footsteps and shouts were coming from the passage outside. Chancellor Benedict made an instinctive move in that direction, and Florin caught a brief glimpse of yet more Moltovian soldiers standing frozen on the threshold. He saw Baron Henried's grim face and Senna's look of alarm, then Benedict wrenched him back and pressed the dagger hard against his throat.

'Come in and join our congenial gathering!' Mimus called to the soldiers in the doorway. 'We're playing an amusing game called "If you stab mine, I'll stab yours!" I'm acting as mediator.'

He rubbed his hands gleefully. 'How do the noble princes feel with an apple-peeler pricking their gullets? No, don't trouble to answer, I wouldn't wish either of you a sore throat.'

So you mock me, do you? Florin thought angrily. If I hadn't made that accursed vow, we would have been out of harm's way long since!

Mimus leapt on to the chest. 'Good, let's play at war,' he cried loudly. 'The most important rule is this: no one must survive. A life for a life, a lion for a wolf, turn and turn about. I suggest we arrange ourselves in order of size. Let us begin with the smallest.' He pointed to the youngest prince, who was clinging to his nursemaid with eyes like saucers. 'It's your turn.'

'No, you first!' Theodo said menacingly. 'I'll throttle you with my own hands!'

'In that case,' Mimus replied, narrowing his eyes, 'let us die in order of foolishness. But be warned, my king: your turn will come immediately after mine.'

He glanced at the queen and Alix. 'Or again,' he said venomously, 'we could die in order of beauty. The princess would then live to see the sunrise.'

Alix's eyes blazed with fury.

The jester was in his element. 'Or we could arrange ourselves according to the colour of our hair,' he said, 'or the length of our noses or the dirt beneath our fingernails—whatever the heart desires. But get on with the bloodshed at last! My sweet king,' he said to Theodo in deferential tones, 'you begin.' He indicated Florin. 'Have the prince killed—and then watch your own sons slaughtered.'

Once more, Chancellor Benedict's dagger increased its pressure on Florin's throat. He felt dizzy with fear. Mimus's buffoonery was amusing no one this time.

'Well, what are you waiting for?' the jester cried. 'The fires of hatred can be quenched with blood alone—cascades of blood. You'll never be at peace until you're all writhing in your own gore, and no holy friar or pious priest will come to pray for your souls. Mimus the jester will sing you an executioner's ditty, but that is all.'

King Philip began to laugh. 'This is insane,' he said. 'Given that we're all such fools, we can surely take a fool's advice. Very well, fool, what do you suggest?'

'What do I suggest?' said Mimus. 'Turn yourselves inside out and let the wind blow through your hearts. Turn the sky upside down and start afresh. Leave the dead to the dead and beg forgiveness of the living. And, since you won't manage any of those things, sit beside the fire and weave baskets!'

As if to underline his words, he jumped off the chest, crouched down on the floor and took some willow shoots from his pocket.

King Theodo was still gazing as intently at Riccardo as King Philip was staring at Florin.

'A bargain, Philip of Moltovia,' Theodo said quietly. 'Safe conduct from Bellingar for your son, your men and you yourself, provided that my son and I and my men can remain here equally unharmed.'

King Philip did not reply at once. With a pensive expression on his weary face he looked from Baron Henried to Count Victor, then back to Florin. At last he nodded. 'First, release the princes.'

Count Victor and Chancellor Benedict converged, each holding a prince by the arm, until their hostages were nose to nose.

'Say an Ave Maria,' Theodo commanded. 'At the word "grace", remove your daggers simultaneously.'

'*Hail Mary, full of grace . . .*'

With a violent jerk, the chancellor released Florin and clutched Riccardo to him. Count Victor followed suit. The two men promptly took the boys by the hand and led them to safety amid their own soldiers' ranks.

Only now, infinitely relieved to have no dagger at his throat, did Florin become aware of the Moltovians' numerical superiority. There were at least three wolves to every one of Theodo's depleted pride of lions. No wonder he had proposed such a bargain!

King Theodo pointed to the door with an imperious gesture. 'And now, leave my castle!'

The sight of his smooth, self-satisfied face kindled an unexpected flame of hatred in Florin's breast. This accursed, treacherous king was still in command. Treachery, murder, incarceration, humiliation—no one would call him to account for those crimes. On the contrary, he was triumphantly giving orders still. Yet it would have been child's play for the Moltovians to take him and his family prisoner and make them pay for what Theodo had done to his father and himself. The time for revenge had come, but the wolves of Moltovia would slink out into the night like whipped curs . . .

When Florin turned to his father, he read the same thoughts in his face. As for the men around him, far from making any move to leave the chamber, they slowly advanced on Theodo.

'I advise you to be gone!' Chancellor Benedict said sharply.

In response, one of the wolves began to beat his iron shin armour with his sword: clang, clang, clang! A moment later all the Moltovian troopers followed suit. Clang, clang, clang! The savage cacophony sounded so ominous that a shiver ran down Florin's spine.

The lions of Vinland had retreated to the farthest corner of the chamber and formed a protective cordon round the women and children. Theodo himself was in the front rank.

Clang, clang, clang! The wolves were hungry—hungry for retribution, and their prey stood ready. One after another, the men raised their swords . . .

Mimus, who had been squatting on the floor throughout this time, plaiting his willow shoots as if the proceedings no longer concerned him, suddenly sprang to his feet.

'Let's play a game!' he crowed loudly.

As if his absurd, squeaky voice had jolted them out of their dreams of vengeance, the Moltovians stared at him soberly.

'One last game,' Mimus went on. He gave Theodo an obsequious bow. 'With you, my sweet king.'

'Go on playing with your willow wands, you old fool!' Theodo rasped.

'But they're for you, dearest king,' the jester said gaily. 'Look!'

When Theodo saw the hoop Mimus had woven out of osiers, his eyes flickered almost imperceptibly.

'You know the game well,' Mimus went on. 'Don't you remember? You made Philip play it day after day, down there in the dungeons.'

Florin was watching his father, who seemed to hold his breath as the jester continued: 'Philip enjoyed it so much, my sweet king, it's high time you enjoyed it too, for once.' Mimus held the willow hoop for Theodo as if he were a trained monkey. 'Come, Your Majesty, jump through the hoop! Hoppla!'

Theodo glared at him venomously. 'I'll have your ass's ears tied to a horse's tail,' he snarled. 'I'll have you dragged three times through the—'

'Do as the jester says!' King Philip broke in sharply. At once, the wolves resumed their menacing tattoo. Clang, clang, clang!

For a moment or two King Theodo's self-control deserted him. Usually so calm and composed, his features became contorted. He turned his head wildly to and fro like a cornered beast, looked at the queen and his children, at his outnumbered soldiers, at the doorway, which was choked with Moltovians. At length, realising that there was no escape, he emitted a sudden bark of laughter.

'Very well, you old fool,' he said. 'I'll do you the favour.'

He was just about to jump when Mimus took the hoop away.

'Wait,' he said amiably. 'Jumping without singing is only half as much sport, so sing us a song, my sweet king. Sing as you jump!'

'You're a dead man, jester,' Chancellor Benedict growled.

But Mimus had eyes and ears for Theodo alone.

'You'll see,' he assured him, 'it's quite easy. I've jumped and sung for you for fifteen years, feeling as snug as a goldfinch in a birdcage. Come, my beloved king,' he said ingratiatingly, 'put it to the test!'

He held up the hoop once more, and—incredibly enough—Theodo began to sing in a loud voice:

> *The Lion of Vinland's men are we,*
> *no prouder army you will see—'*

'No, no, no!' The jester shook his head until his ass's ears flapped. 'Sing us the song that Philip had to sing for you day after day, down there in the dungeons. These men—' he pointed to the Moltovians, 'will beat time for you.'

Clang, clang, clang! While the wolves drummed away, Theodo broke into song once more:

> *Poor King Excrement am I.*
> *Never more to see the sky,*
> *in my royal dung I lie.'*

The men beat time, Theodo sang and jumped through the hoop. Hesitantly at first, then faster and faster. The more he did, the more Florin relished the sight.

Whatever had prompted Mimus to stage this lunatic performance, he was humiliating Theodo on behalf of them all.

> *Poor King Excrement has fleas,*
> *oozing sores upon his knees,*
> *and a thirst that naught will ease.*

> *Poor King Excrement has lice,*
> *shares his meagre fare with mice.*
> *Bread and water him suffice.'*

Mimus lowered the hoop.

'Now that you've heard this fine song, you wolves,' he said, looking utterly exhausted, 'be good enough to return to your forest. We Vinlanders would like to get some sleep at last.'

King Philip was the first to leave the room, leaning on Baron Henried's arm. The others followed him in silence. At the door Count Victor turned.

'One last thing, King of Vinland,' he said to Theodo, who was standing beside Mimus with a face like stone. 'Before you kill that jester of yours, be advised that you owe him your life. Had he not made Prince Florin vow that no harm should come to you, you would have been slain long ago. Kill him in that knowledge!'

Senna put his arm round Florin's shoulders and led him out. As they walked along the passage together, the men around them began to mutter.

'A jester's peace.' The phrase quickly went the rounds. 'A jester's peace, a jester's peace . . .'

The chests in the little antechamber had been smashed, the carpets and the carved portal were burnt to ashes. On the staircase and in the entrance hall Florin saw soldiers lying dead, both Vinlanders and Moltovians.

'Peace?' Baron Henried said gruffly as they walked through the portal and out into the cold night air. 'That remains to be seen. At least we've drawn those mangy lions' fangs for the time being.'

TEN days later Florin rode across the mound of rubble that had once been Bellingar's outer wall.

How absurd a castle looked without walls and watchtowers, he reflected as he gazed up at the lonely wing that housed the royal apartments. Bellingar was bereft of strength like a soft, vulnerable crab stripped of its shell.

One solitary flag bearing the claw-footed lion still fluttered above the building. By contrast, the wolf of Moltovia flaunted itself a hundredfold on the banners and standards flying above the tented encampment that ringed Bellingar on all sides. Baron Henried was right: in this hopeless predicament, held in check by Moltovians and Arelians alike, Theodo could not afford to play false. For the moment at least, peace was assured.

King Philip had recovered surprisingly quickly from the rigours of his imprisonment. This was due partly to the medical skill of the nuns in whose convent they were lodging, and who devotedly tended the dungeon inmates' wounds; but also to a fortifying diet and his own iron willpower. Consequently, he was able to conduct negotiations with King Theodo in person. Florin knew what these entailed: the withdrawal of Vinlandian forces from Moltovia, the restitution of stolen royal property, and compensation for the destruction of Montfield Castle and the noblemen's castles that had also been burnt to the ground. From the little his father said, the negotiations were arduous and laborious. It seemed that Theodo had soon overcome the humiliation inflicted on him by Mimus, because he and his chancellor doggedly contested every last point at issue.

Just as Florin rode through the ruined inner gate and into the castle courtyard, King Philip and his retainers came toward him.

'Negotiations have been concluded,' said King Philip, looking exhausted. 'The armistice has been signed.' He gave a wry smile. 'We shall dispense with a banquet this time. We leave tomorrow morning.'

They were going home! Florin would ride back to Moltovia with Senna and Radbod beside him, even though 'home' would at first be a small hunting lodge not far from the ruins of Montfield Castle. There was nothing more to keep him in Vinland. And yet . . .

'Where the jester is concerned . . .' said his father.

'Yes?' Florin said quickly.

'I endeavoured to purchase his freedom for your sake, but Theodo rejected my offer.' The king gave Florin a searching look. 'I trust you understand, my son. I could not allow a jester to jeopardise our chances of peace.'

'Theodo will torment him,' Florin said bitterly. 'He'll punish him for what he did.'

'But he belongs to him, Florin,' said King Philip. 'He's only a jester, after all.'

'Just as I was only ten days ago,' Florin retorted fiercely. 'You can't fail to hate him after all he did to you, father, but he isn't always spiteful and malevolent.' He paused, then went on: 'Even if he himself has long forgotten it, he does possess a soul.'

King Philip was smiling now. 'We managed to secure him a blanket and an additional meal a day,' he said. 'And now run and tell him so. We'll wait for you here.'

MIMUS barely looked up when Florin entered the stable.

'See to it that Rollo doesn't set eyes on you,' he said gruffly. 'The poor fellow is sorely confused. Ever since he learnt that you're a prince, he's been convinced that Zito was really the emperor of Byzantium.'

Florin barely heard him. His head was spinning as if he had been whisked back to his very first day at Bellingar—as if the time between then and now had never existed. Everything seemed like an absurd dream, just as it had that first day: the stable, the rough walls, the straw on the floor, the Monkey Tower, the animal stench . . . Had he really slept on this straw for a hundred and eighty nights? Had he roamed from one corner of the stable to the other for a hundred and eighty days?

'Why stand there with your mouth open?' asked Mimus. 'Have you come to sing me a song about a fish?'

'We've persuaded Theodo to grant you a blanket and an additional meal a day,' Florin said sadly.

'Fine, then I'll soon be as womanish as Marsus and as fat as Rollo.'

'Listen to me, Mimus,' said Florin. 'Escape! Come with me to

Moltovia—I'll make sure you're beyond Theodo's reach. Then you'll be a free man.' He thought of his dream. If only Mimus could shake off his chains!

But Mimus merely shook his head and smiled.

'If you wish,' Florin promised in a piteous voice, 'I'll make you my court poet!'

The jester guffawed at that. 'Mimus Venerabilis, eh? You put me in mind of the Roman emperor who appointed his favourite horse a senator.' Abruptly, he became serious. 'You do me too much honour, my prince. Old donkeys like me never change stables.'

'But Theodo will never forgive you for making him jump through that hoop,' Florin said anxiously. 'He'll have you killed as soon as we've left.'

'No, he won't,' Mimus replied calmly. 'He may sentence me to a merry reunion with Master Antonius, but he won't forget that he owes me his life. Besides, who would sing at my execution? So don't cudgel your royal brains on my account, you'll be needing them. And now go.'

'What?' Florin stared at him in surprise.

'Go!' the jester repeated brusquely. 'Out of this stable, out of the Monkey Tower, out of my life! I shall dance my feet sore with delight at having finally seen the last of you!'

He gave Florin a hefty shove in the direction of the door.

'Farewell for ever, Prince Mimus,' he called after him. 'You'd never have made a decent jester in any case.'

– THE SEAL –

'WHO DID YOU say?' asked Chancellor Artold.

'A young and incredibly dirty scullion,' Count Marrod replied. 'Believe it or not, he's to receive a royal reception.'

Chancellor Artold pricked up his ears. 'A scullion from Vinland?' he said. 'About the prince's age?'

The chamberlain nodded. 'The grimy lad came riding up on a donkey. Before I could send him packing he produced a royal invitation from his pouch.' He wrinkled his nose. 'I began by sending him to the bathhouse, the barber and the tailor.'

'You did well,' said Artold. 'But rest assured, Marrod, that youngster would have been welcomed here at court even if he were as black as a chimney sweep.'

———————

BENZO, freshly washed and combed and squeezed into a green velvet doublet, looked less than happy as he marched into the throne room hall behind Count Marrod that afternoon. Word of a royal reception for the Vinlandian scullion had spread like wildfire, and his freckled face darkened still more at the sight of so many inquisitive faces. It did not brighten until he caught sight of Florin seated beside his father.

'Hello there, Florin,' he called, waving to him as if they'd just met in the kitchen sepulchre.

'First the king,' the chamberlain hissed.

'This is a great honour, Your Majesty.' Benzo gave King Philip a nod, then grinned at Florin again. 'What's the matter?' he demanded, as the chamberlain intimated, with a vigorous gesture, that he should bow to the king and Florin.

'All is well, Marrod,' King Philip told the chamberlain with a faint smile.

Benzo looked at Florin expectantly. 'You should have ridden here with me,' he blurted out. 'I overtook every horse in the caravan. One of the merchants offered me a whole gold shilling for that donkey of mine!'

Everyone present—chancellor, privy councillors, clerks, pages—was listening with the greatest interest.

'We'll talk of that later, Benzo,' Florin said tactfully. He indicated the assembled courtiers. 'This reception is being held in your honour.'

Benzo looked bewildered. 'Why?'

'Because you helped me,' Florin said simply.

Benzo scratched his nose, looking sheepish. 'Any friend would have done the same,' he mumbled.

'Anyone who helps a king's son is royally rewarded,' said King Philip. He leant toward Florin. 'You do the rest,' he whispered.

Florin rose. In the solemn tone he practised daily with his tutor in rhetoric, he said: 'By virtue of the royal status bestowed on me by God and man, I hereby grant you, Scullion Benzo—'

'You weren't to know,' Benzo broke in proudly, 'but I'm not a scullion anymore. I've been an assistant cook these six months past.'

'Don't interrupt!' Count Marrod cast his eyes up to heaven and Florin suppressed a grin.

'I hereby assign you, Assistant Cook Benzo, the villages, woods, meadowland and ploughland of the estates of Blackwood and Deephole. Moreover, you shall henceforth be entitled to style yourself Baron Darkwood and Deephole.'

Benzo promptly looked suspicious. 'Darkwood? Deephole?'

'They're just names,' Florin whispered. 'Names for a wonderful tract of land some hundred miles from here. Fields, lakes, forests— you'll like it!'

Benzo was far from convinced. 'Baron Darkwood and Deephole?' he said. 'What does it mean? Will I have to live in a dark hole?'

'No, Benzo,' Florin whispered, 'it means that the land is yours from now on. You'll dwell in a castle!'

'But I've no wish to,' Benzo said bluntly. Senna, who was standing behind the throne in his new capacity as Florin's squire, stifled a giggle. 'I don't want a castle, neither in a dark wood nor a deep hole nor anywhere else. Nor have I any desire,' he went on, pointing unceremoniously to Senna and Count Marrod, 'to have to stand around with a broomstick down the back of my doublet like these courtiers here.'

Even King Philip found it hard to keep a straight face. 'Well, Florin,' he said with a telltale tremor in his voice, 'if your gallant friend from Vinland has no wish to become a baron, perhaps he'd be better pleased by the office of assistant kitchen-master, here in Montfield Castle.'

Benzo's face lit up as if someone had placed a candelabrum in front of it. 'Kitchen-master?' he said happily. 'With my own ladles and all that goes with them?'

'Everything,' King Philip assured him. 'However, you'll have to bid farewell to your home at the court of Vinland.'

Benzo didn't have to think for long. 'Sooner or later,' he said, sounding immensely audacious, 'there comes a time when everyone has to go out into the wide world. The scullery maids aren't interested in me and the old kitchen-master spits fire and brimstone—what is there to keep me in Vinland?'

'In that case, assistant kitchen-master-to-be, how say you?' asked King Philip. 'Would twenty gold florins a year be recompense enough for your services?'

For one brief moment Florin thought Benzo would fall over backward. 'You won't regret it, Your Majesty,' he assured the king with a beaming smile. 'After the dishes I'll serve you up, you'll be licking your fingers in your dreams!'

'I don't doubt it,' King Philip said amiably. 'In that case, assistant kitchen-master, adieu.'

Benzo studiously ignored the chamberlain's beckoning hand. 'I have something for you, Florin,' he whispered. He glanced at the assembled dignitaries and added, in a somewhat louder voice: 'For you alone.'

'Er, one moment,' said Florin. He spoke briefly with his father, whispered something to Senna, and rose.

'You mean you can simply walk out on all these fine folk?' Benzo asked in astonishment as he followed Florin out of the throne room.

'Why not?' said Florin. 'You're the guest of honour. Come, I'll show you Montfield Castle—or rather, as much of it as is finished.'

He led Benzo upstairs and along passages. Afternoon sunlight was streaming through big round-arched windows onto the freshly white-washed interior. The outer walls were still encased in scaffolding. Hand cranks and blocks and tackle could be seen, and buckets of lime and mortar were standing in the corners of the rooms.

'How long have you been here?' Benzo asked.

'We moved in three months ago. The builders have been at work for two years. The outer walls have just been completed, together with the throne room and some of the royal apartments. Oh, and the kitchen.'

'But you own more castles,' said Benzo, ever practical. 'Why didn't you wait for this one to be finished?'

Instead of answering, Florin led him over to a window. The countryside round Montfield Castle had been ravaged by fire for as far as the eye could see, but something pale green and shimmering had arisen from the blackened soil: a forest of birch saplings already as tall as Florin himself.

'This is Montfield,' he replied, as if that said it all.

'Your walls are thicker than Bellingar's new walls,' Benzo declared, surveying them with an expert eye, 'and your watchtowers are higher. It doesn't look as if you're counting on a peaceful time.'

Florin shrugged his shoulders. 'My father has yet to recover completely from his long imprisonment. Although the jester's peace is now two years old, he continues to fear some treachery on Theodo's part.'

'And you?' asked Benzo.

Florin gazed out of the window in silence. Should he confess that the sound of a mule's jingling harness made him flinch? That the smell of millet gruel and the sight of striped garments turned his stomach? That he had to don jester's motley in his dreams, night after night, and dance in front of a faceless audience? What must his father's dreams be like?

And yet, to the outside world, King Philip must seem stronger and more powerful than ever. Their return to Moltovia two years ago had become a triumphal progress. Wherever he and his father went, people had stood in the streets and cheered them. During the months that followed, King Philip had travelled the length and breadth of his realm, mercilessly settling accounts with all who had come to terms with their supposed new lord and master: Duke Markward, Duke Vibert, scar-cheeked Count Tillo . . . They had been compelled to look on, grim-faced, as their coats of arms and seals were smashed at a public ceremony. That done, they were ignominiously exiled. The only one to be spared for Radbod's sake was Count Essrin, who had thrown himself at King Philip's feet and begged his pardon.

Now that the dark days of war were over, the inhabitants of Moltovia were filled with confidence. They loudly and happily extolled their king, but he remained unhappy. Unable to endure the sound of music or the sight of dancing, Florin's father spent his nights roaming the royal apartments.

To shake off these dispiriting thoughts, Florin asked: 'Didn't you say you had something for me?'

Benzo smote his brow. 'Yes, of course!' Without ceremony, he rummaged in the pockets of his new velvet doublet. 'A fine old shock she gave me, turning up out of the blue like that,' he went on, fishing out a sealed parchment scroll. 'She made me swear by all that's holy to give it to no one but you.'

Florin ran his fingers over the royal seal bearing the claw-footed lion, then broke it open.

'*Alix, Princess of Vinland, to Florin, Crown Prince of Moltovia.*'

The blood rose unbidden to his cheeks.

'*For weeks and months now, the privy councillors have been pestering me for a decision, their earnest faces suggesting that the weal or woe of all Vinland depends upon it.*'

Florin grinned. Alix had always come straight to the point.

'*Thank God my father is an understanding man—*' Florin snorted contemptuously, '*who will not compel me to marry against my will. But it's all to no avail. Since, to my great regret, Moltovia has no princess to whom Riccardo could become betrothed . . .*'

To her great regret? Florin frowned. Would Alix prefer to join that fat-bellied oaf Prince Cedrik in Frankenland?

'*. . . I wish to ask of you a favour,*' he read on. '*Invite me and my dear Warhorse to spend the summer and autumn with you at Montfield. It will be a trial period. I wish to satisfy myself that your hellish castle isn't too gloomy, that your apartments aren't infested with snakes and spiders,* *and that your fare is fit to be eaten. After that, I will decide . . .'*

Florin frowned again. Who did this pampered princess think she was? Yet her suggestion wasn't foolish. As a guest at the castle she would not only become acquainted with life in Montfield but get to know him, Florin of Moltovia, who was, after all, no longer her father's pathetic little court jester.

'Send me word by messenger. Greetings, and may heaven's blessings attend you. Alix.'

That was Alix just as he remembered her. Had she ever consulted *his* wishes? In fact, they were in the same predicament: his father's privy councillors had been daily impressing on him the desirability of a union between the two royal houses. The peace that now prevailed between Moltovia and Vinland was a young seedling. Having only just sprouted, it needed cherishing; any harsh gust of wind might cause it to wither and die. Alix knew this as well as he did, and she also knew their allotted role, like it or not. Even though Alix wasn't exactly repugnant to him—he admitted as much to himself—she certainly wouldn't give him an easy time. What had Mimus called them? *King Donkey-Ears and Queen Prickle-Tongue . . .*

Alix here at Montfield Castle—what would it be like? Muriel, at least, would dance for joy despite her stiff old legs: a princess and future queen whom she could spoil to her heart's content, and a lady-in-waiting, Wogrim the Warhorse, with whom she would undoubtedly have some splendid altercations. All her dreams would be fulfilled at once.

'You're smiling,' said Benzo. 'Good news?'

'That remains to be seen,' Florin replied. 'Come, assistant kitchen-master, and I'll show you your new kingdom. Oh, yes, before I forget: here at Montfield we use spits only for roasting and ladles for stirring.'

'What a pity,' Benzo said, looking disappointed. 'And I would have been the first kitchen-master schooled in swordsmanship by a royal instructor.'

Florin laughed. 'Well, you're certainly the first kitchen-master to have rejected the title of baron. I'm glad you've chosen to remain with us.'

LATE that night Florin summoned a courier to his bedchamber.

'I have two missives,' he told him, 'which you're to take to the court of Vinland without delay.'

The courier was short and thickset, with bandy legs that seemed to have been shaped by life in the saddle. 'For whom, Your Highness, are these missives intended?'

'This one,' said Florin, dropping some molten wax onto a parchment scroll and sealing it, 'is for the king's daughter.' He took a second sheet of parchment and rolled it up. 'And this one—'

'Your pardon, Highness,' the courier broke in discreetly, 'but that parchment is blank.'

'It is well so.' Florin pressed his seal into the hot wax. 'My seal will suffice.'

'Of course,' the courier said dubiously. 'And to whom am I to deliver this, er, missive?'

'The Master of the Jester's Art.'

'Aha.' The courier clearly hadn't understood a word. 'Where shall I find that exalted personage?' he inquired.

'Ask for the Monkey Tower,' Florin said with a covert grin as the courier finally shut his mouth.

While the wax slowly cooled, Florin regarded the imprint of his seal with a pensive air. Only after lengthy discussions had King Philip acceded to his wish to have a royal seal of his own. Whatever he sealed with it—every letter, every document—now became a little obeisance to one who deserved it.

'This will please you, Mimus,' he murmured.

The seal of the future sovereign of Moltovia depicted King Midas: a young man wearing a crown but adorned with bells and ass's ears.